ALSO BY ANN PACKER

The Dive from Clausen's Pier

Mendocino and Other Stories

Songs Without Words

Songs Without Words

Ann Packer

Alfred A. Knopf   *New York*   2007

To Emily and Will

Prologue

1976

*E*ach evening, the streetlights came on at dusk, and the view out the window changed, from barely glowing kitchens and TV rooms to the houses that contained them, and to the trees that sheltered the houses. It seemed to Sarabeth that for a little while there was a kind of balance out there, an equilibrium. But then, quickly, darkness came down from the sky, and soon the lit rooms returned to prominence, and finally everything else was black, and the world seemed limited to a few bright windows on a street in Palo Alto.

She was at her desk now, doing homework—at John Castleberry's desk, which, like his room, was available for her to use this year because he was away at college. Across the hall, Liz was working, too. The first couple weeks of Sarabeth's living here, they had done their homework together at the dining room table, as they so often had in the past, when Sarabeth lived in her own house across the street. But doing homework together night after night was different from hooking up from time to time, for company or help, and now they studied separately.

Out in the hall, Mrs. Castleberry was talking to Liz's younger brother, Steve, who'd started junior high this year. "Just some math," Sarabeth heard him say. "I'm on top of it." "I know you are," Mrs. Castleberry said. "But don't forget to get on top of those dirty clothes we talked about, too." "I *know*," he said, and though he sounded impatient with her, Sarabeth knew Mrs. Castleberry would just smile her smile, maybe chuckle as she continued on her way. Mrs. Castleberry was so calm.

Her footsteps approached, and she came into view, slowing to wave at Sarabeth. Sarabeth waved back. Even this late in the evening, Mrs. Castleberry's hair was neatly brushed back from her forehead and held in place by a wide headband. Liz had the same thick, slightly wavy hair. Sarabeth's hair was curly and would not be contained.

Mrs. Castleberry's heels tap-tapped their way down the stairs and then changed sound slightly as she headed for the kitchen. The dishwasher started, and the faint noise of the water joined the muffled sounds coming from the TV show Mr. Castleberry was watching in the den. It was a special about NASA; at dinner he'd suggested they all join him for it, and Liz and Steve had nodded solemnly, saying, "Sure thing, Dad," "Wouldn't miss it, Dad," and then broken into laughter. "How about you?" he'd asked Sarabeth, and while she was trying to figure out if he was teasing, and how to respond, Liz said, "No torturing of guests, Dad," and that was that.

He watched TV almost every night—so unlike Sarabeth's father, who as far as she could remember had never in her entire life watched any TV at all. When he was home and not somehow occupied with her mother—assuring her that dinner had been fine, more than fine, good; or saying that while he did like the new painting she'd bought, it was perhaps a little on the expensive side; or asking her to slow down and take a deep breath before continuing a story—times when he wasn't busy with her mother, he cleared off his desk and painstakingly took apart and repaired old and broken radios, telephones, stereos, donating them to the Goodwill once he had them working again. Even last year, with Sarabeth's mother gone, he'd never tried TV for relaxation, for the solace of not thinking; instead, he'd continued bringing out appliances, letting them sit on his desk for days at a time, but only ever looking at them, or poking idly with his special tweezers, no real intention in mind. When Sarabeth helped him pack up the house in August, there were boxes and boxes of old machines for the dump.

Liz had put a record on. Her door was closed, but the album was so familiar Sarabeth didn't really need to hear it to know what it was: the Eagles, *One of These Nights*. "Lyin' Eyes" was starting, and Sarabeth was tempted to wait for the refrain—"You can't h-i-i-i-de your lyin' eyes"—

and then stick her head into Liz's room and say, "That is *so true.*" It was a guaranteed crack-up: Bill Cuthbert had said it to Liz one evening in tenth grade when she was at his house working on a lab report; he gave her a meaningful look as he spoke, as if the Eagles were singing about a truth he'd had to learn the hard way. Sarabeth remembered Liz telling her about it the next day as they rode their bikes to school, Liz's hair whipping behind her, her face full of glee.

Tired of the physics problems she'd been working on, she moved to the bed and opened *Swann's Way,* the English translation she'd gotten from the library—without Monsieur's permission, though he hadn't explicitly forbidden it. "Sah-rah-bette," he had said. *"C'est bien d'aimer Proust, mais il n'est pas lui-même en Anglais."* It's good to like Proust, but he is not himself in English. Of course he wasn't, but she couldn't help herself. And she was reading the French, too, just not as quickly. Monsieur looked the other way for her sometimes, which was sort of nice and sort of embarrassing. Even as she allowed herself to take advantage of it, she longed for next year, for the anonymity of college, when she would no longer be the girl whose mother had committed suicide. She would always be that girl at Palo Alto High School.

Suddenly the Eagles got louder, and Sarabeth looked up to see Liz coming across the hall, *Du Côté de Chez Swann* in her hand. She'd put on her school sweatshirt, green with white letters. "Have you gotten to page ninety-three yet?" she said. "I don't get this at all."

Sarabeth held her book up, cover out.

"You're such a cheater!" Liz exclaimed. She perched on the bed and set her own book down, then reached for Sarabeth's. "Let me see that."

"Then *you'll* be a cheater."

"True." Liz brought her legs up onto the bed and crossed them. She'd pulled her hair into a ponytail but had missed a piece, and it lay in a wave against her neck.

"I'm reading the French, too," Sarabeth said.

"I know."

Sarabeth took Liz's book and flipped through the pages. She said, "Are you kind of tired of French? I wonder if we'll keep taking it."

"Next year?"

"Oui. I'm not tired of speaking it, I'm tired of reading it. *J'adore* speaking it. *Penses-tu qu'on va etudier le francais pendant l'année prochaine? L'an-née prochaine. L'année. Prochaine.* Isn't *l'année prochaine* so much

nicer than 'next year'? Do you think in France when they learn English they're all going, 'Oh, how ugly'?"

Liz smiled.

"Tiens, c'est tellement laide, c'est langue."

Now Liz clasped her hands in her lap. She reclaimed her book and set it behind her. She said, "I saw you talking to Doug outside the office today." She looked serious now, eyes narrowed a little.

Sarabeth felt her face heat up. She knew Liz thought she should stay away from Doug, but if he wanted to talk to her she wasn't exactly going to say no. She'd had some weird times with him last year, but he was being really nice lately.

"Oui," she said. *"Nous avons parlés de les* SATs. Oh, my God. *Des* SATs. But that doesn't sound right, either."

Liz kept on looking. "How was it?"

He'd started the conversation by saying, "SB, you're looking downright foxy these days." But she wasn't going to tell Liz that. "Fine."

"Is he taking them when we are?"

"What?"

"Les SATs."

"Oh," Sarabeth said. "Duh. Yeah."

Liz straightened her long legs. She was in the pants she'd worn to school, sailorlike jeans with patch pockets on the front and back. They'd tried to find a pair for Sarabeth, but they didn't come small enough.

"It's October," Liz said, "and we still haven't taken John's posters down."

Sarabeth looked around the room. Linda Ronstadt was on one wall, Wilt Chamberlain on another. In her room across the street, posters had been forbidden. They would ruin the wallpaper, according to her mother. And they were déclassé.

"I don't really mind them," she said.

"I would." Liz parted her lips and opened her eyes wide. "Do you like me?" she breathed, Ronstadt style. Then she said, "Hey, brilliant idea. I've got those Monet posters in my closet. Let's take these stupid things down and put them up in here."

"But you bought them for next year," Sarabeth said.

"Nothing would happen to them."

"They wouldn't be new anymore. Don't you want them to be new? New room, new life, new everything?"

Liz shrugged, but Sarabeth had gotten herself thinking, and she couldn't not go to the questions, the questions that were always there, waiting. Where would she and Liz be next year? How far apart?

The Eagles stopped singing, and Liz looked at her watch and moaned. "I haven't even started my math."

"Steve's doing math," Sarabeth said—stupidly, but she suddenly didn't want Liz to leave. Time was moving. October now, SATs and applications, December with her trip to see her father, April 15 and the thick or thin envelopes in the mail. Graduation. It would all be over before she knew it.

This night would be over soon. Mr. and Mrs. Castleberry would come upstairs, Mr. Castleberry first, saying, "Goodnight, one and all," as he moved down the hallway toward the master bedroom. Mrs. Castleberry would take her time, stop in on the kids—on Steve first and then on Liz, knocking at her door and then going in and staying for quite a while, ten or fifteen minutes, maybe longer. It had surprised Sarabeth, that Mrs. Castleberry did this. She wondered what they talked about.

"All right," Liz said. "Break over."

Sarabeth sat up. "Do you think he'll get a girlfriend this year?"

"Doug?"

"Steve."

Liz yawned. "If he's anything like John, he already has one." She got to her feet and stood next to the bed, her hands going up to release her ponytail. She regathered her hair and fastened it again, this time catching the errant strand.

Sarabeth reached for Liz's Proust. "What page was it?"

"It's OK. I'm moving on to math."

But Sarabeth had found the place, a page with a long, dense passage, and now she began to read. She felt Liz standing there waiting, but she kept her eyes on the text. After a moment Liz sat again, and Sarabeth slid the book over so they could both see it. She stared down at the page, and at her side Liz did, too. The French nothing now but a trail of black marks.

"Sorry I called you a guest at dinner," Liz said.

Sarabeth looked up at her. "It's OK. I am."

"No, you're not. You're a . . ." Liz's voice trailed off, and Sarabeth imagined the possibilities: "friend," "honorary sister," "near orphan," "beggar," "leech." If she had gone to Baltimore with her father, she'd be none of those things, not the bad but not the good either, and especially not friend. "The nice girls of Baltimore," she and Liz had called the people with whom she couldn't possibly, in a single year, develop anything like the friendship she had with Liz. They—the nice girls of Baltimore—were among the many reasons it had made so much more sense to stay.

"I'm a what?" she said.

Liz patted Sarabeth's shoulder. "You're a you." She stretched her arms over her head, bending from side to side. "OK," she said. "I *have* to get to my math. Nighty night."

Sarabeth raised herself onto her elbows. " 'Nighty night'?"

Liz smiled a wry smile. "It's what my mom says every night. Corny, huh?" She moved to the doorway. "Open or closed?"

"Closed, I guess."

Liz took hold of the knob, gave Sarabeth a little wave, and pulled the door shut behind her.

It was an hour before everyone was settled for the night. Sarabeth waited—until Mrs. Castleberry was in her own room, until all the trips to the bathroom were completed, all the lights off—and then she put on her nightgown and tiptoed to the bathroom herself.

Back in John's room, she closed the door and turned off the overhead so that the only light came from the small reading lamp on the bedside table. She made her way to the window. There were a few lights here and there, but the one she saw, the one she couldn't avoid, was the one directly across the street, the light shining from the room that had once, and for so long, belonged to her parents. That room seemed to be the whole of her view from here. It was to that room that she had most often gone to find her mother, in bed at nine in the morning, at noon, late in the day. It was from that room that she had so often heard her mother, weeping or shrieking. And it was in that room that she had last seen her mother, on a warm spring morning eighteen months ago, when she had poked her head in as usual to say she was leaving for school. Her mother's dark head had not moved from the pillow, but she had raised her hand, and sometimes, even now, Sarabeth wondered what that gesture had meant: goodbye, or go.

part one

1

$\mathcal{S}$ ix o'clock in the morning. It was one of Liz's favorite times of day: everyone else asleep, Brody still motionless in the bed she'd just left, the kids upstairs, in sleep not teenagers anymore but simply larger versions of their younger, childish selves, who, she could almost believe, would wake and seek her for body comfort, as they used to. They were thirteen and fifteen, but she could still open their doors and look at them sleeping: how Joe lay on his back with half his blankets kicked to the side, his mouth slightly open; how Lauren folded her limbs in close, her head sandwiched between two pillows, a fist curled under her chin.

In the kitchen, Liz spooned coffee into the Krups and leaned in for a whiff of the dark, rich smell. She got out four plates and four juice glasses. Moving to the calendar, she did a quick pro forma check of the day, but she knew: soccer practice for Joe, and Brody home a little on the late side because of his tennis game. Lauren did nothing after school this year, and Liz had taken to planning labor-intensive dinners so she'd be in the kitchen if Lauren wanted her. Jambalaya tonight? She'd go grocery shopping after her yoga class.

Outside, the newspaper lay on the lawn, its plastic wrapper wet with dew. She bent over for it, then looked up and down the street. The houses in this neighborhood were at once ample and modest, with lovingly tended small front yards. Sixteen years ago, buying here had seemed a compromise: it wasn't Palo Alto, but it was nice, and the schools were good, and she and Brody reassured themselves that Palo Alto would still be there when they had more money. Now they had more money, but they stayed. They were comfortable here. It was home.

She left the paper in the kitchen and tiptoed through the bedroom to the bathroom. She loved the first blast of the shower on her face; she opened her mouth and used her hands to cup water at her cheeks, her eyes. She massaged shampoo into her scalp, then turned and let the water course through her hair. When she turned back it beat at her nipples, and she twisted them, felt a tingling between her legs. It had been a while since she and Brody had made love, and she was ready. Was he? They were a little out of sync, she sometimes felt.

In the bedroom she began to dress, opening drawers as quietly as she could, though he was beginning to stir.

"Time is it?" he muttered after a short while.

She turned around, saw he hadn't moved. "About six-thirty."

He raised himself up and looked at her, then sank down and lay on his back. She skirted the bed and sat near him on the edge of the mattress. His chest was bare, and she laid her hand over his breastbone, its bloom of graying hairs.

"OK," he said, covering her hand with his own.

"OK," she said with a smile.

She left him and went upstairs to the kids. Lauren was likely to be awake already, and Liz hesitated, then turned the doorknob slowly. She pushed the door open but waited a moment before moving over the threshold.

Lauren was on her back, looking at the door. It seemed to Liz that she had been waiting for this moment, had even girded herself for it: pulling the covers all the way to her chin, making sure her head was in the very center of her pillow. She stared hard at Liz but didn't speak.

"Morning, sweetie," Liz said, but still Lauren didn't speak, didn't react at all. Something was going on with her these days, Liz didn't know what. It was almost as if the last three years had never happened, and she was still twelve: sullen and aggrieved. Though Friday night she'd abruptly changed her mind about spending Saturday in Berkeley with some friends, and Liz knew that at twelve Lauren never would have canceled anything involving even one other girl.

"Almost time to get up," Liz said now.

"I know," Lauren said with a sneer. "I'm not stupid."

Liz pulled the door to and headed for Joe's room. Lauren's tone seemed to have lodged inside her: she felt it harden like a fast-drying coat of shellac on her lungs. Outside Joe's room she took a deep, slow breath to break it up.

Long ago she'd replaced Joe's curtains with blackout shades, and it was very dark in his room, the only light coming from the hallway behind her. She crossed to his bed and sat down. Already he'd turned off the alarm clock that he set, every night, for six-thirty. He was crafty, never just hitting the snooze button but actually sliding the setting to off.

"Joe," she said. His head was turned to the wall, and she put a hand on his shoulder and shook it a little. "Joe."

He burrowed deeper, and as always she felt torn: she wanted to adjust the covers over him, to encourage his sleep, make his bed the nicest place possible; and she wanted, needed, to get him up.

She shook his shoulder again. "Joe."

"I'm awake."

"Right."

"I am. I swear."

She patted his shoulder and left the room, knowing she'd come again in five minutes. She tried hard to make them independent, but there was a cost to her, and some things she couldn't give up. Yet.

In the kitchen she began breakfast. She sliced a pear into a bowl of blackberries, unwrapped a loaf of challah and cut it into thick slices. She put jam and honey on the table, then went back to Joe.

"It's time," she said to his sleeping body.

He hunkered farther, bringing the covers over his face.

"It's time," she said again, shaking his shoulder. "It's almost seven."

"Urf," he moaned, but the position of his body changed, and after a while she could tell he was awake. "No," he said.

"I'm afraid so." She tweaked his foot and then left the room and headed toward Lauren's nearly closed door, but before she could speak Lauren's voice came at her, brusque and preemptive: "Mom, I'm up!"

Liz retreated. Down in the kitchen again, she put challah slices in the toaster and poured herself a second cup of coffee. She sometimes regretted the second cup at yoga, but she missed it too much when she skipped it.

In a few minutes Lauren came into the kitchen. She moved slowly, and her unbrushed hair fell in clumps past her shoulders, collected in the hood of her oversize gray sweatshirt. "Sweetie," Liz said without meaning to, and Lauren gave her a sour look.

"What?"

"Nothing. Hi." Liz put a second round of bread in the toaster and watched in her peripheral vision as Lauren moved around the table and pulled out her chair. When the toaster popped, Liz buttered the new slices, put them all on a plate, and took them to the table. "Here we go."

Lauren reached for a piece of toast and took a bite, and Liz thought, You're welcome. Then she wished she could unthink it. She hated how pissy she felt—it wasn't the kind of mother she wanted to be.

Brody came in, dressed in a white shirt and tie, and she remembered that he'd mentioned a meeting out of the office today. He passed close by her on his way to the coffeemaker, and she caught a whiff of his soap smell, watched as he found a mug and pulled the coffeepot out of its base. His nice broad back seemed broader in the white shirt. He turned and faced her for his first sip, and she thought about how much it had always pleased her to see him in a dress shirt and tie. *That's because he reminds you of your father,* Sarabeth had remarked about this, in her usual perspicacious way.

Now Joe arrived, reaching for a slice of challah before he'd even sat down, then consuming it in two bites and chasing it with a large gulp of juice. He'd shot up over the summer, and he was gangly now, with enormous wrists. She took her seat and watched as he helped himself to fruit, took more toast, pulled his juice glass a little closer: gathered what he needed to stock himself for the day.

He looked up at her as he stabbed a pear slice. "Are you driving us to practice?"

"I'm not sure yet," she said. "I'll drop your gear at Trent's if I'm not. Are you packed?"

"How is our friend Trent?" Brody said as he came over and sat down. "That was quite a play he made on Saturday. That kid can kick." He unfolded his napkin and then unfolded it again and tucked a corner into his collar. He turned to Lauren and said, "Did you know that the entire purpose of the necktie used to be to protect the shirt? Now we have to protect the protector!"

"That's the fullback's job in soccer," Joe said, and Brody winked at Liz as he turned back to Joe.

"You're quick this morning."

"No, I'm not," Joe said, but he smiled with pleasure, a wash of color high on each cheek.

Liz looked at Lauren. She was spaced out, her expression vacant as she played with one of the many thick silver rings she wore. Let's try again, Liz thought, but she wasn't sure how.

"You could get one of those plastic ties," Joe said. "Like for a Halloween costume."

"Maybe I will," Brody said. "That could solve all kinds of problems." He smiled at Liz again and reached for the challah, and she saw there was only one piece left.

She said, "Oops, sorry, I'll get some more of that."

"I can."

"No, no, I will." She slid the last slice onto his plate and went back to the toaster, thinking for a moment that this wasn't the best model for Lauren—or Joe, for that matter. The woman leaping to her feet. But she wanted to do it—she liked doing it. Was she supposed to pretend she didn't?

It was funny: most of the women she knew complained about their husbands' uselessness at domestic tasks, but of course it was they who'd allowed them to be useless. Liz did it, too—complained, too. There was this sisterhood out there, a sisterhood of eye rolling and head shaking and sighing over the helplessness of husbands. Liz had always enjoyed it, the standing around at the kids' schools or soccer games saying, *My husband cannot hang up a towel,* or *I'm going out and leaving my kids with my husband tonight*—before *dinner,* and everyone laughing. With Lauren and Joe older, Liz had less of that: the talking, the standing around. It was a little lonely with the kids older.

Very soon the rush began: Brody looking for his BlackBerry; Lauren disappearing into the bathroom; Joe all over the house at once, searching for his backpack, his math homework, his lunch—oh, wait, he had hot lunch, and he'd just remembered, he needed ten bucks for a student body card—no, today, today was the last day, it had to be today; and then they were all gone.

In the sudden silence Liz sat down again, licking her fingertip and pressing it to the toast crumbs on her plate. She found herself thinking of the brief conversation she'd had with Sarabeth Saturday morning, when she'd called to tell her Lauren wouldn't be in Berkeley after all. Lauren and her friends had planned to stop in on Sarabeth if they had time, and

Liz hadn't wanted Sarabeth wondering all day if they would come. "Oh, too bad," Sarabeth said in response to the news. "I was going to make chocolate meringues." And Liz had gotten a clear picture of the picture Sarabeth must have had, of Lauren and her friends filling her funky little house with their teenage giggles and intermittent high seriousness. Liz was sorry they'd canceled. She'd call Sarabeth after yoga, see if she could come for dinner sometime soon.

Chocolate meringues. That was the treat Sarabeth used to make for Lauren and Joe when they were little, when every few months Liz would load them into the car for a pilgrimage across the bay. In anticipation of these visits, Sarabeth would tape giant pieces of butcher paper to her living room floor, and once the meringues were consumed she'd launch the kids on some labor-intensive drawing project—a giant forest, a city of towers—so that for a while at least Liz could sit on her couch and they could talk. What a respite those conversations were: hearing about Sarabeth's romantic adventures, or learning more about a new project she had going—anything to interrupt the day-in, day-out sameness of life with small children. *I'll trade you,* Sarabeth used to say. *You couldn't stand it for more than a day.* Which was true, of course.

The high school was on the north edge of town, across the street from a little shopping center with a Starbucks, a Subway, and a Jamba Juice. Kids weren't supposed to bring food over from the center, but everyone did, smuggling their Starbucks or Jamba Juice cups into their morning classes. The teachers didn't care, but it was a rule, and if the vice-principal saw you, you got busted. It was called getting cupped. Lauren had seen a freshman guy get cupped before school today, and it was so obvious he'd done it on purpose. It was probably the highlight of his life, proving what a tough ass he was by getting detention in high school.

Lauren was in chemistry, hiding inside her conscientious student look. Notebook open, pen in hand, thoughtful expression. It was ridiculously easy. If she felt Mr. Greenway's eyes on her, she bit her lip as if she were struggling to understand something, then made a mark in her notebook. From far away she would look like she was taking notes, but in fact she was adding details to a picture of a tree she'd drawn yesterday. A Japanese maple. She was terrible at the leaves. In fact, she sucked at drawing. Everyone used to say how good she was, but they were wrong.

Across the aisle and one desk forward, Amanda twisted her copper-red hair around her finger. Her jeans were a little floody, and Lauren saw that she was wearing socks with smiley faces on them, as if she were still in middle school. Amanda could be so weird that way, not caring about stuff.

They had three classes together this fall. "That's great," Lauren's mom had said when Lauren told her, although it wasn't, exactly. It was Amanda, and it was great in exact proportion to how it was not so great: it gave Lauren someone to hang out with, and it made it impossible for her to hang out with anyone else.

"Great." With Lauren's mom everything was either "great" or "too bad." *What would you like me to say?* Lauren imagined her mom asking, and she turned away, then realized that she'd actually turned away, actually moved her head, here in chemistry. She looked at Mr. Greenway, worried that he'd noticed, but he was writing on the board, oblivious. The periodic table hung to his left. Lauren had not meant to look at it, but she'd caught a glimpse—those rows of little boxes, the meaningless letters inside them—and her stomach flipped. It was the middle of October, and she could no longer maintain the pretense that she was going to start getting it soon. Every time Mr. Greenway talked about the periodic table, she thought, OK, listen, but something happened to his voice, like he just *loved* the periodic table, and she couldn't listen. She spaced out. Sometimes she thought of the quilt on her parents' bed, how when she was little she'd lie there and play a game of mentally connecting like fabric with like fabric, a game to explain why the quilt was exactly as it was, as if it had to be. Or she'd think about lunch: where she and Amanda might sit, and whether or not she'd see what's-his-butt.

Who, speaking of: class was almost over. Her heart pounded as she watched the classroom clock click from six of to five of. Just five minutes until the after-chemistry pass. She ran her fingers through her hair, then lowered her head and examined her teeth with her tongue. She cupped her hand under her mouth and exhaled, but her breath just smelled like the classroom, not that she ever got close enough for her breath to matter. Some idiotic magazine article had said you should pinch your cheeks to bring color to them, but color wasn't a problem—her face was always on fire when she looked at him. At the moment she was also sweating between her boobs, which she absolutely hated.

"Lab tomorrow," Mr. Greenway was saying. "Don't forget your

flameproof suits." He smiled his pathetic aren't-I-funny smile just as the bell rang, and Amanda turned and rolled her eyes at Lauren.

"Don't forget your dick brain," she said, meaning Mr. Greenway's, but Lauren was in no mood. She'd missed the before-school locker pass, so she didn't even know what he was wearing today. She preferred this pass to take place out beyond the science complex, under the open sky rather than on the busy covered walkways, where she always felt invisible. Plus she could see him for longer out there, see him leaving his English class if she got out there early enough. Walking that swinging walk. His arms, his legs. She imagined him naked walking like that, and her face got even hotter, if that was possible. Herself naked near him—she wanted to barf.

"Laur-en," Amanda said, and, nearly at the door, Lauren looked back. Amanda for some reason was still at her desk, still putting her stuff in her backpack. Fuck—now the pass would take place on the science walkways, no question. She might even be too late altogether.

"Do you mind waiting?" Amanda whined, and Lauren waited, and by the time she got outside it *was* too late: he was past her, heading for his physics class, wearing his blue T-shirt with the faded red ladder on the back, from his painting job two summers ago. On the front, she knew, just over his heart, it said: JEFF.

2

Sarabeth had a staging job to start in El Cerrito, and she was parked in front of the house, early as usual, waiting for the appointed time. She sometimes thought that the need to be punctual was like a chronic but mostly manageable disease—an asthma, a diabetes, the kind of thing you accepted about yourself, accommodated, all the while knowing it could turn you inside out at any moment. For example: a week or so ago, on her way to a paint consultation, she realized halfway there that she'd forgotten her Benjamin Moore color wheel, and the next fifteen minutes—turning around, speeding home, racing into her house, racing back out, starting her car again—were an ever-escalating torment. The mental equivalent of a quiet summer afternoon into which a platoon of helicopters suddenly flew.

At ten-thirty on the nose she knocked at the door, and husband and wife answered together. Henry and Melissa, according to her notes. They said hello, and she said hello, and then they all stood there awkwardly.

"Please come in," Melissa said, and Sarabeth stepped over the threshold. The first moments were always so hard: as if she'd arrived early for a dinner party—early or uninvited.

Melissa tapped her lips nervously, and Sarabeth said, "I love this room." She glanced around and nodded. "You guys have done such a nice job here."

It was in fact a very nicely proportioned room, but it was jammed with stuff, and in her mind she erased an overly red armchair and matching ottoman, an étagère displaying a lot of Japanese lacquerware, a framed Rousseau poster, a trendy shag rug.

"Thanks," Henry said. "We like it. Although not that much, obviously!"

"Well," Sarabeth said, "there comes a point when you're ready for more . . ."

"Space," Melissa said. "Definitely."

They all smiled, and Sarabeth fished for her cell phone, bringing it all the way out of her purse so they could see that she was hitting the power button. She said, "Maybe we could just walk through first?" and with that they were off.

First was the kitchen, a sunny, remodeled space with a separate eating area on the far side of a peninsula. She imagined clearing the counters, taking the leaf out of the table, bringing in her bentwood chairs. A glass bowl of apples, and she'd be all set.

Next was the minuscule bathroom, which Jim, her friend and employer, had said was slated for a paint job. After that, all it would need would be neutral towels. And a fresh shower curtain, of course.

"And here," Henry said as she stepped back into the hallway, "is the second bedroom, which we use as an office. It's kind of cluttered, we know."

"Cluttered!" Melissa said. "It's a disaster."

Sarabeth averted her eyes as she made for the open doorway. Moving was loss and reinvention and renewal, all at once. And fear. And desire. She felt sometimes that she witnessed moments no outsider should see.

She also saw rooms—like this one—that implied so much history, contained so many snapshot-studded bulletin boards and Magic Markered boxes, that you couldn't imagine the inhabitants ever leaving. Under one of three paper-strewn desks, a single Rollerblade was balanced precariously on top of a sewing machine, and she thought that the story of the missing Rollerblade probably had the potential to introduce her to some of the major themes of Melissa's life.

They showed her their bedroom last. It was a standard first-house bedroom: very small, mostly bed, with dressers crammed against the available wall space and a chair tucked into one corner. Sarabeth stood just inside the doorway and made a mental list.

The dressers would go. The chair would go. The framed family photos on the wall between the two windows would go—as would the wedding picture. She skirted the bed (the busy, flowered duvet cover would go) and took a closer look. An outdoor setting, a bower of white roses, Henry and Melissa with their faces together, looking at the camera. He was nice looking, with good skin and hair, and handsome shoulders, though since the taking of this picture he had begun to go heavy through the jaw.

Stop, she told herself. She could think all she liked about men she met, conflating the best parts of them into some Perfect One, but not even He was who she wanted. Billy was. Still.

Behind her, Henry cleared his throat. "So I guess we'll need to get rid of some things?"

She turned to face them. "Where'd you guys get married?"

They were both silent for a moment, Melissa's finger tapping her lips again as she glanced at her husband. "Back east," she said. "In my grand-parents' backyard."

"Where back east?" This was nosy, but Sarabeth was curious.

"Swarthmore, Pennsylvania. It's just outside Philadelphia."

Sarabeth nodded vaguely, but in fact this was very satisfying: she knew where Swarthmore was and, more to the point, what it was, aside from a college: it was the town where Liz had spent her early childhood.

But she needed to focus. Jim had told her Henry and Melissa were already in escrow on a huge place in Montclair; they needed to get this house on the market *now*.

"You've probably heard Jim talk about a house's bones," she said, "and this house has great bones." She paused for a moment. "Katharine Hepburn bones," she added, and they smiled on cue, as nearly everyone did; how embarrassing that she recycled her jokes, but there it was.

"I'd like to make some suggestions," she went on, "that will enable potential buyers to really see that, but before I start I'd like to hear your thoughts about how you want to present the house, what you're thinking we might do to make it show well."

Melissa nodded happily. It was so easy and important to ask this question, though when Sarabeth first started this work she didn't get the emotional part at all. Early on, she nearly cost Jim a client: a middle-aged woman with a collection of frogs to rival—well, the amphibian population of a hell of a big pond. This woman had plush frogs and ceramic frogs and frogs made of wood and metal and fabric. They were everywhere.

Sarabeth's very first comment was that they should be removed, and the woman went into a great huff, saying she didn't see the value of taking away the house's charm, and did Sarabeth even understand what made a place appealing, did she even know? Jim happened to be there, and when he and Sarabeth exchanged a look—just a quick, careful look, a tiny posy of a look given their vast garden—the woman said she needed to rethink everything, selling at all, moving, really her whole life. In the end the house was listed; the frogs were boxed and put in storage, the bad furniture was removed, and Sarabeth did her thing with window treatments and sisal; but, oh, it had been a warning. Jim was the most loyal guy she knew, but he'd been on edge, and she'd wondered if their old friendship would depend on their new business arrangement and not vice versa.

Melissa said she thought the living room was pretty much OK, the kitchen OK, the office—she and Henry exchanged a glance—a bit crowded, and the bedroom OK. Sarabeth spoke generally about neutralizing the furnishings and opening up the rooms so they could be more clearly seen, and then she told them a very few of the specifics she was considering. Most of it she would save for the next visit, when they'd have begun to think editorially themselves, which would allow them to feel that even her ideas were theirs.

She said goodbye and went out to her car, but as she drove down the street she found that she was worrying a little. One of the few things she had suggested removing was the étagère in the living room, and as Melissa passed it on the way to the front door, she stopped and micro-adjusted the position of a glossy black platter. Sarabeth hoped she wasn't hurt.

Next on her schedule was Emeryville, Mark Murphy's shop. She turned on the radio, and there was a woman's voice, singing: *Look at me, I'm as helpless as a kitten up a tree.* She turned the radio back off, but the silenced song had taken hold, and in her mind she heard *Na na na na, na na nah na, na na na na na na, I grow misty just holding your hand.* She imagined a little girl walking hand in hand with a woman, and it was the day that was misty. They were both wearing dark knee-length coats, as in the sixties. It was like a scene from a movie, piano music on the sound track: you saw them from the back, and you knew they were walking toward something scary or dangerous or sad. Switch to the girl's point of view as she looks up: the woman's face is pale. The girl looks for another moment, then focuses on her feet, the step, step, step of her black maryjanes.

Sarabeth gunned the engine as she merged onto the freeway. It was late morning on a Tuesday, not much traffic. How she lived made sense in a certain way, the bits and pieces of work she did that added up to a living—a life. Sometimes, though, like now, the energy it took to haul herself from place to place seemed out of reach.

Mark Murphy's shop was in a refurbished warehouse in the industrial part of Emeryville. He shared the lease with an artisanal bakery, and as Sarabeth entered the high-ceilinged space she breathed in the aroma of baking bread. He was at his desk, on the phone, but he waved her forward, then held up his forefinger to show he wouldn't be long.

He might be, though—he often was—so she set the box she was carrying on the floor and wandered back to his display area, where a couple dozen lamps were grouped in vaguely roomlike configurations: a few on tables, several standing lamps set near armchairs, wall sconces at almost believable intervals. Mark had done a good job here, and Sarabeth thought it was sort of too bad he was doing so well now; these days, most of his business happened through his handsomely produced catalog, or online, and the showroom was—well, just for show.

"What do you have for me?" he said, approaching her from the front of the shop. He had a way of giving almost everything he said a slight sexual gloss, and Sarabeth blushed lightly. He was attractively tall and narrow hipped, and he wore his Levi's tight.

"It's a new one," she said. "I was thinking about the mocha, and I thought, Let's try something for people who aren't afraid of color."

He tilted his head to the side and smiled his dry, slightly mocking smile. At first this smile had put Sarabeth off—it had taken months for her to realize it didn't necessarily reflect what he was thinking or what he was going to say. Although it could.

"Color," he said. "I'm intrigued."

She headed past him to where she'd left the box. Opening the flaps, sliding away the tissue paper: he was standing behind her now. She took hold of the piece by the wire spokes and pulled it clear of the box.

"Oooh," he said. "That's nice." He pushed papers out of the way so she could set it on his desk. "That is *nice.*"

"Thank you," she said primly, but in fact she was quite pleased. She'd found some handmade dusty-rose paper and fashioned a lampshade unlike any she'd made before. She'd glued braid around the narrow top and the prettily flared bottom, and the shape was almost saucy.

"It's very *McCabe and Mrs. Miller,*" he said. "Kind of 'welcome to our bordello.' "

She cracked a smile.

"But in a good way," he said with a wink. He lifted the shade and looked underneath, his eyes squinting as he faced the high ceiling. The underside, yes: she was particularly proud of the lining. Racing into the future, she wanted to try sea green, apricot. Maybe midnight blue on a perfect cube.

"How much paper did you buy?" he asked.

"Only enough for the prototype." This wasn't quite true—she'd bought all that was left on the roll, three yards and change. But Mark was your classic hard-to-get guy, and she played fire against fire. (And wondered about his twenty-year marriage. Did he have affairs? Or was it perhaps enough to flirt, to be forever sought? His wife, Mary, was a friend of Sarabeth's friend Nina—that was the route Sarabeth had taken to him in the first place—and at the beginning, on meeting him, she had thought: Why didn't Nina tell me they were splitting up? Now she thought: Why didn't Nina tell me they were so solid?)

"What if I wanted to place an order?" he said. "A dozen of 'Welcome to Our Bordello'?"

She suppressed a smile. "I could check back with my supplier."

"Why don't you do that, Sarabeth?" He leaned against his desk and crossed one long leg in front of the other. He had big hands, big knuckles, and his wedding ring nestled in the fine hairs on his ring finger. It had swirls carved into the gold. It said: *We got married back when Zen gardens first got popular.*

"OK," she said. "I'll leave you a voice mail."

She started to put the lampshade back in the box, but he reached out a hand to her forearm, and she stopped. "Do you have a sec?" he said.

"Sure."

He pushed away from the desk and headed toward the back of the shop. Past the display area, he opened a door and led her into a dark workroom. "Come on," he said, crooking his finger. In the back, against the wall, was . . . a canoe? He stepped to the loading dock and hit a button, and a grayish fluorescent light flickered on. He looked up at the blinking panels. "Irony of ironies."

Now she could see: a canoe, yes, but not just any canoe. It was beautiful, long and sleek and glossy, made of a light wood but with a darker wood inlaid into a geometric design on the front. "Wow," she said.

"Pretty, huh?"

"So business is good?"

"I try to do something nice for myself every once in a while."

She walked the length of the canoe, then walked back. "When'd you get it?"

"It was just delivered this morning. You're the first to see it."

At this she looked away from him. She squatted, and when she ran her fingertips over the seams around the inlaid area, there wasn't the slightest alteration in how the wood felt.

"Where do you go canoeing?" she said.

"I tend to like rivers."

She couldn't tell if this was snide or not. "You know, I should actually get going, but thanks for the look. It's beautiful."

He said, "Sacramento River, Feather River. Or if I have more time I go up to Oregon." He watched her in an intent, focused way, and she wanted to say: *OK, you win, I'm not woman enough for you, buddy.* Instead she said, "Does Mary like canoeing?"

He smiled a different smile now, a pained smile she couldn't quite read. "Mary does," he said. "Mary likes canoeing."

Back in the car, she sat still for a moment, watching as a homeless man passed by pushing a shopping cart piled high with bloated bags. Half a mile away was the new Emeryville with its terrifying Ikea, its nightmare version of a suburban shopping mall. Here, in front of Mark's shop, the last thirty years might never have happened.

Seeing Mark always sparked something in Sarabeth: lust, but also loneliness, too. Starting her car, she thought of Henry and Melissa, the brief time with them and the brief times to come and the void that would follow. *My grandparents' backyard.* What did that mean to Melissa? What did Swarthmore mean? To Liz it was the backdrop of early memories, first memories: one having to do with using a big piece of cardboard to slide down a leaf-strewn hill in autumn; another concerning corn on the cob—driving to a farm and buying corn that had just been picked, and Liz's mother cooking it right away and then serving it to the kids at the picnic table in the backyard, steaming ears of corn dripping with butter in the middle of the afternoon. Some of Liz's memories were so vivid to Sarabeth, it was as if they were hers.

She turned her phone back on and called Liz, getting the voice mail at home and then trying her cell.

"I was going to call you in maybe twenty minutes!" Liz said by way of answering.

"Beat you to it."

"I'm in line at the grocery store. Can I call you when I get home?"

"Sure," Sarabeth chirped, but when she'd stowed her phone, she lowered her forehead and rested it for a moment on the steering wheel.

She started the car and headed home, taking Adeline for no other reason than to pass the Berkeley Bowl. The infamous Berkeley Bowl, where she'd met Billy. She'd spotted him at the heirloom tomatoes—this tall man with small gold glasses and thick, gray-blond hair—and she noticed even before they spoke, before that opening remark of his about the tomato that looked like George Bush, that he wore a wedding ring. She laughed at the tomato—it did have these flaplike things on the sides, like ears—and he mentioned a book his kids had that contained photographs of fruits and vegetables that seemed to have faces.

And then there he was at the baked goods. And then in line at the cashier. It was a hot September day, and there was a fresh juice stand, and they bought smoothies and sat on the curb in front of her car and talked for forty-five minutes while her peach sorbet melted and her free-range chicken got busy welcoming colonies of bacteria.

And he was so interested in her! And he thought her lampshades sounded so cool! They met for coffee a few days later, and for lunch a week after that, and then for sex every Monday noon and Wednesday evening for the next thirteen and a half months.

And then they didn't. Now they didn't. It was coming, the anniversary of their breakup. She longed to be someone who could face such a thing with equanimity, who would not joke to her friends, as she had been doing, relentlessly, that when the day came she would mark it somehow: by lighting a candle, calling him, slitting her wrists.

Enough, she thought. Enough.

She was driving. The sky was the intense blue of early autumn, and there were pumpkins on porches—pumpkins already. Halloween was around the corner, and all at once the entire holiday season loomed up on the bare calendar in her mind like a group of massive fortresses coming into view on an otherwise empty horizon.

It came back then, the girl and the woman. Walking in the mist. They were walking *toward* an empty horizon: a horizon that was all mist. She saw them clearly: the girl and the woman walking, and the girl looking up but not speaking, not speaking, never speaking.

3

*B*rody worked at a company called Oiron, where he was VP of business development; he'd been on board almost since the beginning, moving from one position to another as the company went public and grew to its current size of five hundred employees spread over three continents. The best-selling product was Parapet, a comprehensive Wi-Fi security system; Oiron was the name of a fortress in France.

It was Friday now, the end of a long week. Brody was in front of his terminal, triaging the afternoon's e-mails and thinking about tonight, when he and Liz were taking the kids to his favorite restaurant in North Beach, a tiny, crowded place where you could almost taste the garlic from the sidewalk, and the waiters jostled your chair as they passed behind you, and the only difficult moment you could possibly have was choosing from among the twenty-seven different pastas on the menu. He'd discovered it his first year in California; he and a bunch of guys from work had landed there by accident one Saturday night, and his whole concept of Italian food had changed in an instant. He was looking forward to a plate of fettuccine Genovese, the kind with thin slices of potato mixed in with the noodles.

"Dude."

He looked up and saw Mike Patterson standing in his doorway. Mike was big, maybe six feet five, with thick shoulders and arms—high school football, Brody was pretty sure. Mike was in marketing, where Brody himself had been for years; Brody'd been in on the hire, in fact. Mike was a good guy. Brody and Liz had done dinner out with him and his wife several times.

"Who are you duding, dude?" Brody said.

Mike grinned as he came into Brody's office. "My brother put his foot down when his kids started calling their mother dude."

"Joe does that," Brody said. " 'Mom, dude, will you make some brownies?' "

"And Liz?"

"Liz just laughs. You know how she is."

Mike had stopped at Brody's bookcase and was looking at the tennis ball Brody kept on a stand there, a wild shot off Andre Agassi's racquet during a practice session Brody'd happened by at the U.S. Open one year. Mike said, "I'm still shocked you stole this."

" 'Kept it,' " Brody said. "I 'kept' it."

"Sure you did, pal. So are you coming?"

"Where would that be?"

Mike mimed drinking something, and Brody looked at his watch: late on Friday afternoons the helium balloon that was Oiron's usual corporate urgency started making its way to the floor, and to cushion the landing there was generally a beer bash in the cafeteria. "Whoa," he said, "it's later than I thought."

"Brody, it's not about time," Mike said, "it's about the change in synergy. I'm surprised you didn't notice."

"Up yours."

"HR's going to have to schedule another sensitivity-training retreat for us if you don't shape up."

Brody rolled his eyes. "Promise you'll shoot me if that happens."

"I would, but I've already got someone lined up to shoot me."

Downstairs, there were already several dozen people gathered, talking mostly in their work groups, though some ventured laterally across department lines. At the keg Mike drew Brody a cup of beer, then gestured with his head that he was going to try to get to the food. Brody moved to the wall. The beer was thin and foamy and almost tasteless: terrible but in its own way also delicious. He drank half of it in a few gulps, liking the way it felt both warm and cool as it spread through him.

"Brody Mackay, how goes it?"

He turned and there was Russ Conklin, holding not beer but, as was his custom, a bottle of Odwalla carrot juice. Russ was short and muscle-bound and perfectly bald, his head shaved where hair still grew. He was Oiron's founder and CEO, not to mention Brody's boss, but Brody went way back with him, to when they'd been in side-by-side cubes at Wells Fargo twenty-odd years ago. Long after they'd both moved on, Russ had tracked Brody down at another start-up and sold him on Oiron in a five-minute phone call. Actually, Russ had sold Brody on Russ, and it had turned out to be a very good buy.

"Just fine," Brody said. "And yourself?"

"Very well. Give me the ten thousand foot on your conversation with Harker."

Harker was the head of I.S. Solutions, a small software company with some very clever algorithms for the detection and blocking of the latest sniffer devices. Brody'd spent an hour on the phone with him that morning, working out the details of a licensing agreement.

"He's sending it to his legal guy on Monday," Brody said.

Russ raised his juice bottle in a toast. "What I like to hear." He took a swallow and said, "So what are you up to this weekend?"

"Not much. How 'bout you? Cycling to Santa Cruz? Parasailing at Stinson Beach?"

Russ smiled. He'd gotten divorced two years ago, and since then he'd been incredibly active, departing from his workaholic ways for weekend scuba trips, helicopter skiing in the Canadian Rockies. He was also dating like crazy, though Brody suspected he was lonely; it was only after his divorce that he'd begun sending e-mails time-stamped at 3:00 a.m. The witching hour, the hour of Ambien and cable TV.

Brody's phone rang, and he pulled it from his pocket, saw it was home.

Russ clapped his shoulder. "I'll let you get that."

Brody stepped away from the crowd and watched as Russ moved to a group from sales. He answered.

"Is it crazy there?" Liz said.

"Not particularly. We're having our Friday kegger. How're things there?"

"Fine, but we have a wrinkle for North Beach tonight. Joe's game got moved to eight a.m. tomorrow. I'm thinking we should put it off."

"Eight a.m.?"

"I know."

Actually, Brody enjoyed early morning soccer games; that wasn't the issue. He said, "Joe doesn't want to go?"

"Well, he didn't say so. But you know we wouldn't get home till eleven or so. He's got to be at warm-ups at seven."

"True."

"So don't you think?"

Brody considered. Of course it would be best for Joe to get a good night's sleep, but he and Liz had a history of differing on whether or not best mattered all that much. In the grand scheme of things, how important was it for a thirteen-year-old boy to play a soccer game under optimal conditions? When Brody was a kid playing Little League, his parents had barely known when he had a game, let alone made sure he got enough sleep the night before. This was tricky ground, though, because he didn't want to seem like—he wasn't—an uncaring father.

"Yeah, you're right," he said. "We'll do it another time."

"You sure?"

"Definitely."

He put his phone away and looked at the crowd. Just opposite him, a trio of engineers peered down at someone's Palm. They looked as if they'd slept in their clothes, which in fact they might have: there was a big deadline next week, and the feeling of barely controlled frenzy on the third floor was getting stronger with each passing day. It was all Red Bull up there now, and the sharp smells of garlic and sweat. These three guys would each drink a Diet Coke and then go back upstairs, probably be here all weekend. Brody knew that drill inside out: working seventy or eighty hours a week without giving it a second thought because that was what you did if you wanted to go places. Then one day you woke up and went: *Oh. This is my* life *I'm living at this desk.*

The morning air was bright, the grass sopping. Brody helped Joe's coaches drag the goals into place and then watched the boys warm up: stretches, drills, a couple good laps around the field. They were at a park high in the hills, with a clear view west of the coastal range: the rise and rise of its thickly forested flanks. Somehow, you could tell the ocean was right on the other side—maybe because the sky at the top of the mountain was so brilliant. If Liz were along they'd have walked the park's trails until the game began, but these days she tended to skip the early games—so she'd be home when Lauren got up.

There was this thing Brody did sometimes, thinking about Joe: he ran the movie of Joe's life, but sped up. It went slippery infant, chubby baby, toddler, truck lover, math guy, smart aleck, athlete. It was Joe-through-the-ages. Like those old Wonder Bread ads from his own childhood: helps build strong bodies twelve ways. And you'd see a flash series of one kid through the years, wearing the same clothes but getting bigger and bigger.

Right now, Joe was all athlete. The game about to begin, Brody watched him jog in place, touch his toes, jog again. *Ready,* he seemed to be saying. *Ready now.*

The whistle blew, and Joe leaped into play, running wide and receiving a pass from Trent, then dribbling up the side with the opposition giving chase. Joe had moves—he could dodge and feint—and he was fast on his feet, but near the goal something sometimes took over, a hesitation, a lack of focus, and Brody realized he was holding his breath and let it go in a rush.

He headed toward a couple of the other fathers. "Beautiful morning," he said.

"Beautiful," one guy agreed. His son was in the goal, and he seemed to bear some of the tension in his own body: he appeared coiled, ready to spring.

"Got to love these eight a.m. games," said another. He jiggled the keys in his pocket. "This is my twentieth year doing this," he added, almost to himself.

Brody had clocked far less than that, but he was pretty sure he was going on a decade. When had Joe started, kindergarten? Back then Brody had never imagined Joe would continue to play year after year, that soccer itself, the blunt, running, back and forth of the game, would so engage him. In the early years it had been as much about the snack as the game—more, probably. He vividly remembered walking across a muddy field—maybe half the size of this one—carrying a huge pink bakery box while Joe charged ahead and called to the other boys, "We brought doughnuts! You can have glazed, cinnamon, or chocolate with sprinkles, but if you have chocolate with sprinkles you have to finish before you get in your car!" Then, when the game was over, the boys crowded around the box and grabbed. Jostling, sweaty, muddy—like pigs in a litter. Brody felt a great kinship with them, intermingled with a kind of finicky adult remonstrance.

After a while it was halftime. Joe stood with his teammates chugging water, his face red as a steak. Brody gave him a thumbs-up, and he smiled and gave Brody a little wave. He was a good boy, a good son. All the previous Joes lived directly under his skin. It was different with Lauren—or maybe Brody was different. He didn't do the movie thing with her. What he returned to again and again was a certain time in her very young life, when Joe was a newborn, always on Liz's breast, and he and Lauren were their own pair. It was the era when she liked to clomp around the house in his shoes. He read Dr. Seuss to her and cut up cheese and apples for her to eat. She had a special rubber whale, and she squealed with laughter when he made it swim around at bathtime. He loved to make her laugh, he loved to think that she was thinking. But at night, sitting by her crib for a few minutes once the light was off, he'd watch her little body move around, her rump go into the air, thumb into her mouth, and he'd be nearly breathless with the thought that she was still just a baby. He was afraid he asked too much of her. The urge to protect her was enormous.

In the last seconds of play, Joe scored the game's winning goal off a pass from his friend Conor, and all the boys pounded one another with excitement. Crowded together afterward, mud spattered and happy, they did their two-four-six-eight for the other team in a near frenzy of exuberance.

Brody waited for Joe to pack up, and they walked to the parking lot. "Did you see Conor?" Joe exclaimed. "He set that up so perfectly."

"Wouldn't've gone anywhere if you hadn't been ready."

Joe grinned, and Brody squeezed the back of his neck, let his hand rest on Joe's shoulder as they continued to the car.

At home, Liz was at the kitchen table with coffee and the newspaper, her dark hair glinting red and blond in the sunlight coming through the window. She looked over her shoulder, then stood and smiled at Joe. "So?"

"We won, four to three."

"And guess who scored the winning goal," Brody said.

"Way to go!" Liz held out her palm for Joe to slap. "I'm sorry I missed it."

Joe sank onto a chair and peeled off his socks, then unstrapped his shin guards with a groan. His feet were pocked with terry marks, the fine new hairs on his toes sticking to the skin.

Brody looked at the clock: almost ten. "She's not up yet?"

"Not yet." Liz bent over Joe and kissed the top of his head. "Teenagers need their sleep," she murmured into his hair. "In fact, I have a feeling a certain person might crash this afternoon."

"Mom," Joe said, but he was smiling.

Once he'd headed upstairs to shower, Brody sat at the table, and all at once the morning caught up with him. There was a dull ache in his right shoulder—his tennis shoulder—and even his legs felt heavy. "Actually I'm beat, too," he said, and Liz gave him a sympathetic smile.

"Nothing like getting up at six-thirty on a Saturday."

He smiled back at her, but for a strange moment he felt close to tears: something to do with how tired he was, or perhaps with her kindness. She even looked kind: it was in her mouth, in the unassuming gray of her eyes. The first time he ever saw her, this knockout girl with long legs and great hair and a fantastic smile, standing across a crowded bar in the Marina, what he really thought was: She looks *nice*.

He rotated one ankle, then the other. He could do with a shower himself, or a long nap. A long nap with her: the house empty, the two of them lying together. He saw her on top of him, her breasts filling his hands, her face as light as the moon.

"What?" she said. "You OK?"

"Sure. Nothing a cup of coffee won't fix."

They both looked at the coffeemaker: empty. "I'll make a new pot," she said, but he shook his head.

"Actually, don't bother. I'm better off without it. Any plans for today?"

"Just Sarabeth coming for dinner."

"Oh, right." He'd forgotten about Sarabeth—kind of like forgetting about a dentist appointment. Liz was watching him, and he stretched his arms out in front of him, pulled the paper closer for a glimpse of the headlines. He said, "Hey, maybe I'll sand that bench today."

It had been weeks that he'd been promising, and a smile lit her face. "Really?"

"Yeah. It's Saturday, and I'm a man with a power tool. What could be better?"

. . .

Upstairs, Lauren heard Joe's shower go on, and she looked at her clock: 10:17. She'd been awake since eight something, but she was still in bed, or actually in bed again, having gotten up to discover that the only clean jeans she had were a pair she hated. They made her ass look fat, which meant an ugly day. Back under the covers, she'd pulled her nightgown over her nose and sniffed, and though she couldn't smell anything she was sure she stank, because her pits were slick with sweat. It was such a joke that Jeff Shannon would ever look twice at her. He might look twice to bark. She hated how easily she cried—she was doing it again. Tears all over her face. Snot streaming from her nose. She cried without even crying. These days she did. Just quietly, all this stuff sliding out of her.

She sat up and then had to wait for the dizziness to stop before she could stand. Her room had the awful darkness of closed curtains in daytime. She went over and pulled one curtain to the side. It was sunny out, the sky so clear and blue it hurt her eyes. She'd prefer rain or at least clouds. She thought of how her dad used to take her and Joe bike riding: on Saturdays like this, if he didn't have to work, they'd go on these megarides by the reservoir. When Joe was moving along OK, Lauren and her dad would race to the moon. That was what he said: "Let's race to the moon." He always let her win. She knew but didn't know. He'd be panting, he'd be all, "I almost had you." Pretending to wipe sweat from his forehead. And she believed him. It wasn't even like she had to choose to believe him; it just happened. So how did she know now that he'd been faking?

She hardly saw her dad these days. Well, that wasn't really true, she saw him all the time, and for some reason this made her feel worse. Now her shoulders shook a little. Now she was really crying. She got up onto her desk and stared out the window. From the second floor it would be so easy to fall. She meant jump but pretend she'd fallen. She hated these thoughts. She hadn't been thinking about anything before, but now she was thinking horrible stuff. She was crying and crying. She realized that she was pounding her fists against her thighs. If only there were somewhere to go, she needed somewhere to go. She slid off the desk and crumpled to her knees, then lowered her head to the rug. She was crying and crying, as quietly as she could but so hard she felt sick. Her parents were downstairs, Joe was in the bathroom. She couldn't go anywhere.

The picture came to her then, the picture of herself under a heavy blanket, this stiff, hairy blanket like something from the army. It stretched over her, taut like Saran Wrap on a dish in the fridge. Her body was a lump underneath it. She sat up quickly, and bright lights swarmed around her. She crawled toward her closet. She crawled inside, slid the door closed, and sat against the wall, in the space she'd cleared among her shoes. Her stupid blue dress from last year brushed her shoulder. Life was endless, endless.

4

*W*e'll have an early dinner, Liz had told Sarabeth, very casual, don't bring anything, but Sarabeth couldn't not bring anything, so on her way out of town she'd stopped at the Cheese Board for half a dozen cheese rolls. Slowing as she approached the toll plaza on the San Mateo Bridge, she reached onto the passenger seat for the bag and tore off a little bit of one of the rolls—the same one she'd already molested, she fervently hoped. She put it in her mouth and savored the delicious tang, the way it was both soft and crunchy at the same time. These cheese rolls were such a reliable pleasure. She handed her money to the toll taker and floored it out of the gate: water on both sides, the city far to the right in deep shadow, the sun going down behind the mountains.

Joe answered the door, looking about two years older than when she'd last seen him, in August. He was beautiful: Brody's blue eyes, Liz's cheekbones and gorgeous brown hair, her dad's handsome, squared-off chin.

"Hi, there," she said, and he gave her a cute little wave as he stepped back to let her in. "How's life? Are the girls leaving you any time for yourself?"

"It's OK," he said. "You know, school and stuff."

"You playing soccer this year?"

He hesitated. "Yeah."

"Oh, duh," she said. "Of course you are."

Liz came in from the kitchen, smiling widely and wiping her hands on her jeans and then pulling Sarabeth close. She smelled of the moisturizer she'd been using since high school; she smelled of Liz.

She took a step back and looked Sarabeth over. "As usual," she said, plucking at Sarabeth's scarf. "Where do you find these things? I feel so matronly around you."

The scarf was a larky thing Sarabeth had bought at a boutique on College—sheer and stretchy, and imprinted with images and text that looked as if they came from a tabloid newspaper. "California Teen Dating Einstein's Brain" screamed one headline. She'd worn it for Lauren, really. She'd thought Lauren would get a kick out of it.

"Please," she said to Liz. "You're about as matronly as Michelle Pfeiffer." In fact, Liz *was* a little matronly—or if not matronly at least square. Tonight, she was wearing a powder-blue sweater set that could have come from Ann Taylor, even Talbots. "You look great."

Joe was heading away from them, and Liz called, "Did you say hi to Sarabeth?"

"No, Mom," he said, turning back. "I opened the door and just stood there like an idiot."

"Yeah, Mom," Sarabeth said.

"Sorry, sweetie," Liz called, and they both watched as he made the stairs and took them in a few leaps.

"He is too cute," Sarabeth said.

"Isn't he? It actually kills me; I'm afraid he knows it."

"Joe? I don't think of him as conceited."

"No, I'm afraid he knows it and feels he *has* to be. Like it's his job. Come on," Liz said, and as they headed for the kitchen Sarabeth marveled—not for the first time—at the subtlety of the things Liz worried about.

Brody was standing at the counter opening wine, dressed in khakis and a navy-blue crew-neck sweater. Even now, after all these years, Sarabeth was still sometimes taken aback by his—"dullness" wasn't the word, he wasn't dull—his *plainness,* though not in the physical sense but rather in his being *just a guy,* a clean-shaven guy who wore khakis and played a lot of tennis. What did it mean that he was the husband Liz had chosen?

He and Sarabeth greeted each other, and the three of them chatted while Liz set out cheese and crackers. The kitchen smelled of beef cooking in wine, and there were expensive ceramics displayed on shelves, and pots of herbs growing on a ledge in a south-facing window. Sarabeth had to settle in each time, take in the *Sunset* magazine perfection of it all, recognize her own scorn, her own *envy*—and then take all of that and throw it off so she could see Liz; see Liz and herself.

"So how's business these days?" Brody asked her.

"Oh, thriving."

"You got that Web site up and running yet?"

Sarabeth looked at Liz, and Liz tilted her head sideways and mock-glared at Brody. "He's kidding," she said to Sarabeth. "Aren't you, honey?"

Sarabeth didn't care. One of these days she'd enter the twenty-first century, and when she did she'd ask him for help, or ask Liz's older brother. . . .

"Oh, my God," she said, suddenly remembering. "Did I tell you? I somehow got on John's mass e-mail list, and he's forwarding me dirty jokes practically every day!"

"No!" Liz said. "He'll be so embarrassed."

"Don't tell him."

"Of course I'll tell him."

"I want to be on that list," Brody said. "No fair."

Liz flapped her hand at him, then turned back and told Sarabeth that John had called that very morning to report that his oldest had gotten engaged—the first Castleberry grandchild to tie the knot.

"God," Sarabeth said.

"What?"

"I just think it's wrong that someone in my generation could have a child ready for marriage."

"Who says he's ready?" Brody said.

"Touché."

"You know," he went on, speaking mostly to Liz now, "I think maybe I'll head upstairs and check on the game."

"It could use your help."

"That's what I'm thinking."

He took his wine with him, and Sarabeth listened to his footsteps until he'd reached the top of the stairs. The game was a pro forma excuse even if it was a real one: he always gave the two of them time alone.

Whether this was for his benefit or for hers and Liz's, she didn't know and didn't much care. What mattered was that she had Liz to herself for a while.

"So tell me," Liz said.

"Tell you what?"

"Everything!"

Their friendship was a story of stories told, going all the way back to childhood. Sarabeth could still remember the summer day when Liz's family arrived on Cowper Street, when she and Liz were eight. Liz's first story, told that afternoon as the two of them sat on the curb eating Creamsicles: during the long drive across country from Pennsylvania, her little brother had thrown up *seven times*.

"If only there were an everything," Sarabeth said now. "Or even an anything."

"There must be an anything."

"I made a new lampshade."

"What did I tell you?" Liz teased. She twirled the stem of her wineglass and said casually, "For MM?" She worried about Mark—but really, she didn't need to.

"The very same."

"Did he like it?"

"He did. But not as much as he likes his new canoe."

"What?"

"Mark got himself a new canoe. It was kind of strange, really, I was getting ready to leave, and he goes, 'I want to show you something.' And in his workroom he had this actually very beautiful new canoe."

"Only you," Liz said, "would know someone who'd have a canoe at his workplace."

"Unless the workplace was a boat shop."

"Only you would know someone whose workplace was a boat shop!"

Sarabeth shrugged; Liz had a thing about how unusual and interesting her life was. If only it were true.

"So how was it strange?" Liz said.

"I don't know. Because a canoe is so phallic?" Sarabeth waited for Liz's smile. "It was different is all. Mostly I'm in, I'm out, it's all lamps. He made a point of asking if I *had* a second."

"Maybe it was that he showed you something he cared about. He put himself on the line. It would've been hard for him if you hadn't admired it."

"Speaking of phallic," Sarabeth said, and they both laughed.

"Actually, I have something to show you," Liz said, and she motioned Sarabeth to follow her to the garage.

There, in the middle of the floor, in a space cleared of bicycles and skateboards and exercise equipment, stood an old wooden bench: two boards for the back, three for the seat, and a pair of sweet little armrests supported by standards of curved wrought iron. Liz had started doing decorative furniture painting recently, and Sarabeth figured this was her next project.

"I love it," she said. "What's your plan, what are you going to do?"

"I don't know yet." Liz brought her arms close, folding them across her stomach. "That's the hard part."

"It's the fun part," Sarabeth said. "You'll think of something great."

"We'll see. You're the creative one."

"We aren't *ones*," Sarabeth said. "If I'm the anything one, or you are, then that means the other person automatically isn't that thing."

Liz smiled.

"What?"

"I always knew you were the smart one."

They went back into the kitchen, and Liz stationed herself at the drainboard, where a pile of washed potatoes waited. She opened a drawer for a peeler, and in no time there were ribbons of potato skin flying into the sink. Sarabeth stood where she could watch.

"So how is everyone?" Liz said. "How's Jim? And Esther—you haven't mentioned her in weeks."

Esther was an elderly woman Sarabeth had sort of adopted—or was it Esther who'd adopted Sarabeth? For five years now, Sarabeth had been reading aloud at the Berkeley Center for Integrated Living, a result of one of the fortuitous, strange stories that had supplied her with work, a short-term volunteer position reading to the blind becoming a paid—well, gig, actually. Once a week she carried a book of her own choosing to the Center, and people paid to listen to her read from it. Blind and sighted people. Esther was her favorite: at least eighty, thin as a pack of sticks, and possessed of a lovely, uncanny cheerfulness. Nearly every week she presented Sarabeth with a small gift, usually a few cookies in cellophane, sometimes a worn postcard of a painting she'd seen decades earlier at a museum in Europe. She baked the cookies herself: branny, raisiny cookies that Sarabeth never ate, though she took them home and kept them until she received the next bag.

"She's a delight," Sarabeth said. "She's so cute—last week she was wearing this red beret."

Liz grinned. "My mother got red pants."

"Red pants like preppy?"

"More like hottie. Tight, low-cut velvet. She lost weight in Egypt so she's buying all these clothes that'll fit her for like a month."

"Now, now."

Liz had finished peeling the potatoes, and she set them on a board and cut them into chunks, then put them in a saucepan. She filled the pan with water, swirled it around, dumped it out, and filled it again. There was a reason for this, Sarabeth was sure, but she had no idea what it was.

On the counter near her elbow there was a piece of binder paper with a drawing of a leaf on it—a marijuanaish-looking leaf, though surely it wasn't. She held it up for Liz to see. "What's this?"

"Looks like something of Lauren's."

That made sense: Lauren was the artist. She was a wonderful artist, in fact—had been since she was little. The leaf was beautifully drawn, the veins faint but exact.

"Oh, my God!" Sarabeth said. "You know who I just thought of? Do you remember that guy Carl Drake?"

"Oh, my God!" Liz cried. "I haven't thought of him in decades!"

They beamed at each other, Liz's eyes wide with pleasure, Sarabeth feeling something close to an adrenaline rush. Moments like this with Liz, the retrieval of events buried so long they'd become comedy—who needed sex?

"What on earth made you think of him?" Liz said.

"Let me think."

What had? He'd been her just-after-college boyfriend—one of her just-after-college boyfriends—and she remembered being in bed with him, how full he was of dirty talk. *Do you like my dick? Does that feel good on your pussy?* What on earth had she been doing with him? Liking his dick, actually. Then one day she realized there was a difference, and she didn't really like him.

But why had she thought of him? She thought of his apartment, a tiny chunk of an old house near the Oakland border. His room, which smelled of cigarettes and greasy food. His bed. Then she realized.

"Marijuana! He had a huge poster of a marijuana leaf over his bed."

"Ohhh-K," Liz said. "And you thought of marijuana because . . ."

Sarabeth held up Lauren's drawing again. "It's ten o'clock," she intoned. "Do you know where your child is?"

Liz laughed. "That's a *maple* leaf! I wish it were pot."

"What do you mean?"

"Nothing," Liz said, and she returned to the sink, clearly not wanting to say more. Should Sarabeth ask? When Liz was this emphatic she never quite knew.

"All right," Liz said, setting the pot of potatoes on the stove with a clank. "We are getting there." She stood still for a moment, tapping her finger against her chin, then she went to the refrigerator and got out lettuce and a cucumber.

Sarabeth put the drawing down. She said, "I believe the time has come."

"The Wandering?"

"Exactly that."

She had her habits, and one was to spend a little time on each visit drifting through the Mackays' house and garden—as if she were a nineteenth-century landowner who'd traveled to one of the more distant acreages of his holdings, partly to reacquaint himself with it and partly to determine if there had been any changes since his last visit. As if she were a Levin, come to think of it. She was reading *Anna Karenina* at the Center.

Through the family room she drifted, past the huge flowered couch, the elaborate entertainment center, the family photos crowding the horizontal surfaces. At the French doors that let onto the patio, she stopped. She could see Liz reflected in the glass, her arm moving quickly as she sliced the cucumber.

She opened the door and stepped outside. She breathed in the smell of the suburbs. Overhead, the sky was teal blue, starless. She stood still for a moment, then made her way to the wooden glider the kids had given Liz for her birthday one year. She sat down and pushed off with one foot, and the glider creaked as it began to move.

Who cared about Carl Drake? It was Billy who was on her mind. Endlessly. Or if not on her mind, then in it, readily available: the one channel always broadcasting on her mental TV. She saw him in close-up: his thick hair, always so clean smelling; the scar dividing his left eyebrow, where her fingernail fit perfectly; the shallow rise and fall of his upper lip. No other ex-boyfriend had had such a hold on her, not even Roger

Orr, the one guy she'd actually lived with during her spotty romantic career. Was it because Billy had been married? *Was* married?

The shame she'd felt throughout the affair—she'd hated herself, been unable to stop herself, hated herself; even now it overlay all her memories. Did it also make them more insistent?

"Hi," said a voice.

Sarabeth startled, then looked around.

"Up here."

She looked up and saw Lauren leaning out a window, her shape dark against the bright room. "Hi," she called up. "Beautiful night, huh?"

Lauren didn't respond, and Sarabeth cupped her eyes to try to see better. "How are you?"

"Fine."

"What's new? I missed you last week."

Again Lauren didn't respond, but she shifted, her silhouette moving to the left. A phone rang somewhere, inside the Mackays' or close by.

"Want some company?" Sarabeth said.

"Sure."

"I just have to pee first."

Inside, Liz was at the stove, stirring something in a skillet while with one shoulder she pressed the phone to her ear. Sarabeth pointed at the ceiling and kept going. There was a powder room at the foot of the stairs, and she used the toilet, then paused in front of the mirror when she was finished. She had one eyebrow hair that liked to spring away from her brow and call attention to itself, and she wet a fingertip and leaned forward to dab it back into place. She peered into the mirror. She had lines fanning out from her eyes and etched from her nostrils to the corners of her mouth, but what really bothered her were the small indentations beginning to appear in her chin. They were curled like little commas, or maybe parentheses: a full battalion of punctuation making inroads into her face. She straightened up, took a deep breath, and looked again. She was a small, elf-faced woman with wrinkles, but wearing an amusing scarf. It could have been worse, she supposed.

Lauren's room was right at the top of the stairs. The door was closed, and Sarabeth knocked softly, then turned the knob. Lauren was still at the window, and now Sarabeth saw that in order to lean out she'd had to kneel on her desk.

"Hey, you," she said.

Lauren looked over her shoulder, then quickly swiveled around and dropped to the floor. She wore jeans and a gray thermal henley, and her hair fell in unbrushed hunks past her shoulders. Not long ago she'd gone in for the slightly slutty junior movie-star look, three inches of below-the-button belly showing, heavy eyeliner and pale lip gloss, but evidently that was a thing of the past.

"From the patio," Sarabeth said, "you looked like Juliet, leaning out the window."

"Yeah, right," Lauren said, rolling her eyes.

They came together for a quick hug.

"What are you doing up here? Plotting your escape?"

Lauren smiled, or half smiled, anyway. She seemed spacey—much as she had the last time Sarabeth had seen her. Sarabeth wondered if Lauren had a boyfriend, a Romeo she was mooning over. But Liz would have mentioned that, wouldn't she?

"Don't ask me how school is," Lauren said.

"OK, I won't."

Lauren crossed the room and sat on her bed, which was covered by the bedspread she and several friends had made, or doctored, one summer evening when Sarabeth was over. This was two or three years ago: they were sitting around saying how bored they were, as only girls of thirteen could, until finally Sarabeth suggested they take Lauren's existing bedcover, a plain blue coverlet, and decorate it with colored markers and glitter glue. "Lauren's bod right here!" one girl had written. "Groovilicious Girl!" said another note. Sarabeth remembered Liz's initial hesitation at the idea, her own worry that in making the suggestion she'd somehow overstepped.

"So how *is* school?" she said.

"Fine."

"Amanda?"

"Fine."

"You?"

"Fine," Lauren said, smiling at last, though she also flushed a little, her cheeks turning pink.

"Sorry," Sarabeth said. "I'm being an asshole. Let's see. What've you been reading?"

Now Lauren brightened. Long ago, they'd bonded over books: *Harriet the Spy, From the Mixed-Up Files of Mrs. Basil E. Frankweiler.* "Actually," she said, "my mom said I should ask you for advice."

"Please ask me for advice. I love to be useful."

"I need a classic novel for an independent reading project. Something good and not too long. Or boring."

Sarabeth turned Lauren's desk chair toward the bed and sat down. She said, "I think I should go into business advising teenagers on what to read. You're going to pay me, right?"

Lauren fought a smile, and Sarabeth was struck by how pretty she could be, how her smile had always—since babyhood—been beautiful. She had an almost perfect heart-shaped face, with a sweet wide V of a jawline.

"I'm just kidding," Sarabeth said. "Let's see. You definitely can't go wrong with Jane Austen. *Pride and Prejudice? Emma?* Though if you're anything like me you'll end up in a funk, wishing you'd lived back then."

"No way."

"Way. They had it made. The big decisions were, you know, 'Upon whom shall we call today?' I mean, walking around the room counted as doing something."

"What?"

"They're always in the drawing room after dinner, going, 'Shall we take a turn around the room?' 'Oh, no, I prefer to play the pianoforte.' 'I would do my needlework, but I must rest my eyes.' I mean, think about it. They had it good."

"You're weird," Lauren said.

"I know. But how about it?"

Lauren shrugged. "Half the girls in the class are doing Jane Austen."

Sarabeth considered. She remembered struggling with Dickens at Lauren's age, struggling with Hardy. Perhaps what she'd struggled with was struggle itself.

"OK," she said. "I can see this is going to call for deep thinking. What is 'classic,' anyway?"

"Old."

"Probably 'good.' What did your teacher say?"

Lauren sat still for a moment, then got off the bed and went to her backpack, on the floor in a corner of the room. She dug around in it and pulled out an orange binder. "It's just supposed to be something 'good for you,' " she said, making air quotes with her fingers.

"A spinach book," Sarabeth said, and Lauren gave her a mischievous look.

"You mean broccoli."

"Brussels sprouts! Actually, you know what's weird? This is more true of movies, maybe, but sometimes you'll hear about some book, and it'll be a total chocolate-cake book, and then you won't read it for a long time, you'll sort of put it off, and all of a sudden you'll realize it's become a broccoli book. Like, overnight."

Lauren smiled, but after a moment color rose up into her face, and she looked away.

"What?" Sarabeth said.

Lauren shook her head. She turned and stuffed the binder back in her backpack. "Excuse me," she said, and she left the room, and a moment later Sarabeth heard the bathroom door close.

What had just happened? Was she supposed to wait? She heard the water go on; she heard the muffled sounds of Brody's game, coming from the little TV room at the end of the hall. She looked around the room. Next to Lauren's door was a grid of wooden shelves holding CDs, and just above that, drawn directly on the wall by Lauren, was a colored-pencil picture of a big-eyed girl playing guitar. If there were a spectrum of girls' bedrooms, this one would be at the opposite end of the one Sarabeth had had on Cowper Street. Her mother had hired a decorator, for one thing, and she remembered being shown the finished room after school one day when she was about six: the violet-sprigged wallpaper, the fan-backed wicker chair, the silky purple curtains that she'd been told in advance she should try not to touch. She remembered knowing what her mother wanted, standing next to her in the doorway, and how she still somehow couldn't manage to say it, that the room was pretty. "Do you love it?" her mother cried at last, and Sarabeth nodded quickly and said she did.

She moved to Lauren's door and made her way down the stairs. Liz had taken a huge, flame-colored casserole from the oven and was ladling beef and vegetables onto a serving platter.

"I thought this was supposed to be a simple dinner."

Liz looked up and smiled. "There you are." She wiped her forehead with the back of her arm. "I got inspired, what can I tell you?"

Sarabeth reached for the cheese roll bag and held it up for Liz to see. "Hey, I went to the Cheese Board. Got some you-know-whats."

"Oh, that is so nice," Liz said. "We'll die."

Sarabeth set the bag down and found the aluminum foil. She tore off a piece and laid it on the counter, then removed the rolls from the bag, setting aside the one she'd been eating. Except . . . here was another she'd been eating. Now there were two rolls with gouges, which meant someone—she, of course—would have to have one with dinner. But then, no, there were *three* rolls with gouges—she'd ruined three of the rolls.

"I'm such a jerk!" she exclaimed.

"What?"

She gestured at the rolls. "*Ta da.* What kind of guest snacks on her contribution to the meal before she presents it to you? Jesus."

"It's not a big deal."

"It is!"

Liz left the ladle in the casserole and came over. "Now, now." She gathered the rolls onto the foil, turning the torn ones ripped-side down and wrapping the foil over them. "See?" She patted Sarabeth on the shoulder, then put an arm around her and pulled her close. "They'll be perfect with the stew. OK? I'm so glad you're here."

5

*L*iz first heard it in the middle of the night, a sound like rice pouring into a measuring cup, an infinite stream of rice pouring into an infinite cup. Hours later, it was still pouring, the first rain of the season: blurring the windows, blackening the wooden furniture on the patio.

Grumpy because of his tennis game, Brody was hiding behind the newspaper, invisible except for his hands. There had been another bombing in Iraq, fifty-three people killed, but most of the front page was occupied by a human-interest photo of a dog leaping into the air on a beach. Liz recognized the dog as Rexy, a black Lab that had been the recipient of a canine liver-kidney transplant. He'd been in the news off and on, and now he seemed to be thriving, and the Bay Area was supposed to be cheered by this.

Lauren sat at the table without eating. Liz had made French toast, and she watched as Lauren pushed hers around her plate, sliding it first to one side and then to the other, clearing a path in the powdered sugar. Her juice sat untouched, her sliced banana untasted. Liz was up and down, getting herself more coffee and then Joe another helping of bacon, and each time she returned to the table she checked Lauren's plate for progress.

"I'm not going to school today," Lauren said.

Brody lowered the paper and looked at Liz, and she thought: Don't say anything. She turned to Lauren. "Are you coming down with something?"

Lauren didn't respond—she just stared straight ahead, into the space between Brody and Joe.

"Do you feel OK?" Liz persisted.

"I'm not going," Lauren said. "I can't."

Now Brody put the paper down. "What do you mean? School is required. There are truancy laws."

Annoyed, Liz stood and moved closer to Lauren. She held the back of her hand to Lauren's forehead. "You don't feel warm."

"I can't go," Lauren said. Then suddenly she was on her feet, her chair toppling backward with a clatter. "OK?" she shouted. "I can't!" She ran from the kitchen, and in a moment Liz heard her on the stairs.

"What . . ." Brody began, but Liz ignored him and followed Lauren, then slowed so Lauren wouldn't feel chased.

Her door was ajar. She was facing away from it, sitting cross-legged on the floor at an angle that revealed the edge of her face, the thin white cord of her iPod trailing from her ear. Inside Liz, the impulse to advance fought the impulse to stay still, retreat. Let her be, give her some space. At last, she turned and headed downstairs again. In the kitchen she said to Brody, "She's going to stay home for a while—she might go in later."

"Is she sick?"

Liz looked at him. She held his gaze until she was sure he'd look away, but he didn't. Those blue eyes watching her, so stubborn. At moments like this he reminded her of her father, how steely he could be. She remembered her father saying to John once: *Don't say you can't. Say you don't want to try, but never say you can't.*

"It's just one day," Liz said to Brody, and he raised his eyebrows briefly but didn't respond.

When he and Joe were gone she climbed the stairs again. Now Lauren was on her bed, still attached to the iPod. Liz went and sat at her side. "Some days are hard," she said, and Lauren lay still for a moment and then removed one earpiece.

"What?"

"I said, 'Some days are hard.' "

Lauren stared at the ceiling as if she felt nothing at all. Her face was so blank it could only mean she was exerting a great effort to make it blank.

She put the earpiece back into place. She was somewhere Liz couldn't see: she wasn't in the music, but the music was part of how she got there.

"I was going to go to yoga," Liz said, "and then to say hi to Grandma and Grandpa, but I don't have to."

Lauren moved the earpiece again. "What?"

Liz repeated herself, and Lauren shrugged.

Now Liz hesitated, unsure of her next move. Some days *were* hard; one of the great lessons of yoga was that awareness of yourself could be part of how you lived. Observing: the stretch in your hamstrings, the feelings of a hard day. "Sweetie," she said. "Is there anything you want to talk about?"

"No," Lauren exclaimed. Then she got up on her elbows and shouted, "Why can't you fucking *leave me alone?*"

And so Liz did: left her alone, and then left the house, dashing through the rain for her car.

She started the engine but then stayed still, heart pounding. *Why can't you fucking leave me alone?* The words pounded, too. The image of Lauren, Lauren's voice: it all pounded.

All Liz had ever really wanted was to be a mother. This had been her secret: through college, through her twenties. The secret wasn't that she wanted kids; it was that she didn't particularly want a career. It was the early eighties, every woman wanted a career; at least every woman who'd gone to Stanford, as she had. But not Liz. She held various jobs, but kids were going to be her career, Lauren and Joe were her career—her work, her life. Which meant she shouldn't feel so entirely *reamed* now by what had just happened. She ought to be able to take this kind of stuff in stride.

Rain poured over the car, and she backed out of the driveway and headed down the street. It was almost as dark as evening, and the cars she passed moved slowly, headlights on, wipers racing back and forth. She hit a huge puddle, and a sheet of water whooshed up behind her.

The parking lot at Yoga Life was almost empty. Inside, the shop was quiet, its rolled mats and stretchy clothing and books on practice neatly arranged for the day. In the studio, Liz put her things in a cubby. Only eight other people, which was nice, though not so nice for Diane.

Who was in the middle of the room, talking to someone Liz didn't recognize. Diane's short gray hair was newly cropped, and she wore a simple black unitard that hugged her long legs and revealed the muscles of her strong, square shoulders. She was like a goddess, Liz always thought. Or an Amazon. The names of certain yoga poses made so much sense, given Diane: warrior, hero. In her gentle way, Diane was both of these.

Liz took a spot near the front. Until yoga, she'd thought of exercise as a way to make her body look better; now she understood about feeling better. And yet, she was very quiet about it. Diane talked sometimes about how yoga calmed the mind, and Liz thought it had calmed hers to the point where she no longer needed to say so much.

But she was not calm today. She tried to stay with Diane, but she kept thinking about Lauren, seeing and hearing Lauren. "Your teenager will use whatever is available to upset you. She'll use what you give her." This was from a book called *How to Be Your Teenager's Best Friend and Other Follies of Parenting Adolescents.* Liz had liked the title—she knew women who did that, tried to be one of the girls with their daughters, just another companion for shopping and gossip, and she knew it didn't work—but the book itself was a disappointment, nothing but the usual draconian nonsense. Give orders, and expect full compliance. End of story. Chapter 2 was called "It's All About Limits." Which limits would the author say Liz was failing to set? *You can't talk to me that way?* As far as Liz was concerned, she might as well say *You can't be unhappy.*

Lauren was unhappy.

After yoga, Liz rolled up her mat and returned to the car. She thought of going straight home, but she'd told her parents to expect her, so she continued to Palo Alto, to the senior complex where they'd been living for the past six years. She still sometimes ached for the old house on Cowper Street, but they didn't seem to miss it; they were too busy living their surprising new lives of foreign travel and bridge tournaments and choral singing—the kind of retirement you might read about in a brochure. Where, Liz sometimes wondered, had these gregarious people been hiding inside the reserved shapes of her reserved parents?

The rain had slowed to a sprinkle, and when she entered the central courtyard she passed a uniformed worker sweeping puddled water toward a storm drain.

"We finished the album," her father announced at the front door, his reading glasses hanging from a cord around his neck. "It's all ready for you to see."

A month earlier, he and her mother had taken a Penn alumni cruise up the Nile, but Liz had only seen a few snapshots. As she followed him in, she said a silent goodbye to the idea of a quick visit.

"Perfect timing," her mother said as she emerged from the tiny kitchen. "Did Dad tell you? We just finished the album."

They spent a few minutes talking, but it was clear to Liz that her parents needed her to look at the album *now*. It was happening, of course—they were becoming her children—but at times like this the transformation seemed sped up. And in fact, the first picture was one Liz had taken herself, of the two of them and their luggage standing on the curb at the airport, looking for all the world like Lauren and Joe on the first day of school, posing on the porch with their backpacks.

She flipped through the pages. Standing in front of the Pyramids, or against the rail of the cruise ship, her parents looked older than they did in life, almost frail, but so game it was touching.

"It's all on the computer," her father said. "If you want any copies, it's a snap."

"Great," Liz said.

More photos, and she came to one of her mother fanning herself with a palm frond. Across the table, her mother leaned forward and peered at the photo, then turned to Liz's father and said, "Remember how much water we drank that day?"

"Listen to this, Liz," he said. "If they served you an open bottle you had to send it back. That's how contaminated the water was."

"Or how paranoid you were," Liz joked, but neither of her parents smiled, and she felt bad.

"Oh, honey," her mother said. "After Mexico we just don't take any chances."

Liz's father disappeared into the kitchen, and Liz fought an impulse to look at her watch. She wondered what Lauren was doing. She'd almost snapped at Lauren, had certainly felt a kind of automatic urge to snap: to get into it with Lauren, yell, the kind of thing Lorelei had done to Sarabeth every day of her life. Often without even so small a provocation as *Why can't you fucking leave me alone?* Liz remembered a day when she and Sarabeth were playing with glass animals at the top of the stairs, and Lorelei, passing them in her stocking feet, had somehow managed to step on a tiny elephant. "What's *wrong* with you?" she'd shrieked at Sarabeth, as if the entire thing had happened according to Sarabeth's design.

Liz's father emerged from the kitchen with a tray of drinks—a trio of tall aqua glasses accented by orange wedges.

"Oh, good idea," Liz's mother said. "Wait'll you try this, Liz, you're going to love it."

Liz accepted one of the glasses. The drink was cold and dark and ice-less, and it tasted like a fruit drink of some kind, but oddly strong and sour, or maybe strong and sweet-and-sour; Liz wasn't sure. "What is it?" she said.

"It's a gaboo," her parents replied in unison, and they both laughed.

"The Russells invented it," her mother explained. "You make tea and chill it, then you add fresh lemon juice and peach Torani and just a tiny bit of bitters and bar sugar."

Liz took another taste. Since when did her parents know about bar sugar? Her father was wearing an argyle vest! Yet even the aqua glasses were very contemporary, and she wondered what had happened to the tumblers they'd always had—what had happened to *them.*

Outside, the rain seemed to have stopped, and through a torn place in the clouds she could see a pale, watery blue. On the other side of the sliding glass door there was a patio, but it was too small for much beyond a tiny metal table and two chairs. The big house on Cowper Street with its huge, tree-filled yard, its sunny kitchen, its rooms upon rooms—how could they not miss it? *It was so much work,* her mother had said blithely one day, as if the entire meaning of leaving were located in the extra time she had now. It had been a lot of work, of course, but Liz mourned it in a way that her parents seemed not to share. Perhaps it was a truth of life that the house you mourned was the one where you became yourself.

At the end of the day, Brody stood below the baseline of a tennis court at the Peninsula Club, waiting for David Leventhal's first serve. The courts were barely dry enough to play, but in Brody's view barely dry enough was plenty dry enough; he didn't let much get in the way of tennis. And yet, crouched and ready, he felt oddly delinquent, as if he were playing hooky from something. Why, when he played every Tuesday at exactly this time? Then he realized: it was the darkness. Daylight savings time had ended Sunday, and he and David were starting under lights for the first time in months.

"Long," he called of the first serve.

On the opposite side of the court David grimaced and practiced his toss again: once, twice.

The second serve was in, and Brody hit it down the line, a stretch for David's backhand, but David was fast and he made it. No chance now, pal, Brody thought, and he charged the net and pounded the ball past David's feet.

"Nice," David called.

Brody moved to the ad court. He'd taken off his sweatshirt, but he wasn't quite warm yet, and he danced a little from side to side.

David slammed in a serve he couldn't return. "Speaking of nice," he called back.

His shoulder hurt, but he tried to ignore it. The only thing to do was give it up for a time—give tennis up—and he wasn't going to do that. Tennis was beautiful, it was so pure: the connection, over and over, with the ball. It was hit and hit again, your heart pumping blood—as if it were wellness itself—to the farthest reaches of your body. He had run for a while, but running was so boring. Tennis was the thing. Had been since he was thirteen. He could still remember his first few times playing, in junior high, how it just felt right, the racquet in his grip. Other guys he knew said the same of golf: the clubs just felt right. His first racquet, the sweat-curled leather wrap. Andrew Drayson, his best friend. They played and played, got better and better. In the space of three or four months they went from absolute beginners to the best in their grade, then their school. In high school they fought over and over again for the number one spot on the singles ladder. Every match was vastly different yet superbly recognizable. Every match, every set, every game.

"Mackay," David called after an especially long point. "My cardiologist thanks you for this."

"No problem," Brody called back. "I'll send you a bill."

Afterward they showered and dressed. David had a trial starting, and he'd head back to work now, drive through Taco Bell on the way. His wife liked to say that she was a double court widow. Brody and Liz had met them when both couples lived in the city. Very long ago now.

"Kids?" David said as they packed up and left the locker room.

"Fine," Brody said. He thought of Lauren at the breakfast table, of Liz letting her skip school—he'd heard on the way to the club that she'd ended up staying home all day. He thought Liz could be too soft; she thought he could be too hard. But what good did it do, staying home from school? Hiding from your problems.

"Yours?" he asked David.

"Everyone's doing great. I still can't believe this is Caitlin's last year home."

They'd reached the clubhouse door, and Brody held it for David and then followed after him. The night was black, enveloping. Through a stand of trees he could see, far below, part of a runway at SFO, marked by lights. He thought of misty nights in the city twenty years ago, the sound of a foghorn as he headed home from work. Liz waiting for him in the small apartment they shared.

He waved to David and headed for his car. Stowing his bag in the trunk, he thought again of Lauren at breakfast: hair hanging by her face, shoulders rounded. And the sound of her chair falling backward, wood banging against wood. It almost scared him, how much he wanted her to snap out of it—whatever "it" was. This moodiness that took over.

Through dinner he kept an eye on her. She was placid, and Liz had whispered, before the kids came into the kitchen, that she'd cleaned out her closet during the afternoon, filling three garbage bags before she was finished—a good sign, Brody thought.

After dinner the kids went upstairs to do homework, and he and Liz sat in front of the TV. There was a news report on, and they stared silently at the footage from Iraq: charred vehicles, cloth-draped bodies, bloody children.

"Turn it off," Liz said, and he pointed the remote at the screen and killed the picture.

"I'm weak," she said.

"It's upsetting."

"I feel like I should be able to watch."

"Honey." He moved closer and put his arm around her, and after a moment she leaned into him. She smelled a little of shampoo, a little of the lasagne she'd served for dinner.

She said, "I got started on the bench this afternoon."

He pulled away to look at her. "Yeah? How's it going?"

"It doesn't really look like anything yet. I was priming it, and Lauren came in and said, 'How sweet. You can put it outside at Christmastime and pretend it got snowed on.' "

"She did?"

"She was just kidding."

"Yeah, but—"

"It was fine," she said, patting his leg. "It was nothing."

He sat still for a moment, thinking there was more to say but also that he didn't want to argue. He didn't even know what the argument was. He reached for the remote and turned the TV on again. He surfed until he found *Law and Order,* or maybe one of its clones. He remembered David Leventhal once saying that the ABA was going to have to sue NBC for libel; litigation wasn't nearly as interesting as the show made it out to be, but applications were up at law schools all over the country, and as a result the economics of the entire enterprise had been placed in peril.

He lowered the volume and turned to Liz again. "Do anything else?"

"Visited my parents. They can't wait to show you their Egypt pictures."

He smiled.

"And I talked to Sarabeth—she's going to a gamelan concert tonight."

Sarabeth was always doing something just a little hipper than anything he and Liz would do on their own, and every third or fourth time Liz would get a bee in her bonnet and they'd end up at some warehouse in Alameda, watching naked people write on one another or something. On the plus side, it gave him some great stories for work.

"You know those Indonesian chimes?" she said. "And gongs?"

"Yeah, yeah." He reached for her hand, interlacing their fingers. "Sounds like fun. Hey, I was thinking about the city today. About walking home from work."

"Nostalgia?" she said.

"No, I was remembering the foghorns."

"Sounds like nostalgia to me."

He swung his legs onto the coffee table and leaned back. Thinking of those days, of the guy he'd been: what a striver, what a go-getter. That guy never could have imagined this life. What had that guy wanted? To be sharp, aggressive, confident, canny, smooth. To be Russ.

There were footsteps on the stairs, and Joe came in, twiddling a pencil between his fingers. At dinner he'd still been amped up from soccer practice, but he looked tired now. Brody liked it that Joe had practice on Tuesdays this year—his own tennis day. He figured Joe's legs felt the same way his did.

"Hey, bud," he said to Joe.

"I'm starving."

Liz pulled her hand free from Brody's and scooted forward. "Want some more lasagne? I can heat some up for you."

Joe thought for a moment. "Nah." He went into the kitchen for a box of crackers and brought them to an easy chair near the couch. He stood to one side of the chair, turned around, and fell straight back into it, his legs swinging way up and then folding over the padded arm. "Sweet," he said.

He sat quietly, stuffing crackers into his mouth, his bare feet moving a little.

"Is your homework done?" Liz said.

Joe glanced at Brody, then looked at his watch and said, "I think it needs a little longer."

"Wise guy," Brody said.

They all sat there: Joe chewing, Liz shifting to the end of the couch and resting her feet against Brody's thigh, Brody holding the remote loosely in his hand. Above them Lauren's floor creaked, and he heard the sound of her desk chair scraping across the floor. At dinner she'd said she had a lot of chemistry homework tonight.

"Dad," Joe said suddenly, mouth full, "guess who's going to the Yankees."

Brody tried not to smile. "Not this again."

"No, he is," Joe said. "Trent told me. He is."

"Barry Bonds is not going to the Yankees. It'll never happen."

"I don't know," Joe said. "I think you're in denial."

"Better da Nile dan da Hudson."

"Errrr," Joe protested, but he smiled and stretched, then got up and tossed the cracker box onto the coffee table. He went back to the kitchen, filled a glass with milk, drank it down and filled it again. When it was empty, he burped loudly.

"Honey," Brody said to Liz, happier than he had any reason to be. "We forgot to teach the kids manners."

In a little while the house shifted into its penultimate nighttime form: both kids in their rooms, the dishwasher running, Liz upstairs scouting for small tasks and saying goodnight. Brody remained on the couch, in no hurry to move because once he did he'd have to set his alarm for 4:30 a.m. He had a 6:50 flight to Seattle.

He thought again of the apartment he and Liz had shared in San Francisco: the two small rooms, the tiny kitchen, the balcony with its narrow view of the bay. He remembered how strangely thrilled he was by his first sight of Liz's makeup in their shared medicine cabinet, how it seemed to prove something important.

When he proposed they were on the living room couch eating take-out Chinese. He'd been thinking about it for weeks but hadn't had a plan;

what got him to speak was a conversation he'd had at the office that afternoon. One of his coworkers had said, more or less in passing, that people chose their spouses for the flimsiest of reasons, and when he asked what she meant, she insisted that she'd married her husband because he had a nice blue shirt. And that her friends had reasons like: because he gives a great back rub, because his sister's really nice, because he can order wine in a restaurant. Right then and there Brody thought: because she has a great laugh. She did—a wide, unencumbered laugh that was tantalizingly at odds with her calm demeanor. And that was her reaction, over the Chinese food. She said yes and cried a little, and then she laughed and laughed.

6

Sarabeth's house was set behind another, larger house, on a flag lot without its own driveway. This meant she had to park on the street, which should have been easy—it was a tiny, quiet street—but the parking situation was completely out of hand. Berkeley being Berkeley, there had been petitions to limit the number of cars per house that could park on this block, petitions to formally disallow rules about how many cars per house could park on this block, flyers left in mailboxes urging more considerate parking ("Dear Neighbors: Please, if you park in a space next to a driveway, take a moment to think of the rest of us and park within a foot of the curb cut"), and even, rumor had it, an enraged letter from one party to another about the immorality of a single family's owning two SUVs.

All of this was on her mind as she made her morning tea, because last night, coming home from dinner with Nina, she'd had to park way down the block, and she couldn't quite decide if she was shameless enough to go out in her pajamas to retrieve the book she'd left in her car.

She wasn't, quite.

Instead, she carried her tea to the front window and watched the familiar sight of the Heidts doing their morning relay. The Heidts were the family of five that lived in the house in front of hers; it was their driveway she used to get to and from her house.

Bonnie came out first and started the car, an old white Volvo station wagon. She was followed soon after by her husband, Rick, who carried three-year-old Isaac and his fire truck lunch box. As Rick buckled Isaac into his car seat, Bonnie got out of the car and headed back to the kitchen, only to step aside as Chloe and Pilar burst from the door and raced down the steps. Chloe was ahead, but she stopped abruptly, made an extravagant gesture of displeasure with her arms, and then turned and trudged in the direction from which she'd come. Which left Pilar, apparently free now, to set down her backpack and spread her arms wide and twirl.

She was Sarabeth's favorite—six years old and impossibly winsome. A couple days ago, she'd accosted Sarabeth on the sidewalk and said, "Guess what we did at school today," and though Sarabeth had been on her way out, she'd been helpless to resist the conversation.

"Let's see," she said. "Did you learn a new song?"

Pilar rolled her eyes. "We have singing on *Mondays.*"

"Silly me."

"Guess," Pilar said, bouncing on her toes and smiling a smile crowded with tiny white teeth. She was wearing too-small purple leggings and a pink turtleneck, and a ribbon of white belly showed where they didn't quite meet. She also had green paint in her hair, which was probably a clue.

"Was it good or bad?" Sarabeth said.

"Good!"

"Did you learn how to stand on your head?"

"We made a real train!" Pilar exclaimed, and she turned and raced away.

Mornings were very regular, and once Rick had pedaled off on his bicycle, and Bonnie had backed the car out of the driveway and headed off to drop the children at school, Sarabeth returned to her kitchen with her empty mug.

It was the day she'd been dreading, the one-year anniversary of her breakup with Billy, and yet she felt OK. Maybe it would end up being like turning forty: lots of trepidation beforehand but the day itself absolutely fine. She was even feeling unusually sanguine about her house, which was in a state of serious ill repair. There were days when she worried over the old wiring, the dilapidated roof, but today she looked around her living room and thought that the structure didn't matter that much because she really liked her stuff: her braided rag rugs and flowery armchairs, the curlicue wrought-iron shelving she'd rescued from an ice-cream shop that was going out of business. She liked her stuff.

At ten, Jim pulled up in front of the Heidts' driveway in his shiny white Lexus, and she waved from her watch point at the window and headed out. She was joining him for part of the weekly realtors' tour, as she sometimes did when she had time.

"Sweetness," he said as she got into the car, and they leaned together and kissed cheeks, his close-trimmed gray-white beard bristling her a bit. The radio was tuned to his customary classic rock station, and he reached for the volume knob and turned it down. In certain moods, he would leave the volume high, sing along at the top of his lungs to "Helpless" or "Brown Sugar."

"You look charming," he said, tweaking the hem of her skirt, a flippy knee-length print with bright orange and yellow flowers scattered across a black background. "Are you debuting this or have I just not seen it?"

"This would be its second outing."

"It's cute. Very I-may-not-earn-much-but-I've-got-style."

"Ouch."

"Sorry." He waited for her to fasten her seat belt, then pulled away from the curb. "I'm pissy because I'm furious at Angela. She asked me to take these clients of hers this weekend, which is fine, but it's like, I'm doing her a favor, not the other way around."

"That Angela," Sarabeth said.

"I know. Life is too short for this bullshit."

"Working with Angela?"

"Caring what she does. What she thinks."

"That's right," Sarabeth said. "It's what we think of ourselves that matters."

"Please shut up," he said, but a cheerful look had appeared on his face.

They made their way to Cedar and then to Shattuck. The rains of the last few days had stopped, and a tiny green shoot of happiness sprouted somewhere inside Sarabeth. She loved Jim, had loved him since the day she met him, in the living room of what was now her house. He had stood there handing out flyers in a way that seemed to say he was both a serious businessman and a completely approachable, funny, ironic guy playing the part of a serious businessman. He had a talent for heartfelt duplicity.

"So there's actually a very cool place on tour today," he said. "Or reportedly cool. An in-the-hills contemporary with really high-end finishes and wraparound decks, and Richard Misrach's view."

"Ha," she said. "Doesn't Richard Misrach have Richard Misrach's view?"

"It's like next door or something. Just up the hill. I'm not sure."

"But I mean, having that view would just be having that view."

"Yes," he said. "And your point is . . ."

"Never mind," she said with a giggle. She had no idea what her point was. More likely, she didn't have one.

On they went. Today is the first day of the rest of your life, she thought, and then: Well, maybe the second. But she was fine, she was fine; she was good.

They arrived in Elmwood and drove past one huge house after another. Sarabeth thought of the show of Richard Misrach photographs she'd seen at the Berkeley Art Museum a few years back, a show of maybe two dozen photographs of the Golden Gate Bridge taken from the deck of his Berkeley hills house. They'd been shot at all different times of day, over the course of a year, maybe longer, so that the color and light were astonishingly varied and evocative. Early morning shots of the bay at its palest blue, the bridge at night forming a scallop of lights. They were amazing, and as Sarabeth moved from photograph to photograph she felt herself transported, into an enchantment that was laced with something darker, awareness of the passage of time, maybe, the end of the museum visit looming and somehow signaling the end of life itself, creating an interval of grief-shadowed exaltation.

Jim parked, and they made their way to a two-story house set way back from the sidewalk, at the end of a path that curved past a variety of ornamental grasses. At the door, a group of three was just leaving, and Sarabeth saw that it included a man she sort of had her eye on, Peter Something, though today he seemed kind of ordinary, just a guy leaving a house. A clean-cut guy in khakis.

The listing agent was Rita Lassining, whom Jim called RL, or Realtor Lady, and she did indeed play the part very fully, never a hair out of place. Today she stood at the dining room table with her smoked salmon and her flyers, in a tobacco-brown blazer over a high-collared gold silk blouse that was like a display stand for her impeccably made-up face.

Jim said hi to her, and she said he should make sure to look at the master suite, and he whispered to Sarabeth, when they had moved out of earshot, "That's a signal to *not* look at something else."

But there was nothing to not look at. It was a beautiful house, beautifully staged. Sarabeth's little bag of tricks seemed paltry indeed here. She recognized the hand of Bethany Chen—or rather the linen sofa of Bethany Chen, the damask curtains of Bethany Chen, the gorgeous cherry dressers of Bethany Chen. Sarabeth's staging materials could fit in one room and in fact lived in a storage unit not much bigger than her bathroom; Bethany Chen's staging materials occupied, according to rumor, an entire apartment in Oakland. This kind of thinking, though: Jim was right, life was too short for it.

But something had changed. She felt it as they drove from house to house, as they looked at the view that was like Richard Misrach's view and saw . . . the Golden Gate Bridge. Yep, there it was.

When they were finished touring, Jim dropped her at home. She'd been planning to work on lampshades, but she was suddenly incredibly tired. She kicked off her shoes and lay on her living room couch, her old purple velvet couch that was bald in places and also a little lumpy. And yet, it was her couch, her couch in life. That this was true seemed wrong, even unfair.

Whatever she'd possessed this morning was gone.

She turned onto her side and stared at the fireplace. On the mantel was a row of seven unmatched silver candlesticks, one of which had belonged to her parents, had been part of a pair that had sat on the Cowper Street mantel for most of her childhood. She had separated the pair, she could no longer remember why, though the symbolism was pretty obvious.

She thought of a recurring dream she'd had in her twenties, of her parents' wedding, in which her father stood at the altar with his back to the aisle, and her mother walked in on her hands. A dream about how wrong they'd been for each other—upside down, backward—though she had also come to see, with the help of a therapist, that, walking on her hands with her dress falling around her fingertips and her underwear showing, her mother was basically going down the aisle crotch first, and her father by turning his back was saying no thanks. The therapist was on the Freudian side, or perhaps that was Sarabeth, dreaming the dream.

Where was the other candlestick? She had no idea. She might have given it to someone, might even have thrown it away. She stared at its mate—its twin. It was so pretty: a slender stalk holding a flowerlike petal on which rested a tiny cup to hold, most beautifully, a plain white candle. Last time she'd used it, Billy had brought her a box of just such candles as a present, and they'd gathered all the candlesticks she owned, set them here and there around her bedroom, and turned off all the lights in the house. Lying with his arms around her, surrounded by flickering candle-light . . . it was nearly too painful to think about it, and yet here she was, thinking about it. Remembering.

That evening, when she took her place in front of the microphone in the community room of the Center for Integrated Living, she was queasy with dread. She was a hundred and seventy-two pages into *Anna Karenina,* the longest book she'd ever brought here, and the idea of con-tinuing all the way to the end, chapter after chapter, Thursday night after Thursday night, struck her as literally impossible. There they all were—Esther, Harry and Melba, Dick, Stuart, Sylvia, at least sixty people and perhaps ten guide dogs, who were waiting, too, Sarabeth knew—and she couldn't fathom how to find her voice.

"Good evening," she managed, and as one the crowd said good evening back.

"It's great to see you all," she continued, and she waited for another idea to come to her, more chat, anything, but her mind was blank, appar-ently less likely than the endless book to help her. *This is Sarabeth,* Jim had said to someone today. *My partial stager.* And now, as if she'd never heard the phrase before, had never joked about it before—and, oh, the jokes were endless, given the plenitude embedded in both "partial" and "stager," let alone in "stage"—as if she were considering the phrase and its application to her life for the very first time, Sarabeth felt pinpricks inside her eyelids and wished as fervently as she'd ever wished for any-thing that there were some part of her life, some part of herself, that was whole.

7

*A*manda had this idea, and Lauren thought she might be desperate enough to try it. Just go up and say: *Hi, I'm Lauren.* It was
so insane to think she could even do that, but how insane was it that he
didn't even know her fucking name? *Hi, I'm Lauren.* Right, like she
wouldn't be shaking and sweating. *Hi, I'm Lauren. From the library? Do
you, uh, have a towel I can borrow?*

It had been six months since the day at the library, half a year, and
nothing had happened since then, nothing. He probably wouldn't even
remember by now. It was during midterms last spring, and she was at
the library downtown, sitting at a computer, when he walked up and
glanced around and without hesitation took the terminal next to hers.
She knew who he was, but only in the sense that he was one of the hot
guys at school, though not at all the hottest. But hot, no question—tall
and broad shouldered, with pale, clear skin and lips that looked carved,
like a statue's. Her heart raced, slowing only after he'd been there for
several minutes. Then, for a while, they both worked; she tried from
time to time to sneak a peek at his monitor, but she couldn't really tell
what he was doing. After about half an hour he got up. Without thinking
she looked at him, and he gave her a little wave and said, "Knock 'em
dead."

Knock 'em dead.

She still couldn't really believe it. It wasn't a big deal, but it was so nice: like, he knew she went to his school, he knew she had midterms. It blew her away.

But what a joke it was now. She had done nothing but smile at him since then. And she didn't even smile every time she saw him. He probably thought she was crazy. Or that she had some kind of spastic mouth or something. Or, more likely, he had no idea she existed.

She was sitting with Amanda on a bench in front of the office—a total loser lunch location, but whatever, sometimes it was better just to be yourself, as her mom would say. Amanda had stretched out on the bench and was lying there with her eyes closed—which Lauren would never, not in a million years, do at school. She sat nearby, zipping and unzipping her backpack like an idiot. She was getting her *Howards End* paper back in English today. She couldn't imagine why Sarabeth liked that book— Lauren had hated it, which had made the paper agony to write. She would probably get a B and some comment about how it was well organized, as if she'd turned in her dresser drawer. What, she wondered, would it be like to get a D on a paper, or an F? You probably couldn't get an F if you turned something in, but could you get a D? She imagined Ms. Freiberg approaching her, the stack of graded papers held close to her chest so no one could see anyone else's grade. The look on her face as she stopped at Lauren's desk, full of pity and worry. Lauren's heart pounding. And then the shame. A D would clinch it, clinch everything. It would be like having a giant D on her chest for "dummy," "dope," making an announcement like that A in *The Scarlet Letter.*

Amanda sat up and gave her a strange look. "What?"

Lauren turned away. She felt like crying, and she roped it, roped it, roped it back in. She hadn't even gotten her stupid paper back yet. "Nothing," she said.

"What'd you say?"

"No-thing."

Amanda shrugged and reached for her pack. She unzipped the front pocket and took out a foil package. "Want some dry-roasted edamame? They're rich in isoflavones."

"Ew," Lauren said. Amanda's mom was always buying weird foods; she'd had anorexia as a teenager and so was overcompensating or one of those words. "No, thanks."

"Let's do something this weekend," Amanda said. "Do you want to go shopping tomorrow? I totally need shirts."

Lauren imagined the mall, imagined herself trudging around, the place all echoey, the smell of the food court. She said, "My mom said I have to do chores tomorrow." She often pretended her parents were stricter than they were. She sometimes even got pissed at them for what she'd told Amanda they'd said. She knew she was a horrible daughter.

"Sunday?" Amanda said. "Or next weekend? We could do the Berkeley thing." She said this super casually, but now Lauren was mad: she'd screwed everyone by blowing off Berkeley last month, and Amanda was pretending it was no big deal? It wasn't even fair; they could have gone without her.

Why? everyone kept saying. Why? She hadn't felt like it, that was why. The only bummer had been missing the visit to Sarabeth. Sarabeth was so completely different from Lauren's mom—it would've been cool to take everyone to her house. Sometimes Lauren imagined what it would be like having Sarabeth for a mother, how she'd be so easy to talk to. In high school, for example, she'd had a killer crush on a guy named Doug—Lauren had overheard her and her mom laughing about it once. Later, Lauren had asked her mom for details—she was just curious—but her mom had gone into her whole Sarabeth-and-her-dead-mother thing, and Lauren had changed the subject. She hated it when her mom talked about Sarabeth's mother. Or Sarabeth-and-her-mother.

Lorelei. Sarabeth pretty much never talked about her—the only thing Lauren could remember her saying was that her mother had called Lauren's mom's family "the Castleberries" instead of "the Castleberrys." Lauren wasn't sure how she did this—with her tone or something—but the idea seemed to be that she was a snob. Lauren had seen a picture of her once, in a shoe box in her mom's closet, and she didn't look like a snob at all. She was standing outside Sarabeth's old house, across the street from where Lauren's grandparents used to live, and she looked kind of shy. She was small and pretty and dark haired—though her eyes made Lauren want to look away.

"Yo," Amanda said. "Earth to Lauren?"

Lauren looked over. Amanda's hair was orange in the sunlight, and her freckles really stood out today, especially this big one in the middle of her chin. "What?" Lauren said.

"Next weekend? You're sure spaced."

"Whatever," Lauren said, but she was impatient now, because there he was, over by the gym. He'd gotten his hair cut recently, and she still wasn't used to it. It was geeky but sort of cute. He was so cute. But he was so skinny. If she ever sat on his lap she'd totally squish him. She thought of her ass spreading on his lap—she was disgusting.

The bell rang, and she packed up, said goodbye to Amanda, and made her way to English. Ms. Freiberg was already at her desk, the papers in a neat stack in front of her. She waited for the tardy bell and stood up. There were still people coming in, but she started talking about how it had been a really good group of papers, people had chosen challenging books, there were some good theses, well supported, although some people, she said, eyes locked on the back wall, had not taken enough time, and they probably already knew who they were.

She began at the first row of desks. She had the papers in order, so that as she approached each person, that person's paper was on top of her pile. Lauren's heart pounded as Ms. Freiberg got closer.

"Lauren," she said with a smile, and she handed Lauren her paper.

Lauren held the paper to her chest before she looked at it. The first page, two comments in red ink; the second, a long note in the right-hand margin; the third, more notes and a couple of words circled; the fourth, a smiley face on the left, near the bottom; and the fifth, the last: three inches of red ink followed by a C minus in a big red circle.

She sat still, but she was going to cry, she was going to cry in just a second. Then the feeling passed, and the inside of her body was hot, her stomach roiling. She shoved her stuff into her backpack and stood up. Her face was on fire. Ms. Freiberg was at the far side of the classroom, just a few papers left.

"Lauren?"

She couldn't speak. She was standing there in front of the entire class, and it wasn't impossible that she would puke right now.

"Are you ill?" Ms. Freiberg said.

Lauren managed to nod.

Ms. Freiberg returned to her desk and scribbled something. "Here," she said, handing Lauren a hall pass. "Go to the nurse, OK?"

Lauren took the pass and headed for the door, knowing everyone's eyes were on her. How obvious was it that this was because she'd blown the paper? Completely obvious. Her face was covered with sweat, and when she opened the door and got outside, the cool air was an astonishing relief. She stood there for a moment, trying to slow something, her breathing, the nausea. But she still felt queasy. She shouldered her pack and made her way to the office. She lay on the nurse's cot and stared at the acoustic panels of the ceiling while the nurse called her mom. The nurse gave her a cool cloth for her forehead while they waited.

Lauren's mom was freaked. She came bursting into the nurse's room in her painting clothes fifteen minutes later, a totally worried look on her face. Lauren wished she'd stayed in class, but now that her mom was here she was definitely going home.

"What's wrong?" her mom said.

"I just started feeling really sick."

"To your stomach?"

Lauren nodded. It wasn't so bad, actually. In fact, she wasn't sure she felt sick at all anymore.

"Do you feel like throwing up?"

"Mom!"

"There's a stomach thing going around," the nurse said. "I've seen a lot of this."

"Well," Lauren's mom said, "let's get you home."

She went to sign Lauren out, and the nurse took the washcloth and helped Lauren sit up. "It'll pass in a couple days," she said. "Maybe faster if it's food poisoning. What did you have for lunch?"

"A turkey sandwich."

"With mayonnaise?"

Lauren's mom was back. "OK, sweetie," she said, and Lauren's face got hot again, but she stood and followed her mom out of the office. They walked to the car in silence, her mom casting glances at her every so often. At home she escorted Lauren to her room.

"Resting will help," she said. She pulled back the bedspread on Lauren's bed and plumped the pillows. "We have ginger ale—you could try sipping that."

"Whatever," Lauren said, and her mom gave her a curious look before she left. Lauren got into bed, then felt weird lying in bed in her jeans. She took them off and pulled on some boxers. She was a complete fraud. What was she supposed to do, lie in bed all afternoon? It wasn't even two o'clock.

Her mom came back in with a tray. There was a glass of ginger ale and some saltines, and a little flower in a bud vase. "I'll put these here," she said, setting the tray on Lauren's bedside table. "Just see if you can rest, OK?"

Lauren nodded. She sort of wished her mom would sit with her.

"Do you want me to bring you a bucket?" her mom said, and Lauren felt her eyes fill.

"No, thanks."

Liz returned to the garage, where she'd been working on the bench when the nurse's call came. It was so strange; she couldn't remember the last time Lauren had come home sick in the middle of the day. Maybe she did have food poisoning, since it had come on so fast. In a strange way, Liz sort of liked the idea that she was up there, not feeling well. Not feeling good, as both kids used to say. *Mom, I don't feel good.* It had been all she could do not to sit on the side of Lauren's bed just now, to stroke her shoulder. But Lauren would have no truck with that these days.

The bench was in the middle of the garage floor. She'd known from the first moment she'd seen it what she'd do: a lively plaid of yellow, green, and blue, topped by a sprinkling of tiny flowers. Fresh, pretty. Springlike. Very different from the things she'd done in the class she'd taken: the footstool she'd sponge-painted dark green over black, the picture frame on which she'd carefully stenciled a winding vine.

Why had she told Sarabeth she didn't know how she was going to paint the bench? Maybe because she couldn't quite believe it would work. Right now it was solid white, with lines of blue paint and other lines of blue painter's tape running this way and that. Mondrian on a bad day, Sarabeth might say.

Liz went back to the kitchen for the phone. "How do you feel?" she asked when Brody answered.

"Fine," he said rather briskly.

She hesitated; she hadn't started this quite right. "Lauren came home sick. Her stomach. I was just wondering if you had anything."

"No, no," he said. "Sorry, I'm fine. Did she throw up?"

"No, she just said she felt queasy. She's pretty flushed, too."

"Maybe she has a bug."

"Evidently."

They said goodbye, and she stood still for a moment, listening for sounds from Lauren's room. Nothing. She headed up the stairs: Lauren was deeply under her covers, eyes closed, fists tucked under her chin. Good, Liz thought. She's asleep.

But Lauren was not asleep. She had gone to the bathroom, and the trek across her bedroom floor, and out her door to the wide-open upstairs landing, and on into the cold, tiled bathroom—this had gotten her feeling awful again. Her hideous face in the mirror, and she, she just couldn't stand anything. She wished she could take some medicine, except what could she take? What was there for this? She wanted to take pills and pills of it. A wave of nausea swept over her, and she made for the toilet, but nothing happened. What if, in front of her parents, she started to rant and rave? What if she couldn't stop?

Back in her room, she crawled into the closet and slid the door closed and sobbed. Her pack was out there in the middle of her room, the C-minus paper inside it. What if her parents found out? *You got a C minus? What happened?*

She leaned against the wall. There was more room in here now, she'd gotten rid of a ton of stuff, but she sort of wished she hadn't. There was too much room. She heard something and cracked the closet door, then opened it and dashed for her bed. Just in time: her mom came and stood in the doorway and looked at her. Go away, go away, Lauren thought, and her mom went away.

A C minus was worse than a D. If she'd gotten a D it would have been like: *Oh, you must not have understood the assignment* or something. A C minus was *You suck.*

She had taken in only about half the comment on the last page, and when she heard her mom close the garage door, she got up and went to her pack. Back in bed with the paper, she read all of Ms. Freiberg's notes. "It's interesting," Ms. Freiberg had written at the very end, "that the paper, in its shortcomings and disorganization, reflects an aspect of one of the book's most important themes, the contrast between Helen's passion and Margaret's reason. You may revise this if you'd like. Please see me—I think I may be able to help."

Whatever the fuck Ms. Freiberg meant, there was no way Lauren was revising it. The book sucked, especially the parts about Leonard Bast. What a loser. She lay back down and began crying again. It was awful, she couldn't stop: she was crying and crying and crying. She rolled over like that might help, but of course it didn't.

The phone rang at some point, and a quick glance at the clock told her school was out. Was it Amanda calling? She might be wondering where Lauren was. Lauren half wanted to yell to her mom that she was awake, but it might not be Amanda; Amanda might not even have noticed that she was missing. Amanda was getting friendly with some theater people, and she might be happily hanging out with that dork Christa Baker, talking about *drama.* If Amanda got all theatery Lauren would be screwed. She could imagine Amanda being one of those tech people, doing lights or sound or painting sets or whatever. Lauren hated plays. She'd taken a theater class when she was ten, and it was the most embarrassing experience she ever had. One day you were supposed to act out being an animal, and Lauren had to go into the middle of the room and pretend to be a penguin in front of all these people. Remembering it, she almost laughed, and for some reason that made her feel worse. Tears streamed down her face.

Liz had a chicken roasting in the oven when she went upstairs a little before six-thirty. Roast chicken, mashed potatoes, green beans: one of Lauren's favorite dinners, in case she felt up to eating. Lauren's door was closed now, and Liz knocked and waited and knocked again.

"Lauren?" she called. She opened the door, and Lauren jerked up to sitting, her face red and tear streaked, her mouth wrenched downward.

"Oh, sweetie," Liz said. She hurried to the bed and sat down, and Lauren fell against her. "Sweetie, what is it?"

Lauren shook her head, but her body heaved and heaved, and Liz felt tears running into the neckline of her own shirt. She stroked Lauren's back. "What?" she said, and then, "There, it's OK, it's OK." Something was terribly wrong, and yet how glad she was that Lauren was allowing herself to be held. This body in Liz's arms: she barely knew it anymore.

She put her hand down on something crinkly.

Lauren pulled away, and they both looked down at a pile of papers halfway under Lauren's pillow. Lauren pushed the papers farther under and scooted back.

"What's that?" Liz said.

"Nothing."

Liz looked at Lauren, and suddenly she knew: it was the English paper, the independent reading project paper. Lauren had done badly. Or probably not badly, probably just not as well as she'd hoped. It was there, under her pillow, the paper she'd had to write about the book she'd hated. Liz had tried to tell her that she should read a bit of it before committing, but Lauren could never be warned; she had to hurtle forward, the consequences be damned. Why was that? Had Liz or Brody modeled recklessness? Or had they, in modeling caution, somehow encouraged the opposite?

Lauren wiped her sleeve over her face. Her lips were as red as if she'd spent the afternoon kissing. She stared at Liz and sighed. She lifted the pillow and threw it past Liz to the floor. She made a little gesture of pushing the papers toward Liz, and it took all Liz had not to reach for them.

"Is there something you want to show me?" she said instead.

Lauren pushed them closer. She stared at Liz. Finally she picked them up and held them out for Liz to take.

"Your paper?" Liz said, because she'd been right: "Two Sisters in *Howards End*" read the title on the top page.

"I failed it," Lauren said.

Liz glanced through the pages, taking in the quantity of red ink more than the content. On the last page, below a long comment, there was a big red C minus in a circle.

"Is this what you're feeling bad about?"

Tears streaming again, Lauren nodded.

"You hoped for a better grade?"

"Duh," Lauren said, and she bowed her head and sobbed again.

Liz hesitated and then put a hand on Lauren's shoulder. "I think you had high hopes for it. And you worked hard on it."

"Mom," Lauren cried. "I'm probably going to get a C in chemistry!"

She was struggling in school. That's what it was. Liz felt the lifting of a huge burden. Lauren was having a hard time with her schoolwork. Academics had always been easy for her, but they weren't this year.

Liz said as much, and as she talked Lauren settled into a peaceful kind of listening that suggested she was actually taking in what Liz was saying: that it was especially hard to be challenged when you weren't used to it, that struggle in one part of life could affect confidence in others.

"I hate to see you put so much pressure on yourself," Liz said. "It's OK if you don't get good grades, you know."

Lauren nodded, and after a while she wiped the tears from her face with the edge of her sheet. The color in her face had bled away, and she looked pale and composed, except for her ruby lips.

"I'm roasting chicken if you think you might be able to eat," Liz said.

"I don't know."

"Well, I hope you'll feel like coming down, honey." Liz reached out a hand and ran it down the back of Lauren's head. "About twenty minutes," she added, and she left the room and headed downstairs.

The potatoes had begun to boil. From outside, Joe banged into the garage, and she heard him huffing as he shucked off his cleats and shin guards. He came into the kitchen and inhaled deeply.

"Chicken?"

"You just have time to shower."

She opened the oven door and pressed a cooking fork into one of the chicken's thighs. The juices were clear already, but she doubted it was done. So many of her mother's rules had turned out to be untrue. Perhaps the significant thing was that Liz had expected otherwise. She wondered how Sarabeth was; they hadn't spoken in a few days. Was it thinking of her mother as fortyish and the queen of a family kitchen that had brought Sarabeth to mind? There was a memory that Liz returned to often, a summer afternoon in the Cowper Street kitchen a year or two before Lorelei's death. She and Sarabeth were sitting at the table, drinking Tab with lemon, when Liz's mother came in with groceries. She moved around putting things away, and Sarabeth watched, and it was the first time Liz understood how alone Sarabeth was: watching her watch the incredibly ordinary actions of a woman taking care of her family. At the time, Liz hadn't really understood what was going on, only that she had an urge to distract Sarabeth with conversation and an equal urge to remain silent. Around the room Liz's mother went, paper-wrapped meat into the refrigerator, fruit into a colander to wash, a box of cake flour set aside for later. And quietly, almost reluctantly, Sarabeth following her every move.

Brody came in, and Liz turned to greet him.

"How's she feeling?"

"She wasn't sick—she was upset about a grade."

A look of compassion came over his face, and she realized she'd been worrying about what he'd say. Brody was a good father, though. The snapping, the occasional rigidity—they were not the true him; they were sparks flying off the stress of his work. Of course he would feel for Lauren.

"Poor thing," he said, and he kissed her and then, surprisingly, kissed her again, his hands on her back pulling her close. They parted, and then she moved forward and kissed him, taking his upper lip into her mouth and massaging it with her tongue.

"Well," he said when the kiss was over and he'd pulled away and was looking at her.

"Well yourself."

They stared at each other, and then Liz laughed and said, "Isn't life funny?"

Brody went into the half bath to pee, sounding like he hadn't peed all day. After, he would change his shoes, taking off his oxfords and putting on the soft moccasins he wore around the house. Soon they would all appear, Brody, Joe, and Lauren—Liz knew Lauren would come. The kitchen with its food smells would draw them. They would sit down, and the food on the plates as they gathered together would say: *Yes, this is OK, we're all OK.*

By ten o'clock Brody was in bed with his laptop, sending off a few last e-mails. The house seemed quiet for a Friday night. Liz was upstairs saying goodnight, and he could hear her knock on each child's door, could hear the murmur of conversation. He'd been in a meeting when she phoned this afternoon, and he'd been short with her, or so he'd felt. He hadn't known, of course, that it wasn't just a check-in kind of call. A guy in Seattle had said during lunch Wednesday that his wife called him from one phone when it wasn't urgent, from another when it was. Which prompted someone else to say that when his wife really needed him, she sent him a text message.

Liz came in and kicked off her shoes, and he closed the computer and lowered it to the floor. "How is she?"

"OK. But really tired—they have so much pressure on them. Good thing we never moved to Palo Alto, those schools are much worse."

"You know, it's good practice for life."

She was at her dresser, unfastening her watch, and she glared at him in the mirror. She put the watch down and turned to face him. "Maybe *managing* stress is good practice, but feeling it isn't."

He didn't see how you could learn to manage it without feeling it first, but he didn't say that. "She'll be OK," he said instead.

"I know."

She went into the bathroom, and he heard the water running, the sound of the electric toothbrush. After dinner, Lauren had brought him her chemistry book, and he'd spent an hour with her, going over several chapters. She'd even made a joke, something about how much easier it would be if the element names started with "um" instead of ending with it. "Then you could just say 'um . . .' and the teacher would figure you were on the right track and say, 'Good job.' " They'd had a nice moment together, laughing at that.

When Liz came back out, she began to undress, pulling her shirt over her head, taking off her jeans. In her bra and underwear she turned to face him, a troubled look on her face. "Will she really?"

"Yes." He held out his hand, and after a moment she came and took it. He tugged lightly, coaxing her to sit. Her bare thigh was near his sheet-draped hip, and he lifted his fingers to her clavicle and stroked the hard bone, then moved his thumb to the soft flesh in front of her underarm. He reached behind her and unclasped her bra.

"You old pro," she said. She shrugged the bra straps from her shoulders, and in an instant her breasts were released: their roundness, how pale the skin was compared with the dark plums at the centers. "Maybe I'll just skip my pajamas tonight."

He moved over for her, and she got in next to him, reaching to turn off the light.

"Do you suppose they're asleep?" he said.

"Lauren might be by now. Joe was still knocking around."

They lay facing each other. She touched his forehead, his temple. He turned his head slightly and sucked her forefinger; he liked the way her nail felt against his tongue. She made a little noise, then scooted her hips forward until they were pressed together. They pressed and pressed until he was fully hard. He rolled onto his back and pulled off his pajama pants and jockeys, and now they pressed again, her silky underwear wrapping around the head of his erection. This moment was a particular favorite of his: entering her a bit, pushing against her underwear, sensing the wetness. After a while she rolled onto her back and pulled her underwear off. There was a crash from upstairs, from Joe's room, and they laughed a little. "Literally knocking around," he said.

Sex and children, he thought. Sex was for making children and for finding your nerve endings until you were lit up and glowing. Children, meanwhile, were for sex; they were growing, not without challenges, but someday they'd start having sex, they'd have orgasms, make babies, and you and this woman would keep doing this quietly, outside the reproductive spotlight, body to body, until it was time to stop.

"There," she said. "Oh God, yes."

Brody and Liz fell asleep, drying slowly, coming apart slowly as they sank until only their ankles touched. They slept best when they slept naked, their bodies having climbed and climbed.

Joe was asleep, too. He slept the deep, restorative sleep of the well-exercised athlete. He wouldn't remember his dream, but if he did he wouldn't find it noteworthy. In his dream he was merely sleeping, Joe-the-dreamed in the very same position as Joe-the-dreamer, on his back, arms stretched wide. Joe-the-dreamed lay in a bed very like Joe-the-dreamer's, but the bed was far from anything, in a place that was a little like endless blue sky and a little like time suspended. Joe-the-dreamer watched over Joe-the-dreamed, and Joe-the-dreamed dreamed nothing. This was a dream he would have on and off throughout his life, whenever he was worried.

Ten yards away, Lauren wasn't sleeping. She was wide awake, lying in bed, trying as hard as she could not to move. She felt a little as she had once when she was drunk, one night last year when she slept over at Amanda's. Amanda's parents were out of town, and her sister, Corinna, had a friend over, too, and the four of them drank screwdrivers and watched *The Silence of the Lambs* on DVD. The room had spun that night, and it was almost as if it were spinning now.

Not moving seemed to help. Forgetting her body seemed to help. Keeping watch on the clock seemed to help, because she could tell at a glance that despite how it seemed, time really was passing.

8

$\mathcal{S}$arabeth's motto was "A bad movie is better than no movie at all," and while it wasn't true that she'd see absolutely anything, she rarely went more than a week without seeing something. Once, in her twenties, she attended eleven movies in seven days, and even now she viewed this less as proof that she'd had way too much time on her hands and more as a personal best.

The Heidts had people over most Sunday afternoons, which coincidentally—or maybe not?—was one of her favorite times to go to a movie. Thus it felt very familiar to be standing as she was now, staring out her living room window at the seven or so kids playing in the Heidt backyard while the minute hand on her watch ticked toward the time when she absolutely had to leave.

But she lingered. Through the Heidts' kitchen window she could just make out someone moving around: Bonnie, no doubt, whom Sarabeth understood to be quite the cook; she had even knocked once at Sarabeth's door and asked apologetically if Sarabeth had any star anise she could borrow. Dumbfounded and flattered, Sarabeth went into her kitchen and pretended to look.

Pilar had brought outside with her a zoo's worth of stuffed animals, and Sarabeth watched as she arranged them on a blanket, with a refreshing disregard for potential interspecies problems: giant floppy lion next to fuzzy pink flamingo, T-shirted Babar surrounded by little yellow chicks. Her hair was in braids today, short little braids that stuck out just below her ears.

The back door swung open, and now Bonnie stepped outside. She wore an orange polar-fleece vest over a red turtleneck, a lot of color even for her. She was the type of fortyish woman whose sexless personal style owed as much to kindergarten as to spinsterhood, and Sarabeth wondered what she'd been like at the time of her romance with Rick, if even then she'd clothed herself in brightly colored, shape-hiding garments; eschewed makeup; air-dried her hair. What would a person like that have worn for a wedding dress?

Liz had worn her mother's gown, but with the sleeves removed and the neckline altered to expose her gorgeous shoulders. Sarabeth had had so much fun with her in the months leading up to the wedding: racing around the city looking at lace, flower arrangements, who-knew-what-all. It was during that time that the idea of making things had really taken root in Sarabeth.

She had to get going. With a nod at Bonnie, she hurried down the driveway and out to her car, then sped through the orangest of traffic lights toward the theater.

Nina was there ahead of her, waiting with her hands in the pockets of her leather trench coat, her strawberry blond hair framing her face in ringlets and waves. She shook her head indulgently as Sarabeth ran up.

"You do know you're two minutes early."

"Leave me alone!" Sarabeth panted, only half kidding.

They made their way through the empty lobby and on into the darkened theater. It was a sunny afternoon outside, and there were only six or seven other people in the place.

The lights went down, and Sarabeth felt herself sink in as she waited for the first preview. That wide grass-green preview screen—she gladdened each time at the sight of it. Six previews, seven, there could never be too many. She liked the fact that, during the previews, she often forgot what movie she was going to see.

Which was what? Oh, right: the Canadian film about sibling incest, or at least that was what the press was all about—maybe they were just being sensationalist.

"Remind me to tell you about Mary and Mark Murphy," Nina whispered, just as the first preview started.

Sarabeth turned to her. "What?"

Nina shook her head. "After."

Sarabeth opened her mouth, then closed it again. What about Mary and Mark? What? She found her heart was pounding, and she was glad she'd seen this preview before. She thought of Mark and the canoe, a few weeks ago, and his odd, pained smile as he said, *Mary does. Mary likes canoeing.* What was up? Mary was a law school friend of Nina's, but whereas Nina had gone to work for the state, Mary was in private practice. She and two other Boalt graduates had their own firm, and she specialized in divorces. "Berkeley divorces" was the phrase in Sarabeth's mind. Meaning enlightened. Was Mary going to have her own Berkeley divorce? Impossible, Sarabeth thought, but of course nothing was impossible. And Mark had seemed odd, with the canoe. Preoccupied.

Two and a half hours later the lights came up, and Sarabeth and Nina turned to each other with their mouths agape.

"Oh, my God," Sarabeth said.

"The thing with the ax."

"And he was so *gross* at the end—that noise he made."

The press had been scant preparation for the movie. About an hour in, after they'd had sex on every surface imaginable, the brother had chopped off the sister's hand with a wood ax. Things got worse after that, and at the end, the sister finally murdered, he wandered naked through the house, pulling on his penis and emitting a sound, half screech and half growl, that no human should be able to make or have to hear.

"Watch those taboos," Nina said with a mischievous smile.

"Stop," Sarabeth said, but she smiled, too: Nina had a pet theory about the reducibility of all narrative art. At their book group, Sarabeth usually figured it was time to wrap things up when Nina started throwing out possible summarizing slogans.

They made their way up the aisle and through the lobby. It wasn't until they were standing outside the theater, trying to decide where to eat, that Sarabeth remembered what Nina had said just as the lights went down. "Wait, wait," she said, pulling Nina out of the way of the passersby, "what about Mary and Mark?" Her heart was pounding again, and she was annoyed with herself for being so eager, or looking so eager—whichever, she was annoyed.

"Oh," Nina said, eyes wide, "I completely forgot. This is so amazing. They're leaving for China on Wednesday."

"China?" Sarabeth said, and then she remembered: they wanted to adopt a baby. They were going to adopt a baby, evidently. "You mean it's happening? Mary must be so happy." She herself, on the other hand, was strangely sad; or perhaps she was simply moved, given the long story of infertility, drug treatments, failed IVFs, and despair that she'd heard, in installments, from Nina. Mary had been through the wringer. Sarabeth sluiced a tear from under her eye and forced herself to smile.

"It's intense, isn't it?" Nina said. "She's taking at least a year off work."

"I'd better make some lampshades," Sarabeth joked, "or they'll go broke."

They stood on the sidewalk, people walking past them: full of purpose, or so it seemed.

"So dinner," Nina said at last. "Do you want to go to Frisée? I could go for one of those little pizzas—maybe they'll have the goat cheese and sun-dried tomato."

This struck Sarabeth as inordinately funny, and she laughed a nervous, giggly laugh she feared would get out of hand.

"What?" Nina said.

Sarabeth shook her head and laughed harder. It was just . . . goat cheese and sun-dried tomato pizza. It was . . . Mark and Mary going to China to adopt a baby. It was . . . a movie about sibling incest, dismemberment, and murder. It was a yard full of children, and the idea that she might have star anise!

"What?" Nina was saying, her hair surrounding her face like a flame. "Sarabeth, what? Are you OK?"

"Oh, I'm fine," Sarabeth said, but she had imagined herself in Bonnie Heidt's kitchen, and a feeling of intense unhappiness overcame her.

9

She had the dark look around the eyes that Liz didn't like, the faintly hollowed cheeks. And she spoke a little too quickly, as she often did in times of difficulty. Trying to outrun herself was how Liz thought of it.

"I wonder how they'll manage," she kept saying. "I wonder if maybe they're too old."

They were at their usual Thai place south of Market, sitting at their usual table. The phone call that had brought this dinner into being had readied Liz for a Sarabeth in bad shape, but not this bad, or not this apparently bad: she looked a little as she had in the weeks after her breakup with Billy. She was very sensitive to loss—as how could she not be? Though what she was losing if Mark adopted a baby, Liz couldn't quite see. Maybe just an idea. A wish. If you'd been through what she'd been through, that could be a lot.

"Do you think they're too old?" Sarabeth said. "I mean, just from an energy standpoint?"

The answer, of course, was no, but what effect would that have? Put another way, would Sarabeth be better off hearing how hard it would be? Or how wonderful? This dilemma was as familiar to Liz as the restaurant, the food, the melancholy look on Sarabeth's face. Liz felt it was important to be truthful, but she also felt there was generally more than one truth, and the choice of which to deliver could help or hinder.

"What an adventure," she said, skirting the question altogether. "Imagine, you go on a trip and return home with someone you're going to know for the rest of your life."

The waitress arrived with their soup, and they leaned away from each other while she filled their bowls, the tangy, orangey milk of the broth and the little curled bits of chicken.

"*Tom ka gai,*" Sarabeth said. "This should help."

Liz raised her wineglass. Years ago, they'd been in the habit of going to a different restaurant every time they met—the latest hot spot or some out-of-the-way gem Sarabeth had discovered—but in the last few years they'd settled here, and it was more honest somehow: their dinners weren't about going out, they were about getting together, and as if to prove it they ordered the same food every time.

"Hey, how's Lauren?" Sarabeth said after they'd both had their first taste of soup. "I never heard how she liked *Howards End.*"

Liz thought of Lauren's tearstained face last Friday, when she got her paper back. The way she'd allowed Liz to hold her, the way she'd allowed herself to be held. The next day, it had been as if none of it had ever happened.

"She didn't," she said. "She had a hard time with the paper."

"Oh, I'm sorry," Sarabeth said. "I should have suggested something else. I feel bad."

"Don't be silly. She has to have these experiences."

"You really think that?"

Liz remembered resisting Brody's saying about the same thing: *It's good practice for life.* What did she think? Did she wish the kids had no challenges, no disappointments? What a pointless wish that would be, like wishing winter wouldn't come, or illness, or death. But in a way she did wish it, because she hated the suffering.

She spooned up some broth and glanced around the restaurant. It was starting to fill, a SOMA crowd of thirtyish high-tech types. The women wore low-slung jeans and clingy featherweight sweaters, a far cry from the kind of thing Liz had worn when she was their age and working. Suits, it was then. Jackets with shoulder pads.

"Never mind," she said. "Let's talk about you. How's *Anna Karenina?*"

Sarabeth smiled and leaned forward. "Last Thursday? Esther comes up to me afterward and says, 'Dear Sarabeth, this is the highlight of my week.' And she hands me three incredibly old Hershey's kisses—like, with the little white tags practically gray."

"That's so sweet," Liz said.

"Isn't it? I always feel like she's handing me a tiny piece of her life."

"Maybe she is. So someone will have it when she's gone."

"Oh, that's sad," Sarabeth said, setting her spoon down and sinking back into her chair. "And beautiful. You always say things that are so true."

"Please."

"You do. Billy noticed it, did I . . . did I ever tell you that?" Sarabeth kept her eyes on Liz for a moment, then colored and looked away.

Liz thought of her one and only encounter with Billy. She had always feared, especially as they grew older, that Sarabeth would find her way to a married man, but she'd never imagined someone as dangerous as Billy, as adept at hiding his treachery behind a veil of compassion and intelligence. She'd also never imagined how distressing it would be for *her,* nor how reluctant she'd be to meet him. Sarabeth had begged for months, and finally, when Liz could make excuses no longer, she drove to Berkeley and had the most awkward and stilted lunch with the two of them, Sarabeth trying so hard to be at ease, Billy as full of himself as she had expected, and the idea of his family hovering everywhere. Leaving afterward, she had shaken his hand and said, "It was so nice meeting you," when what she was thinking was: You monster.

"I'm sorry," Sarabeth said now.

"For?"

"Bringing it up. Actually, making you do it in the first place."

Liz shook her head. Looking at Sarabeth's tiny white face, her unruly hair, the curve of her narrow shoulders—she had a renewed awareness of how much Billy had meant to Sarabeth, saw how much Sarabeth was still in anguish. She wished she had some way to lift it—lift the misery off Sarabeth the way you could lift a mesh dome off a bowl of potato chips, straight up, without jostling the sides of the bowl.

In a few minutes the waitress arrived with their red curry beef, and they waited while she cleared away the soup. From a stamped tin tureen she spooned rice onto clean plates, then ladled the *panang* over it.

"I've been thinking," Sarabeth said once she was gone, "maybe I should invite her to tea. Esther, I mean. Like I could take her to a place with scones and real china, and we'd sit there and talk about life. But I'm not so sure I should. It's like, do I want to change the relationship?"

"That's a good question," Liz said. "It's like my mother and Mrs. Nudelman."

"Your mother and Mrs. Nudelman what?"

"When she got sick. My mother took her lunch every day. You didn't know that?"

"I don't think so," Sarabeth said. And then, "God, Mrs. Nudelman. I haven't thought of her in years."

She had lived across the street from Liz's family, right next to Sarabeth's: an old lady in a small Spanish-style house fronted by the most beautiful garden. Long before Mrs. Nudelman fell ill, Liz's mother had been friendly with her, asking her for advice on growing tulips in California, bringing home jars of her kumquat preserves. Then the roles changed.

"What did she have?" Sarabeth said.

"Cancer."

"Did we know that?"

"I don't think so. Or if we did, we didn't know what it meant." Liz pinched up some rice in her chopsticks and dabbed it in the sauce. It was strange: in childhood the idea of cancer had been so terrible it had been almost without meaning. And that somehow made it not terrible—made it nearly nothing. She thought of how knowledge accumulated in layers rather than linearly, how you learned the same things over and over, but differently each time, more deeply. This made her think of rain, sprinkling lightly, dampening the earth; and then sprinkling again and pouring down, and the earth taking it in and getting wet with it, drenched with it. And then, over time, gradually drying out again, as in old age the mind sometimes cleared itself, and memories—and knowledge—were lost.

"Do you ever dream about Cowper Street?" she asked Sarabeth.

"Not that I remember. Do you?"

"I dream about our backyard. The orange trees. I don't exactly dream about them, but I kind of dream their smell."

"That smell!"

"Our own little madeleine moment."

"But in reverse."

Liz leaned back and felt herself relax. She was always glad when she and Sarabeth talked about the past; she thought of it as good therapy for Sarabeth. Liz sometimes even brought up Lorelei: *Remember the time your mother played Monopoly with us for six hours? Remember when your mother taught us how to make popovers?* She had to be careful, though, because so many moments that for her had been harmless, even fun, for Sarabeth had been—or had, in retrospect, become—very fraught. *Remember the time your mother modeled that silky gray dress for us? And we thought she looked so beautiful?* In response to which Sarabeth might say, bitterly: *You mean the one she ripped to shreds because she thought my father didn't like it?*

Sometimes Liz felt it was best to pretend Lorelei had never existed.

After dinner they stood together outside the restaurant, clutching their coats close. They were almost directly under the freeway, and the sound of cars on wet road was everywhere.

"So a week from tomorrow," Liz said. "Are you sure you don't mind bringing your same salad?"

"Of course I don't mind. Anyway, the kids love it."

"That's not a good reason—would you rather bring something different?"

"Liz," Sarabeth said. "Are you sure you don't mind making your same turkey?"

"OK, you got me."

They hugged and parted, and Liz started the long walk to the garage where she always parked. It unnerved her a little, being alone in the city at night, and she kept a brisk pace, her purse tight at her side. The buildings she passed were dark and warehouselike, though a few had lights on upper floors and company names etched on the narrow glass sidewalk-level doors. Stopped at a crosswalk, she was joined by a big guy in a leather jacket, and her heartbeat hammered until the light changed and he took off ahead of her. She passed a seedy-looking doughnut shop with a single old man sitting hunched over a cup of coffee, and then an empty lot in which she could just make out the forms of several homeless people lying in sleeping bags. She was ashamed of herself, being afraid of such unfortunate people.

In the van she felt better. As she made her way to the garage exit she thought, for some reason, of those orange trees on Cowper Street, with their hard, shiny leaves. There'd been lemon trees, too, that produced lemons with incredibly thick skins. You'd cut one open, and there'd be half an inch of white pith surrounding the tart fruit. Her mother had made lemonade with them. Liz remembered the summer when she and Sarabeth were thirteen, how day after day they sat under the big tree in the backyard and read aloud the advice column from *Seventeen* magazine, all the while sipping from tall glasses of homemade lemonade. If John had a friend over they'd read in loud voices, trying to attract the boys' attention. If Steve had a friend over Liz would tell them not to come out back, and Steve would pout and tell their mother, but in the end Liz and Sarabeth would be left alone, the yard theirs. How long ago that was, when you could be at once so dramatic and so innocent.

She paid the garage attendant, and soon she was on the freeway, doing sixty, heading home. Already, there were Christmas billboards up: Gap scarves, De Beers diamonds clipped to the branches of a fir tree. "How do they get those signs up there?" Joe had asked at age five or six. "With an airplane?"

She switched to 280, drove past the neon of the Serramonte Center, along the rim of the vast, light-dotted bowl that was South San Francisco. The airport became visible, then the wide, irradiated mouth of the Valley. And then the freeway twisted to the west, and soon there was little to see from the road but the darker dark of the hills, the lighter dark of the sky.

No one knew where she was right now—not precisely, not with complete certainty. She approached the turnoff for 92, the road to Half Moon Bay, and she imagined a piece of herself splitting off, taking the turn in an alternate van, the two of them heading up the mountain, other-Liz and other-van, the twists and turns of the narrow road. She followed them to the top, then stopped at the first point on the downward stretch where the ocean became visible. From there she leaped to the distant beach, soaring downward with her arms spread, and she remembered a moment in college, in a class on twentieth-century poetry that Sarabeth, from across the bay, had urged her to take because the professor was a famous poet herself, visiting just for the quarter. There was a long poem that the professor had read aloud, and at the end it was something or other about birds going "downward toward darkness, on extended wings," the words themselves dark and majestic as they filled the Stanford classroom. "They're on extended wings," the professor said when she was finished reading, "but they do go down." All these years later Liz remembered the moment vividly, the professor with her little voice, speaking of the biggest things there were. The chill she felt as she listened.

· · ·

November was always rainy, but Lauren thought this year was worse than usual. Rain and rain and rain, cold air on her neck, damp seeping through her shoes to her feet.

She was in math, and a steady stream of water leaked down the windows, blurring the view. She had math last period every day, and as if math itself weren't bad enough, Aimee Berman sat across the aisle from her. Today she had a huge hickey on her neck, and she was pretending to be embarrassed by it. At lunch Lauren had seen her covering it with her hand and laughing with her girls. They were huddled under the overhang in their idiotically matching outfits: skirts over bare legs, despite the weather. Aimee's was this ugly plaid thing, but on her it looked good. Her legs were so perfect, it was like they weren't even real.

She also had dyed blond hair—and not just streaks, or one color this month, another next month, but seriously, professionally dyed blond hair, and she had had it since sixth grade, according to someone Amanda knew. Like, in fifth grade her hair had been brown, and then suddenly. The person Amanda knew had said the dyed hair was Aimee's mother's idea, which Amanda thought was sad. Amanda was always thinking things were sad when Lauren was grossed out. Lauren always had the wrong attitude.

Which was probably why Amanda was dumping her. Before Lauren's mom had left for the city last night, she'd suggested Lauren call Amanda to see if she wanted to go to a movie Saturday, and against her better judgment Lauren had called. Amanda, it turned out, was "busy." There was this horrible long silence as Lauren gripped the phone. She felt seasick. Finally Amanda said, "How about Friday?" and it was all Lauren could do not to tell her to go fuck herself. She said she was busy Friday, and when she saw Amanda before school this morning, she lied and said she needed to spend lunch in the library.

Because of Thanksgiving, next week was just Monday, Tuesday, and Wednesday, and Lauren didn't know which was worse, a full week of school or a four-day weekend at home. Her aunt and uncle and cousins were coming up from LA: Steve and Kelly would sleep in the guest room, Austin and Parker would get Joe's room, and Joe would get the foldout in the upstairs TV room. Lauren wasn't exactly affected, but she always felt kind of squished anyway.

Then there was the bench. Her mom, for weeks, had been painting an old bench with the dorkiest plaid pattern. Who ever heard of a plaid bench? And the colors were just awful, bright like kids' colors. Lauren had asked her if she was going to cover it while Steve and Kelly were visiting, and her mom had been like, Why? It was going to be mortifying. Her mom's furniture painting was so pathetic. What was the deal, anyway? Didn't she have enough committees to keep her busy? Lauren thought it was all a way to copy Sarabeth and her lampshades, except Sarabeth's lampshades were cool.

She looked across the aisle again. Aimee had her cell open, hidden behind her propped-up math book, and her thumb was busy punching buttons, texting someone in another class. She looked up and gave Lauren such a cool stare that all Lauren could do was look away, her face on fire. In her peripheral vision she saw Aimee return to her cell—probably to key in "OMG! Tht girl Lauren nxt 2 me is fugly."

Mr. Pavlovich had asked a question. Lauren knew not because she'd heard it, but because the atmosphere had changed. Everyone was alert, listening now whether they appeared to be or not. Chalk in his dusty fingers, Mr. Pavlovich scanned the room for a victim. He was the only one of Lauren's teachers who regularly called on people who weren't raising their hands, and Lauren tried for a look of slightly confused attention. He scratched the side of his pockmarked neck, leaving a smudge of chalk dust. "Aimee?" he said.

Aimee's face didn't change, but her hickey seemed to get a bit darker. She was actually a little on the dumb side, and all at once Lauren felt sorry for her. If she'd known the answer herself, she would have tried to find a way to pass it to Aimee.

"I don't know," Aimee said. She stared hard at Mr. Pavlovich, and now *his* face changed a little, reddening as he ran a finger across his upper lip. The moment seemed endless, and Lauren honestly didn't know which of them would prevail. Mr. Pavlovich should, but Aimee was Aimee and even he knew that. Was he thinking he wanted to fuck her? Maybe he *was* fucking her and had crossed a line by calling on her. When Amanda's sister was in tenth grade, a PE teacher was discovered to be having an affair with a freshman.

The bell rang, and the whole thing collapsed, Mr. Pavlovich's uncertainty, Aimee's strength, Lauren's idea that any of it was interesting. She loaded her stuff into her backpack and left the room. The only person Aimee was fucking was Tyler Moorhouse, Jeff Shannon's best friend. Actually, they weren't necessarily fucking, which was all about Aimee's cred, since Tyler was a senior. Tyler and Jeff were probably leaving their math class right now. God, had Aimee been texting Tyler? Until now Lauren had never thought that every last period Aimee could be texting Tyler and saying stuff about her that he would say to Jeff. She suddenly saw herself as possibly more visible to Jeff than she'd ever considered. What mean stuff might Aimee have said? Lauren's heartbeat felt crazy, and she paused for a moment to catch her breath. If Aimee was telling Jeff stuff about her, then she wasn't starting on level ground; she was starting *down*. She was screwed. In fact, she might as well ask him out, have him laugh in her face, and call the whole thing over right now.

She stopped at a drinking fountain and gulped water, really thirsty. Straightening up, she wiped the back of her hand across her mouth and turned, and there he was, right behind her, waiting for a drink: with his tall, lanky body and his chiseled mouth and his incredible blue eyes. "I'm Lauren," she blurted, and then in complete mortification she bolted, speedwalking halfway to her locker before she realized he'd be passing by on the way to *his* locker and she absolutely couldn't be standing there dialing her fucking combination when he walked by, not after the way she'd just humiliated herself. She stopped and turned, thinking forget it about the rest of her stuff, and there he was, coming right at her, and he stared into her eyes and gave her a long, knowing smirk.

Liz was having a bad morning. She was out of half-and-half. She'd burned two batches of toast. She'd been counting on Brody to take the kids, but he had to get to work early for a conference call. And Lauren: Lauren had done it again.

I'm not going to school today.

Liz was in her closet, shoving her feet into shoes, and as soon as she got home from dropping Joe, she and Lauren were going to have a talk. *Sweetie,* she would say, *I'm getting worried about you.*

Which was a lie. She wasn't getting worried, she was worried—she hadn't had an unworried day in two months, if not longer. The school-work explanation had been as empty as empty could be. Lauren should see a therapist. And Lauren would not want to see a therapist.

Back in the kitchen, Brody and Joe were as she'd left them, in twin states of ill repose. Brody had the paper open, but it might as well have been upside down for all she believed he was reading it. Joe was eating an English muffin with his head so low it was practically on his plate.

"Liz," Brody said, glancing at his watch and getting up from the table.

She looked at him.

"I'm really sorry. If this were something I could skip . . ."

"Forget it," she said. "Go. It's fine."

He waited a moment, then gave her a perfunctory kiss and left the house.

When Joe was ready she went up and told Lauren she'd be back soon. There was a heavy fog outside, and the air was cold and damp. She looked up and down the street, and there wasn't a person visible, not a single sign of life anywhere. Days like this, the rest of the world, even the next block, seemed entirely hypothetical.

"What a morning," she said as she stepped up into the van, and from the passenger seat Joe looked over at her with nervous eyes. Lauren these days—how was it for him? "Oh, sweetie," she said.

"Just drive."

The school was up in the hills. The drop-off line started a block back, and you inched forward, more and more slowly as the first bell approached. Liz recognized a number of people, or recognized their cars: the khaki Sienna, the silver Odyssey, the massive dark orange Hummer. It was a community of vehicles. "Vehicular mayhem" came a phrase to her mind.

The car in front of Liz moved forward, and when she'd closed the gap Joe opened his door and jumped out. "See you later," he mumbled, and she watched as he dove into the stream of kids heading for the school. All those kids, all those backpacks: they reminded her of nothing so much as ants marching along, each with its own burden. Childhood was hard, mainly because you hadn't learned perspective. Nothing was real beyond the present. The unknown future wasn't comfortable or uncomfortable—it simply didn't exist.

She needed a little more time, and once she'd circled the school she headed north rather than turning south toward home. Thank God it was Friday; she didn't think she could stand another day in this week.

She found a parking place right in front of Starbucks, but the line was long so she ducked into the bakery next door and bought a loaf of bread first. Back at Starbucks, she waited in what was now a longer line, then realized only after she had her coffee that she was out of decaf and would need some for Thanksgiving. She stood in the beans line while the counter person tried to cope with the fact that she was being asked to work, here at her job. She was probably eighteen or nineteen, surly, and so slow it had to be intentional. Liz understood clearly that this would not bother her so much if she didn't fear Lauren would end up just the same.

Finally, a pound of beans in hand, she left the store. She got into the car and thought: It doesn't have to be like this.

Then she realized that she had it, the thing to say to Lauren. *It doesn't have to be like this.* With concern, with hope, and without pressure. She had just the right thing to say when she got to Lauren's room.

But Lauren wasn't in her room. For many hours she had fought an idea, and now the fight was over and she was grateful. The worst possible decision had turned out to be a great relief. She had done it, and she lay in the empty bathtub (she had not wanted to leave a mess), and bled, and sank into the thing the pills were helping her with, the not feeling, the not thinking that was going to help her with not being, because being was not . . . working . . . for her. . . .

Warm where her wrist touched her face.

part two

10

*A*fterward, Brody would not remember the drive to the hospital, the adrenaline blast to his system, the way his hands kept slipping off the wheel as he sped across intersections where yellow lights were going to red. The entire thing would be lost to him, and in moments when he wasn't plagued by other things he would be plagued by the idea that he might have hurt someone, that he didn't know he hadn't hurt someone on his breakneck race.

What he started with, what his memory would start with, was the emergency room waiting area, where Liz's parents were watching for him, both of them.

"Where is she?" he said, and Marguerite tried to take his hands, and the image of her hands—her soft, wrinkled, slightly arthritic hands as he pushed them away: this was flash-printed onto his mind.

He sprinted past them and pushed through a pair of swinging doors. All he'd really gotten on the phone was: *Lauren, hurt herself, ambulance, hospital, now.* He dodged an elderly man on a gurney, and there was Liz, turning and seeing him and bursting into tears.

Again, all he could say: "Where is she?"

"Brody," she cried.

He remembered himself and took her in his arms, felt her weight against him, felt, as he pulled away, her hair detaching from his cheek, where the dampness of her face had made it stick.

"Where?" he said.

"God," she wailed, but then she indicated a door, and he pushed through it and saw: Lauren's bare legs, three people standing over her, machines and an IV bag.

"Sir," the one man said, "you can't come in here."

"I'm her father." He moved for a better look: her eyes were closed, and there was a tube in her nose, something black smeared all over her face. "What happened? Is she unconscious?"

"Sir," said one of the women. She was doing something between Lauren's legs, and Brody looked away.

"OK, I'll go," he said. "But just tell me . . ."

The man—Brody took him to be the doctor—faced him. "Your daughter had a drug overdose. We're monitoring her vital signs and giving her activated charcoal to absorb the toxins."

"A drug overdose?" Brody said. This was impossible; Lauren didn't do drugs. Everything was happening too fast. "What do you mean, what did she take?"

"Tylenol. And apparently some Benadryl. The medicine cabinet was empty when your wife found her."

Brody's pulse raced. He knew from somewhere that too much Tylenol could be really bad; that was why the liquid stuff you gave babies came in such tiny bottles. He put his palms together and took a deep breath. He had to slow down. He turned away, only to realize that he'd been looking at Lauren's left wrist and that it had been wrapped in a bloodstained bandage. He looked back: the other wrist, too.

"Oh, my God," he said. "She slit her wrists?"

The doctor was studying one of the monitors. "The cuts are the least of it—we'll stitch her up in a minute. It's her liver we're worried about."

"Her liver?"

"Why don't you wait outside? We'll talk in just a bit."

To Brody, the lights were suddenly far too bright, and a wind roared past his ears. Then things were normal again.

"OK," he said. "I'll wait outside."

In the hallway, Robert and Marguerite had joined Liz. As soon as she saw Brody, she broke away from them. "What'd they say? Are they pumping her stomach?"

"The doctor said he'd come talk to us in a minute."

She put her face in her hands and wept. "No, no, I can't stand this." He touched her, and she jerked back. She looked at him and cried: "I went to get coffee."

He had no idea what she meant, and he turned to Robert and Marguerite. Was there a coffee machine in the waiting area? Did she *want* coffee?

"After she dropped Joe at school," Marguerite said. "She went to get coffee before she went home."

"No," he said. He took hold of Liz's shoulders and bent to look in her eyes. "Oh, no." He meant *Don't do this to yourself,* but a terrible sound came out of her, and she wrenched herself away and sobbed harder.

"You didn't know," he said.

"I did!" she shrieked.

"Honey." He reached for her again, but she pulled away. "Liz. Where did you find her?"

"Stop!" she cried. And then: "In their bathroom!"

He tried to picture the inside of the medicine cabinet in the kids' bathroom, but all he could come up with was some very old Johnson's Baby Shampoo sitting stickily on a glass shelf. There was Tylenol in there? Benadryl? He remembered bribing Lauren to take Benadryl when she was four or five—for every tiny sip she got a jelly bean. Joe stood nearby, waiting for a jelly bean or two of his own.

The door behind him swung open, and he turned. One of the nurses came out, and behind him Liz and Robert and Marguerite moved forward, almost as one. They crowded behind him, and he had a sense of himself as not just their spokesman but also their protector. "What?" he said, but the nurse just held up her forefinger and kept going.

After several hours in the emergency room, Lauren was moved to the pediatric ICU, but it was a while before Liz fully registered the change, how it was calmer here, and quieter; and the light, thank God, was dim. Lauren had a tiny room to herself, and she said over and over again that she wanted to go home: she said it crying, not crying, crying again. She couldn't go home, though, and so Liz wouldn't, and so it was Brody who left at ten to pick up Joe from Trent's house, where he'd spent the evening.

Joe. Sitting in the dark next to Lauren's sleeping body, Liz thought back to the middle of the afternoon, when Brody had left for the first time, to meet Joe after school. The plan had been for Brody to call once he'd told Joe what had happened, but it was Joe who called, saying "Mom?" when she answered, his voice breaking slightly on the single syllable, and it had taken her long moments to be able to speak.

Light from the hallway bisected Lauren's face. Liz leaned forward and ran her hand over Lauren's hair, then held the backs of her fingers over Lauren's mouth to feel her breath. Terrible things had been done to her today, following the terrible things she'd done to herself: they'd punctured her veins for IVs, pumped bottle after bottle of charcoal into her stomach. By far the worst was the vile liquid they'd made her drink, four separate times—it was sulfurous and repulsive and necessary to counteract the effects of the Tylenol on her liver, which remained, even now, in great danger.

She could go into liver failure. She had to keep drinking the horrible stuff, every four hours through the weekend, and she could still go into liver failure.

Liz leaned back in her chair and tasted salt at the back of her throat. How could she have allowed this to happen? How could she have let the last months happen, sitting by while Lauren fell? She was on a tiny island, surrounded by the vast ocean of her guilt, and the water lapped and lapped at her ankles, its undertow strong enough to pull her in should she somehow avoid the headlong dive she kept imagining. All that kept her out was how much Lauren needed her now, how much more than ever, though she'd not need her now if only Liz had had an ounce of sense, a gram, in the last few months. What had she been doing this fall? Yoga! Painting a bench! In her mind she slammed a mallet against the bench, splintering the wood; she threw paint remover on it and watched with pleasure as it burned through her gay colors. She reached into her body and tore at her muscles, then plunged her fingers into the crevices of her joints and ripped at them until they were permanently damaged.

Then she thought: Is this how Lauren lived? Ravaged by self-hatred? And she wept again.

A sound woke her sometime later to the bed she had improvised, her upper body curled in a chair, her legs reaching under its wooden arm to rest on the metal frame of Lauren's bed. She was incredibly sore, her mouth dry and sour. Lauren was still asleep. How soon before they came to draw blood again? To administer the next dose of the disgusting stuff.

She pulled her legs back and sat up, moving as quietly as she could. Slowly, painfully, she stood. She edged out of the narrow space described by the chair, the bed, and the table, and she went into the windowless bathroom. She hit the light and hid her eyes for a moment, then stared at herself in the mirror. She was wrecked, hideous. Then she realized that was exactly what she was looking for, evidence that this had undone her, and she turned from the sight of herself and wept. She eased herself onto the closed toilet and sobbed at her own self-pity, and she sobbed at it all: Lauren, Joe, Brody, her parents, her family, her life, her home, her child, her child. She sobbed and sobbed. And then, after a while, there came a moment when it ebbed, and she watched herself through it curiously, unwilling to allow a single moment of falsity; she felt she could cry, but only if she couldn't not cry. She couldn't not: it was back and she sobbed again. But it slowed, and it faltered, and after a while she *could* not, so she stopped. She mopped her face with a hand towel. She began to feel composed, and she glanced at her surroundings, *a hospital bathroom,* and then she was going into the bathroom again, the kids' bathroom yesterday, Lauren bleeding in the bathtub, and she began to cry again. This happened several times, the slowing and the fresh onslaught. Finally, in a lull, she went to the sink and ran cold water over the towel and pressed it to her eyes, and because the coolness felt so soothing she bathed her eyes with handfuls of water, then dried her face and ventured the mirror again. *You,* she said to herself.

11

$\mathcal{S}$arabeth had made a rule for herself that she would never drive down Billy's street, and she'd followed it to the spirit if not quite to the letter: she'd driven by only twice since the breakup, once just a week or two afterward, on an afternoon when she knew he'd be teaching; and once at five o'clock in the morning, when no one in his family could possibly be awake. On this Friday evening, though, two days after her dinner with Liz, she happened to be in Rockridge, just blocks from his house, and she felt such a strong pull in that direction that it alarmed her. She imagined stopping out front, cutting the engine, getting out. She'd lean against her car and look: at the handsome craftsman styling; the wide, deep porch; the long driveway back to the garage in which were kept, she knew, the family's four bicycles, hung on a wall rack that Billy himself had built.

She remembered the look Liz had given her across the table Wednesday night when the subject of Billy came up. A look that seemed to say: *I know.* Liz knew, and somehow that allowed Sarabeth to keep driving.

She was on her way to a read-through of a play written by her book-group friend Miranda, and while she'd envisioned a borrowed house with a large living room, what she found instead was an elegant concrete cube, fronted by a beautifully landscaped garden illuminated by carefully placed yard lights. TEATRO MIO, said a discreet plaque on the front door.

Teatro Mio. My theater?

Billy had been an actor when he was younger; he'd liked to quote Shakespeare to her, lines from the romances as they lay in bed together, Henry V's battle cry as he returned from the bathroom and stood naked in the doorway: "Once more unto the breach, dear friends, once more." This on an occasion when he had to head back to campus for a department meeting. She recalled his ironic smile, the way he stood naked in the doorway, entirely unselfconscious. He was generally naked the entire time he was at her house; she'd never been with someone so comfortable with his body.

Nina was already in the lobby, standing with the two Karens—doctor Karen and dentist Karen, as Sarabeth thought of them, even though she'd known doctor Karen—Karen Grimes—for twenty-five years, since long before she was a doctor or needed to be distinguished from any other Karen.

She hugged each of them, tried to bring herself to them, but all of her leaned toward Billy. They were talking, and she let herself go, to his strong arms, his whispering voice. . . .

"Sarabeth," Nina said. "Weren't you thinking about getting tickets?"

"Tickets?"

"Hello? To go hear the Nigerian guy?"

Sarabeth had a vague memory of a talk Nina had mentioned, but she couldn't remember anything else. "I guess maybe I was," she said. "But I never did."

It was warm in the lobby. There were twenty-five or thirty people milling around, and she eyed the door, wondered if she had time to go outside for some air. "Hang on," she said to the group, but as she edged away from them a bell rang, and she turned and saw that Miranda had appeared.

Miranda was one of the quieter members of the book group, and she generally dressed to match her personality, but tonight she wore a sapphire-blue silk dress, and her honey-colored hair was piled on top of her head. What was this going to be like? Sarabeth didn't know Miranda very well, had not understood until this moment how much must be at stake for her.

Miranda climbed onto a chair and rang the bell again, and when the crowd fell silent she smiled and said, "Please join us."

The theater consisted of four rows of steeply banked seats in front of a bare stage. Sarabeth followed Nina in and sat down. What *was* this going to be like? The whole thing had started with *The Hours,* which the book group had read and unanimously loved back in the late nineties, and then loved again when the movie came out.

"I kept wanting them to meet each other," someone had said as they sat together afterward, in a café near the theater.

"I know," someone else said. "Actually, I wanted Virginia Woolf to meet Mrs. Dalloway."

"Mrs. Dalloway? You mean the modern-day Clarissa?"

"No, Mrs. Dalloway the character."

"But Mrs. Dalloway wasn't even in it."

Miranda had taken the bait. A museum administrator, she was finally curating her own show, hanging not paintings but people in the hopes of making a meaningful convergence. Writers meeting their own characters; that was the task she had assigned herself.

When everyone was settled, a man came out onto the stage, dressed in a dark suit and carrying a script. Focus, Sarabeth thought as he began to speak, but into her mind came a picture of Billy reading stories to his boys, or washing dishes while She read the stories, and she couldn't focus. What is he doing right now? What, right now? This was a game she had played with herself—against herself—throughout the affair. She would imagine him shooting baskets with the boys, standing in front of a classroom of students, practicing tai chi with his Sunday morning group, and anywhere he might be, no matter how unlikely it was that his wife would be with him, Sarabeth imagined Her too, penetrating some fourth wall to stare back at Sarabeth.

He never said he was going to leave her, and that was not the issue; Sarabeth did not expect him to leave her. The issue was, she was sad. *I love you,* he would say, *I love you, I love you,* and she knew it absolutely: they were a great couple, someone might have thought who saw them only through a keyhole, with 99 percent of the picture hidden. When he was with her he was fully with her. She wanted to have dinner with him at a restaurant? No problem, he said, and they met for dinner at a restaurant in the city, no big deal. She wanted to have a whole night together? No problem, his wife was taking the boys to LA, and he stayed all night three nights in a row and woke her with kisses on her shoulder each morning. Nothing she wanted was impossible, except all she really wanted: total ownership. *We're here for such a short time,* he said to that—meaning on earth, meaning in this state of being alive. This was his way of telling her not to be greedy, not to long for something you couldn't have when what you did have was so nice. But she was greedy.

"Greedy?" Liz had said. "It seems pretty normal to me."

Up on stage, the man in the dark suit had been joined by a second man in a dark suit. The first man had been talking for quite some time, and while Sarabeth had missed most of it, she had an impression of confusion. From *Mrs. Dalloway* she remembered insane Septimus Smith sitting on a park bench and thinking he heard an important communication in the roar of an airplane passing overhead. The idea of hearing something unreal had always terrified her.

"It shall be the end of me," said the second man angrily.

"They said they would come," said the first man. "I believe they will come."

And two more people did come, another man in a dark suit and a woman in a long, droopy dress and spinster shoes. Virginia Woolf at last. Stones in her pockets, madness . . . As a child, Sarabeth had thought "madness" was a word for unmerciful rage.

You can't even get mad, Billy had said, toward the end. *Has it occurred to you that you're angry at me?*

They were in an unpleasant therapy-speakish few months, where, as at the beginning, they had to have sex as soon as Billy arrived at her house—now because if they waited they'd devolve into weepiness and cajoling. Shortly before the end, he showed up late one Wednesday night and said in a tone of the deepest misery: *I can't do this anymore.* He didn't mean cheat on his wife; he meant tolerate Sarabeth's unhappiness.

"We *are* you," Virginia Woolf was saying to one of the dark-suited men.

Sarabeth had to leave. She caught Nina's eye and tapped her forehead by way of explanation, then half stood and sidestepped past dentist Karen.

Losing Billy had ruined her. Or maybe it was being with him that had ruined her. Why had it happened? Why had she had coffee with an obviously married man? Why had she sat on the curb in front of the Berkeley Bowl with an obviously married man? Why had an obviously married man talked to her at the heirloom tomatoes?

Because you were so pretty, he said once. *And you looked so sad. I wanted to make you laugh.*

In her car, five blocks from his house, Sarabeth cried. Sad won him and sad lost him, and through it all time passed. She was on the down-slide to fifty, and she was alone, alone. What had been happening, up on the stage? What had Miranda been saying? *We* are *you.* Flaubert had said it first, but maybe it bore repeating. Mad Septimus Smith and all the characters in all of literature, Anna, Levin, Vronsky: they *were* their makers, painful parts of their makers. Made to bear too much, but known.

Across the bay was Liz, who truly knew Sarabeth. Thanksgiving was six days away. Sarabeth's own makers were long gone, and whether or not they had ever known her was a moot question because they didn't know her now: her mother had been dead and gone for decades, her father dead for years and long gone before that. Gone, too, was her lover, the love of her life, and oh, she had loved him so, his kindness, his focus, his lightness—maybe his lightness most of all, the way his self, mind, soul, essence, whatever could move about so easily, his body moving easily through her house, not as if entitled but as if free, that was it, he was so free. So much was gone, but still Sarabeth had Liz.

The weekend crept by. She called Liz a few times, but there was no answer, and she didn't have the heart, or maybe the energy, to leave a message. She canceled a Saturday afternoon shopping date with Jim and Donald and instead moped around the house. She wished she were the type of person who could rent a slew of movies, or eat massive amounts of sugar, or take soothing aromatherapy baths when she was unhappy, but it seemed she could only feel unhappy, one minute at a time. Billy, and her loss of him. It was so hard to find someone you actually liked, someone you loved: Why had she let it go? Why hadn't she tried harder? She had suggested this to him, one of their last times together—*I could try harder*—and it was the one time she saw him cry. He cried like a man, just the liquid eyes and nothing else.

Sunday morning she almost threw it off. She woke to rain, the *thip, thip, thip* of it as it hit the ground outside her bedroom window, and she burrowed under her covers and for a moment thought that to fall back asleep on a Sunday morning in late autumn when it was raining was a minor pleasure of a certain, specific order, like the pleasure of the first bare-legged day of spring, when you'd just shaved your legs, or the pleasure of a spoonful of peach sorbet at the height of summer.

Peach sorbet reminded her of Billy, though, and she couldn't get back to sleep. She stayed in bed for another hour and a half and then got up and crept into the kitchen, to the miniature but somehow engulfing work of making tea.

It was during phases like this that the disrepair of her house most bothered her. In the late morning she spent a despairing half hour contemplating the horror that was her bathroom—not just the water-ruined windowsill in the shower but also the filthy radiator and the bug-filled light fixture and the incredibly ugly aqua tiles, any number of which were chipped. She could distinguish between the radiator and the light fixture (both of which could be cleaned, theoretically) and the windowsill and the tiles (neither of which could be repaired without a great deal of money and trouble), but she was powerless to take on either kind of problem.

All afternoon she avoided her living room window so as not to have to see the lit-up inside of the Heidts' house and their Sunday company. Toward dusk she returned to the bathroom and ran water for a bath. While the tub filled, she fingered the abalone shell that rested on the glass shelf above her sink. Billy had brought it to her from Tahiti; its color was the shimmery blue-green of the ocean when the sun was low. Their reunion after that trip had marked what was in retrospect the beginning of the end. He'd had a glorious time. The boys had spent hours every day in the water and had come back with their dark hair blond and their pale skin deeply tanned. To Sarabeth it was excruciating.

She began to undress, and the phone rang. She stepped out of the bathroom and looked at her answering machine. She knew she needed to get outside herself, but how, when it was she who was keeping herself in? Nina had called three times, but she hadn't answered, hadn't responded to the increasing concern in Nina's solicitous messages; and the apologetic e-mail she'd sent Miranda had brought a concerned call to which she had not responded either.

Her outgoing message finished playing, and the answering machine beeped.

"Uh, Sarabeth," said a man's voice. "Liz wanted me to call you because, uh, this is Brody, Brody Mackay, and Liz wanted me to call you because something's happened, and—" He sighed, and, staring at the phone, Sarabeth trembled.

"Lauren tried to hurt herself. She did hurt herself. She's in the hospital, and Liz wanted me to let you know. Thanks, bye."

Something was terribly wrong in the physical world—it was as if Sarabeth's house had turned sideways. She reached for a chair and sank onto it. *Lauren tried to hurt herself, she did hurt herself.* What did that mean? It had to mean what she thought it meant, but it couldn't mean what she thought it meant, because that couldn't have happened. Sarabeth's heartbeat was crazy—it wasn't so much fast as incredibly loud. Lauren couldn't have done that. Done what, though? She didn't know what Lauren had done. She needed to call and ask.

But: *Liz wanted me to let you know.*

Why hadn't Liz called? The house turned sideways again, and Sarabeth ran into her bedroom and dove onto the bed. She put her fist to her mouth and gnawed at her knuckles and sobbed. She had to go to Liz right now, but she didn't know if she could.

She had to, though. She kicked off her sweatpants and pulled on jeans. If she was going to drive across the bay she needed to eat, and she ran (why was she running?) into the kitchen and grabbed a bag of rice cakes. At the front door, though, she stopped, overtaken by dread. In seconds she was back on her bed.

She reached for the phone, then hung up at the sound of the dial tone. She should be in her car already. She should be approaching the freeway. If she went right now she could make up for the time she had lost. But went where? Where was Liz? What she needed was to call Brody back and ask for more information. But would he be home? Wouldn't he be with Liz, wherever she was? And if they were together, why hadn't Liz placed the call? This again, insistent now: why hadn't Liz placed the call?

Because she couldn't.

Sarabeth felt a wave of dizziness. She sat up, then quickly lay down again, her heart hammering. She could not see Liz that upset. She couldn't. *This isn't about you!* she screamed at herself, but terror came down over her anyway, and she gave herself up to it, trembling, panicked, paralyzed.

12

$\mathcal{S}$ unday night was the first night Liz and Brody were both home at bedtime. She rummaged through her dresser, past her pajamas, until she found what she hadn't known she was seeking: her old gray knit pants from the Allen Allen catalog, so worn that the so-called cotton cashmere was as pilled as real cashmere, and the seat and knees ballooned. She pulled them on, then found a ragged T-shirt for a top.

She got into bed next to Brody. Joe had gone up early, pleading homework; he'd been asleep when she went to say goodnight.

Brody turned off the light and rolled to face her. She lay still, letting the darkness settle, letting herself settle into the darkness. The exterior walls of the house felt too far away, and then, after a while, not quite so far. Brody put a hand on her shoulder, and she tried to force herself to relax. She would not make love, but she could be touched. And she could touch. She reached for his hand and held it. "I'm—"

"Shhh," he said, "don't," and she withdrew her hand and turned away.

"It's just," he said, but then he fell silent, and she waited for more. After a while it was clear there would be no more, and she tried unsuccessfully to remember what she'd been going to say, but it had been replaced by anger.

"Sorry," he said at last, and she waited for herself to soften, face him again, stroke his cheek. She didn't.

"Sorry about what?" she said coldly.

"Never mind."

"What?"

"That I don't want to talk."

"Who's talking?"

"Liz."

They were side by side, both on their backs, cold as corpses. She felt herself exhale heavily. He touched her hand, and in a second she was on top of him, pressing her mouth against his, straddling his leg and rubbing herself against his thigh until in almost no time she was about to come. She was incredibly aroused, gaping, half an inch from a firestorm. "Oh, God," she cried, and she felt for his penis, but it was completely limp, and she let go. She ground herself against his leg again, and then she came with a loud, sighing groan.

She lay where she was, half on top of him, panting. "Sorry," she said.

He stroked her back. "It's OK."

She reached for his penis again, but he caught her hand and held it away, and she moved off him and faced the wall. Outside, a tree branch scraped against the house, driven by the wind. She felt sticky, and not just between her legs. Had she showered today? She remembered combing her wet hair in front of the TV and the 49ers had been on, so evidently she had. Before leaving the hospital to come home, she'd asked Brody to call Sarabeth, but she'd forgotten to ask, when she returned, if he had done so. Obviously not.

Lauren's liver was going to be OK, but Lauren—Lauren was not OK. Dr. Porter, the psychiatrist in charge, had said that she'd consider releasing her to Liz and Brody's care, but she strongly recommended Lauren be admitted to the adolescent psych ward instead.

"For how long?" Liz had cried, and Dr. Porter had pulled her glasses from her nose and said, "Until she's less of a danger to herself."

At night the hospital was full of secrets, but in the morning the secrets were gone and it was just busy. Lauren wasn't scared anymore, or she was scared in a different way, of the terrible real things that would happen rather than the terrible unreal things that wouldn't. She would not be attacked in the dark. She would not suffocate in her sleep. But she would leave this room, in a few hours, and with school going on, going on without her, she would go to a place where there were crazy people.

In her peripheral vision she saw the woman whose job it was to watch her. The woman had a magazine, but Lauren didn't want to turn her head to see if she was reading it. She didn't want to look at her at all.

The woman was a "sitter." It was hospital policy that someone watch Lauren to make sure she didn't try to off herself, which was ridiculous because she wouldn't do that *in a million years*.

Girls burning themselves with lit cigarettes, boys pacing the halls and thinking they were God. It was going to be a nightmare. She'd have a roommate who'd probably sneak some guy in and fuck him while Lauren lay awake in the next bed, and some bitch of a nurse would dole out pills in little paper cups. And school would go on without her; it would go on and on.

She needed to get back—before people found out. She could say she'd gone on a business trip with her dad. Or she could say she'd had . . . pneumonia. Only how completely idiotic was that when she hadn't even had a cold? She remembered math, Aimee Berman telling Mr. Pavlovich that she didn't know the answer, Jeff at the water fountain, Jeff smirking. And then Thursday night at home, lying awake, thinking about . . .

He hadn't meant it, the smirk—hadn't meant that he knew everything about her feelings and found her and them disgusting. She blew everything out of proportion. Here, now, in the hospital: she was mortified. She'd heard there was an operation you could have to make you sweat less; was there one to make you blush less? Couldn't someone sever some nerves? At once her wrists hurt, and she looked down at them, lying at her sides, wrapped in white bandages. It was almost as if they weren't hers, except they hurt. At least she didn't have to drink the stuff anymore. It had been so disgusting, thick and viscous and smelling like rotten eggs. A wave of nausea came over her just thinking about it: this hot, foul feeling in her stomach. She didn't know how many times she'd puked the stuff up—when she did they made her drink more. Or they stuffed a tube in her nose and pumped it in. She'd had diarrhea like crazy. Her stomach boiled, and she thought, No, and then she barfed on herself.

She sat up and swung her legs to the side, but it was no use: she heaved and barfed again, all over her lap, her bare legs, the floor. The sitter was standing now, looking at Lauren with her pig face pink, eyes wide. Where were Lauren's parents? Where where where?

"Go ahead," Brody said, "take him if you want—that's fine."

Joe was upstairs getting his backpack, and Brody was watching Liz across the breakfast table, waiting for her to decide what she wanted. Minutes ago, she'd asked him to drive Joe, but now she thought maybe she would. Make up your mind! he thought. It's not that big a deal!

"You know, maybe I actually *should*," she said. "Since I drove him on Friday. To sort of—normalize things."

They exchanged a look—nothing would normalize anything—but he played along. "Yeah, why don't you? It might be good for you, too."

"I think I will." She went to her purse and got out her keys. "You'll be ready when I get back?"

"Absolutely."

Joe came into the kitchen, struggling with the zipper on his backpack, stopping at the table for a last bite of toast. "Ready," he said to Brody.

"Actually, Mom's going to take you."

Joe's face changed a little, a slight dimpling above his left eyebrow that signaled surprise, disappointment, something.

"That OK?" Brody said.

"Sure."

"I don't have to," Liz said.

"God, it's fine, can we just go?" Joe blushed and then said, in a softer voice: "I don't want to be late."

When they were gone Brody got up and cleared the table. He loaded the dishes into the dishwasher, wiped the counters. Apparently there would be paperwork at both ends; the transfer could take most of the day.

He went into his and Liz's room. He yanked at the covers but stopped short of making the bed. He opened the curtains, then opened the window for good measure. *The outdoors is a big place to heat.* That was his mother, back when he was a kid. Even then he'd had a thing about fresh air. He stood at the open window, waited for the feel of the cold outside to reach him.

In five minutes Liz would be back. He found his laptop and logged into his e-mail. He'd checked his BlackBerry a few times over the weekend, scanned the sender names and subject lines, but he hadn't read anything. Now he selected a few e-mails at random and just glanced. Kathy, his assistant: ". . . don't know if you'll be . . ." Fred Rodriguez from sales: ". . . unless we increase cross-sell activity . . ." Tim Hilliard at Secur-Soft: ". . . follow up on our conversation of . . ." Kathy again: ". . . really worried, know you'll be in touch when . . ."

He heard the front door open. "Brody?" Liz called.

"In here." He closed the laptop and set it aside. He was almost to the bedroom door when she appeared.

"Ready?" she said.

"Yeah."

She stood there with her purse hanging from her forearm, a troubled look on her face.

"What?" he said.

"Should we be doing this? Is it the right thing?"

The psychiatrist had said hospitalization significantly reduced the likelihood of repetition, and that was enough for him. Though Lauren's wails when she found out had nearly cut him open.

"Well," he said doubtfully, "we could bring her home," and to his relief Liz looked alarmed.

"I suppose we could," she said. "But—"

"We already told her she was going."

"Yeah." She stayed still for a moment and then began digging around in her purse. "OK," she said as she produced her keys. "We'd better go then."

It was the worst day of Liz's life. The place was shocking in the way the impossible could be shocking: Were she and Brody going to leave Lauren here? Leave her? In a room with barred windows? Near a lounge full of dinged tables and stained linoleum? Among kids who were so plainly sick it made Liz's stomach hurt?

And there was a terrible smell—like maple syrup and gravy and urine combined.

At home afterward, the sky drained of color, Liz puttered around in the kitchen and did not answer the phone: not when her parents called, not when it was her brother John from Philadelphia, not when it was her brother Steve. Thank God for caller ID.

Lauren hadn't even cried. They'd delivered her up for whatever would happen—talking, Dr. Porter had said, groups, support, help, the words themselves acquiring a kind of menace as they were spoken—and she'd barely looked at them when they left. "It's not uncommon," the intake nurse said, "for kids to clam up when they first get here."

At dinner, Joe leaned over his food, chewing quickly, strands of wavy hair falling onto his forehead.

"Joe," she said, suddenly unsure whether or not she'd told him about Thanksgiving.

He looked up. "Yeah?"

"We're not having Thanksgiving. The dinner. With Steve and Kelly and the twins."

"You told me."

Across the table, Brody twirled a forkful of spaghetti. As he chewed he began right away to twirl another.

"It'll still be Thanksgiving," she said. "Obviously."

Brody looked up. "I'm sure Joe wasn't thinking the president would rescind it."

"The president?" she said, her face warming.

"It's a presidential order every year. This day of November shall be the Thanksgiving holiday."

"It's the fourth Thursday."

"Not automatically. And I think it's the fourth Thursday after the first Monday."

"That would be automatic."

"It's proclaimed every year," he said. "According to a formula."

Joe cleared his throat, and she came to her senses. Bickering—how foolish. The question was what to do on Thursday: on Thanksgiving. She wished they had something other than the feast to mark the day, a habit of actually giving thanks somehow. Though perhaps that would be harder.

"What are Grandma and Grandpa doing?" Joe said.

Liz's mother had been the first to mention it. "What should I tell Steve and Kelly?" The question had flustered Liz not because she hadn't thought of it but because she had. She was ashamed of having wondered even briefly if they should go on with their plans.

"I guess they'll be at the condo," she told Joe.

"Can I go over there?"

"Is that what you'd like?"

Brody sent her a look across the table, but what was he trying to say? Nothing—what he'd been saying all day. He'd been silent on the drive to the hospital, silent on the drive back home.

She didn't want Joe with her parents, she wanted him here, but she assumed that what she wanted was wrong and therefore in need of correction. So Joe should go. Or maybe they all should, she and Brody and Joe. Her mother had offered. But that felt wrong. Maybe Brody and Joe? She didn't know where "should" was coming from—from how things felt or how they ought to be.

After dinner she went into her bedroom and closed the door. She had to call Sarabeth. She was glad Brody hadn't—it was something she needed to do herself, for herself and for Sarabeth. When she said the words to Sarabeth she would cry, which was probably why she hadn't called yet. Sarabeth would cry, too. For a moment, looking at the phone, she saw Sarabeth's little house as a refuge, much as Joe seemed to see her parents' condo; she imagined driving there now, telling Sarabeth not on the phone but face-to-face in Sarabeth's living room. Sarabeth's house was too small, though, too quirky-pretty. Arriving there tonight, with her monstrous news: Liz would feel grotesque, a giantess.

She punched in the familiar numbers and listened to the ring. "It's me," she said when Sarabeth answered.

There was a pause before Sarabeth said hi.

"Listen," Liz said. "I have to—"

"I know I'm horrible," Sarabeth said. "I'm so sorry."

Puzzled, Liz hesitated for a moment, then started again. "I have something to tell you."

"I know," Sarabeth said. "There's no excuse."

"What do you mean?" Liz had the strangest feeling that Sarabeth meant for Lauren, for what Lauren had done—that there was no excuse for that. But that made no sense, because Sarabeth didn't know. "I have something to tell you," she said again. "Something bad."

Sarabeth inhaled sharply. "Oh, no."

"Lauren—" Liz said, but before she could say any more, Sarabeth burst into tears.

"Oh, no," she cried. "Oh no, oh no, oh no."

Liz waited. In a moment, something would become clear. She was on the edge of the bed, and she reached for a small pillow and held it on her lap.

"How did she do it?"

"Do what?" Liz said.

"Hurt herself. Did she—not make it?"

Liz brought the little pillow to her face. She breathed in and out, the familiar smell of Tide. She said, "You knew she hurt herself?"

"Brody called me. He said you wanted him to tell me. Wait—you didn't know that? That's what you were going to tell me? And she's—OK?"

"Brody called you?" Liz said.

Sarabeth was silent.

"When?"

"Yesterday," Sarabeth whispered. "He left a message."

"So you already knew."

"I was going to call you."

"But I beat you to it."

"Yes."

"I have to go," Liz said, and she hung up the phone.

In seconds it rang, and for some reason she answered it. "I'm so sorry," Sarabeth said. "I'm incredibly sorry. Can't we talk? I don't even know what happened to Lauren. What happened? How is she?"

"Here's what happened," Liz said. "She slit her wrists, took most of a bottle of Tylenol, and is now about to spend her first night in the psych ward of the hospital." *And you knew for an entire day and didn't call me.* "I can't talk right now."

"Liz."

"I can't talk right now. I can't talk to you now."

She hung up and lay back on the bed. She closed her eyes, then rolled onto her side. She felt for the little pillow, down near her hip where she'd left it; she brought it up and put it over her ear. Large pillow below her head, small above. She imagined a wedding cake, with her own sideways face in place of the middle layer. Something to slice.

13

$\mathcal{S}$ arabeth opened her front door and stepped onto the porch. It was very cold, and she shivered and crossed her arms tightly over her chest, but she didn't go back inside. She had wept and wept in there, moving from room to room, from couch to bed to floor. She had come out here to stop.

. . . slit her wrists, took most of a bottle of Tylenol . . .

Quickly, she crossed the porch and braced herself against the post. At the Heidts', all the upstairs lights were on, and she focused on the bright windows, imagined Bonnie and Rick up there putting the children to bed. Chloe, Pilar, Isaac. Girl, girl, boy. At the Castleberrys' it had been boy, girl, boy.

. . . slit her wrists . . .

. . . slit her wrists, took most of a bottle of . . .

She pressed the heels of her hands to her eyes and wiped them on her pants. She took a deep breath. There was wood smoke somewhere, faint and far away.

What had happened to Lauren? She remembered Lauren abruptly leaving her bedroom when the two of them were talking last time. She remembered thinking Lauren was dressing differently, that Lauren was a little spacey. And what did she do? Recommended a book. Recommended a book that had ultimately caused Lauren trouble. Oh, and had a small tantrum over the condition of the cheese rolls she'd brought.

She put her face to the cold post. *This isn't about you,* she said to herself again, but it was baritone deep this time: wobbly, distorted, vanishing. She was worthless. All day today she had told herself she would call, but she had not called. All day today she had thought she should drive over with food, but she had not driven. And again, now, still: she wasn't driving. Liz had saved her, saved her a thousand times over—it was the central truth of her life. Had it been inevitable that she would one day fail Liz?

A blade across the tender, pale skin. She pulled back her sleeve, felt the tendons where they surfaced close to her hand. Taut chords, strings on a violin. She found a tendon just to the side of the base of her throat and turned her head so she could pinch it between her fingers.

Lauren couldn't have meant it. Liz couldn't bear that.

Liz couldn't bear this.

She made her way down the steps to the little scrap of walkway that led to the Heidts' driveway. She paused. To her left was their garage, to her right their driveway and their car. The wind shifted, and she thought she felt a drop of rain on her forehead. She backed up and sat on her bottom step.

She should have taken food.

On Cowper Street, the day after her mother died, so many people brought so much food she couldn't get it all into the refrigerator. She remembered finally giving up and just randomly stowing it: in cabinets, drawers, the cold oven. Then when people finally left, even Liz and her parents gone home, she retrieved the improperly stored dishes and scraped into the garbage creamy chicken and noodles; broccoli and rice; thick, tomatoey rafts of lasagne. She left the empty dishes in the sink until, in bed at last, she thought better of it and went back downstairs to wash them, thinking that she didn't want her father to come upon them in the morning when he sought the small solace of a cup of coffee.

All this time later, all these years later. She brought her feet up and wrapped her arms around her shins, then lowered her forehead to her knees. After a while, she felt a drop of rain on her scalp, and then, some time later, another. She looked up again. Invisibly, barely audibly, it was raining. She heard it on the leaves, slow, and on the Heidts' driveway. It hadn't rained since yesterday morning, when she'd woken to the sound of it and had for a moment forgotten Billy, forgotten the long hours she'd spent thinking about him Saturday evening, Saturday afternoon, Friday night.

She longed to tell him about Lauren. Why?

Because she knew him, that was why. She knew what he would do. He would hold her, stroke her hair, make it easy to cry. The very things she'd failed to do for Liz.

14

*L*auren had to get out—she had to get out. This was all such a mistake, such a nightmare. During breakfast she sat by herself and tried to think of how to explain that this was all wrong, and she tried not to look at the other kids. Her roommate, Abby, was across the room, at a table full of very thin girls. Abby was very, very thin, and though Lauren hadn't asked, she knew Abby had an eating disorder. She was like a biology lesson on how little of the body was bone. Bone was all she was, and there wasn't much of her. Her collarbones jutted, and her face looked like a drawing in a kids' book, pointy, all nose and chin.

Lauren felt like a blimp. Sitting here, she felt her stomach bulge over her jeans, her ass spread across the seat of the chair. The food was horrible—dried-out scrambled eggs and canned fruit. Tonight she would order what she wanted to eat tomorrow; last night, her first, she'd stupidly refused today's menu. Her wrists hurt, and the bandages were getting raggedy and gray. No one would have to wonder what she was doing here.

She had started taking an antidepressant. You had to build up to the full dose, and there were side effects sometimes and then you tried something else. Nausea could be one. Light-headedness. Those were things she experienced anyway, though, so how would she know? Also, what was it supposed to do? Her life was her life.

After breakfast there was a meeting led by the nurse Lauren had talked to when she arrived, Kitsy. She was this short, round woman with glasses and incredibly frizzy hair. After this meeting, Lauren was going to tell her she was in the wrong place.

Kitsy had everyone pull their chairs into a circle—twelve girls and five boys. It was so much like a movie Lauren wanted to laugh. Besides Kitsy, there were a couple other adults—mental health workers—and Lauren couldn't imagine why anyone would want to work in a place like this.

Lauren was between Abby and a guy with curly hair. He smiled at her, and there was something about him: something not quite matching between his eyes and the rest of him. She looked away.

"Some of you have met Lauren," Kitsy said. "She arrived yesterday." Kitsy smiled at Lauren, and Lauren's cheeks burned. Turning to a girl with bleached streaks in her hair and inch-long, grown-out roots, Kitsy said, "Would you like to start?"

"Whatever," the girl said with a shrug. She had heavy black eyeliner circling her eyes and a silver stud in her lower lip. She smiled a weird, almost sexy smile at Kitsy. "I'm Callie," she said.

"What's your goal for today?"

"Talk to my foster mom, I guess."

"That was your goal yesterday," said a guy across the room.

"Bite me."

There was a silence, and Lauren waited to see if Callie would get in trouble for this. There were time-outs here, and there was also a reward system for good behavior, like if you were good you could go to the cafeteria and choose your own pukey food.

"Morgan?" Kitsy said as she looked at a big-boned girl with stringy white-blond hair.

"I want my sister to visit me."

Something ran around the group, shock or something.

"Can your sister visit you?" Kitsy said.

Morgan stared into the center of the circle. As Lauren watched, her face changed: it went from blank, to scared and miserable, to blank again.

"Your sister can't visit you," said another girl in a sort of pissy way.

Morgan looked at Kitsy. "I know."

"It's very painful," Kitsy said, and then there was a long silence. Lauren wondered why Morgan's sister couldn't visit her. Maybe Morgan had done something awful to her.

"Do you have a more realistic goal?" Kitsy said.

Morgan shook her head, which seemed to be permissible; the next girl ran a hand through her incredibly short, boyish hair and began to speak.

"I'm Casey," she said, "and one of my problems is I cut myself." She paused and stared right at Lauren's wrists, and Lauren felt her face burn. "I'm working," she continued, "on why I do that. My goal today is to talk to my doctor about it some more."

Kitsy nodded at Casey and then looked at the guy next to her, a tall, skinny beanpole with greasy black hair hanging to his shoulders. He said he was going to try not to listen to his voices, and Lauren's stomach lurched: there were crazy people here. What a moron she was, being surprised by this. The guy blinked and then looked into his lap and picked at his thumbnail. The curly-haired guy was next, and then it would be Lauren's turn, and she had to figure out how to tell them that this was a mistake, that she shouldn't be here.

The curly-haired guy said, "I'm Lucas, and I'm going to try not to punch the wall." A half laugh ran around the circle, as if he actually might punch the wall, and he turned to Lauren and gave her a bright smile. He was sort of cute, in a totally un-Jeff-like way.

Kitsy looked at Lauren. "Would you like to tell us about yourself?"

Lauren shook her head.

"You have to say something," said Casey, the short-haired, cut-herself girl. She was staring at Lauren's wrists again.

"This is a mistake," Lauren said. "I shouldn't be here, I didn't mean to do anything."

"Yes, you did," Casey said.

Lauren got up and started toward the hallway leading to the bedrooms, but one of the adults, a guy with black nerd glasses, caught up with her.

"Hey," he said, not exactly like *hey you* hey, but not exactly hi. She stopped.

"I shouldn't be here," she said. "I shouldn't."

"A lot of kids feel that way at first."

"Yeah, well *I shouldn't.*"

"The thing is, you are."

She looked down, and to her horror tears streamed from her eyes.

"It feels terrible, doesn't it?"

Lauren put her face in her hands and sobbed.

"This is our morning check-in," he said. "You don't have to say anything you don't want to say, but I need you to come back to the circle."

It was the longest day of Lauren's life. After the meeting there was school, and the woman in charge said she was going to call Lauren's teachers to see what Lauren should be working on, which made Lauren cry again. Her school couldn't know! Did everyone in the world have to know? She'd made a mistake. She hadn't even meant it. The other kids looked at her and whispered.

At lunch Lucas sat next to her and talked almost nonstop—about his schoolwork, his friends, his whatever. His T-shirt said GOT COCAINE? but the COCAINE had been markered the same color as the shirt, dark blue, and it almost didn't show up. His shirt looked like GOT ——? and it only made you want to get closer to see what he was hiding.

"Are you allowed to wear that?" Lauren said.

"We're working on it."

"My mom would never let my brother wear a shirt like that."

"No, here," he said. "We're working on it here. I have substance abuse issues," he added, sort of sarcastically but also like he meant it. "I have bipolar disorder."

After lunch there was another group thing, and Lauren tried to make herself invisible. This was something she'd been good at for a long time— she was almost completely invisible at school—but here they wouldn't leave her alone. She told them the truth, that nothing was wrong, and Casey, whom she now hated, said, "Yes, it is." Fucking bitch, Lauren thought, but it was different from thinking Aimee Berman was a fucking bitch, because with Casey—Casey staring at Lauren, staring at her wrists—there was something weird, like she didn't just think Lauren was a loser, she actually wanted to prove it.

Some kids went to do yoga, but Dr. Porter wanted to see Lauren, which was a relief because there was no way Lauren was doing yoga. In the other part of the hospital Dr. Porter had talked to Lauren for a while, and to Lauren's parents, and she'd said she would see Lauren again here in the psycho ward, but now she was introducing Lauren to someone else, Dr. Lewis, and he was going to "treat" Lauren. Dr. Porter was old, like sixty, and she had gray hair that fell to her shoulders and little gold glasses and a white coat. Dr. Lewis was a lot younger, though he had little gold glasses, too, and a white coat, too.

"We'll find a place to talk," he said to Lauren, and she shrugged, because what else, that was all anyone did around here. They went into a little room. She was feeling really tired, and when this was over she was going to her room to rest. "Room time," someone had called it at lunch. One of the thin girls, but Lauren couldn't remember her name. In fact, there were way too many people here, and Lauren didn't care what their names were, she just had to get out.

"I'm hoping to help you," Dr. Lewis said once they were seated at a table. "I'm guessing you've been in a lot of pain."

Lauren looked at the door. There was a little window in it, with a wire grid dividing it into tiny squares. The big windows behind her were covered by bars. All the windows to the outside were covered by bars.

"Lauren?" he said.

"It was a mistake. I didn't mean to do it."

"Do it?"

"You know." She looked at him, but he just sat there waiting. "What I did," she said, and she lifted her bandaged arms from the table and then let them down again.

"What did you do?"

Of all the fucking things, why was he torturing her? She moved her arms to her lap. "As if you didn't know."

He made a steeple with his forefingers. "I know what I heard about," he said, "but I don't know what you experienced. I don't know how you would describe it."

He was a freak. How she would "describe" it? Then again, if she told him, if she just said the words, could she go?

"I slit my wrists," she said, bringing her arms up from her lap and laying them on the table again. "And I took some pills."

"How did you slit them?"

"With an X-Acto knife."

"What's that?"

"It's like a craft knife," she said, not believing how weird this was. "Kind of like a box cutter, only smaller, with a smaller blade."

"Do you know why you slit your wrists and took some pills?"

"I didn't mean to."

"You must have been feeling pretty bad."

"No, I wasn't," she said, and she burst into tears and buried her face in her hands. "I wasn't, I wasn't!" She let herself go, and now she cried and cried. This fuckhead looking at her, the nurses, the other kids. Everything was completely screwed. She was completely screwed. Last Friday at breakfast, when she said she wasn't going to school—why hadn't her mom said she had to?

Liz should have told Lauren she had to go to school last Friday. She should have seen, that day when Lauren was so upset about her English paper, that Lauren was in serious trouble. She should have understood, the first morning Lauren stayed home, that something was really wrong.

She was in the kitchen cleaning out the cabinets. She hadn't cleaned them in months, or possibly decades. Out came everything, boxes of cereal and cans of tomatoes and coffee mugs and honeycomb candles and beer glasses and dinner plates, and Liz scrubbed the shelves with sponges and 409. Joe was at soccer; Brody was trimming the ivy on the back fence. In an hour they would have an early dinner, the nature of which she couldn't fathom at this moment, and then she and Brody would go visit Lauren. Without Joe. "It's better," Dr. Porter had said, "if siblings don't have to see the ward. It can be pretty upsetting for them."

Joe had asked again about going to her parents' on Thanksgiving, and it had been decided that all three of them would go, and that her mother would make roast beef. It was so absurd Liz wanted to scream. Why was roast beef OK and turkey not? Yet it had been her idea, her compromise. Everything was twisted. Life was full of pretense. How she felt now, the oddness of going on living when it seemed you shouldn't be able to: it was a little like how she'd felt after 9/11. Each morning that fall she'd pored over the *Times,* reading the newest news and then, when she could no longer avoid it, poring over the "Portraits of Grief" and weeping. The house empty, everyone gone: she did this only when she was alone. Weeping and weeping and weeping. And then folding the paper closed and somehow, impossibly, going about her day. She hadn't been flying those planes, though. What she'd felt then was pure: pure grief. She hadn't been flying this plane, either—she'd basically abandoned the controls and taken a seat at the back of the cabin, by the window, through which she'd gazed idly at the passing scenery, not a care in the world—and what she felt now was impure grief, polluted, hellish. She squirted 409 on a bare shelf and attacked the grime as if it were her very self.

Later, at the hospital, Lauren rushed to hug her. She was in hysterics by the time Liz let go. They sat in a corner of the lounge, and Lauren begged through her tears to be taken home. "It was a mistake," she kept saying. "It was a mistake."

"Sweetie," Liz said. "It won't be for very long. Tell us how it's going."

"Everyone hates me."

"Why do you think that?"

"Because it's true!" Lauren cried, and she bowed her head and sobbed harder.

Across Lauren's bent shape, Brody gave Liz an opaque look, and she thought: What? What do you want me to do?

"Did you talk to Dr. Porter?" she asked Lauren.

Lauren straightened up again. "She put me with a different doctor. A man." The look on her face changed. "Why did you let me stay home?" She turned to Brody and cried, "You're the one who said school was required!" Then she stood and bolted from the room, and one of the nurses gave Liz a sad smile and followed after her.

"God," Brody said.

They leaned back in their chairs. Across the room, a girl with very short hair was looking at Liz.

Suddenly her cell phone rang, and she pulled it from her purse to shut it up. It was SARABETH HOME, for the third time in the last several hours, and she hit SILENCE and then turned the phone off. Sarabeth had called this morning, and they'd talked for a while, but that was all Liz could take. Of course this was hard for Sarabeth—Lauren making a suicide attempt, even a suicide gesture? It was impossible. But Liz *didn't have time for that right now.*

The nurse came back into the lounge. She made her way to Liz and Brody's corner and sat in the chair Lauren had occupied. She was a beautiful black-haired woman with light brown skin and a diamond stud in her nose. "Lauren is very sad," she said, her voice lilting a little with an Indian accent. "She feels really terrible, and we need to help her."

Tears pushed to the rims of Liz's eyes, and she fought to keep them from falling.

"Most kids here go through a lot of different feelings," the nurse continued. "Sad and confused and angry. Sometimes Mom and Dad are angels, and sometimes they are devils."

"And right now we're devils," Brody said.

"Lauren needs some time," the nurse said. "Here she has very good doctors and staff." She smiled and brought her palms together, and Liz had nearly moved her own hands before she understood what she'd been expecting the nurse to do: bow her head and say, *Namaste.*

Namaste.

I bow to you.

It's the acknowledgment, Diane had said once, *by one soul of another soul.*

Liz imagined herself bowing to Lauren, acknowledging Lauren. Had she somehow failed to do that? She couldn't think of anything more important for a mother to do.

On Wednesday, Brody finally went into the office. Technically, the company was already closed for the Thanksgiving holiday, but there were a lot of people around, in jeans instead of khakis, or sweatpants instead of jeans—letting it be known that they weren't really here, not officially. Kathy sat at her desk until twelve-thirty, then came to his doorway with an apologetic look on her face.

"Go," he said. "Kathy, really."

"I don't have to. Do you want me to wait and see if anything comes up?"

He went to the door and hugged her, his gray-haired fairy godmother of an assistant, his genius of organization. A good assistant, Russ had said once, was someone who brought you a hose at the first sign of smoke. Kathy brought him a hose, a fire extinguisher, a bag of sand, a tarp. . . .

"I'll be fine," he said. "See you Monday. Have a great weekend."

"You, too," she said. "I mean—"

"I know, Kathy," he said. "It's OK. Thank you."

When she was gone he returned to his desk. He had dozens of e-mails to deal with, but he could do that at home. He began going through the stack of papers that had accumulated on his desk.

A knock sounded, and there was Russ, standing in the doorway. His version of dressing down was a dark blue shirt with the top button unbuttoned, no Zegna tie. His shoulders pushed at the shirt fabric, thick like a wrestler's. Ugly-sexy, Liz had called him once. Or had it been Sarabeth, drawing a conclusion based on Liz's description? Brody was a little surprised Sarabeth hadn't been over, though maybe Liz had asked her to wait.

"Come on in," he said to Russ. "I thought you were out of town."

"Not till tomorrow morning—I'm on the first flight to Cabo with my youngest." Russ came in and sat in Brody's visitor's chair. "I'm so fucking sorry, man. How is she?"

Brody thought of Lauren's rage last night, of the way she'd come back to the lounge at the last minute and clung to Liz, begging her not to leave. He said, "It's hard to know. They only started Prozac Monday."

"Prozac can really help." Russ looked very certain, and Brody wondered if he was speaking from some kind of personal experience. His kids were older than Lauren and Joe, pretty much grown, but there was a son who'd had difficulties and apparently did again, or still. Rumor had it he was back at home, living with Russ's ex-wife in the eight-thousand-square-foot house in Woodside that she'd gotten in the settlement. Patty. Liz had always liked her, had enjoyed talking to her at company social events. On such occasions now Russ was generally accompanied by a woman half his age: gorgeous, and never seen again.

"I don't know why you're here today of all days," Russ said. "Seriously. Go home."

"I needed to come in."

A look came over Russ's face, and he said, "Oh, of course. Are you OK? I mean how could you be, but—"

"I needed to get some stuff for the weekend."

Russ nodded quickly. "Right, right." Then he said, "Listen, take whatever time you need, OK? Really, I mean it."

He stood, and Brody stood, too. Was he supposed to say thank you? He didn't need Russ telling him he could take time. But yes, he was supposed to say thank you, and he did so as he walked Russ to the door.

He left a little later, calling Liz to say he'd pick up Joe. The bell rang as he walked through the middle-school gate, and within seconds a first wave of kids spilled past him, forcing him to the edge of the walkway. He waited, and a second, larger wave approached, the kids so developmentally disparate that some looked like college students while some still looked like—still were—children.

It was Joe's last year here; he'd join Lauren at the high school next fall. *Lauren Mackay's brother, Lauren's little brother, Lauren's brother:* Brody imagined whispers and felt a spark of anger at her.

Joe appeared with Trent. They walked without speaking, simultaneously speeding up to pass a slow mover, stepping to the left to get around a couple of stalled girls.

"Joe," Brody called.

Joe kept going; it was Trent who slowed down, glanced over his shoulder, stopped. He said something to Joe, and Joe turned. For a moment, he had the what'd-I-do? look of his much younger self. Then he made his way over.

"Thought I'd come get you," Brody said.

"OK."

"How was school?"

"Fine."

The contours of worry on Joe's face: Brody felt so powerless he might as well have been made of air, water. He imagined a man-size dump of water splashing onto the pavement where he stood.

"We can give Trent a ride if you want," he said, but Joe shook his head.

"That's OK."

They walked in silence, Joe with his hands in his pockets, head down. The walkway split, the crowd thinned, and there was Trent again, just ahead of them, his backpack hanging from one shoulder.

"Come on," Brody said. "Let's see if he wants a ride."

Joe glanced at Brody and then lengthened his stride toward his friend.

"Trent," Brody called. "Want a ride?"

Trent turned, eyes wide. After a moment he shrugged his assent.

They continued, and immediately Brody knew he'd made a mistake. They were silent, all of them: walking the rest of the way to the car, getting in and buckling their belts, driving the roads to Trent's house. Lauren everywhere and nowhere, both at once.

That evening, in the crowded hospital lounge, she was nearly silent. Brody and Liz weren't meeting with her psychiatrist until Friday, and he half wished they wouldn't have the chance to see her again until after they'd talked to him.

Much later, when they were home again and Liz and Joe were asleep, he left the upstairs TV room, where he'd been trying to work, and tiptoed downstairs to the kitchen.

From the doorway he could see the digital clocks on the stove and microwave: 2:04 and 2:05. He could never perfectly synchronize all the clocks in the house, though he thought about it at every daylight savings time change, every power outage. Now they were 2:05 and 2:05. Red numbers glowing, the faint buzz of the emergency flashlight plugged in next to the door to the garage. It was quiet, dark. He felt himself a darker shape in the transparent darkness of the night. Himself, impermeable. He imagined the kitchen from outside, the dark windows seen from a neighboring house, the thin light that would suddenly appear if he opened the refrigerator or turned on the fluorescents under the cabinets. This light would imply someone standing there. Himself, standing here. He thought of Liz asleep, of the stairway to the upstairs: the room he'd just left, the guest room, the kids' bathroom, Joe's room, Lauren's. In his mind he climbed the stairs and looked in on Joe, Joe's chest rising and falling, the sound of his breathing a tonic to Brody, a treasure. In his mind he opened Lauren's door, then backed away.

He moved to the couch and stared at the blank TV. The remote was on the coffee table in front of him, and he picked it up and studied the buttons, wondered how loud the sound would be if he turned it on. He didn't want to wake Liz. He didn't want to watch TV. He put the remote back and stretched out. He had not called his mother yet about what had happened. She was actually no older than Robert and Marguerite, not in years, but she was older in spirit, in mental flexibility—and she was too old for this. She hadn't visited since Brody's father died, and Brody thought it was because the Bay Area frightened her, the congestion, the energy. She still visited his sister in Cincinnati. In fact she would be there for Thanksgiving tomorrow. Today.

At the fridge he poured himself some milk and gulped it. Then, in the garage, he found clean shorts on the dryer, shoved his sockless feet into his tennis shoes, and headed to the car. The streets were empty. Each house was snug, dark, safe. At the high school he parked behind the courts. He made his way to the nearest baseline. He lined up his cans of balls behind him, tossed his racquet cover to the fence, grabbed a couple of balls, and settled into serving position.

He started with his toss. Ball in one hand, racquet in the other, both in front of his chest, he brought his arms down and up again, and the ball continued into the sky and came back down into his hand. Ten times he did this, fifteen. He liked the rhythm, the swing of his arms moving down together and then separating and sweeping upward. The pain in his shoulder asserted itself, but he moved through it. He bounced the ball a couple of times and did four or five more tosses. Now he was ready. He held the ball, the racquet, he swept his arms down and up, and he slammed the ball into the service box. And the next one. He hit all the balls he had, his target the outside corner of the box, and he nailed it and nailed it again. He was sweating lightly now, despite the cool air. He circled the net and collected the balls. From this side of the net he worked on his ad court serve, reaching down to the cluster of balls, grabbing two at a time, shoving one into his pocket, and hitting the other. Back on the first side he tried it with his eyes closed. Later he changed the target spot. He hit his mark or not—it no longer mattered. What mattered was the darkness, the solitude, the late hour, the cool air, and the motion, over and over again, of his arms.

15

*H*er tea was very hot, and then it was not so hot, and still they didn't come out. Sarabeth was at the window, and the Heidts' Volvo was in the driveway, and neither moved. What was going on? Was someone sick? But that wouldn't keep them all home, would it?

In the kitchen, her coffeemaker hissed. In a while it hissed again, and though she found it difficult to move away from the window, away she went: to fill a mug, stir in a knobby brown lump of sugar. She was a creature of habit: she had tea first and then coffee, every morning. She carried her mug back to her lookout, but still there was no sign of the Heidts.

Surrounding her, filling her, was what Lauren had done. And what she herself had done, had failed to do. "It must have been really hard for you," Liz had said on the phone Tuesday morning. "It's so understandable that you'd have trouble with this." Warm, she'd been. Forgiving. But when Sarabeth called again—and she called again several times—Liz didn't answer.

It felt almost like a weekend, and she was tempted to have her weekend breakfast of lemon pound cake. Instead, she returned to the kitchen and started toast. On the shelf behind the toaster an old gift of Esther's had gathered dust, and she reached for it across the heating slots. She unwrapped the cellophane and pressed the surface of one of the cookies.

Hard as a rock. She had no idea where she'd left off in *Anna Karenina*, but she'd figure it out before tonight. She had quite a group these days—more even than she'd had for *Madame Bovary*. Adultery. You might not commit it yourself, but you were sure going to be interested in it.

Guilt is a useless emotion. Billy was always saying that—being philosophical, telling her to let it go. As if it were so easy! As if it were morally acceptable. He'd hardly been speaking from a neutral position.

She popped the toast, and though it wasn't as dark as she liked, she plucked it from the toaster and spread it with almond butter. At her table she ate quickly, three or four bites. There was a feeling in her chest that she didn't like—from eating too fast? "Esophagus" had been a favorite word of Lauren's in early childhood. To hear it spoken or to speak it herself had sent her into fits of giggles.

How was Liz surviving? She had sounded calm on the phone, but she couldn't be calm; she couldn't be anything but devastated. "No, thanks" had been her response to Sarabeth's offer to drive over. "Nothing, thanks" to what Sarabeth could do to help. Someone else might just go, but not Sarabeth. Was she respecting Liz's boundaries? Or being a bad friend? A worse question: Would Liz be talking to her if Sarabeth *hadn't* failed her so horribly? Confiding in her, telling her how she felt? Had Liz ever truly depended on her? Sarabeth thought of when Ted, Liz's boyfriend before Brody, broke up with her, one of the coldest, out-of-the-bluest breakups she'd ever seen. Liz had gone underground then, and Sarabeth had worried and wondered why. But she hadn't forced herself on Liz. Hadn't said: *I will not leave until you are well again.*

She went to take a shower, and it was there, waiting for the water to heat, thinking maybe she'd call Jim about touring, that she realized: today was Thanksgiving. There was no tour today. The Heidts were home because there was no work today, no school. It didn't matter where in *Anna Karenina* she was, because the Center was closed today, a fact she had known, had owned, once upon a time. "See you in December," she'd said at the end last time. "That's marvelous," Esther had said as she hobbled out of the room. "Marvelous."

Sarabeth shut off the water and sat on the closed toilet. How could she have forgotten Thanksgiving? When had it happened, when was the last moment she'd known? She wondered what she should do. What were the Mackays doing? How odd that she had not thought of it on Tuesday, talking to Liz. Heat filled her face, and she felt sick with shame at the possibility that if she'd remembered she might have asked Liz if dinner was still on.

She took her shower, dried off, returned to the bedroom. For an hour or so she lay on her bed and read, until at last she got up and made her way to the living room window. She had begun to hear voices a while back, and in fact the Heidts' yard was full of children—at a quick count nine of them, all wearing paper headgear appropriate to the holiday. Chloe had on a black-and-white pilgrim hat, while Pilar and Isaac both sported elaborate feather headdresses. Had Bonnie made these hats in advance of the party, or would each child have been welcomed with the opportunity to make one for him- or herself?

It was after one o'clock somehow, and Sarabeth went into the kitchen and made tuna salad, thinking, as she always did, that no-drain vacuum bags of tuna were among the world's greatest inventions. She ate six huge forkfuls standing at the sink, then covered the bowl and stashed it in the refrigerator.

She wandered into her workroom and gazed at the carton that had arrived yesterday. She thought of opening it, but she knew what was inside—two dozen ring sets—and she had no desire to see two dozen ring sets. She crouched at her scrap box and dug through it until a piece of shiny silver paper caught her eye. She began folding it, randomly she would have thought, but then she recalled the cootie catchers she and Liz used to make, origami-like structures of folded paper that you could ask questions, and she realized she was folding with them in mind. Deep inside you wrote answers: "yes" and "no" and "maybe," say, or "dentist" and "hula girl" and "teacher." She remembered one of Liz's, where the question was "Who will you marry?"; Sarabeth chose a flap, and Liz opened it for her, and they both shrieked with laughter because what was written there was "Steve." "At least we'll be sisters," Sarabeth said, and Liz said, "We already are."

She abandoned the paper and returned to her bedroom. She took up a volume of Hemingway stories and began reading "Hills Like White Elephants," but the cloistered conversation made her restless, and she closed the book and instead thought of the pale hills, the heat, the dust, the drone of insects. She had never been to Spain. Her father had offered to take her to Spain *and* France one summer, but she'd declined. It was the summer after her freshman year at Berkeley: he was in Baltimore, and she told him, truthfully, that she'd just rented a room in a house and wanted to get used to living there before school started up again in the fall. She was working at a café, reading a lot. It wasn't bad. But after that, after she passed up his offer, their communication fell away with surprising speed, and when he died a few years later, just two months after being diagnosed with pancreatic cancer, her life in some way got simpler. It had been hard, being cowitnesses to a disaster.

The children had fallen silent, and she went to investigate. The Heidts' yard was empty; she figured they were inside eating. Would there be a separate children's table? She thought of the holiday dinners of her childhood, how much she'd disliked sitting at the children's table, how she'd felt suspended in time, waiting for her parents to claim her again. Once, a man looked over from the adult table and told her not to eat with her fingers. She was eating a roll, but she was mortified anyway.

She would have been wearing a fancy dress; her mother bought her two each year, one for Thanksgiving and one for Christmas. Velvet or silk. She wasn't allowed to put them on until the holiday in question arrived, and then only at the last minute. Beforehand, she would watch her mother's preparations, the brushing of her hair, the fastening of a necklace, and when her mother was all ready—perfect from top to toe, and very beautiful—they would go together into Sarabeth's bathroom, and under her mother's terrifying gaze Sarabeth would carefully scrub her hands in preparation for putting on the special dress.

Liz didn't do that kind of thing. She was such a good mother. One Thanksgiving Joe wore his soccer uniform. Another year Lauren decorated the table with rocks and pinecones from the backyard, and then placed among them her collection of rubber trolls. Sarabeth's mother would have died before allowing a table of hers to look like that. Actually, she had.

It was remarkably warm, and Sarabeth thought that if she had a private porch she'd sit outside and read. If she had a private porch, she might have a *place* to sit outside and read; as it was, she'd barely swept. She sat on her top step and looked at the Heidts' yard: a single abandoned feathered headdress lay on the lawn. She wondered if it was Pilar's.

With a creak, the Heidts' back door opened, and out came some of the children, Isaac and some of the other little ones, holding cupcakes. Isaac glanced at Sarabeth; it was not typical for her to be on her porch. He set his cupcake on the sandbox ledge, stood next to it with his feet side by side, and with a great whoop jumped into the sand. Another boy stood outside the box eating his cupcake, eyeing Isaac's from time to time.

With another creak the door opened again, and now Pilar emerged with another girl. They both carried cupcakes, the girl in a pilgrim hat, Pilar's head bare. "My feathers!" she cried, and she set her cupcake on the patio table and hurried to rescue her headdress. She gave Sarabeth a funny little wave as she settled the feathers on her head. She turned and went back to the table for her cupcake. Sarabeth wondered if she should get up and go inside, but it was so nice and sunny, and there was nothing inside but tuna and Hemingway, and so she stayed. Pilar and the other girl were talking quietly, while the sandbox now contained Isaac and three other kids, each of whom had frosting around the mouth and a big plastic truck in hand. "Beep, beep," they said. "Rrrrrm, rrrrrm."

Pilar approached the sandbox. She wore a purple jumper over a patterned turtleneck, yellow tights, and very elfin purple-and-green mary-janes. She stopped and surveyed the younger children's work, then continued past the sandbox toward Sarabeth.

"Hi," Sarabeth called, and Pilar waved again.

"Happy Thanksgiving," she shouted. She approached the jasmine that separated the Heidts' property from Sarabeth's, picked her way through it, and in a moment was at the base of Sarabeth's steps.

"Happy Thanksgiving to you," Sarabeth said.

"I'm a squaw," Pilar announced, touching her feathers. "My mom said I could be a squaw with extra feathers if I wanted."

Sarabeth pondered this for a moment, then remembered that only the chief wore lots of feathers—and did the women wear any? "Why not?" she said.

"Thanksgiving is for being creative."

"I should say so."

Pilar was eating her cupcake between statements—or eating the frosting, anyway, a business requiring tongue and lips but no teeth.

"How's your cupcake?" Sarabeth said.

"Good. The frosting is chocolate and the cupcake part is pumpkin, which isn't very good but is better than pumpkin pie."

"You don't like pumpkin pie?"

"Blech," Pilar said with a shudder. "My brother and I hate it. My sister likes it so-so. My brother threw up last time we had it, but he might have been getting sick anyway, we're not sure."

"It's hard to know what's caused by what."

Pilar held the cupcake out, empty of frosting, its surface shiny wet. "Want the rest?"

"No, thanks," Sarabeth said, "but it's nice of you to offer."

"On Thanksgiving you're supposed to be nice to people," Pilar said. "It's a day of caring and sharing. My sister and I aren't allowed to fight unless we have to."

"I see," said Sarabeth.

"Did you make any friends yet?"

"Excuse me?"

"My mom says that's why you look at us. Because you're lonely."

Heat flooded Sarabeth's face, and her stomach churned. She turned away from Pilar and breathed hard. Pilar stood there, just over her shoulder, but Sarabeth couldn't move. She was sick, sick. Yet she feared she was upsetting Pilar, and with great effort she turned back. Pilar watched her solemnly, the only evidence of disturbance the fact that she was plucking crumbs from the cupcake and dropping them to the ground. Sarabeth tried to think of something to say.

"It's Thanksgiving for the birds, too," Pilar said.

"It is. You're sharing with them."

"Bye," Pilar said, and she made the jasmine in two long steps, leaped over it, and strode through the yard and into the house without a moment's pause.

Sarabeth went inside and locked the door. Her living room was so dark she could hardly see. She closed her eyes and by feel—touching first the plant table by the door and then an armchair—she found the couch and slowly eased herself onto it. She lay down, resting her head on a throw pillow she'd made by embroidering flowers onto a pink silk handkerchief and wrapping it around a pillow form. Against her face the flowers felt scratchy, and she pulled the pillow out from under her head and tossed it to the floor. She hesitated a moment and then with her feet grabbed the white lace pillow at the other end of the couch, took hold of it, and tossed it to the floor, too. She sat up quickly, and when the room stopped spinning she crossed to the mantel and moved each of the seven silver candlesticks to the floor. From her bedroom she got the wire-and-mesh Eiffel Tower that held her earring collection, then went back for the majolica plate on her bedside table, where she kept ChapStick, lotion, and a notepad and pen. On the living room floor there was now quite a collection of stuff, and she added the Eiffel Tower and the plate, which she'd bought at some antique store in the city because she'd felt she *had* to have it—whereas she felt like kicking it now. She brought in a few more things from her bedroom, then turned her attention to the bathroom. From the wall she took a paper silhouette of a woman carrying an umbrella. With her free hand she put a wire basket of soap balls into Billy's abalone shell, and she carried all of this into the living room and set it on the floor. She went back to the bathroom for the little pink dish Liz had brought her from France, one of her most beloved possessions: an opalescent pink oval in the middle of which had been painted the words *Je rêve.* I dream. Liz had bought it for her at a flea market in Montpellier. She set it on the floor and went into the kitchen, where she gathered a blue glass bowl, her two favorite mugs—one still holding an inch of this morning's coffee—and a creamer in the shape of a cow.

On the couch again but sitting up now, she surveyed the things on the floor. This was her life, a life of talismanic objects. Or it had been. The truth was that the pillow with the amateurish embroidery was nothing. The wire-and-mesh Eiffel Tower was nothing. Billy's abalone shell, Liz's pink dish—they were neither Billy's nor Liz's, they were her own, and they were nothing. What did these objects know? They had been endowed with meaning, even power, but to do what? They were entirely empty now—so much matter that didn't matter. Not even worth the effort to kick or destroy. The company she keeps—was that a book title? The company Sarabeth kept was a collection of inanimate objects she kept for company, and she saw now with a mixture of disgust and grief that they'd been empty all along. *No,* she should have told Pilar, *I haven't made any friends.* She had feared, always, that at some moment she would understand that she was not a sprightly gal in a little house, a free spirit, creative and bohemian, but rather an eccentric, a crank. Here it was. The moment was upon her, it was now. She had a floor full of junk, and she watched people.

16

*A*t meals all week, Lucas sat with Lauren. He talked to her and
talked to her, telling her his story: how since he was twelve he'd
been drinking and doing drugs—"for fun and profit." Sometimes, all of a
sudden, he'd get silent or crabby, but mostly he talked nonstop. He told
her about the night not long ago when, after a period of wakefulness that
had lasted two days, he found himself walking the sound wall on 101 at
2:00 a.m., cars rushing below him, wind in his face. It was incredible up
there, the perfect balance his feet found on the narrow wall, the impene-
trability of his glee. Cops came to both sides of the wall and shone
Maglites at him, though, and now here he was, locked up. His parents
didn't give a fuck, he told Lauren, though she was sure they did.

It was Saturday now, and for some reason he hadn't been at breakfast
or check-in. Because of the weekend there was no morning school, so
people were just hanging out, in the lounge or in their rooms. Lauren was
in her room. She was on fifteen-minute checks now, and she'd just been
checked, so she headed for the bathroom. People used bedsheets to hang
themselves—Lucas said it was the only way. Lauren thought you ought to
be able to drown yourself in a toilet, but you'd need a lot of willpower.
She had no desire to kill herself, but she couldn't get anyone to see that,
so she was stuck. Last night she'd met with Dr. Lewis and her par-

ents, and it had been awful, her mom looking petrified, Dr. Lewis saying, "It's hard to acknowledge problems" and "Maybe you can each start by saying how you feel right now." Her dad sitting there like he'd rather be anywhere else.

The drug was making Lauren really thirsty, and she turned on the water and used her hands for a cup. Outside the bathroom she paused, then headed to the lounge to see if Lucas was around yet. Sometimes he switched subjects—from himself to the other kids—and that was interesting, too. At bedtime one night Abby had told Lauren that she shouldn't hang out with Lucas, but then she'd refused to say why. Abby pretty much didn't talk to Lauren.

In the last bedroom before the lounge, she saw through the open door that Callie was in there making out with Turner. Callie looked up just as Lauren passed, and she ran her tongue over her upper lip and gave Lauren a sick smile. Total time-out if they were found, but they probably wouldn't be: everything here was at the wrong speed. According to Lucas, Callie had been sexually abused for years. Whatever, she was gross.

In the lounge, Abby and the other anorexics were folded onto the couches in the corner. It freaked Lauren out to look at them, but at the same time she was always staring. They were tall and short, blond and brunette, but for some reason none of that really registered. What registered was their likeness to one another. Their bony bodies.

Casey and another girl who cut herself were playing cards with Ivan, one of the non-nurse staff people. He was tall and green eyed, and Lauren thought Casey was in love with him.

Lucas was sitting alone, reading something. Lauren crossed the room and sat opposite him. He was wearing a T-shirt with a bloody face pictured on it, along with the name of a band. He looked up, then looked back at his book.

"Where were you at breakfast?" she said.

He didn't respond.

She waited a bit, but he read on, not looking at her. She said, "What are you reading?"

Again, he remained silent, but he raised the book so she could see the cover: *Ramona the Pest* by Beverly Cleary. She laughed, but rather than laugh with her, he looked up and gave her a quick, mean look, then returned to the book.

"What?" she said. "I'm sorry."

He stayed slouched, face lowered. Lauren had read *Ramona the Pest* in first grade—he couldn't be reading it for real, could he? She wouldn't have laughed except she thought that was what he was expecting.

"I always loved that book," she said, but he still didn't move.

Lauren felt sick, and she glanced around to see if anyone was looking. Casey was. Casey was entirely evil—she hadn't let up on Lauren since the first morning. Now she gestured for Lauren to come to the card table.

Lauren shook her head.

Casey gestured again: a quick, insistent *com'ere* with her arm. Her short hair was going in all directions this morning, and Lauren wondered if maybe she did that on purpose, to look more messed up. Casey was very into how messed up she was. And yet, she was probably leaving soon.

"Lauren," Casey called.

Now Ivan looked, too. Lauren glanced at Lucas, then got up and crossed the room to their table. Ivan was holding the fourth chair out for her.

"How's it going, Lauren?" he said.

"OK."

She waited for Casey to tell her that she *wasn't* OK, but instead Casey said, "Lucas is down today."

"Down?"

"It's his disease. He's way down."

"But his medications," Lauren began. The whole thing with Lucas was, it was treatable. With drugs. "I thought—" She turned and looked at him, and all at once she understood that he wasn't actually reading the book. She even understood that holding it like that, to look as if he were reading it, was hard work. And, as if to confirm this, he closed the book and slumped deeper in his chair.

"Does Dr. Porter know?" she said.

Ivan scratched the side of his neck. "We'll let her know when she checks in."

Lauren stared into the center of the table. They were playing some kind of card game where you discarded into a pile, and the most recently discarded card was the jack of diamonds. She stared at the card, and all of a sudden she was thinking about Jeff Shannon. And that made her think about being in bed at home on a sunny weekend morning, hearing noises downstairs, seeing that line of light around the edges of her curtains. She saw herself in her closet, crying. What on earth was wrong with her?

Liz was at Safeway. She never shopped on the weekend, but she was out of milk, out of Wheaties, so here she was. Brody had taken Joe to a soccer tournament in Foster City—she was going to meet them over there this afternoon. She felt bad about not seeing the whole thing, but sometimes it was just too much. Did it disappoint Joe, her not always being there? In the last week he had been quiet, hard to read. Mute on the subject of Lauren.

"It's not about your guilt. It can't be." This was what Dr. Lewis had said to her and Brody last night, out in the corridor after the session with Lauren was over. Liz had understood him to mean that in order to help Lauren they must focus on Lauren, and she knew he was right. But at home afterward, moving from room to room, all she could think was that this was the place where she'd catastrophically mismanaged things, and they might have to move to recover. She started to say this to Brody, and he looked at her as if she were crazy.

The Safeway was nearly empty—it was the weekend after Thanksgiving; everyone was at the malls. Liz moved down the aisles, grabbing cereal, bread, rice, mayo, salad dressing, and on down her list. Tuna—she took a couple of the no-drain vacuum bags, remembering a funny Sarabeth soliloquy on the new technology of tuna, the breakthrough potential of the new packaging, how if tuna were traded on the stock market it would be skyrocketing. And why did that make her think of the time Sarabeth confessed that she always confused Nasdaq with NASCAR?

She hadn't heard from Sarabeth since the cell phone calls she didn't answer Tuesday. "You didn't want to invite Sarabeth?" her mother had asked over the roast beef on Thursday. Liz had shrugged, but a bad feeling had lingered, and here it was again. She felt in some sense duty-bound to call Sarabeth, but also enraged that it should have to be she who called. So what if this was hard on Sarabeth—what was Liz supposed to do about it?

Tuna casserole had been a great favorite of Joe's long ago, and she grabbed a third vacuum bag, deciding on the spot that she'd make tuna casserole tonight. She found the soups, added a can of cream of mushroom to her cart, then went back to the pasta aisle and got a cellophane

bag of wide egg noodles. Tuna casserole, spaghetti and meatb
those dishes from the kids' childhoods. Had she lost something,
those recipes aside?

In produce she despaired over the wilted weekend fare. Why pay
money for lettuce that looked like that? She found the least objectionable
red leaf she could, then skipped fruit altogether, thinking there were a few
bananas left at home, some oranges, and she just didn't have the heart to
spend any more time here.

Foster City soccer tournaments were a Thanksgiving weekend staple,
and Brody had spent many a late-November weekend exactly where he
was now, in his collapsible chair under a crisp blue sky.

Joe had played well this morning, but the noon game had been a disaster, 7 to 1, and Joe had been especially clumsy. Grouped under a small
cluster of pine trees before the start of the day's final game, he and his
teammates were being lectured by their coach, and Brody kept his eyes
averted lest he see the coach look too often at Joe.

His shoulder was killing him. He got up from his chair and twisted
side to side from his waist, then walked toward the tennis courts. There
were lots of doubles games going on, plus two serious guys about his age
running each other to pieces. A pair of teenage girls made up the only
other singles game, and from several courts away Brody watched them
until he realized he was studying their bodies, not their strokes. He
turned his back and leaned against the chain link. He remembered the
smell of girl sweat from the times in high school when he and Andrew
Drayson had played mixed doubles, how girls' sweat smelled different:
cleaner, grassier. He and Andrew would smirk at each other across the
net: at their superiority to the girls, at their desire and cockiness, at their
intimate knowledge of the other's fear. Later, they might sit on the bench
near the girls' locker room and watch the girls come out, their legs no
longer exposed by their little white skirts. Brody and Andrew would pretend they were not on that bench for any particular reason, but the girls
would laugh knowingly, say, "Fancy seeing you guys here," and Brody
and Andrew would make stupid jokes and elbow each other, and fail,
each time, to ask the girls out.

Andrew was still in the Cleveland area. Brody had seen him only
once in the past couple of decades, at the twentieth reunion of his high

school class. He and Liz had flown out for the weekend, leaving the kids with Liz's parents, and they'd had a surprisingly good time catching up with people, dancing under a disco ball, drinking Tom Collinses because that had been the favorite illegal drink of Brody's youth. Andrew had gotten very, very fat and only laughed when Brody asked if he still played tennis. It made Brody sad now to think of it—not Andrew fat, not Andrew no longer playing, but that he himself hadn't known until that night what had become of Andrew, hadn't wondered. Flying home, he'd thought that his best friend had vanished into a fat guy in a huge navy-blue blazer, and he'd wondered if Andrew's best friend had vanished, too.

A couple fields down, Joe's team was starting to warm up, and Brody returned to his chair. If only Lauren had played soccer, this probably never would have happened. She had played as a very little girl, but a year or two after Joe started, she stopped. As far as Brody knew, the only exercise she got was in PE. Liz had always been dead set against forcing, or maybe even encouraging, the kids to try things, and as a result Lauren had no passions. *They need to be allowed to make their own choices.* Yeah, but what if they didn't make any? Brody was certain a sport, or even a hobby, would have made a difference.

"Hey, there," said a voice, and then Liz was touching his shoulder and unfolding her chair next to his.

"You came," he said.

"I said I would."

"And you did."

The game was about to start, and Joe stood at left halfback, his face flushed from the jog around the field. For a moment he seemed to be looking at Brody and Liz, but from so far away it was hard to tell. Liz waved, and Brody stifled an impulse to tell her not to distract him.

"Your mother called," she said.

He turned to look at her. She was wearing a zippered fleece jacket that he'd bought for himself and then rarely worn, the color a brighter blue than he liked.

"Hello?" she said.

"I heard you." He glanced at the field. He'd told his mother and sister on Thursday evening, in a call that had lasted only a few minutes. "What'd she say?"

"She wanted to know if there was anything new."

"And?"

"And I told her there wasn't." She crossed her legs and looked away from him, and he knew he was being an ass.

"I'm sorry."

"Forget it."

"Was she still in Cincinnati?"

Liz nodded.

His mother, when she heard the news, had gasped and then fallen completely silent. "Oh, my dear," she'd finally said. After some confusion Marilyn had come on the line and asked for the whole story, and Brody had thought simultaneously that it was just like her to intervene, and that he was incredibly relieved that she had.

The whistle must have blown, though Brody hadn't heard it; Joe had the ball and tried for a pass, but a kid on the other team intercepted.

Brody thought about last night, the meeting with Dr. Lewis. Every word out of his mouth had been followed by an equivocation. The Prozac was important, but long-term psychotherapy might be even more important. Talking was vital, but some teens needed medications before they could make use of it.

And if it was all about drugs and therapy, then why was she still in the hospital, five days later?

"I wonder," he said, but before he could even get the thought out, Liz stiffened beside him.

"We have to," she said.

"What?"

"Keep her there. Let the setting help her."

There'd been a time when her ability to anticipate what he was going to say had delighted him, even as it had occasionally frustrated him that he couldn't do the same with her. Now he found it annoying. Was it so hard to let him finish a sentence? And: *Let the setting help her.* That was Dr. Lewis's phrase.

"Maybe that's not what I was going to say."

"Was it?"

He shrugged.

"Honey," she said. She put her hand on his arm and left it there, and after a while he began not to mind it. He stared at the game. It was late November, sunny and clear and sixty degrees, a day the Midwest couldn't fathom. The bay was blocks away, the ocean just on the other side of the mountains, the country's most beautiful city a half hour north. All of this

Brody knew. *This is why we live here,* people said at all times of the year. *This is why we wouldn't live anywhere else.* Was it more dangerous, though, here in the Bay Area, where it was so beautiful and so temperate? What if he had stayed in the Midwest? Where hardship came every year in the form of frozen pipes and cars that wouldn't start and months of cabin fever. Did a certain kind of ease pave the way for trouble?

17

*I*t was Sunday morning, and Sarabeth's living room was filled with a pinkish glow. Her skin was pink. The *New York Times* was pink. Her life was going to be pink, because she'd hung a red tablecloth over the living room window, and it was going to stay there for all of time.

She was never going to look at the Heidts again.

She lay on her couch. Across the room, a little charcoal drawing of a bird hung on the wall, and she stared at it, wishing there were something between her and that bird. She wanted to call Liz. The bird had an eye. She reached into her purse for her cell phone and then held it and looked again at the bird. It had been drawn with an economy of strokes: head, beak, feathers, twiggy feet. There was pressure in her chest as she scrolled to Liz's home number. It had been five days since the Tuesday morning phone call that had seemed to right things, Liz sounding so sympathetic and forgiving. On each of those days Sarabeth had wanted to call Liz, and had wanted Liz to call her, and had done nothing.

Joe answered. His voice was changing, its pitch today that of the man he would become.

"Joe?" she said, and then "It's Sarabeth, how are you?" and then "I'm so sorry about your sister."

"Thanks," he said.

There was a silence, and she realized she'd spoken too quickly, hadn't given him any time to respond.

"Hang on," he said, and she lay there with her cell phone held to her ear, looking at the picture of the bird, then at the pile of pointless belongings still strewn across the floor below it. The pink dish from Liz was pinker in this light.

"Hi," Liz said.

Tears spilled from Sarabeth's eyes. "Hi."

Liz was silent, and Sarabeth wiped the tears away and sniffed.

"Are you crying?" Liz said.

"No," Sarabeth said, but it was a throaty, nasally "no," and now she did cry.

"What's up?" Liz said a bit stiffly.

"I'm sorry," Sarabeth sobbed.

"It's OK," Liz said. "I told you, really."

"No, I mean for this."

"I don't even know what 'this' is."

Not just stiffly: coldly.

"Nothing," Sarabeth said. "I'm sorry to bother you."

"You're not bothering me."

"How is she?"

"The same."

Sarabeth waited, but that was it—that was all Liz was going to say. She let go of the cell phone and let it balance on the side of her head. She put her hands over her face.

"What are you upset about?" Liz said.

"Nothing," Sarabeth said, her hands still half over her mouth, the phone wiggly on her head. "I'm sorry to bother you," she said again.

"You're not bothering me," Liz said, "but you're baffling me, and I can barely hear you."

"Oh, my God," Sarabeth said, and then the phone slipped off her ear, and though she grabbed at it she failed to catch it, and it fell to the floor. Retrieving it, she saw that the call had been cut off. Redial, she thought, redial, but she'd never mastered the ins and outs of this phone, the shortcuts, the easy-dials. She set it on the coffee table and yearned for blankness.

18

$\mathcal{L}$ucas had not spoken to anyone in two days. It was schooltime on Monday, but he was off somewhere with Dr. Porter, who had arrived in an uncharacteristic hurry just as check-in was ending.

One of Abby's friends had left yesterday, and there was a new girl no one had seen yet—Casey had mentioned her at breakfast. Casey knew everything. She was leaving Wednesday, after almost three weeks. She'd been here the longest of anyone.

Today marked a week for Lauren. She sat at a table doing a math worksheet. The idea of Mr. Pavlovich getting a note that she was out . . . she didn't want to think about it. Nor about Amanda, who had called yesterday and said how much she missed Lauren and cared about her. Nor about her parents, visiting last night, coming again tonight, not *doing* anything for her, nothing at all. Did they *want* her to be in here? They must. Better here than bugging them at home.

Lucas came back in, followed by Dr. Porter. His face was the same as it had been since Saturday, lifeless and black eyed. He sat on a couch and stared off into space. Dr. Porter spoke quietly to Kitsy and then left; she'd be back in the afternoon. What did she do in the mornings, anyway? If she had kids, she'd be more likely to *work* in the mornings and *not* be here in the afternoons. Then again, if she had kids they'd be around thirty.

Lauren couldn't imagine having a shrink for a parent. *What was that like for you?* .

Actually, her mom was full of that shit. She fucking studied it, she had books about parenting. When Lauren was little, she was always talking with other moms about naps and stuff, "boundaries," "limits," who knew what all.

Lauren put her pencil down and went over to one of the windows. Someone had stuck a Hello Kitty sticker on the glass, and she picked at an edge until there was a lip she could pull. She tore away half the sticker, then scratched at the rest until all that remained was the thin white underlayer. She looked at her fingernails, imagined what it would be like to attack her cuticles the way some of the other kids did. There was this one guy, Angus, with fingers that were puffed like doughnuts around the tiny, bitten plates of his nails. No guys cut themselves, though—as far as she knew. From the window she glanced at Lucas. He was looking at her, and she gave him a little wave. His face stayed the same, but after a moment he beckoned for her.

"What?" she said, approaching the couch. He beckoned again, and she stepped closer, then sat on the edge of the chair next to him. It was a square yellow armchair, vinyl—this was the first time she'd sat in it. In fact, it was where *he* usually sat.

He inhaled, as if to speak, but then he just sighed and let his head fall back.

"Are you OK?"

He looked up, looked right at her. His eyes were wet, and she didn't know if that meant tears or something else, something she'd never heard of that had to do with bipolar disorder. He was taking a mood stabilizer, according to Abby. Abby knew all about the different medications. She knew that Lauren was taking Prozac without Lauren's ever having told her. "How'd you know?" Lauren asked, and Abby said, "After a while you get to recognize all the pills."

The wetness pooled and fell onto Lucas's cheeks. Lauren put a hand out and then, after a moment, pulled it back. She looked up and saw three or four people staring at her. One of the nurses gave her a sad smile. All at once she had to get out of there, and she stood up and raced for her room and slammed the door behind her.

In a moment Ivan opened it. "Lauren?"

"Go away."

"Do you want to talk?" He locked the door open, pushing the doorstop into the bracket on the wall. "It's hard to see a friend so down." "He's not my friend," Lauren said. She was near tears again, furious. "He's not my friend!" she yelled.

Ivan gave her a sympathetic look, and she flung herself onto her bed and buried her face in her pillow, waiting for him to go.

But even once he was gone, she was still there. She sat up after a while. Went to lunch. Went to group. In art she doodled with her colored pencils, making rainbows and hearts and four-leaf clovers, as if she were some dopey little kid. Dr. Lewis appeared for her session, and she followed him to their meeting room. He was incredibly geeky. He'd have been laughed out of her school. He wore horrible plaid shirts—orange and green, say, or purple and brown. Purple and brown! Maybe he was color blind. He had really dorky shoes, too, loafers with tassels. He wore a wedding ring, and she figured his wife was a bigger dork than he was, someone who would wear a ski turtleneck as a top, someone who would wear a fake tortoiseshell headband. Probably they were each the only one ever to have liked the other.

"How are you feeling?" he said once they were seated.

"Fine," she replied, as always; she didn't know why he wouldn't get the message.

"How was the weekend?"

"Fine."

"Your day today?"

At this she just shrugged.

He picked up his clipboard and flipped through the pages. She planted her elbow on the table and rested her chin in her hand. He always kept her for exactly fifty minutes. This struck her as unfair, because a lot of people got through therapy in much less time.

"So you got a call from Amanda?"

"Who are you, my mother?" She hadn't quite meant this, and she shook her head. "I mean, what, do you have a record?"

"I remind you of your mother?"

"No! You're nothing like my mother."

"What's she like?"

"She's fine." She stared at him, at his ugly plaid shirt. He wore a tie with little squiggles. He didn't speak, just waited. "She's nosy, if you really want to know."

"Maybe there are things you want to keep hidden."

"There are not!" she exclaimed, but all at once she was thinking of Lucas in the lounge this morning, beckoning, and the tears in his eyes and on his cheeks. Fuck if she wasn't about to cry again. Then she was crying.

"I think there are some things that are really painful for you," Dr. Lewis said. "Lots of teenagers feel they need to keep painful things hidden."

Lauren shook her head, but something had happened, something between her and Dr. Lewis, just now; she had no idea what it was, but she couldn't say no anymore, she just couldn't.

"I cry all the time," she sobbed.

"I think that's what sad people do."

"I'm not sad," she said, but then she looked up and saw him watching her, and she said, "I am, I am, I am." And she lowered her head and put her hands over her eyes and said, "I am."

Not quickly, not smoothly or continuously, Lauren began to make progress. Monday evening she wept again, but differently. She was miserable. She hated school, hated herself. Liz's heart broke as she listened, then broke again as Lauren fell into her arms and wept harder. It was toward exactly this—Lauren admitting her unhappiness—that Dr. Lewis had said they were working; what Liz hadn't anticipated was how painful it would be.

On Tuesday Lauren showed her and Brody a drawing, and again Dr. Lewis was present. They were in a small room, sitting on chairs around a Formica table. Liz had a squeezed feeling in her chest that she was trying to ignore. She wanted to be calm. Whatever Lauren needed, that was what she wanted to be.

Lauren set the drawing on the table and turned it so they could see. She'd drawn four figures with the general shapes of humans, but they'd been heavily charcoaled, the shading filling in and jagging over the outlines.

"They don't have faces," Brody said, and Liz shot him a hard stare. What was he thinking, saying something like that? She looked at Dr. Lewis, tried to read his reaction, but his face was neutral, as always. It was funny: he wasn't good-looking in any of the usual ways—he was too thin, and he had eyebrows so sparse his eyes had a spooky, naked look—but he was attractive anyway. Maybe because he seemed so wise.

"I wonder," he said thoughtfully, "if this picture was a way for Lauren to explore some feelings without words."

Exactly, Liz thought. She wished he would talk more; she hoarded what he said, went over and over it in her mind. She longed to corner him with questions, and it was only the sheer unmanageable number of them that kept her from doing so. Lauren making progress meant Lauren coming home soon, which was both exactly what Liz wanted and also terrifying. *What should I do if she says this? What should I say if she does that?* The idea that she was a skilled parent had dissolved, exactly when it was what she most needed to be. Skilled? She was hapless, uninformed, inadequate. She had friends who'd gone through this kind of thing postpartum, the feeling that to be a mother was going to take resources they just didn't have, but she had not felt that. It had been just a matter of taking care. The world of care, it turned out, was vaster than she had ever known. She didn't think she could do it.

When she and Brody got home he went straight to the family room couch and aimed the remote at the TV. She stood watching him for a moment, then began stacking the bowls and platters that people had left, full of food, on the porch. Her friend Julie had offered to get them back to their owners, and she carried them to the front hall and set them by the door, so she'd remember to put them outside in the morning.

She headed up the stairs to find Joe.

"Enter," he said in response to her knock, and she was briefly cheered, or charmed; he could do this, surprise her with evidence of some kind of elastic inner life.

He was on his bed with a book, lying on his stomach with his saggy jeans showing a couple inches of boxer waistband. His shoes were on, but she didn't really care—she didn't want his life to be a cacophony of correction.

She sat at the foot of the bed. "What are you reading?"

He looked over his shoulder and turned the book so she could see: *Catcher in the Rye,* of all things. He was just a little way in. She wondered if he'd known before he started what it was about.

"Is that for English?"

"Just reading it."

Sarabeth had read it at his age, over and over again; for a while there, nearly everyone she knew was a big phony.

Liz had been harsh with Sarabeth on the phone Sunday—she knew she had. She'd barely slept Saturday night, tossing and getting up for water and tossing some more. When Joe told her Sarabeth was on the line, she was lying down, not sleeping but in a lulled state. She'd almost asked him to take a message. Clearly she should have.

"Do you know any big phonies?" she asked him now.

He thought for a moment. "Mrs. Graham."

"How so?"

" 'OK, persons, let's get into our small groups for some Civil War brainstorming.' "

"How is that phony?"

He scooted toward the head of the bed, turning and leaning against the headboard. He had Brody's sapphire eyes and smooth, beautiful skin. This boy of hers, this boy. Were many women as moved by their sons as she was by Joe? It wasn't the kind of thing she discussed with other mothers.

"Well," he said, "first of all, 'persons.' I mean, we're people. But she's also so hyper, like if she doesn't call it brainstorming we won't go, we won't be motivated. It's like: *We're in school, just tell us what to do.*"

"Annoying."

"Yeah."

She hesitated. "What's Holden's sister's name again?"

"Phoebe," he said, but a guarded look came down over his face, saying *Don't*.

She had to. "Yours will probably come home in a day or two."

"She will?"

Liz nodded.

His face stayed in neutral, but he'd set the book down and now he picked it up again and held it in his lap, forefinger between the pages marking his place.

She said, "How are you doing, sweetie?"

"OK."

"I know we've already talked about this, but—it's no one's fault."

"I know."

On top of his bookcase were some family photos she'd put in special frames for him when he was younger: one with little wooden train cars along the top, another with a baseball and a soccer ball glued onto opposite corners. In the train frame the four of them were on the beach in Carmel. In the sports frame it was Christmas Day, and Lauren and Joe were posed on brand-new bikes, and Joe was looking at Lauren while Lauren beamed.

What should she say to him now? What would Dr. Lewis say?

She sat where she was, and after a while his body seemed to relax, and he began to read again—or pretended to, anyway. How would it be when Lauren got home? What were they trying to get to? She heard him turn a page. If she could just sit near him while he read, if she could just stay for a few more minutes.

The image of Lauren's drawing lingered in Brody's mind. People with no faces—no detail at all, just messy shading. Her drawings were usually so careful and precise. She drew a lot of plants, studied the leaves in the backyard and captured the stems, the veins. Years ago it was pictures of animals.

He remembered a time when she was four or five and so shy that the arrival of company would literally bring her to her knees. She'd put her hands on the floor and crawl over to him, maybe meow a little as she rubbed against his lower leg. "Got a new kitty?" the company would say.

He glanced at the French doors, the black night behind them. The days were growing shorter and shorter. Tonight he would go again, to the tennis courts at the high school; he'd gone every night since the first time, last Wednesday. Late, long after Liz and Joe were asleep. The first few nights he went to bed first, then got up once Liz was sleeping soundly. After that, he just stayed up. "I'm not really tired," he told her. He sat in front of the TV, or with a book, but in fact he was waiting for her to be gone. Begone, he thought one night as she lingered in the family room doorway, talking on and on about something that didn't matter. Be gone.

His shoulder was worse than it had ever been. One night, warming up, he'd thought he shouldn't continue—his shoulder hurt that much. Another night a cop pulled up, got out of his car, and strolled to the fence. Something rose up in Brody—a wish to meet the cop in some dark encounter—but the cop just watched Brody for a moment and then said, "Insomnia?"

He heard Liz on the stairs, and in a moment she came in. She said, "Wow."

" 'Wow'?"

"I'm so tired." She stood in the middle of the room, and he saw the last ten days on her lined face, in her disheveled hair. He felt exhausted himself, and determined not to say so.

He muted the TV and looked at her. "She needs to come home."

"She's going to."

"Do we disagree?" he snapped. He knew he sounded pissed off, but he didn't care: he was sick of her attitude, so patronizing. "I don't think we disagree, and yet—"

"And yet what?"

"You're doing it again right now!"

She stared straight at him. She wore a V-neck top, and the skin it exposed looked dry and creased. Her throat, her neck—she loved to be kissed there. She would giggle, twist, writhe. Her body had not changed much; her legs were as fine as when she was thirty. He hated her, though—hated her guts.

After a little while she came over to the couch and held out her hand. He took it. She pulled, and he stood and followed her to their bedroom, watching himself as if from a distance, curious more than anything else about what would happen next. What happened was that she undressed him and undressed herself, and they both got into bed. What happened after that was that he lay there while she stroked his abdomen, his thigh, his penis. And then, in an instant, he was rock hard and on top of her, and he pushed into her with a hope that it would hurt, and he thrust hard when he heard her gasp. He put a hand over her mouth and held it there while he pumped—four times, maybe five—and then exploded into her, his mind going black for the briefest wonderful moment until he came back to himself, and his body lost the feeling of satiety second by quick second, and his fury pulsed back through him.

"Jesus," she said, but he didn't wait for more—he got up and pulled on his clothes and left the room.

19

$\mathcal{S}$ arabeth began eating scrambled eggs: once a day, twice, even three times on one occasion, though she only picked at the third plate, vaguely disgusted. It was atavistic; it went back to the time right after her mother's death. She had entered the Cowper Street kitchen one evening to find that the gifts of food that had seemed so endless had in fact ended. The refrigerator contained condiments and sour milk. The bread box held one last greenish banana muffin. Even the staples were nearly gone: all that remained in the soup cabinet was a single tin of lobster bisque that had been there for something like a decade.

Up until then she and her father had been scavenging among the donated food and the dwindling staples, sometimes together but more often alone; she had even found him early one morning eating cold beef stew straight from a Tupperware. She saw on this evening that it had to stop. They had to deal. Real cooking was for the moment beyond either of them, and so she bought and scrambled eggs: with milk or without, plain or with chopped tomatoes, with grated cheddar or a pad of cream cheese. She learned that her father liked his eggs very dry, and she discovered that if she got hers out of the pan early and put them on a prewarmed plate that she set over simmering water, they could both eat them as they liked.

That endless but fast-disappearing year when she was in eleventh grade, and her mother was dead, and he had not yet decided to move away: what a strange, impossible year it had been. Mostly they avoided each other, she upstairs and he down, she at school and he at work, but from time to time they went to a movie together, often an old Hitchcock movie being screened by one of the film societies at Stanford, and in the dark, staring up at the beautiful and troubled face of Joan Fontaine or Ingrid Bergman, they were joined in something vast and unspoken.

The transfer to Baltimore happened quickly, went from unlikely possibility to done deal in mere weeks. The therapist Sarabeth saw when she was in her twenties had remarked that it had been a kind of preemptive strike on her father's part, to leave Sarabeth before she could leave him, and though Sarabeth argued that he'd wanted her to go with him, she supposed that in some way the therapist was right. It hadn't felt like a strike, though. It had felt like mercy.

They packed the house in August, during a heat wave. Her mother's clothing was already gone, and they emptied the kitchen cabinets into boxes, sorted through books, labeled furniture BALTIMORE or STORAGE or GOODWILL. It was into a carton marked STORAGE that the silver candlesticks had gone, along with a fancy Limoges vase that Sarabeth's mother had bought for herself at Gump's, in the city. The vase seemed to stir something in her father. He picked it up and rotated it, looking at it this way and that. He said, "This made her happy for almost a week," and Sarabeth stood there hoping he wouldn't say more, nearly holding her breath until he put the vase down again and began wrapping it in newspaper. That evening, she slid her bare feet into flip-flops and carried her belongings across the street to the Castleberrys' house.

Thursday morning she watched for Jim's car, thinking she had neither the energy to tour with him nor the courage to cancel. When he arrived, she kept her eyes focused straight ahead, away from the Heidts' house, as she headed down the driveway to the car. Needlessly, since the Volvo wasn't even there.

"How are you?" he said as she got in.

"Fine."

When he'd called last night, she'd been in bed already, at seven-fifteen. *Were you asleep?* he'd said. Now he watched as she arranged herself in the seat, put her purse on the floor, buckled up.

"No offense," he said, "but I don't believe you."

She wondered if she could tell him: about Lauren, about Liz; about how horrible she felt, how desperate to call Liz again, and how afraid. She looked at him, Jim in one of his trademark colorful sweaters, all swoops and jags of green and tan and brown, and while she had always been able to tell him anything, she was too ashamed.

She said, "It's just Billy misery."

"Honey, since when? I'm so sorry, what happened?"

"Nothing. I was in Rockridge at this one stop sign, and I just—"

"You had a relapse?"

"Yeah."

"Oh, honey." He reached for her hand and held it. "Why didn't you call me?"

"Because it's so boring. It's pathetic."

"It's not, it's the human condition."

She was able to smile at this, and he gave her hand a little shake and let go to put the car in gear. He said, "Let's go on tour, shall we? We'll have ourselves a morning, all right?"

The sky was pale with cold, and pedestrians hurried along the leaf-strewn sidewalks in layers of sweaters and knit hats, the Berkeley version of winter wear. Jim told her about a harpsichord concert he and Donald had attended, about a friend of theirs who was giving up on the Bay Area and moving to Oregon. At a huge house in the hills, the group of realtors that often included Peter Something didn't include Peter Something, and Jim said, "He broke his leg."

Sarabeth tried to seem interested, but she couldn't even remember Peter Something's face. She had first noticed him during Billy: decided he was cute and moved on. Post-Billy, cute became more interesting. She found out that he was single. But she'd never even spoken to him.

"Rock climbing," Jim added. "Do you get that?"

"I guess. The challenge?"

"Yeah, but the discomfort. The terror."

"Some people are into that."

They toured the house, got back in Jim's car, drove to the next property. Jim's niece in Southern California was about to have a baby, and he told Sarabeth about his sister's near-daily phone calls to update him on the condition of her daughter's cervix. "She will never live this down," he said. "That's a promise."

After the last property, he excused himself to make a phone call, and

Sarabeth leaned against the car and waited for him. She felt the chill of the air, looked at the thinning winter trees, and there was something so familiar about how she felt: it was as if she were hearing music she'd known long ago and forgotten. A song, maybe, but what were the words?

Jim came back. He said, "Do you have time to look at a new listing with me?"

It was an apartment in Adams Point, a third-floor condo with all the character of a Days Inn motel room. The owner had bought it after getting divorced, only to decide that she couldn't live without a yard. Sarabeth didn't understand how that could happen. How could you not know that about yourself?

Her name was Helen. She wore the kind of baggy black pants and tunic that Sarabeth thought of as no-clothes—the kinds of things you wore when you had given up. In a sad attempt at style, she'd tied a colorful batik scarf around her neck, but this highlighted rather than overturned the general impression of misery. Was Sarabeth, by chance, projecting? She was, of course.

"This is going to sell so fast," Jim said as the three of them stood together in the entryway. "The only tricky thing is that there's another unit coming on, but I don't think it's nearly this clean. Come on," he said to Sarabeth, "wait'll you see."

Helen had owned the place for two years, but it looked like two months, two weeks. The furniture was all new and so bland as to defy the idea that an actual person had chosen it. The walls were worse: hung with framed reproductions of Impressionist paintings that were so familiar you didn't even see them.

Sarabeth smiled at Helen. "It's lovely."

"Thank you."

The kitchen was a galley with nothing on the counters but a folded red dishtowel. The bathroom could have been taken from a plumbing showroom, right down to the unused soap. It wasn't until they got to the bedroom that Sarabeth saw anything interesting: a rather lovely antique rolltop desk. It made the room way too crowded, but it would work well in the living room—an improvement for both spaces.

"So where are you going?" Sarabeth asked at the door, and Helen retied her scarf before responding.

"I'm not sure—a little cottage, maybe."

Sarabeth got a look from Jim. They said goodbye to Helen and descended the stairs in silence. In the car she turned to him. "What was that?"

"I'm exercising good boundaries. She wants to sell her condo, I'll sell her condo."

"And then she'll be on the front page of the *Chronicle,* fished out of the bay under the bridge."

"Sarabeth!"

She fastened her seat belt. Her own age, that's what she was thinking. Helen was about her own age.

"Did you take me there to show me how much worse my life could be?"

"No!" he exclaimed. Then he looked over at her and sighed. "Well, maybe a little."

She stifled a giggle. "Oh, God."

"What?"

"It could be."

He started the car and headed back to north Berkeley, neither of them saying much as they drove. At one point his phone rang, and he silenced it without so much as a glance to see who was calling. When they arrived in front of the Heidts' driveway, he put the car in park and pulled her close.

The Volvo was back. She said goodbye to Jim and stood eyeing the distance to her front door; then she took a deep breath and walked as naturally as she could past their house, past their back door, past their yard, and up onto her porch.

Inside, she went straight to her bedroom and lay down. Tonight was a Center night, and she opened *Anna.* Went back to what she'd read two weeks ago. Read ahead. She was ready. She saw herself as globally ready—*Anna* fully in mind, lampshade paper on order, a new listing to stage (barely). Globally ready and locally absolutely idle.

What if she called that Helen and said: *Who are you, what was your life, what happened?* She tossed *Anna* aside. Again, the idea of distant music, familiar and sad. A song without words.

20

She couldn't get used to it. Her room, the family room, the kitchen; her mom, dad, brother—how could you live somewhere your entire life, go away for two weeks, and return a stranger? She wasn't the stranger: they were; it was. It was her first day home, late afternoon, and she sat at the kitchen table with *Glamour* while her mom made dinner. "The Moves That Make Him Crazy"—she didn't want to read that. She didn't want to read "Movie Star Arms in 8 Weeks." Why eight, when you got right down to it? Why not nine? Or ten? *Forget it, if I can't have them in eight I won't do it.*

Her mom kept looking at her—over the salad spinner, a steaming pot, the wooden board where she cut bread. Lauren felt twitchy. She didn't want to be alone in her room, but she didn't want to be looked at, either. In group earlier this week a new girl had hidden her face in her hands and said, "Stop looking at me, stop looking at me." Later, when Lauren had her session with Dr. Lewis, she told him about this, and he said, "You felt a connection with her. It's hard to be looked at. But I think it's also hard not to be looked at." And at that Lauren had begun to cry.

"How's it going?" her mom said.

Lauren looked up. Her mom looked like shit. And why did she have to ask questions all the time?

"Fine," Lauren said, and her mom got this stricken look on her face, which she then tried to hide with a fake smile. It was all so bogus.

Lauren's scars were a vivid, wet-looking red, four on her left wrist and two on her right. She could no longer remember doing it. All she remembered was being in her room beforehand while everyone was downstairs finishing breakfast and getting ready to leave. She hadn't slept at all. All night, her two options had run through her mind, but when she thought of going to school she still thought of the other, whereas when she thought of the other, as horrible as it was, that was all she thought of. At around two she got out of bed to figure out what to wear in the morning, but searching for the jeans she looked best in and a sweater no one would notice, she felt the pull of the other as the only logical choice, the one that would solve all her problems, not just the current one about how she could face Jeff after the catastrophe of blurting out *I'm Lauren.*

"There's a difference between wanting to die," Dr. Lewis had said, "and wanting to stop suffering."

Lauren didn't really have a right to suffer, was the thing. When she thought of Lucas, when she thought of Callie, even Abby—Lauren knew she had it lucky.

"Would you set the table for me?" her mom said. She was at the stove again, stirring whatever was in the steaming pot.

"OK." Lauren closed the magazine and set it on the counter, then went to the place mat drawer. She had never really thought about it before, but her mom was sort of freakily well organized. And her dad— had he always been so pissy? Coming in from the hospital earlier today, he'd tripped over the little rug in the hallway, and you'd have thought her mom had put it there on purpose, the way he rolled his eyes at her and kicked it back into place. In the middle of the afternoon he'd left for a couple hours of work, and Lauren was pretty sure he was glad to go.

She distributed the place mats, got napkins and silverware.

Her mom said, "So how are you feeling about the partial stay?"

Starting Monday, Lauren was going back for partial hospitalization— days at the hospital, nights at home. Which part of how much that sucked did her mom not get?

"Whatever," she said.

Her mom was still at the steaming pot. She looked at Lauren for a long moment, then she picked up the pot and carried it to the sink, where she released a cascade of steaming water and peas.

"What are you doing?" Lauren cried.

Her mom gave her a weird look. "Draining the peas," she said, and only then did Lauren realize there must have been a colander in place to catch them. She was a basket case. Partial hospitalization? She never should have left.

The evening was slow for Brody, creeping. At dinner Liz worked way too hard to keep a conversation going, and as a result every word she uttered struck him as false. Christmas was coming! Robert and Marguerite were going to be in a big concert! Joe's soccer team had won an invitation to a tournament over winter break! And of course they were going to Tahoe!

After dinner, Joe asked for a ride to Trent's, and Brody took him; he and Liz had agreed in advance that forced family time would be a mistake. Liz had rented some movies, and when Brody got back, Lauren chose one for the three of them to watch.

Much later, after Joe was home again and everyone else was asleep, Brody left his laptop, where he'd been trying to catch up on work, and made his way to the garage. He'd taken to leaving his tennis shorts and shoes in there, a change he felt sure Liz had noticed, though she hadn't remarked on it. They were on a shelf above the dryer, and he reached for them, shucked off his khakis, and pulled them on. He slid his feet into his tennis shoes without bothering to change his socks. Dark socks for tennis—what an iconoclast he was.

"Where are you going?"

He turned, and there was Lauren, standing in the doorway to the kitchen.

"Honey," he said. "Gosh, I didn't hear you."

She was flushed and tousle haired, her nightgown sweeping the floor.

He said, "Can't you sleep?"

"I was thirsty."

"Want some water?"

"What are you doing?"

There was nothing for it: he had his shorts on, his shoes. "I'm just going to hit some tennis balls."

"In the middle of the night?"

He turned away. The garage was a mess, or seemed so because of the bench Liz had abandoned, which sat on newspaper in the middle of the floor, partially painted, perhaps never to be completed. One evening he'd brought it up, meaning to offer help of some kind—a hand in moving it out of the way if nothing else—but she'd seemed furious at the mention of it, and he hadn't gone on.

"Yeah," he said to Lauren. "In the middle of the night."

"Where can you hit tennis balls in the middle of the night?"

The realization of what he was going to have to say hit him hard. He did not want to do this, did not want to utter the word "school."

Instead he said, "What would you like to drink?"

She lifted her shoulders. Her nightgown, he realized, was a castoff of Liz's—it was possible he himself had given it to Liz one Christmas. "Lanz" came the brand name out of nowhere. He remembered now that Liz had worn these nightgowns—Lanz nightgowns—for years, so unsexy they were almost sexy. A longing for her swept over him, but in her presence these days he felt something like its opposite. Maybe not revulsion, but something close.

"Juice?" he said to Lauren.

"I'll get it."

She moved away from the doorway, and he hesitated a moment, the darkness outside the garage calling to him with its promises. He left his racquet on the dryer and went up the steps to the kitchen.

She stood in front of the cabinet where the glasses were kept. Her hair hung past her shoulders, blondish brown, tangled. She wasn't moving. Had she truly wanted to kill herself? *Kill* herself?

"Laurie?" he said.

She bowed her head, and in a moment her shoulders were shaking. He crossed the room and turned her, pulling her close. "It's OK," he said. "It's OK."

Pressed against his chest, she shook her head. "I can't go back."

He thought of the other kids: anorexic girls, a boy with a vacant face, another ranting about bin Laden. "It won't be much longer," he said. "I promise. Just a week or two."

"To school," she cried.

He stepped back, hands on her shoulders, and looked into her face. She was terrified.

"Why?"

"Because it's horrible," she wailed, and she covered her face and wept. "There was this girl—she cut herself all the time. She used scissors if she couldn't find a knife."

"What?" He was shocked. "Didn't anyone do anything? Go to a teacher or something?"

"Not at school, at the hospital! I mean, she didn't do it at the hospital—that's why she was there."

She was tired, exhausted—he'd only just realized it. He needed to calm her down, get her back to bed.

"Laurie," he said.

"You were going to my school, weren't you?" She wiped her face with her sleeve. "To hit the balls."

He hesitated. "Yeah."

"It's OK." She moved to a box of Kleenex and plucked one out. "I don't care." She blotted her eyes and blew her nose. "But I want to go to the hospital all the way until Christmas, OK? Please? Otherwise I might have two or three days of school right in the last week. I don't want to go back for a few days and then have a huge break."

"I can see that," he said. He knew his insurance wouldn't cover it, but maybe he could work it out. "I'll look into it, OK? I'll try to make it work."

She stood still for a moment and then crossed the kitchen and poured herself some orange juice. She drank it in an unbroken series of gulps and set the glass near the sink. "I'm going up," she said.

He heard her on the stairs, heard a creak from her bedroom floor. Going in there that first day, when he came home from the hospital; he'd left to fetch Joe but had stopped at the house. Her room had been unusually tidy, just her backpack in the middle of the floor and a pair of jeans slung over a chair, as if she'd intended to go to school. He had stood there for a long time, not entirely unaware but not really aware, either, that he was postponing, little by little, the moment when he would first see the bloody bathroom.

21

$\mathcal{S}$arabeth wanted, she needed, to find out what was happening with Liz and her family, and several times a day she reached for the phone, only to draw her hand back, terrified that she'd burst into tears at the sound of Liz's voice. She hated herself for her cowardice, but what if Liz sounded cold again? How would she bear it? And wasn't it the case that if Liz wanted to talk, she'd call Sarabeth?

One thought chasing another, catching it, swallowing it.

She lay on her couch when she was not in bed. For a while, she had books and magazines with her, but she didn't read much, and a low point came when she realized it was not the book or magazine but herself—she couldn't concentrate. This had never happened before, not for days, and she wept about it, then stopped, then wept again. You couldn't die of this, but if it got worse you could decide you couldn't bear it, and then what?

This. At times it was loud, at others quiet. When it was loud, it used her own voice to snarl out her failings one by one. There was her failing as a friend. There was her failing as an income earner. Her failing as a house-keeper, a homeowner. These days she failed at personal hygiene, at the small job of feeding and watering herself so that as she lay in bed she became light-headed at times and thirsty beyond tolerance. She was a failure at coping with failure, because what she felt was that most disgusting of things, self-pity. She was a failed lover, many times over. She had failed, in fact, at being an adult.

The quiet was different. It was more like being ill.

Saturday, almost a full week since the terrible, brief conversation with Liz, Sarabeth mustered all the courage she had and called Liz's parents.

Robert answered. "Sarabeth!" he said. "Now there's a voice I like to hear. No, no, you're not disturbing me at all."

And then, "Gosh, you haven't heard from her? She's pretty overwhelmed, but it's really fine to call her."

And then, "They brought her home yesterday, actually. I'm surprised you didn't— Listen, call Liz, really. My gosh. Hey, I'd put Marguerite on, but she's out Christmas shopping."

She thanked him and hung up. Lauren was home. That was what mattered: she was home.

Nina had reported that the Murphys were back from China, and a couple days later, on a cold afternoon, Sarabeth drove to Mark's shop with a new lampshade. Nina had said they were exhausted, but even so Sarabeth was surprised by the deep hollows in Mark's cheeks, the slight hoarseness she heard in his voice.

"Look," he said, and he led her to a picture of the baby, who had silky black hair and a round face and dark, lively eyes.

"She's so cute," Sarabeth said. "What's her name?"

"Maud. Maud Li-Wei Murphy."

She looked up at him, tried to read his expression. His eyelids had a dark cast. "How are you?" she said. "How is it?"

"Intense."

"Intense as in . . ."

"Intense as in intense."

She hesitated and then knelt in front of the box she'd brought; she didn't want to pry. She pulled out her new piece. It was steep sided and gray-green, with long narrow slices cut out on the diagonal. "Silvered with Rain" was how she'd been thinking of it. She tried to remember if it had been before or after the weekend of Miranda's play, of Brody's phone call, that she'd made it. She recalled being in her workroom; she recalled the sound of rain.

"Wow," Mark said, sucking air into his mouth. "That is beautiful."

The slices were as narrow as she'd been able to make them: slivers, hairs. At the time, she'd especially liked the way it looked when it was illuminated, the paper a cool, silvery green, warmer where the slices of lining lightened the light.

Before. She'd started it the night of her dinner with Liz. Up late in her workroom, thinking about Mrs. Nudelman, about Cowper Street, while rain drummed the roof.

"You've been busy," he said.

"Not as busy as you."

He took a deep breath and sighed. She wondered if he'd say more now, if she asked again. Intense in a good way?

She licked her lips. "Is she sleeping?"

"She is sleeping. And waking. And sleeping. She has not, to quote our pediatrician, established an age-appropriate sleep pattern yet."

"She's how old?"

"About eleven months. She is believed to have been born last January fifth."

Believed to have been born. Sarabeth thought about this, the enormous unknown of this child's life. How that unknown would be part of her life—and part of Mark's and Mary's lives—forever.

She wondered if Mark had had to negotiate with Mary for time here today. There were two kinds of new mothers, Liz had once said: the kind who saw her husband's work as a gift to her, and the kind who saw it as a crime against her. Liz was firmly in the first category, of course.

"Hang on," she said, and she went back to her car for the other thing she'd brought, her baby gift.

"What's this?" he said.

"Just a little present."

He opened the box, and color rose slowly into his cheeks. "I can't believe you did this."

"What? It's nothing."

"Please. It's not even close to nothing. Thank you so much."

With the remains of the dusty-rose paper, she'd made a little lampshade for the baby, using the razoring technique but making hearts instead of thin diagonals.

Mark was staring at her, and all at once she was embarrassed: it was too forward, to have brought him something, especially something she'd made. She should've bought a little wooden rattle. She said, "The sleep thing's normal, right? I mean, given everything? The changes, the travel—"

"Sarabeth, stop. This is *so kind* of you. I can't thank you enough."

"Well, I had some paper left over from those 'Welcome to Our Bordello' shades."

He put his hands on his hips. "You're not one of those people, are you? Just say 'You're welcome.' "

"You're welcome."

"Now say, 'I give it with love and from the fullness of my heart.' "

"You're going too far, Mark."

"You're right." He put the lampshade on a base and turned the lamp on: glowing hearts in the dim winter light. "Ever wonder who you'd be," he said, stepping away for a better look, "if you were you but raised somewhere else?"

"Like China?"

"Or next door. Or Italy, or an orphanage, or a hut. How much of yourself would remain?"

"There'd be no one to observe it—to compare."

"But if there were."

"Environment is everything."

"Biology is."

"Two things can't be everything."

"Maybe together they can," he said, and he touched her hip as he moved past her to turn the lamp off.

But, no: that hadn't happened. Had it? No, she thought, and then yes, and then no. *Something* had happened, though; heading for her car a little later, she felt stirred, as if she were a bowl of soup and he a spoon. This was a feeling she knew well, from Billy and a couple of guys before that, and especially from reading about people—about women mostly— to whom such things happened. About Anna, poor soul. Anna had been whisked. Beaten.

Stop, she commanded herself. Mark had not touched her, at least not intentionally. She was conjuring things to make herself feel good, wanted. Because she wasn't.

By seven-forty that evening she was in bed. The winter solstice wasn't for a couple of weeks, but if she hadn't known better she'd easily have believed tonight was going to be the longest night of the year. How many more hours of darkness? How much sleep could she manage? She couldn't remember the last time she'd masturbated, but the idea was boring, even repugnant. The last time she had sex: a year ago November 2.

Since then sex had been a gaping hole in her life, and in all likelihood so it would remain. She recalled a period when Nina didn't date for years and someone asked how she tolerated the celibacy. "I take Zoloft," she said, not untruthfully.

Was Lauren taking an antidepressant? Sarabeth knew what she needed to do: she needed to muster the courage to call Liz. No matter what might happen, she needed to call. Robert had said to! But what did Robert know.

Her mother had had all kinds of prescriptions, but from what she knew they weren't so effective. Obviously they weren't. The same therapist who'd called her father's move preemptive had told her that she hadn't metabolized her mother's death—as if it were some food she had yet to digest. But she had, she knew what had happened: Lorelei had been unhappy her whole life, and she had taken the step of putting herself out of her own misery. She had euthanized herself. What was unmetabolized about that?

She had been a pretty girl, Lorelei—her father's prize. She had spoken of him frequently, and with reverence. "Papa," she'd called him; not even "my papa," just "Papa," as if, in some strange way, he'd been Sarabeth's father as well. "Papa loved me in burgundy." "Papa took me to Central Park every Sunday afternoon." "Papa liked me to sit at his feet while he was reading." About Lorelei's mother, on the other hand, Sarabeth knew almost nothing. She'd had some illness, the nature of which was a mystery. Sarabeth had an impression of a woman in a bed, but it was very vague. Who, after all, had Lorelei been but a woman in a bed? And who, these days, was Sarabeth?

22

Christmas loomed. Ordinarily there would be a tree up by now. Ordinarily Liz would be done with her shopping by now, would be focused instead on helping Lauren and Joe do theirs, on transporting them as needed to the malls, suggesting gift ideas for her parents. She'd be wrapping presents during the day and baking at night.

Instead, she was watching Lauren.

The moment of saying goodnight each night (entering her bedroom uncertainly; what would she be doing? how would she seem?)—this was what Liz returned to constantly, looking for some kind of knowable, even progressive story. But there was none. Lauren was in her pajamas or not, listening to her iPod or not. She was sort of cheerful or not.

Goodnight, sweetie. Goodnight, Mom. It could be as little as that.

Last night, she'd been in bed already, reading, and for a moment it had been for Liz as if five years had vanished and Lauren was the child who saved up her confessions and worries to hand over to her mother at bedtime. Not that she'd said anything, but Liz had imagined it. She'd tried to tell Brody about it afterward, about how the picture had been so vivid, but his lack of interest was palpable. Had he left the room while she was in the middle of a sentence? She thought he might have.

She and Lauren were on their way home from the hospital. An ordinary Wednesday afternoon, but there was a ton of traffic, and it would only get worse as December progressed. Lauren stared out the window.

"Would you like the radio?" Liz said.

"If you want."

Liz reached for the power button, then changed her mind. Turning on the radio was too much like saying: *We aren't talking.*

"I talked to Grandma earlier—she sends her love."

"OK," Lauren said. "I mean, thanks."

They'd come by on Sunday, Liz's parents, but only to say hello; they were on their way to an afternoon concert in the city. "Stop back by on your way home," Liz had said, and they'd demurred so fast she knew they'd discussed it beforehand. Later that night, already irritable, Brody had muttered something about overkill, and when she asked him to repeat himself, he said, "Stop being such a program director. Your poor parents. Things have to happen in their own time."

It was almost dark when she and Lauren finally pulled into the driveway—almost dark and barely five o'clock. On the way into the kitchen she called up the stairs to see if Joe was home. "Want to come have some hot chocolate?"

"No, thanks," he called back.

"What about you?" she said to Lauren. "Hot chocolate? I was thinking I'd make myself some tea."

"No, thanks."

Liz filled the kettle and set it on the stove. She wanted to check the voice mail, but having Lauren with her felt a little like having a guest. Did Lauren sense that?

Depression, Liz had read recently, was anger turned inward, and she wondered if Lauren was angry now, specifically, right at this moment, though of course that wasn't how it worked: it wasn't lively, targeted anger; it was submerged, indiscriminate anger, something very unlike the feeling you might have when suddenly provoked.

She got herself a bag of English breakfast tea. When the water boiled she poured it into her mug and then went to the phone. The stutter tone sounded, and she pressed MEMORY 1 and MEMORY 2 and learned that she had one new message. She hit the 1 to hear it, and the automated voice said it had been sent today at 1:38 p.m., but then, instead of the message, there was more from the automated voice, and suddenly Sarabeth's voice saying, "Sarabeth Leoffler." And then, "Hi, Liz, it's me. I've been thinking about you, and I was just wondering how things are going. Let me know when you can. Bye."

For days Liz had been feeling she should call Sarabeth. Now Sarabeth had beaten her to the punch.

"What does it mean," she said as she put the handset back in the charger, "when a message comes with an introduction of who it's from?"

Lauren looked up from the newspaper. "What?"

"I just got a message from Sarabeth, but it wasn't just her voice—there was an automated voice beforehand saying it was a message from Sarabeth Leoffler, but 'Sarabeth Leoffler' was in Sarabeth's voice."

"She undergrounded you," Lauren said.

"What?"

"She didn't actually call you—she sent you a voice message."

"You can do that?"

"Duh. Then you don't have to actually talk to the person." Lauren thought for a minute. "That's sort of weird from Sarabeth."

"Tell me about it."

"What do you mean?"

No, Liz thought, don't tell; and then, somehow addressing Dr. Lewis: Or should I? "We're having some problems," she said.

"You and Sarabeth? That's so weird."

"How?"

"I don't know," Lauren said with a shrug. "You don't *have* problems with your friends. You're not a kid."

"Adults have problems."

"Yeah, with their mortgages. Or with us. Or, you know, with their husbands or wives." At this last her voice dropped a little, and she looked away.

"Or with alcohol," Liz said. "Or with authority. Or with anger, or anxiety, or depression."

Lauren gave her a quick look. "Is it about me?"

"Sweetie, no," Liz said. "Of course not." She kept her eyes on Lauren, commanded her face to behave. And it wasn't about Lauren; not really.

Lauren looked away for a long moment. "Is she coming to Tahoe?" she said at last, turning back.

Sarabeth coming to Tahoe for Christmas was very occasional—it was crowded up there in winter, only the main house open, the cabin closed till May or June. And this year Liz's parents were so nervous about the whole thing, Liz didn't want to complicate matters. "Should we go?" her mother had asked on the phone this morning. "Should Steve and Kelly and the twins? Are you sure you don't want just your family? We'd all be fine with that, you know."

But her mother's fear had nothing to do with it. Neither did how much space there was. Sarabeth wasn't coming because Liz didn't want her to.

"Not this year," she told Lauren.

"Because of your fight?"

"It's not a fight," Liz said, but Lauren gave her a quick, knowing look, and Liz understood that in fact it was.

In a while Lauren left the kitchen, and Liz got started on dinner, browning chicken breasts, slicing vegetables for a quick sauté. It was so dark out; the windows were like mirrors intended to reflect the room back at her, a picture she didn't want to see.

In a little while she heard Brody's car. "Boy is it cold," he said as he came in. "Bet we'll have a frost tomorrow." He seemed about to approach her and then changed direction and went to the mail instead. He flipped through it slowly and then turned, his face organized into a look of careful neutrality.

He said, "Something smells delicious."

She said, "Just chicken."

This was how they often talked these days, in code. He had just told her that he was not disinclined to see her in a favorable light, and she had replied that that might be true, but that he hadn't convinced her.

"Kids upstairs?" he said.

"Yeah."

All I can do is repeat myself.

In that case you haven't *convinced me.*

He ran his hands over the sides of his head. His hair wasn't going gray so much as losing color, fading. It was the color of putty now, whereas it had been a light brown before. He gave his bad shoulder a tentative roll, and she saw him wince.

How foolish that they were in this state, how stereotypical. *Well, the daughter ended up OK, but the marriage . . .*

What did she want from him? For an intense moment she craved Sarabeth's company, not her voice on the phone but her self, across a table. Sarabeth was so smart—what would she say? What *did* Liz want?

Brody wanted time to pass. Not hours or days, but great swaths of it; he wanted it to be April, July. This made him sad: the last weeks before Christmas had always been his favorite time of year. He remembered the snowy downtown streets of his childhood, getting out of his mom's station wagon for a quick run through the frigid air into the drugstore. The huge backseat door, and if you didn't look first you might put your feet down in four inches of slushy water. At home there was an air of expectation; he and his sister were better friends at this time of year than any other. A year older, she generally ignored him, but in these weeks she'd put a finger to her lips and lead him to a closet where a giant shopping bag had been shoved under a shelf. "Stop, idiot," she'd whisper if he made a move toward the bag, and he'd stop, and then they'd stand there companionably for another moment or two.

After dinner, he watched TV with Liz and Lauren for half an hour, then went upstairs with his laptop. In the little TV room at the end of the hall, he plugged into an outlet and downloaded the e-mails that had come since he left the office. He glanced at a couple of news sites and then, on a whim, picked up the phone and dialed his sister's number in Cincinnati. It was after eleven there, but she was always up late.

"How's Mom?" he asked after he'd reported on Lauren. "I've talked to her, but I can't get a read on how this whole thing's affecting her."

Marilyn was silent for a moment, and he braced himself for a worrying story. But she said, "You know what keeps going through my mind? Not that this is an answer, but Dad couldn't have stood this. Dad."

Brody thought about this. His father had been the sentimental one in his parents' marriage; it was he, not Brody's mother, who'd cried at Marilyn's wedding. Brody would never forget the sight of his dad's face when he came to the pew after tucking Marilyn's hand into the hand of her husband-to-be: a tear on each cheek, his mouth contorted by the effort to conceal his feelings. Once he was seated, Brody's mom passed him a tissue from her purse and then took his hand and held it for the remainder of the ceremony.

He'd loved being a grandfather. Marilyn had waited to have children, so Lauren was the first grandchild, and Brody and Liz took her to Cleveland when she was just five months old. Every evening that week, Brody's dad came in the door from work, spread a cloth of some kind over his dress shirt, and sat holding the baby until dinnertime.

"She's really quiet," he said to Marilyn.

"Does that scare you?"

"Not by itself."

"Oh, Brody."

He reached for a paperweight on the far side of the desk, and the movement caused the phone to slide sideways, setting off a bell somewhere in its innards. The phone was at least ten years old and had all the heft of a plastic pencil holder; he made a mental note to get a new one as soon as possible.

He said, "The whole thing could've been so much worse."

"You mean she could have succeeded?"

"Or done serious damage to her liver. She could be on a transplant list right now."

"Oh, how awful."

"Or she could have damaged the tendons going into her hands," he went on, but he was thinking how strange it was that the word "succeeded" could be used in this context. Succeeded. A successful suicide should be an oxymoron. He remembered Liz telling him about Sarabeth's mother, early on in their relationship; she said Sarabeth was *the daughter of a suicide,* and he was confused for a moment, thinking she meant Sarabeth was the daughter of—the offspring of—an *act* of suicide, in the way someone might be the offspring of an extramarital affair, or a May-December romance, or a drunken night.

If Lauren had succeeded, he'd be the *father* of a suicide. The creator, the primogenitor, of a horrible act.

23

*L*iz didn't call back. Not Wednesday evening, not Thursday or Friday. This possibility had not occurred to Sarabeth, and its fulfillment lodged in her gut and began to grow, a noxious weed sprouting terrible new leaves by the hour.

The phone didn't ring at all until late Friday afternoon, and it was only then that she understood the trade-off she'd made: in order to get voice mail (in order to be able to call Liz without the danger of speaking to her), she'd finally gotten rid of her ancient answering machine, but with it she'd also gotten rid of her ability to screen her calls.

Answer? The phone stopped after the third ring, and the decision was made for her. She waited awhile and then lifted the handset, pressed TALK, and heard the stutter tone. She called in and heard a message saying that the Paper Place was calling a second time to alert Sarabeth Leoffler that her prepaid order had arrived.

The phone was silent for the next several hours. When it rang again she was in bed, or not quite in bed but *on* bed, dozy, her overhead light still blazing. She let the voice mail get it.

"Uh, Sarabeth," said a voice she recognized as Mark Murphy's, strangely gravelly as it played back to her a few minutes later. "I'm calling about something nonprofessional, just a question for you, really, and if you get this by, like, ten-thirty, could you call me back? I'm on my cell. Thanks, bye."

What was this? She felt a flutter of curiosity, the first flutter of any kind she'd felt in days. It was almost nine-thirty. Where was he? If at work, why ask her to call the cell? If at home, why ask her to call the cell? If neither at work nor at home, why call her at all? She punched in the numbers and waited.

"Sarabeth," he answered after one ring. "Hey, how's it going? Thanks for calling me back."

"Sure."

"The thing is—actually, can you hang on for a sec?"

"OK."

"One sec," he said, and there were loud voices that got louder as she held on. And then silence.

"Sorry about that," he said, coming back. "Noisy bar."

"You're in a bar?"

"No, I'm outside a bar."

"Oh. Ha."

"Bunch of idiots watching hockey in there."

"So why were *you* in there?"

"Sarabeth, Sarabeth," he said. "Too many questions. I'm the one with the question."

"So you said."

"But—oh, can you hang on again for a sec?" This time he didn't wait for her assent but did whatever he had to do without further comment. She had no idea what was going on, but she was very curious, almost unbearably curious.

"Sorry," he said. "Another call came in."

"What's going on, Mark?"

He blew a raspberry. "Crazy night is all."

She heard herself sigh. Was he drunk? Her curiosity began to shift, toward annoyance.

"Sarabeth," he said. "This has not begun well. Do you have a minute?"

"Yeah."

"What's your address again?"

"My address?"

"It's something I have to ask you in person."

"What is this?" she exclaimed. "What's going on? Are you drunk?"

"No," he said. "Good question, fair question, but no. Can I come over?"

She looked around the room, certain it, she, the entire house, smelled to high heaven. "I'm in my sweatpants," she said, and then regretted it.

"Not a problem. Is this OK? I'll be fifteen minutes, twenty max."

She gave him her address and then hung up and sprang into action, a cover-up job, since real cleaning wasn't possible and she had to leave at least five minutes for her body. She kicked some of her discarded clothing under the bed, tossed the rest into the closet. She pushed open windows, ran for the kitchen, moved the piles of dirty dishes into the refrigerator and then back out and into the oven in case he wanted something to drink. Passing through the living room, she saw for the first time in days the array of objects still cluttering the floor. Fuck, she thought, but kept going. In the bathroom she took the fastest shower in history, no time for her hair, then dried off and put on a different pair of sweatpants, clean, and a pale green funnel-neck sweater for which she'd spent far too much last winter.

It had been ten minutes. She had another five or ten to go, and she hurried to the bathroom mirror, where she discovered that her hair was revoltingly dirty. She should have washed it—so what if it would have been wet when he arrived—but it was too late now. She brushed it and worked the impossible curls, then pumped on hair spray to get it to stay in place. Lipstick? Too studied for a woman in sweatpants. She felt tremulous and ran for the kitchen and a piece of bread, and she was wiping butter from her lips when he knocked a couple minutes later.

"Sarabeth," he said from the doorstep. He was unshaven, untucked, unsmiling. She'd forgotten the porch light, and all was black behind him. She permitted herself a quick glance at the Heidts': no sign of life.

"Sorry," she said, flicking on the light. "Come in."

In his shop the ceilings were about twenty feet high, and while she'd known he was tall, she hadn't known quite how tall. He came in and instantly made of her house an elves' hut. He was seriously tall, taller even than Billy, who was six feet two. She led him to the sitting area and waited for him to choose the couch before settling into a chair herself. His giant knees nearly touched the coffee table.

"So," she said. "You have a question."

He rubbed his bristly cheeks, then spread his arms along the back of the couch. Hollow cheeks, a twitch in his eye: he looked terrible.

"Got a beer?" he said.

"You couldn't have asked the bartender that?"

A tiny smile flitted across his lips. "That's not the question."

"It's *a* question."

"There you go. I've always found you to be very insightful."

She went to the kitchen for a beer. For herself she got a glass of tangerine-grapefruit juice. She'd been on a tangerine-grapefruit juice kick for several days. Her pee had started to smell of it.

He'd left the couch and was squatted at the spread of stuff on her floor. "Having a garage sale?"

She held out the beer, and he stood and took it, then went back to his seat. She remained standing.

"This is very hard for me," he said.

"I'm intrigued."

"Do you think—" He stopped and sighed hard. "Do you think there's such a thing as evil?"

He was perfectly serious. He watched her as he sipped from the beer bottle, watched her as he put it on the coffee table. After a while she returned to her chair. Her juice glass felt cold, and she reached it toward the coffee table, then changed her mind and set it on the floor at her feet.

She said, "I don't know."

"I don't know, I've-given-it-a-lot-of-thought-and-haven't-figured-it-out? Or I don't know, it-doesn't-interest-me-I-don't-care?"

"Don't know that either."

He reached for his beer. He sat looking straight ahead, rolling the bottle back and forth between his palms. She knew she was in his peripheral vision, knew he was highly aware of her presence. She really didn't think he was drunk, but he was something. *Had* he meant to touch her, the other day at his shop? She saw herself lying on the couch, exactly where he was now: an hour ago, all afternoon, most of yesterday. It was almost as if she'd left an imprint, almost as if he were sitting on her, and with this idea came an intense longing to be fucked.

He looked over at her. "What's with your hair?"

"My hair?" she said, her face warming. "Nothing is with my hair. My hair is very much alone. Well, my head is sort of with my hair, but you couldn't really say they're together."

"Sarabeth, what's wrong?"

"What's wrong with you?"

He scooted toward her. "I went to SFMOMA today—I was playing hooky. And there was this thing in the gift shop that made me think of you, this necklace—different-colored puff balls on a thin cable."

"I'm flattered."

"No, it was cool—it made me think of you lampwise, not jewelrywise. Like it could be a pull."

"Oh."

"But it had a name. I mean, a little card near it. And guess what it was, guess what it was called?"

She shrugged.

"It was a Fudabi Schmuck."

She giggled; she was feeling odd, almost high. "What does that have to do with evil?"

"I don't know—I guess it made me think of Hitler."

"He was definitely a Fudabi Schmuck."

"The biggest," Mark said. And then, "I really want to kiss you. I've wanted to kiss you since the day we met."

"Mark, don't."

"Don't kiss you?"

"Don't say you want to."

"Too late."

She stood and backed away from him. Her heel knocked against something, and she looked down as one of the silver candlesticks fell over. She said, "You're married."

He shrugged, then held up his palms as if to say he couldn't deny it.

"What is it?" she said. "What's going on with Mary?"

"Maud is going on with Mary. And Mary is going on with Maud. They're going on and on and on."

"And you feel left out."

He tipped his head back and stared up at the ceiling. His knees were splayed, and the crotch of his jeans had an inviting roundness to it. She looked at his Adam's apple, watched it bob and then go still.

Her heart pounded. She went and straddled one of his legs, then sat and kissed him, kissed him, the warmth of his lips, the taste of beer, his heat—

She was insane. She scrambled off and said, "You have to leave."

She could see that he'd begun to get hard. He stood and swiped at his erection, ran his hand over his chin. He gave her a broad, collusive smile, but he couldn't keep it going; it melted off him and he was simply unhappy. Back to him she went, and on tiptoe she kissed him again, moving her lips until his moved again, too. "I'll think about it," she said, and then she made for the door and opened it, and after a moment he raised his eyebrows and gave her a little wave and left.

She thought about it, for days. Picturing his forearms, she thought about it. Picturing the fade on the thighs of his jeans.

As an antidote she went to movies. She even sat through a documentary about the politics of famine, the longest 107 minutes of her life. She was shallow, callous; she couldn't deny it. As if to make sure there could be no doubt, she went straight to Walgreens afterward and spent an hour reading gossip magazines.

Then she forgot a staging.

"Uh, honey?" Jim's message said. "That condo?"

It was Wednesday morning, the day before the open house; she was beyond screwed. Her mover was busy, so she went to her storage unit, gathered everything she could fit in her car, and sped to the condo building, where the loading zone out front was occupied by a painter's truck.

Just what she needed.

She parked around the corner, grabbed what she could carry, and headed back to the building. At least Helen's furniture was bland rather than garish. And the rolltop desk might turn out to be a lot lighter than it had looked. It might even come apart.

Helen had left the place spotless, though there was a closed-in 409 smell that Sarabeth would have to banish. She dumped her stuff, took a very brief peek at the desk, and went back to her car for the rest of what she'd brought.

DIAMOND PAINTING, said the writing on the side of the painter's truck. Were they going to park there all day?

Back upstairs, she began by taking down the Impressionist posters, and right away the living room looked better. Into a closet they went, along with Helen's cheerful Marimekko throw pillows, which Sarabeth felt sure had not been in the condo two weeks ago. (Had Helen bought them for the sale? Did she not understand staging?)

In the bedroom, she took Helen's unfortunate nylon-backed bedspread off the bed and replaced it with her own nice ivory matelassé coverlet. She tried different combinations of shams and pillowcases. Was she brave enough to face the desk?

It was in the corner. The top was rolled up to reveal a warren of cubbyholes—empty, thank God. The writing surface was slanted, with a little tray at the bottom to catch pencils and pens. The base was made of two banks of drawers, also thoughtfully emptied.

Standing at one end, she hooked her fingertips under the half-inch lip and tried with all her might to get the desk even a couple inches off the floor.

She was ruined. What was she going to do? Whom could she call? Not Jim. Nina was at work. She couldn't call Mark, ha-ha.

She locked up and went downstairs. There was a little Mediterranean food shop on the corner, and though it was barely 11:00 a.m. she got herself a falafel pita and sat eating it on a low wall. Leaving the desk in the bedroom was the only option, but the more she considered it, the worse it seemed. People would take one look in there and think: no. Jim would take one look and fire her. *Honey,* she could imagine him saying. *I'm really sorry, but we are over.*

She bit off another mouthful. The cool chunks of cucumber were soothing next to the hot, oily falafel.

Back she went. On the second floor, the painters had stretched a tarp from the stairwell all the way to the open door of the unit where they were working. They were responsible painters, then. She'd seen some who left so much paint on the access, they could have billed for it.

She had forty dollars in her wallet. Would painters be insulted if they were asked to help move a piece of furniture for forty dollars?

Slowly, in case she changed her mind, she moved toward the open doorway. It seemed rude to place herself where she could see in, so she stopped short and reached around for the door, knocking as best she could given that the door moved as soon as her knuckles touched it. She waited and then tried again, this time knocking on the outside wall.

She heard footsteps, oddly uneven footsteps: first the sound of a hard shoe, then a soft thump, then the hard shoe again. This did not exactly jibe with a painter, and when someone appeared it was not a painter, it was Peter Something, in a pressed white shirt and khakis, and a cast on one leg.

"Oh," Sarabeth said.

He gave her a quizzical look, his straight, dark eyebrows coming together, his head tipping slightly to the side. "Can I help you?"

"No," she said. "It's just—I thought there were painters here."

"There are."

She looked down and saw his toes poking out of the cast. They were sexy toes, actually, with clean, squared-off nails. Was he cute? *Shut the fuck up,* she told herself.

"I'm upstairs," she said, "and—" She looked past him into the apartment. "Wait, are you listing this place?"

"Next week. Why, you interested?"

She explained her situation, why she was there, what she needed— she was pretty babbly, but he hung on till the end.

He said, "Well, that's both quite a jam you're in and also highly resolvable."

"It is?"

"Which one do you question?" He smiled and said he'd be right back, and he left her on the doorstep and disappeared into the bedroom of what appeared to be a mirror-image version of Helen's place. She heard him speaking Spanish, heard another voice, heard laughter.

"They're going to quit for lunch soon," he said, coming back. "They'll come help you then if that's OK."

She stared at him, embarrassment beginning its long, vinelike climb up her insides. She was aware that even if she knew what to say, she might not be able to say it.

"I'd offer my services as well," he said, "but under the circumstances—" He gestured at his leg.

Still she stared.

"Is that OK, then? Half an hour or so?"

"Yeah, no, it's just—" She took a deep breath. "I'm completely mortified."

He gave her an incredulous look. "Why?"

She shielded her eyes for a moment, her face on fire. "Sorry," she said, "this is absurd. It's just—I feel like a little kid. I needed someone to take care of my problem, and it happened."

"To me you had a problem and pursued a solution and found one." He had a sweet look on his face, a look that was both gentle and amused, and she felt herself begin to relax. "Like an adult," he added.

"Oh, so you're nice."

He grinned and pulled a card case from his back pocket. "Peter Watkins. Coldwell Banker."

"Sarabeth Leoffler. Um, home sale design."

"Really? I thought you were one of us." He gave her a long, apprais-

ing look. "OK, then," he said, "half an hour or so," and she thanked him
and waved and turned away.

I thought you were one of us.

He'd meant one of us realtors, of course, and his saying so meant he
recognized her, but all she could think, her earlier despair returning, was
that the real mistake he'd made was in thinking she belonged to the community of the competent.

She was in bad shape. To make matters worse, when she got home she
had a message from Mark. "Hi, Sarabeth. I'll bet you know who this is.
Nothing important, just saying hello." She pressed 3 for erase and hung
up so quickly, the handset fell from the charger. She hurried to her room,
got into bed, and pulled the blankets over her head. Early on with Billy,
tortured with indecision but unable to stop herself from seeing him, she'd
fled Berkeley one Friday afternoon when his wife and kids were going
away for the weekend and he'd said he could spend the entire time with
her. Forty-eight hours! She hightailed it to the Mackays', and Liz gave her
a glass of wine and dinner and the guest room, where, once everyone else
was asleep, the two of them sat together on the bed, legs crossed, and
talked and talked. "I'm worried about *you*," Liz said. Meaning not Travis,
not Zeke, not Her, though when Sarabeth brought them up Liz said she
couldn't imagine it not affecting them as well. "But I don't know them,"
she added.

It had been October, maybe November. Rain falling: thumming the
roof, rattling the leaves on the trees.

"You think he'll hurt me?"

"I can imagine a lot of things that might make you suffer."

"But I'm suffering now."

"I know. I wish you weren't."

Liz didn't tell her what to do. Not until much later, when some kind
of impatience had taken over, or moral disgust, or something. "Why am I
still doing this?" Sarabeth had asked her, and Liz had said, "Why *are*
you?" In other words *stop*—and so for a while Sarabeth didn't tell her any
of what was going on.

What would Liz think of Mark's visit? She'd be horrified. Or was that
wishful thinking, the same thing as wishing Liz knew? As wishing she'd
called back.

It had been a week to the day since Sarabeth had sent her the voice message.

"Jim?" she said into the phone a little later. "Can I come over?" And then she blurted out the entire story of Lauren and Liz.

Jim and Donald lived way up in the Oakland hills, in a house they'd built on the site of a house they'd lost to the '91 fire. When she arrived half an hour later, she found they'd made a space for her in the short, steep driveway, and they both came to the front door to welcome her.

"I told Donald," Jim said. "I hope that's OK."

"Of course," she said, and Donald enfolded her in his long, skinny arms. She stayed close for an extra moment, breathing in the wool smell of his sweater.

In the living room Jim poured her a glass of red wine, and then he and Donald settled on the couch while she took a seat on the floor, on the thick rug that lay in front of the fireplace.

"So what's next?" Jim said. "What are you going to do?"

She was surprised by this. "Nothing. There's nothing I can do. I can't call again."

"What do you mean? That's ridiculous, of course you can call again."

She looked away. Behind the couch, a sliding glass door led to a wonderful multilevel deck: the number one item on the wish list Jim and Donald had given their architect. They told stories about how invigorating it had been to start over, to get *exactly the house they wanted,* but she couldn't imagine how they'd borne so much loss. Among many other absences, they now had no pictures of either of them from birth to the day of the fire.

"I'm sorry," he said. "I'm not sleeping well. I'm so tired it's affecting my social skills. Why do you feel you can't call again?"

It had to do with respect, with not being the kind of person who hammered and hammered. She didn't know how to explain this, though. She said, "I've been really tired, too. Do you suppose we have chronic fatigue syndrome?"

"Everyone's tired," Donald said. "Haven't you heard? It's the new depressed."

"Where does that leave depressed?" Jim quipped, and Sarabeth smiled and rolled her eyes, but she couldn't muster the energy to take it any further.

On the coffee table there was a platter of bread and cheese, and he slid it toward her. "Eat. Want any of this? Or I can cook you something."

"Oh, I'm fine, thanks."

He sliced off a piece of Brie and put it on a cracker. "Here."

She let him hand her the cracker, and after a moment she took a bite. In her mouth there was texture, the cracker crunching, the buttery smoothness of the Brie, but she didn't taste much of anything.

"You could write her a letter," he said, and she shrugged.

"I suppose so. Actually, I think I just have to wait."

Donald cleared his throat. "I've been thinking that your mother must feel very close right now. Her death, I mean."

Sarabeth felt a caving sensation in her chest. It did and it didn't. She did and she didn't. The fire crackled, and in the quiet afterward she heard the faraway barking of a dog. She brought her glass to her lips and let the rich, dark wine bleed across her tongue and into her throat.

"I'm sorry," he said. "Did I overstep?"

"No, of course not," she said. "It's fine."

And it mostly was. There had been times when she hadn't talked about it—in college, in her early twenties—but she'd gained some distance somewhere along the line. She had even, in her mid-thirties, had a friend whose father had killed himself, and the two of them had done little *other* than talk about it—to the point where they had a kind of routine going, the suicide sisters, that they performed for and with each other. It had made them fast friends for a time, and then embarrassed and awkward former acquaintances ever after. "My mother didn't leave a note." "My father left a note and didn't mention me." An integral part of the routine was competition.

"Let's go into the kitchen," Jim said. "I'll make some pasta."

"I'm—"

"Come on," Donald said. "He won't do it just for me, and I'm starving."

Jim stood and offered her his hand, and she let him pull her to her feet. He'd been so nice about the condo earlier, praising her when the job she'd done was merely adequate.

She followed him into the kitchen. While he and Donald moved from refrigerator to sink to stove, she sat at the table and glanced at some of his work papers—flyers for the condo, comps on a house in Kensington, a stack of photocopies of a newspaper article about the housing market.

"Top-Priced Bay Area Communities" read the heading of a sidebar, and she looked, as she always did, for Palo Alto: the median price for a house was $1.2 million.

She had, from time to time, thought of asking Jim to figure out what her family's house on Cowper might fetch in the current market, but she didn't really want to know. *Gazillions* would be the answer. And it wouldn't matter, because it had been necessary for her father to sell it when he did. Necessary in every way.

Life on Cowper Street, life in that house, with its elegant, unlivable rooms. What she remembered was a fear of displeasing her mother, of her mother becoming angry at her—or angry at herself, which was just as bad. There was loud anger in the kitchen, where plates could be broken, and silent anger upstairs, where Lorelei simmered and sulked. Sarabeth remembered hysterical anger in the garage, when she hid once behind a wheelbarrow and wasn't found for a long time.

Toward the end, Lorelei changed. She became quieter, and she cried a lot. She was almost always in bed when Sarabeth left for school in the morning, and the last thing Sarabeth did before heading out was stop in and say goodbye. Very occasionally there was something lovely about Lorelei in bed—the stack of pillows, the crystal carafe of water—and at such times Sarabeth could feel drawn by the room, by the idea that Lorelei might absorb peace from the room, even by Lorelei herself. On the last day, though, it was just a mess: curtains drawn, abandoned clothing all over the floor.

Sarabeth hadn't discovered the body, but only, she sometimes thought, through sheer determination not to. When she returned home from school in those days she occupied herself with avoiding the parts of the house where she might come in contact with her mother. On that day, the kitchen bore traces of her mother's having been up for a while: there was an unsuccessful soft-boiled egg lying near the sink, most of the yolk congealed on the counter. Sarabeth cleaned it and then took her homework to her father's small office off the living room.

She worked. The house was very quiet, as it could well remain until he got home. Liz was still at school—she was on the yearbook staff, and they were working furiously to get the final pages finished and off to the printer. From her father's desk, Sarabeth had a narrow tree-impeded view across the street to the Castleberrys' front door, and she was simultaneously watching for Liz and listening for Lorelei. She would realize many years later that she had made a deal with herself, the deal being that when she saw Liz she would go and check on Lorelei. Life was usually best when Liz was home—best best when Sarabeth was over there with her—but on that day, as she looked up again and again to see if Liz was pulling up across the street on her bike, she was relieved each time to see nothing but the Castleberrys' front door.

Cowardly then, cowardly now.

Though she had called Liz. She had. She had agonized, and then she had called. And now . . . it was true, what she'd said to Jim earlier. She just had to wait. Waiting was, after all, something to do; it was its own small kind of solution.

On the other side of the cooking island Jim chopped shallots, and Donald stood at the sink washing lettuce. They had been together thirty years, longer than any other couple she knew. Jim looked up. For a moment, he seemed surprised that she was watching him, and then he gave her a smile and waved at her, and she waved back.

24

Christmas was ten days away, and Liz could delay no longer. Thursday morning, after dropping Lauren at the hospital, she headed to the mall to do her shopping. Every bit of it, with any luck.

It was hard to park, at not even nine o'clock. She cut the engine and wrote out a list, trying to put the things she wanted in the order in which she'd arrive at the stores that sold them, reminding herself as she did this of the short interval just after her father's retirement when he took over the weekly grocery shopping: he memorized the layout of Safeway and wrote his lists in aisle-by-aisle order, starting with meat and ending with produce. The novelty wore off, though, the pleasure of being so efficient, and soon Liz's mother was the shopper again.

They'd come for dinner Sunday night, and her father had talked a lot, as he always did under pressure, and her mother had contrived to spend almost the entire predinner period working in the kitchen—Liz wasn't sure she addressed a single word to Lauren all evening. Except when she came in: she rushed at Lauren and cried, "My girl," hugging her tightly but avoiding eye contact altogether.

Liz got out of the van and locked up. Seventeen was the number of items on her list, but it wasn't as bad as it looked: she was going to get iTunes gift cards for all the nieces and nephews.

The list had her starting at Nordstrom, though, and she had not bargained on the ground-floor bustle, on the women in Santa hats spraying perfume, on the young mothers trying to push writhing, stroller-bound toddlers from counter to counter, their chipper determination weakening already. In front of the entrance to the up escalator an elderly couple stood in a paralysis of befuddlement that Liz saw might last several minutes. The elevator instead then, but to reach it she had to make her way through men's shoes, and the gleaming wingtips, the truffle-brown oxfords, the Rockports, the Børns, the Josef Seibels, the Mephistos, the Johnston & Murphys—she was overwhelmed by them, by their pathos. There was something so touching about men's shoes, how huge and hopeful looking they were. She gave a hovering salesman a go-away glance, and she lifted a shoe to her face and breathed in the smells of leather and cork. She set the shoe down again. Brody's feet were gigantic; he was barely six feet tall, and he wore a size twelve. Her second or third date with him, twenty-odd years ago, she'd blurted out something about how big his feet were—totally out of the blue—and then she'd burst into mortified laughter. What a goof she'd been then. She remembered it as if it had been someone other than she sitting beside him at Candlestick Park, watching the Giants, happy she could impress him with her baseball expertise.

The woman Liz had been then, the girl—she'd hung out in bars, gotten drunk most weekends, dated men who were about as dependable as puppies. Her adult self more closely resembled her teenage self than it did that person. She'd even slept around some, though in a moderate, good-girl way; despite her efforts, she was pretty much of a fuddy-duddy even then. She'd meet guys and want to cook dinner for them, but they had trouble sitting still long enough; they'd be like *chew, chew,* and then *Wow, that was great, wanna go out?* Brody was older, solid. He knew what he wanted. He wanted who she'd have become if she hadn't detoured into the semiwild life; and so she detoured out of it and became herself.

She gave up on Nordstrom for now, instead entering the vast terrain of chain boutiques. They were all around her: Papyrus, Brookstone, J.Jill, Claire's, the Body Shop, See's Candies, Sunglass Hut. In the atrium she looked up and saw that the sky was a wicked shade of near white. She felt out of kilter, chided herself for beginning to lose her resolve.

She walked. Walking was good, and walking quickly was even better; it was something like an antidote to despair.

Despair in a store.

This was a phrase of Sarabeth's: it was what you felt when you had time, money, desire . . . but you couldn't *buy* anything. Counterintuitively, you prolonged your stay, waiting for something to change. It wouldn't.

How long ago had Sarabeth called Liz—undergrounded her? It was last week sometime; Liz wasn't sure when. The holidays were always so insane.

She arrived at the Apple store. There were about ten people in line, and she understood it would only get worse, but she couldn't make herself go in. You could get iTunes cards almost anywhere now, couldn't you? She walked on, slowing only as she approached the Santa area, and then there he was, Santa himself: sitting on a huge sherbet-colored Candy Land version of a throne. It was like a prop for a play, a movie: *Santa, the Musical!*

The photographer's assistant was dressed as an elf, an elf holding a clipboard; Liz watched as she bent to help a very young woman with a stroller. Liz decided to watch one Santa visit, wait through one photo op, then turn around and get to work. But when the young mother at last lifted up her child, Liz saw not the toddler she'd expected but a tiny sleeping newborn, dressed for the occasion in a fuzzy red suit and a long, fur-trimmed red cap, and Liz wanted to scream: she felt she might well scream.

She headed for the nearest exit. Outside, she discovered that she'd been sweating; she felt it as the cool air hit her face. She found a tissue in her purse and blotted her forehead, her upper lip. She watched people coming across from the parking structure, women mostly, alone or in pairs. Women chatting, women with handbags hanging from their forearms. She backed up until she'd reached the rough surface of the mall building, and she closed her eyes. Barely moving, she turned her head back and forth until she felt the stucco scraping lightly against her scalp.

They sat in a circle. The faces were mostly different from when Lauren had started, more than three weeks ago. Casey was gone. Morgan was gone. Angus was on partial but absent today. Abby was gone—back to intensive care because her vital signs had tanked. Lucas remained, but he was gone, too—gone to Lauren, anyway: he had avoided her since the day she was released from inpatient. Today there were two new kids: a boy with bruises on his face, a girl with bandaged wrists. Ivan was leading, and because of the newcomers he went through the privacy rules yet again. Wrapping it up, he said, "And finally, we won't tell your parents what you say here unless we feel you're in imminent danger."

"And all you have to do to keep him quiet," Callie said, "is give him a blow job."

She was a few seats away from Lauren, on one of the ugly corduroy couches, and she made a point now of looking at Lauren and sliding her tongue back and forth over her top lip. This really bothered Lauren, which was probably why Callie did it. Dr. Lewis said sometimes abused kids felt that the only way to connect with people was to be sexual. This morning, Callie had told Lauren that when she was in seventh grade she'd sold hand jobs to boys during audiovisual presentations. Lauren didn't know why Callie came to her with these stories, but in some psycho part of herself she was sort of flattered. "I think it's human nature," Dr. Lewis had said about this, "to be curious about the ways people can get into trouble."

Ivan looked around the room. "Does anyone have a reaction to what Callie said?"

"Slut," said a boy named Nick.

"She was pissed," Lauren said. Her face warmed, but she went on. "Because you can just walk out of here, and we can't."

"I didn't say that," Callie said.

"It's true, though," Ivan said. "I can just walk out of here. What do you have to do to walk out of here?"

"Work," Nick said.

Ivan nodded, but Lauren thought this wasn't really true. Some people stayed because there was nowhere else to go. Callie: her fourth foster mom had said she was finished. Lucas: his parents couldn't be reached, seemed to have vanished, and the only other potential adult in his life was a great-uncle in Utica, New York, who was trying to figure out if he had enough money to send Lucas to boarding school.

Lauren, in fact, *could* walk out of here—did walk out of here each afternoon, and would walk out of here for the last time tomorrow. Something had happened, though: she wanted to stay. Not just until Christmas, but for the rest of high school. Her parents and the school district had decided that she didn't have to return to school until January, but January would come faster than she could stand, and she didn't want to go back. To her dismay, tears edged out of her eyes.

"Lauren," Ivan said, "do you have something you want to share?"

"Her ass," Lucas said.

Everyone turned to look at him; he'd barely spoken all week. Lauren felt sick.

"Wow," Callie said at last, breaking the silence, "that was really hostile," but she said it like a Valley Girl, *rilly hostile,* and Lauren felt worse.

"Lauren?" Ivan said.

All eyes were on her except Lucas's. "What did I do to you?" she heard herself say. She regretted it immediately and pinched her eyes closed for a moment.

"Yeah," Callie said, "what did she?" and Lauren wondered if in some part of her fucked-up self Callie was actually on her side.

The group was silent. Ivan was watching Lucas, and now he brought his hands together in front of his lips and said, "I think there are some questions for you, Lucas."

"Fuck you," Lucas said.

Ivan tapped his hands against his chin. "I'm hearing a lot of anger today."

Lauren stifled a giggle, then melted into tears. She sat there crying: fat assed, ugly, pathetic.

Lucas shoved his chair back a few feet. Now he was outside the circle but not outside the group—to leave the group he'd have to leave the room, and that wasn't allowed.

"What does anger feel like?" Ivan said.

"Like you want to kill someone."

"Like someone wants to kill you."

"That's fear."

"Maybe for you."

"Sometimes anger goes with feeling hurt," Ivan said. "Sometimes kids say angry things to each other when they're hurting."

"Gag me," Callie said, but Lucas blushed and stared into his lap, and Lauren remembered the moment a few days before she was released when he sort of cried in front of her. She remembered the way the tears clung to his eyes, tiny pools in front of a look of sadness that was there and then not there and then there again, like even inside himself he didn't know how he felt. When the tears finally surged, they trailed slowly down his cheeks, but the rest of him looked just the same. And what did she do? She left the room.

Someone began talking about something else, and she let herself go—not more crying, but a spiral into what she and Dr. Lewis called the Bad

Feeling. It was where she'd been living for a long time. She knew it very well: like a room, like a jail cell. It was the place where she hated herself the most. It was the place where she could feel like puking at any time.

But: your parents gone, no forwarding address. She couldn't imagine it.

Lucas stared into his lap.

When the session was over everyone stood. Some would go to art, some to yoga, some to music. Some saw their shrinks. She'd seen Dr. Lewis first thing this morning, and though she'd stood, too, she hung around the emptying circle, looking half at Ivan and half at Lucas, who had not moved.

Lucas knew she was still there—she could tell, maybe from how determined he seemed not to look anywhere but down. Ivan was on his feet: watching the dispersing kids, glancing at Lucas, smiling across the ring of chairs at Lauren. Was it the same day Lucas cried that she thought the jack of diamonds looked like Jeff Shannon? Ivan had been playing cards with Casey. And now Casey was gone. On her last day, she'd motioned Lauren into her room and pulled up her pant leg to reveal a huge number of cut marks on her shin—some faint and white, some crooked, some shiny red. She said, "You have to decide every day not to do it."

Lucas leaned forward and rested his forearms on his legs. Lauren walked around the outside of the chairs and sat on the one nearest him. He looked at her, then looked away again. She didn't know what to do— she felt sort of idiotic sitting here, but she wasn't going to just leave him, not this time.

The Oiron holiday celebration was in a ballroom at the Palo Alto Sheraton, on the last Saturday night of the party season. There were several hundred people there, eating and laughing and sipping better champagne than you'd think would be served at a corporate party, because Russ's brother-in-law owned a winery in Napa.

But Brody couldn't really enjoy it. Liz hadn't wanted to come, and they'd fought over whether or not it was OK to leave the kids—to leave Lauren—home alone. "What do you think will happen?" he'd asked her, and the answer had hung in the air between them, unspoken.

They'd spent the first part of the party together, but now she was on the other side of the dance floor, talking to Mike Patterson's wife. In bed last night he'd approached her, just a hand on her hip, but she'd stiffened and moved away. They hadn't made love in a long time—certainly not since Lauren had come home. Maybe not since the night he left the bed as soon as he was finished.

That night, the way he was: he remembered a period early on when she sometimes wanted it that way. "Be rough with me," she'd say. "Fuck me." Proper Liz! Other times, she'd tell him to pretend they'd just met. Or either of them might whisper to the other, "You're not allowed to move until I say so." They were adventurous then, playful. Now you couldn't even call what they did making love. Or not always, anyway. Plenty of times it was just having sex. Like having lunch. Just something you did because you needed to.

He scanned the ballroom. Russ was standing near the bar with an exquisite young Asian woman, who had the most perfect mouth Brody had ever seen. She was maybe twenty-five, and she gazed at Russ with a dreamy expression on her face, as if she'd float away if he removed his arm from her waist.

A waiter passed with a tray, and Brody helped himself to more champagne. He knew he should eat, but he felt stubborn about it, imagining Liz would tell him the same thing.

He looked at Russ and his date again. How would it be to have a girl like that—to feel, even briefly, less your usual self than her happy idea of you?

He headed over to a group from sales, arriving in time to hear one of the guys say, "And so we rode the chairlift back down the mountain and returned her equipment, and now when I go skiing, she goes to a spa."

This was met by much merriment.

"Separate vacations! The secret of marital success!"

"My parents spent four weeks apart every year."

"Whether they wanted to or not."

"Oh, believe me, they wanted to."

Brody smiled and moved on. His parents would no sooner have taken separate vacations than lived separately. They were midwestern. His dad called his mom Sarge, as in *Yes, ma'am, Sarge, right away, Sarge.* Winking at Brody, making sure he understood it was just a joke.

"Here's the man we need."

Brody turned to find three of his colleagues standing in a small cluster, and he shook hands with each of them, good party handshakes.

"What's your guess on the cost of this thing?" Bruce Sellers said.

"Who cares?" said Rajiv Chaudhari. "It's a write-off."

"Oiron company party," Brody said, "sixty-five thousand dollars. Employee happiness, priceless." He thought for some reason of last year's party: dancing with Liz as it got late, the mingling smells of perfume and sweat. He looked over to where he'd last seen her, but she was gone.

"Rumor has it," Bruce said, "he's going to one of those private Caribbean islands for Christmas."

"No, he's buying one."

"As a present for her?" Tony Blank said, and they all looked over at Russ's date. "I'd buy a country," he added, and they all chuckled.

Brody drained his champagne. What *would* Russ do for Christmas? He thought of Russ's former house in Woodside, of a dinner party he and Liz had attended there one December, when the entire estate was strung with little white lights. There was a butler, or at least Brody and Russ had a joke about there being a butler; to this day Brody didn't know whether the guy had been hired for the occasion, as Russ insisted, or not.

He imagined Russ driving by the house this week, looking at the lights, continuing on.

Tony said, "Hey, d'I tell you guys about my new toy? Early Christmas present from my wife? She got me a Ski-Doo snowmobile."

Bruce said, "Screw you, my Yamaha's better."

"Why'd she give it to you early?" Rajiv said. "Don't tell me there's another wrinkle to this Christmas thing."

"Come off it," Bruce said to Rajiv, "we know you grew up in LA," and Rajiv grinned.

Brody stood with them for another five or ten minutes, talking about Christmas plans and work gossip and who was skiing where. A little later, drunk and hungry, he found Liz in the hallway to the restrooms. She was studying a framed newspaper article about old Palo Alto—or was pretending to, anyway.

"Ready to go?" he said.

"Sure." Her phone was in her hand, and she opened her purse and dropped it inside, then closed the purse with a snap.

"You called home?"

"Everything's fine."

"Excellent," he said, and a look of disgust came over her face.

"You're smashed."

"So?"

"Just making an observation."

They made their way back to the ballroom. The dance floor had filled, and he imagined the heat, the way the music would feel in his legs.

From across the room Russ waved, then met them near the door. "Taking off?"

"We've got to get home," Liz said.

Russ hesitated for a moment and then took hold of her hands. "It's been such a hard stretch for you guys. I want to tell you again how sorry I am—I'd do anything to help." He leaned forward and kissed her cheek, then stepped toward Brody and pressed his lips against Brody's cheek, too. "Take care, you two. I'm glad you came."

At the car, Liz held out her hand for Brody's keys, and he almost gave them to her. "I'm fine," he said instead. They both got in, buckled up. He wanted to say something—*I've got it covered, Sarge*—but she might scoff. He backed out from the spot, taking care to make every move as smooth as butter. He cut through Stanford, remembering the day early in their relationship when she showed him around her old haunts, and how his curiosity about her life as a college student told him he was getting serious.

He looked over at her. She was staring straight ahead, eyes so firmly on the road she might as well have been the one driving. They passed the golf course: trees on the left, trees on the right, darkness everywhere. His cheek tingled, and he brought his fingers up to touch the spot that Russ's lips had grazed.

It would be freezing, but Lauren's dad wanted to go to the beach. Lauren could tell her mom wasn't all that into it, but she was going along, all fakely cheerful about how nice it would be. As for Joe—he just shrugged. That was pretty much all he did anymore. "Whatever"—all he said. Last night, watching TV with him while their parents were out, she'd had this feeling of wanting to say something, but she hadn't known what, and he was zoned out, or zoned into the show—just zoned.

"How about you, Laur?" her dad said. "You game?"

Last Sunday, after going with her parents and Joe to get a Christmas tree, she'd spent the afternoon reading dumb magazines and trying to make herself call Amanda. Today would be the same. She'd talked to

Amanda once during the week, but it was too weird. Amanda had told her something about Jeff Shannon, and though Lauren knew Amanda was trying to help, trying to keep her up-to-date, she didn't want to hear about it. Jeff Shannon was probably waiting to torture her when she got back. Waiting to smirk again, make her feel like a dog. The jack of diamonds. What was the hardest thing to scratch? A diamond. Lauren felt she couldn't scratch Jeff, couldn't affect him. This was Dr. Lewis's idea, and it was sort of like an English paper and sort of true.

"Lauren?" her dad said.

"Sure, OK."

They gathered sweatshirts and blankets. In the van, her dad set two bottles of Poland Spring in the cup holders and drank them in quick succession, before they'd even reached the freeway. Lauren was behind him, Joe behind their mom, his whole body angled toward the window.

"A week till Christmas," their mom said, looking back. "Any last requests?"

Lauren considered. She'd asked for clothes so far—and a new cell phone, to replace one she'd lost. It was kind of a sneaky request; how could they deny her a new cell phone now? But whatever.

She shrugged.

"Joe?" her mom said.

He looked up. "Yeah?"

"Is there anything you want for Christmas that you haven't told me about?"

"Oh. Nah."

They took 92 up the mountain, the road twisty and surrounded by forest. At the top, the Skylawn Cemetery. Today, a funeral procession blocked the way, and for a while they just sat there, waiting. At last they crossed the intersection and began the descent to Half Moon Bay. Lauren could see the ocean, steel colored under a gray sky. It was going to be ridiculously cold on the beach. What were they going to do, huddle on blankets, count the minutes until they could reasonably leave?

Down they went, slowly, slowly, slowly: there was a lot of traffic.

"Kind of late for people to be coming over here for trees," Lauren's dad said.

Lauren saw her mom open her mouth as if to disagree, then close it.

"Joe," she said, turning around again, "do you want to miss school Friday and head up to Tahoe Thursday afternoon?"

"OK," Joe said. "Whatever."

"Hang on," Lauren's dad said. "I have to think about that."

"So do I," Lauren said. Her mom swiveled her head and went all concerned looking, and Lauren said, "I was kidding," which she in fact had been, but she could go with it as serious—she kind of liked it, actually.

They reached the flats on the ocean side, and now they wound past nurseries and Christmas-tree farms. They passed the pony ride place, and Lauren registered it not so much as the pony ride place but as the place about which they always used to say, *There's the pony ride place.* She remembered coming over here to the pumpkin festival once, with her mom and Sarabeth, just the three of them. Sarabeth had bought her a little wooden witch riding a broom that had bristles of real straw. In the hospital, Lauren had kind of hoped she'd see Sarabeth when she got home, but if her mom and Sarabeth were in a fight, who knew when that would happen. And what kind of weird fight were they in? Her mom wasn't the fighting type.

At last they reached the light at Main Street. The clouds were darkening: massing over the horizon, coming inland to mingle with the high fog.

They took their usual access road to their usual parking area. Outside the van, the wind was ferocious. They ducked their heads, rounded their shoulders, shoved their hands into their sweatshirt pockets. At the path, Joe took the lead; Lauren was in the rear, just behind her dad. The water was vast and dark, edged by a long, wide stretch of beach. They were at the top of a cliff, and Joe picked his way through beach grass and shrubs until he came to a steep, narrow trail down to the sand.

Her mom was afraid of heights. Or no: of falling. Without a look back, Joe skipped his way down, but her mom only glanced back over her shoulder and then hesitantly took a single step. She waited, then brought the other foot after her and stopped.

Help her, Lauren thought, but her dad didn't move.

Again, her mom moved one foot, and then, very slowly, the other. There was a turn in the trail now, and Lauren couldn't see the angle of descent, but her mom's stillness told her it was getting steeper. Her dad put his hands on his hips.

Her mom stepped down again, but now she slipped a little and gasped, and she reached a quick hand to the ground to steady herself. "Ow," she exclaimed, and she pulled the hand right back and looked at it, then clapped her palm against her jeans and stared straight ahead.

"Dad," Lauren said in a low voice.

He turned.

"Help her."

"She's OK."

She couldn't stand it. She stepped past him and said, "Want a hand? I can go ahead of you, you can hold my shoulder."

"Just go on down," her dad said in a nice-enough voice, but it was like that was it, no choices, Lauren had to go. Her mom smiled at her—*it's OK*—and Lauren shrugged and made her way down. From the beach she looked back up. Her dad was in front of her mom now, her mom's hand on her dad's shoulder.

Joe came up. "What are they doing?"

"They're coming."

With the toe of his sneaker he lifted a piece of seaweed and flung it away. He looked straight at her with a question he'd never ask, and she felt her face warm and looked up again. Her parents had taken another step or two, but they had a ways to go.

"Come on," she said, and she and Joe started toward the water, as if there might be something to see in it that they couldn't see from where they were now.

To Brody, Liz's hand felt light—as if she didn't want to trust him with her weight. He took a step, then waited for her to follow. Another, and she hesitated and then came, too. He remembered a time, maybe twenty years ago, when she had ridden him piggyback. "I'll make you fall," she'd laughingly warned him, but he'd turned his back and reached for her thighs, and she'd gone along with it. They were south of Carmel, cypresses black against the blue sky, a cold wind freezing Brody's ears. Were they married yet? He didn't think so. She was heavy. At the steeper parts it took all his leg strength to brace them against falling. Point Lobos, that's where it was. On her back was a little knapsack of food, and once at the water's edge they sat on a high rock and ate sandwiches and Oreos, bought—the Oreos—by him because she'd said at some point that she couldn't stop eating them once she started, and he wanted to see this, evidence of a ravenous appetite. On the rough rock, she proved it. She ate twelve Oreos, sixteen. Then she lay back and groaned happily, and he bent over her and licked the black crumbs from the corners of her mouth.

"Thanks," she said now, as they reached the beach.

He turned back to face her. "Sure."

"Cold?"

"You bet." He offered her his hand, and after a moment's hesitation she took it. The kids weren't in sight. They crested the high point of the beach and stopped, looking at the ocean. It was not so dark from here—more foamy, green-gray. Two men and a young woman—a girl?—walked away from them, to the south. In the other direction, Lauren and Joe headed north, paralleling the waterline, Joe several feet ahead of Lauren. As Brody watched, Lauren bent to look at something in the sand, and, without turning around, Joe paused, too.

Liz seemed about to speak and then didn't. They stood there watching their children, hands still together. This trip to the beach, Brody thought, this day in the cold air. Couldn't it help them all?

25

$\mathcal{L}$ ike most of their cohorts in the choral group, Liz's parents had dressed in Christmas colors, her father in a dark green sweater with reindeer on it, her mother in her red velvet pants and a sweater appliquéd with a Christmas tree. Though held at a church, the program had been billed as multicultural, and hanging above the singers was a banner reading CELEBRATE YOUR HOLIDAY in a dozen languages.

Liz and Brody and the kids were in a pew about halfway back. Brody and the kids seemed to be on autopilot, but when the sing-along part of the program started, Liz tried to hum along and then actually joined in on her favorite, "Deck the Halls." To her surprise, the mere act of singing lifted her, and as the verses continued she raised her voice. She remembered one Christmas when she was a very little girl, standing with her family on the porch of their house in Swarthmore and listening as a group of caroling neighbors filled the night air with song. Afterward, back inside the house, she took hold of Steve's hands and did a ring-around-the-rosy with him, she was so happy.

Cookies and cider were served in the community room once the concert was over. Liz's parents rushed to say hello, and again her mother couldn't look at Lauren. "It was wonderful," Liz said. "Didn't you think so, Lauren?"

Lauren nodded. That afternoon the two of them had gone to get Lauren an outfit for this occasion, and she looked pale but pretty in the long-sleeved lacy black dress she'd chosen, in the pointy-toed pumps Liz had bought despite the high price and the fact that they looked like something Carrie Bradshaw would wear.

Liz's father commandeered Joe for a raid on the refreshments, and when they were gone, her mother said to Lauren, "Grandpa's so glad you're here, dear."

What was she thinking, saying something like that? Why not *I'm so glad you're here*? Liz glanced at Brody, but he seemed not to have heard. He saw her looking, though, and he leaned close and murmured that he was going to get some air. "Go for it," she murmured back. Since Sunday at the beach, things had seemed better between them. They'd decided to leave for Tahoe on Thursday, which—their having made a decision together—had felt like a step in the right direction.

She told her mother this now.

"But that means you'll have to open the house," her mother said.

"I think we can manage."

"But Dad and I were going to drive as far as Auburn Thursday night and then get up there Friday morning to open it for you."

"Is that your preference?"

"Well, no, but I thought it would be yours. You always used to like to come into a house with heat. You said it was hard to arrive with kids and groceries and presents and have to get the house in order before you could do anything else."

"That was when the kids were little," Liz said, and then she stopped herself: there was no point to this. "Festive sweater," she remarked.

"Isn't it fun?" her mother said with a big smile. "There's a wonderful shop in Los Gatos that has all kinds of things like this. I could go back and see if they have one in your size."

"That's OK," Liz said. "I mean thanks, but I seem to have a ton of holiday clothes already."

They stood for a long moment without speaking. Lauren looked bored, but also as if she didn't dare venture away.

"So we'll be ten," Liz said.

Her mother looked surprised. "I thought eleven."

"Where'd you get eleven?"

"Isn't Sarabeth coming?"

Liz felt Lauren looking at her. "Actually, I hadn't invited her."

Her mother's eyes widened. "No? After Thanksgiving I would have thought—"

She broke off talking, and Liz smiled at Lauren in what she thought was an encouraging, don't-mind-her way, but Lauren remained impassive.

"The goods are good," Liz's father said, rejoining them with a plate of treats in one hand, a Styrofoam cup of cider in the other. "Cookie?" he said to Lauren.

"No, thanks. Actually, I have to go to the bathroom."

"Do you want me to go with you?" Liz said.

"*Mom,*" her father said, and he elbowed Lauren for a smile she didn't give.

Liz watched as Lauren navigated her way through the crowd, then she forced herself to turn back to her parents. They were old: they were old and grief stricken and trying. At the moment, however, she could not spend another minute with them.

She said, "I think I'll check out those goods myself."

Plunging into the crowd, she squeezed past white-haired singers and well-dressed men and women her own age and doted-upon young children with sticky fingers and the kind of excitement that would make bedtime difficult.

At last she reached the food. There were thick squares of dark molasses-heavy gingerbread, butter cookies decorated with red and green sprinkles, powdered-sugar pecan balls, and fudge with walnuts. Someone had made tiny Christmas-tree cakes, iced in green and finished with silver dragées, and Liz helped herself to one of these. She took a big bite: the cloying sweetness of canned frosting. How poignant it was to think of these elderly people providing treats for their families and friends. She thought of Esther, the old woman who brought Sarabeth bad cookies and old postcards. Last year at Christmas Sarabeth had made dozens of little books to give as gifts, each with a loop of golden thread so it could be hung on the limb of a tree if the recipient desired. She gave them to Esther and her other listeners at the Center, to her friends, to her clients. She used scraps of lampshade paper supplemented by several sheets she went out and bought for the occasion. Liz's was in the shape of a leaf, the cover cut from red leather. When Liz opened it, she saw that each page was made of a different color of tissue paper, reds going to oranges to yellows, to lovely spring greens at the very end.

It was too warm in this room. Brody had been right: air was what was needed. Liz chucked the cake and made her way to the door, pulling her coat on and rearranging her scarf to swathe her neck and throat. The church was in south Palo Alto, just off Middlefield. She followed a path to the front but didn't see Brody. The neighborhood was festooned with Christmas lights—on trees, fences, rooflines, several herds of wire reindeer. She took her cell phone from her purse and turned it back on. She had bought a very snazzy new one for Lauren, and for a moment she rued her own, twice the size it needed to be, scuffed from sharing space in her purse with keys, pens, the metal clasp of her wallet.

She found the number and pressed CALL, and the phone rang three times and then switched to Sarabeth's recorded voice. Was it the same message as ever? The words were the old words, but they seemed different somehow: tinged with dullness.

After the concert, Joe went to his room to do homework while Lauren lay on her bed and did nothing at all. She had some assignments for school, but there was no hurry. That there was no hurry was actually how she felt a lot these days. Time was surprisingly slow.

She pulled up the left sleeve of her dress and moved her fingertip along one of her scars. She was worried about Jeff Shannon, worried and freaked out about seeing him, no matter what Dr. Lewis said about how you never knew what another person was thinking. She wondered if she could hide from him somehow once she was back at school, and if she could successfully *make* herself hide if that was what she decided to do. It would be just like her to decide to hide and then change her mind at the last minute, or not even really change her mind—more change her feet, her legs, go where she hadn't intended to go. She was worried about school in general, and as she stroked the next scar she thought of it: the first view you got of the main building facing the street, the loadies and other class cutters hanging out on the curb, already gone; then the inner terrace, where the jocks and cheerleaders stood near the big oak tree, all of them smiling all the time, like they were in some group toothpaste ad; then the library, the science wing, the gym. She didn't want to go back, didn't see how she could when she was so ugly. She stroked the next scar: she was so ugly. Her mom had bought her this dress and it was like, why bother when she was so ugly? She was so ugly and she was such a loser. Such a loser, such a loser: it was like a line from a song, and she hummed it over and over as she stroked the last scar. The scars all felt the same, almost silky, the only difference their lengths. The third one was the longest. She didn't know which cut she'd made first, but she kind of thought it must have been the third one. She touched the scars again and thought of: Jeff Shannon, school, how ugly she was, what a loser. The Jeff Shannon scar was about an inch long, starting at the base of her thumb and angling diagonally down her wrist. The school scar was a little longer. How ugly she was—that was the third one, almost two inches long, more sideways than diagonal. The last was barely half an inch, but at times it had been the most painful because the cut was so deep. They went: Jeff Shannon. School. How ugly she was. What a loser. The scars were raised and paler in color than they had been. She stroked them again and then switched hands, pulling back her right sleeve to expose what she'd done there. Not as much—just the two cuts, and with her already damaged left hand, so they weren't very deep or long. She ran a finger over the first scar, then the second. She pushed the sleeve back over them. She touched the scars on her left wrist again, keeping her fingertip slow, keeping the pressure light. Jeff Shannon, school, how ugly she was, what a loser.

She heard the dishwasher go on downstairs: her mom was heading for bed. Soon, when her mom was asleep, her dad would sneak out to play tennis. Lauren heard him almost every night: leaving or returning, the sound of the garage door, his steps in the empty kitchen. Her mom didn't know about it, she was sure. Her mom, who had always known about everything. She never went to yoga anymore, never talked on the phone. Joe hardly talked at all. She wondered again: Had he been like that before? Leaving the church tonight, he'd said, "Bye, Grandpa," and for some reason it had made Lauren want to cry.

She sat up slowly. What she knew now was that she had low blood pressure. Well, that was one thing. She had low blood pressure, so she couldn't stand up too fast. She thought of it as a kind of secret, a valuable secret she'd keep hidden from anyone who might enjoy the sensation, that spinning, the yellowy light.

At her closet she took off her new dress and hung it back on the store hanger. She peeled her nylons over her hips and butt and thighs. She hated the way nylons looked after you'd worn them, lying on the floor with all the roundness of your ass preserved. It made her want to throw them away.

She did love her new shoes, though. She pulled on a nightgown and then sat in front of her closet and brought one of the shoes to her face. The smooth black leather, the beautiful new-leather smell. They were so pointy. They totally squished her toes, but that was OK. They had straps and narrow, high heels—they were actually very *Sex and the City,* though she hadn't said that to her mom.

On her way to brush her teeth she paused outside Joe's room. His door was ajar, and she could hear his pencil tapping on a book. She pushed the door open a little. She thought he'd notice, thought he'd say something, but he didn't—probably too into his homework, maybe even listening to his iPod. She pushed it a little more. Just a little more after that, and she could see his feet at the end of his bed. She waited. It was weird that he hadn't said anything. She pushed it open all the way, thinking she just wanted to see what he was doing, just wanted to see if he was reading or what, listening to music or what, and he was sitting there staring right at her.

"Oh, sorry."

He shrugged. A textbook was open on his lap, and the pencil he'd been tapping was still in his hand.

"What are you doing?" she said.

"Math." He sat there for a moment, then he held up the book for her to see.

She remembered when she was in eighth grade, when she'd had that algebra book. Sitting at the kitchen table, her dad trying to help her, and how she couldn't, couldn't, couldn't get it. "I hate math," she said.

Joe kept his eyes away from her. At her grandparents' concert, coming out of the bathroom a little before her dad found her and said it was time to go, she saw Joe standing by himself across the room, hands in the pockets of his khakis, looking like he could stand there forever if he had to.

He'd changed out of his nice clothes, into sweats. His hair was long for him, dark.

"Are you going to ski?" she said, though it was a stupid question; of course he was.

"Yeah," he said. "I guess. Are you?"

"I guess. Kelly and Mom won't."

"Probably not."

Ski mornings in the Tahoe house, everyone walking around in long underwear and sweaters, waiting until the last minute to put on their wind pants. Her mom and her aunt in their bathrobes, holding cups of coffee. And her grandma, too. Her mom and her aunt used to ski, but not her grandma. She would stay at the house and make stew for dinner, or layer cakes because the twins loved them. It was going to be weird to see her aunt and uncle and cousins after what had happened. She wondered what they'd done for Thanksgiving instead. If they were mad at her.

Joe had the same look on his face as earlier, at the church: he could sit like this forever. He wouldn't have to say anything. He wouldn't care if she did. She wasn't like that at all. She had to say something, felt it as if the words, whatever they might be, were accumulating pressure inside her, until she—or they—would burst. This made her think of Lucas, and she wondered, for the zillionth time, what was going to happen to him. "What are you giving Dad?" she said.

"I don't know. A sweater."

"I'm giving him a tennis shirt."

Joe tapped his pencil once, then two more times. Still his face was blank. She felt ridiculous all of a sudden. Left his room and went into the bathroom, where she closed the door and turned on the water. Why was she here? She stared at the mirror as the water began to warm and steam. She couldn't figure out if she looked like herself or not.

It was hard for her to get to sleep. Dr. Lewis had said it could be the Prozac, but it had been hard before. She lay in bed and listened as the nighttime sounds came. Joe in the bathroom. The TV downstairs. Much later, the click of the garage door.

Falling asleep was letting go—Dr. Lewis had said that, too. Letting go of the wish for sleep. Sometimes she felt she was close, but then she would notice she was close and *that* would wake her. "Ah, yes," Dr. Lewis had said with a smile. "That old trick." Yesterday, for the first time, she'd seen him at his office in Burlingame. Mondays at four-twenty—that was going to be her regular time. She would also see him Thursdays at three-fifty. His office was in an old house, and she'd sat on a nice leather chair and talked to him across a blue rug, and it had been stranger than strange.

Lauren dipped and rose, dipped and rose. It seemed that she would never sleep, but with each dip she lost consciousness, first for just a few seconds, then for longer and longer. She didn't know that she slept, and so her sleep was not restful. It felt like no sleep at all.

Liz's was the opposite, a sleep so deep she didn't stir when Brody came in. She was far gone, dreaming of little girls in Christmas dresses. He was chilled from sweating in the cold night air, and he showered, but still she didn't know a thing. She didn't know when he got into bed, didn't know when he turned from one side to the other, his shoulder aching, his mind restless until he took himself to the top of Keyhole and pointed his skis down the mountain.

Joe was thinking of skiing, too, or dreaming of it. Not a specific run, more the swoops and jumps, the fine tailspray of powder. He might wake—he often did lately—and if that happened he'd bolt upright and then get out of bed. Waking in the night was new, though he recognized something very old in it, and whenever it happened he half expected the hall light to go on, his mom or dad to hurry in, tying the belt on a bathrobe, saying, *Shh, shh, what is it, you had a bad dream, it's OK.* Or not saying that, not saying anything. Sometimes he remembered things he wasn't sure had ever happened.

If he woke, he would turn on his desk lamp and open his astronomy book. It was a textbook, kind of dry, but he liked it, liked reading it, especially at night. He had another astronomy book, about the constellations, but the constellations didn't interest him; they were too much like fairy tales, myths, fantasies of the kind Trent read. Stars were just stars, as far as Joe was concerned. Not parts of stories.

26

She parked at the end of the block, in front of a house where a party seemed to be ending: people spilled down the walk calling goodbye, happy holidays, see you in the New Year. She'd been at a party, too: her book group's annual gift exchange. Locking her car, she could feel the glass of wine she'd drunk, a band of warmth across the bridge of her nose and onto her cheeks.

It had been a strange evening. For the first time in weeks she'd known exactly what Liz was doing, and because she'd known, she'd been unable to stop picturing it: Liz in a church in Palo Alto; Liz and Brody and Lauren and Joe, lined up in a pew; Liz in a dressy top and maybe her diamond earrings, holding a program in the way she always held programs, with both hands, her thumbs forming a triangle on top of the paper; Liz waving at people, nudging Brody to wave, waving some more.

It was on Sarabeth's calendar was how she knew. "Rbt & Marg concert." *Of course it'll be boring,* Liz had said back when she first told Sarabeth to mark the date. *You should come.*

The night was cold and damp. Sarabeth walked past the Heidts' house, which was decorated with colored lights along the rooflines and a grove of giant candy canes at the edge of the front yard. Last Christmas they'd gone away for a week, and she hoped they were going away this year, too.

She turned up the driveway. She'd forgotten to leave a light on, and her house was almost invisible. Back from the street, hidden from the moonlight by trees, it was little more than a dark mass. She passed the Volvo, slowing as the light from the street ebbed. She was just a few yards from her steps, picking her way along the walk, when a figure loomed up before her, someone on her porch, and she screamed.

"It's me, it's me," Mark said, stepping toward her. "God, I'm sorry. I didn't know how not to scare you. I knew this was going to happen."

Her pulse raced, and she turned her back on him and burst into tears.

"Sarabeth, I'm so sorry."

She sobbed into her hands. She heard someone call her name, and she looked up to see Rick Heidt standing in his kitchen doorway, the room lit behind him.

"Oh, Rick," she called. "I'm sorry. I'm OK."

"We heard a scream."

"I thought I saw something. But it was nothing."

"Are you sure?"

On her porch, a creak suggested some movement by Mark—deeper into the darkness.

"Yes, I'm fine. But thanks so much."

He waited a moment before moving back into the kitchen. "Anytime, you know. We're here."

Once his kitchen light was off, she turned around. She could see Mark now, his tall body outlined against her front door. She said, "What are you doing here?"

"Waiting for you."

She found her keys. Taking a deep breath, she stepped up onto the porch, then stood next to him as she unlocked the door. Inside, she groped for the light switch. He was still outside, and she flipped on the porch light and gestured for him to come in.

He hesitated. "Is it OK?"

He looked more put together than the other time—shaven, less hollow eyed. He wore a red plaid scarf around his neck.

"I got your message," she said.

He inhaled and lifted his shoulders, then sighed and let them drop. Nothing would happen: she decided it in that moment. Knew it. Decided it.

"I'm going to have some tea," she said. "Mint. Would you like some?"

"Please."

She led the way into the kitchen. There were dirty dishes on the counter, two pieces of apple browning on a cutting board. She took her kettle and filled it, then set it back on the stove. "Hang on a sec," she said, and she moved past him through the doorway, to the stuff on the living room floor. She picked up the two mugs and brought them back into the kitchen. She turned the water back on, waited for it to get hot, and then washed them thoroughly. She faced him.

"Have you cheated on her before?"

At once he shook his head. Then he put his fingers over his mouth and said, "Sort of."

"How do you sort of cheat? Does it depend on the meaning of the word 'is'?"

He half smiled. "She knew about it."

"She gave you permission?"

"It was more a matter of looking the other way."

"I'm sorry," she said. "It's none of my business." She got out the tea bags, tagless little paper squares. She dropped one in each mug.

He was standing in the middle of the room, his coat still buttoned, his lips pale and chapped. He unbuttoned his coat, loosened the plaid scarf. He went and leaned against the wall. "Can I ask you a question?"

"Sure."

"You live alone here. It doesn't seem like you date. I'm just wondering—" He broke off talking and shrugged. "I mean . . ."

"You're wondering what I do for sex?"

He barked out a laugh but didn't correct her.

The kettle began to whistle, and she turned around and switched off the gas. She thought of the dreams of his naked body, of his hands all over her, that had gripped her for at least a week. She faced him again. "I have a vibrator."

His cheeks reddened a little. "And that works for you?"

"Not that well. I haven't figured out how to program it to say it loves me."

He smiled, but after a moment he moved to the table and sat down and put his face in his hands.

She filled the mugs with water and brought them over, set one near his elbow. Taking the chair opposite his, she said, "I did it for over a year. Guy with two kids."

He looked up. "And a wife?"

"And a dog and a cat and a hamster."

"Really?"

"I think they had a goldfish."

He lifted his mug. "I guess it wasn't a good idea, huh?"

"Not for me."

He blew into his tea and sipped noisily, then put the mug down and rested his chin in his hand. He looked closely at her, and she saw creases bracketing his mouth, the way his cheekbones jutted out under his eyes. It came to her that she didn't know what his face looked like, not really.

He held out his free hand, and she put hers in it. "What's she like?" she said.

"Which one?"

"Either."

He thought for a moment. "She's wiggly. And sticky. And when I give her a cookie she makes this excited little squeak, like a monkey."

"I assume this is Maud."

They both smiled. After a moment he squeezed her hand and let go. He picked up his tea and blew into it again.

"Are you guys talking?"

"Mary and me? Sure, about diapers. And soy milk, and blackout shades." He took a sip of tea. "Actually, that's not true. But it's hard to have much of a conversation about how freaked out I am. I mean, who has time?"

Sarabeth thought of the years when Lauren and Joe were young, how she'd almost lost Liz then—had felt, many times, that she *had* lost her. But then she'd miraculously call at a time when the kids were sleeping, or at preschool, and Liz would say, "Oh, thank God, I've been dying to talk to someone who doesn't need something from me."

Had she lost Liz now?

She looked at Mark again, his big hands wrapping the mug. She said, "What did you talk about before?"

"Nothing," he said with a shrug. "Everything."

She blew into her tea. Steam still rose from the surface, and she wondered how he'd been able to drink his. She brought her mug close to her mouth and just held it there, letting the warmth bathe her upper lip.

"Mark?" she said.

"Don't tell me it'll be OK."

She didn't. Instead, she looked at his hands, at the bones of his wrists. She imagined a life of talking about nothing and everything: a consummation—how did it go? A consummation devoutly to be wished.

With a sheepish smile, he dug into his jeans pocket and tossed something onto the table. It was a condom. She put her mug down and reached for it. After a moment she opened the package and pulled the condom out. She brought it to her nose, and it smelled like plastic, which it was. She and Billy had used condoms, condoms and her diaphragm simultaneously. No risks. She remembered a time when she tried to roll the condom off him, during sex; she just wanted to feel him inside her, no latex between them, just once. She'd just finished her period, which he knew. But he pulled out and rolled off her right away, then sat up and said in a voice so firm it scared her, *No*.

Mark took the condom from her. He pinched the tip and unrolled it little by little. When it was open he laid it on the table between them. It was odd to see one open on a table, the blousy shape, the thinness. After a moment, he turned it so the tip was facing her. "Pow," he said.

They talked a little more, and then she saw him out and cleaned the kitchen and got into bed. It was very cold. She thought of getting a heating pad, but she knew her body would warm the sheets after a while—slowly, the way a single body did. Everyone was in bed now: Jim with Donald, Liz across the bay with Brody, Mark with Mary. She didn't know what to do with it, how she could see bodies in beds and how she was one. It was dizzying to go up and down like this: others as if from far above, and herself here. She saw a pool of light on the couples, light in the spaces between them, the spaces they defined by lying together. It was in a light like that that she wanted to live. With Billy the light hadn't fully existed because she'd been unable to keep it with her when she was alone. Or it had existed, but it was a false light, light like a false spring, flowers blooming too early and doomed to die. She thought her mother had been a flower sort of like that, a flower that lacked the support of a stem: all blossom, already browning at the edges.

When the weak December sun woke her eight hours later, she was thinking this again, seeing it: tender petals tinged by their unhappy fate, evident if you looked. She lay in bed, and her room—her life—seemed a place she had wandered into by accident. Bedroom to bedroom, dust to dust. On Cowper Street there must have been a time when her parents had lived together in a pool of light, but she could not remember it. Always, they had been separate, and she separate from them. And yet this morning she had a feeling of some other story than the one she knew. What if she could find it and furnish it with happy times? What would she put in it? Her mother and herself, on the floor with blocks, building and laughing. Her parents holding hands on the living room couch. Her father taking her to the park while her mother stayed home and happily cooked the family's favorite dinner. She could invent all kinds of things, and once invented they could take on substance, mass; they could go head to head with what she knew. Which, then, would be more real? Her mother and herself on the floor with blocks, building and laughing: could she say absolutely that it hadn't happened? Her eyes welled, streamed. She lay in bed, got up, ate, returned to bed. Minutes turned to hours. Still she stayed in bed, while shadows moved across the floor, tracking the progress of the day.

In the evening she got up. She went into her workroom and calmly began cutting bits of scrap paper into squares. Last year she had done nearly this, made tiny books as gifts. Tonight she was on to a lampshade. "Patchwork," she would call it. On a white background she glued the squares: some were translucent, some were opaque; some of the colors were pale, some were dark, some were bright. What she liked was the way they looked together, how each was its own but also part of what they all were together. In randomness there lay a secret order, or so it was sometimes nice to think. She left the work to dry, ate bread and fruit, got back into bed. She slept fitfully, waking to images of Lorelei and herself, of Liz and Lauren, of Mary and Maud. The men were standing against the walls of her bedroom, guarding her. Rick Heidt was there, too.

In the morning she took a bath, lifting one leg and then the other to shave away the long wiry hairs of winter. She sank under the water, lifted her head, and thought fleetingly of Glenn Close in *Fatal Attraction,* bursting from the bath, a woman who had been stirred, whisked, beaten to a frenzy. By passion, by desperation.

She got out of the tub, dressed, went into the kitchen. Why the same thing every day, why tea and then coffee? She wanted cherry cider; she didn't know why.

She bundled up and left the house, out for the first time since Tuesday. It was Thursday now, and the world was as busy as ever—busier, because Christmas was just three days away. Andronico's was mobbed with couples and families, everyone pushing carts loaded with food. She collected cherry cider, out-of-season asparagus, and a miniature key lime pie. She didn't even need a basket.

Her hair was still wet, and as she walked home she felt her toes going numb from the cold. What would she do when she got back—drink cider, peel asparagus, return to the patchwork lampshade? Something she'd possessed earlier was gone again now.

She was panting lightly when she got home, her breath just visible in the cold air. The Volvo was gone. Up the empty driveway she walked, into her house, into her kitchen. She thought to check for messages, thought she hadn't been gone *that* long, lifted the handset anyway. To her surprise, the stutter tone. She realized she wanted a message from Mark, and she put the handset back in the cradle. But she couldn't live this way.

She lifted the handset again and got to her voice mail, and the voice said, "Sent. Tuesday. At nine-seventeen p.m." Tuesday? she thought, but then there was no more time to think because Liz's voice was saying: "Are you there? It's me—Liz. Sarabeth? Are you there?" There was a pause, and then she said, "I miss you. Call me." And standing in her kitchen, Sarabeth burst into a thousand pieces of bliss that rained lightly and colorfully onto the floor.

part three

27

*I*t was so foggy on the freeway that Liz stayed in the slow lane, heart hammering, wondering if it had been a mistake to go out. She couldn't see anything but the road just ahead, and she flinched whenever a pair of headlights loomed up behind her. She began watching for exits, for a way down out of the hills, down to the streets of Hillsborough or Millbrae, where she would be able to see houses and find a safe way home. She would not take such an exit, but she watched anyway.

It was the first week of January, and she was on her way to have dinner with Sarabeth. They had talked a few times over the holidays, and for quite a while once Liz was back from Tahoe, but they hadn't seen each other since . . . *since.* Liz was eager to get things back to normal.

The fog lifted as she approached Colma, and she sped up, feeling for a moment that she could leave her fear behind, though of course the feeling of it stayed with her, beating through her bloodstream. Again, the thought that she should have stayed home. How did agoraphobia start? She had begun thinking differently—or maybe just more—about mental problems. What defined paranoia? Or obsessive-compulsive disorder? She could not go to bed until the kitchen was spotless.

In the city, she parked in her usual garage and walked the three long blocks to the Thai place. She passed people slouched in doorways holding signs that asked for money. There were times when the truths of the world—its reports on the multitude of ways there were to suffer—pressed in so hard that she felt she couldn't bear it. What did it mean that she did bear it? What was the wall inside her made of that it kept such truths away?

At the restaurant she was seated and ordered wine. She hoped it would be OK, seeing Sarabeth. Their phone conversations had had a strained feeling. Would seeing her feel strained, too? The part of Liz that hated the fog, that hated the way she feared the fog, hated this, too.

The door opened and Sarabeth rushed in. Evidently it had begun to rain; Liz watched as she struggled to close an umbrella, head bent to the task, though Liz also had the impression that she was hiding.

At last she looked up. Her face was tiny and white, her hair curling wildly around it. As she searched for Liz, she bit her lip.

Liz raised her hand, and Sarabeth saw her.

"I'm so sorry," she said, rushing over. "I couldn't park."

"You're not late." Liz stood, and they both hesitated for a moment before they hugged. Sarabeth felt thin, but it was hard to be sure—she pulled away quickly.

She shrugged off her coat and then, avoiding Liz's eyes, looked over at the hostess stand. "Duh," she said, and she carried the coat away.

She *was* thin, and when she came back, Liz saw that there were dark crescents under her eyes.

"Sit," Liz said.

Sarabeth pulled out her chair and sat. She said, "So how's it been so far? School, I mean."

Today had been Lauren's third day back, and as on the first two she had moved slowly and reluctantly through the familiar morning rituals of getting ready. On the other hand, each afternoon she'd seemed easier than the previous, and tonight, as Liz was getting ready to leave, she even complained a little about her homework. Liz took it as a good sign that she would mention school at all.

"You know, I'm not sure," Liz said. "I can't really tell. And I can't imagine ever trusting my judgment again anyway, so—" She shrugged and reached for her wineglass.

"You will," Sarabeth said.

"What?"

"Trust your judgment again."

"No, I won't!" Liz had spoken more emphatically than she'd

intended, but this was the truth: she would never have full confidence in herself again.

Sarabeth looked alarmed, and Liz knew she should say something, but what? This was exactly how she'd felt on the phone. She had a script in front of her, but she couldn't quite read it. Couldn't speak it.

The waitress approached, and for a while there was business to occupy them: Sarabeth's wine order and then the question of whether or not to order dinner now, too. Liz hoped they would, then swallowed the wish when Sarabeth told the waitress they needed more time.

"How are you?" Sarabeth said when the woman was gone.

"How are *you*?"

Sarabeth's eyes filled, and Liz felt bad; she'd sounded testy, turning the question around without answering it. Why couldn't she be a nice, reasonable person? She leaned forward and said, "Really, how *are* you? You look thin, have you been eating?"

"I'm fine," Sarabeth said. "Tell me more about Lauren. Was she OK about therapy Monday?"

At Tahoe, Lauren had said she didn't want to go back to Dr. Lewis, but on Monday morning she'd just nodded complacently when Liz reminded her she had an appointment after school.

"She was fine with it. It was kind of strange, really, given how adamant she was over Christmas."

"Maybe she didn't mean it."

"Like it was a pro forma thing?"

"Or a test."

Liz took a sip of wine and thought of Tahoe, how flat Lauren had seemed. On the phone Monday morning, returning Liz's call, Dr. Lewis had suggested the flatness might have been Lauren's strategy for coping with the time till school started again—anesthetizing herself because she was anxious. Which had made Liz feel it might have been a mistake to go to Tahoe in the first place. She remembered the first day up there, how she'd chosen not to ski and then spent the entire time worrying, puttering around the kitchen with her mother and Kelly when what she really wanted was to get to the slopes herself, hitchhike if she had to, to see how Lauren was. She'd skied the entire rest of the time, freezing, her legs killing her, but with Lauren never far away.

She looked at Sarabeth again. "*Are* you eating? I haven't seen you this thin in a while."

"I am now."

"What do you mean?"

"Here she is," Sarabeth said, and she looked up as the waitress arrived at their table.

By habit, Liz opened her menu. Appetizers, Soups, Curries, Noodles, Rice: she imagined ordering something different this time, pad thai, for example, or *green* curry beef. She looked up and saw that Sarabeth was waiting.

"The usual?" Sarabeth said, and after a moment Liz nodded.

When the waitress left, she fingered the base of her wineglass. What was happening at home right now? She reached into her purse and looked at the face of her phone, worried she might have missed a call. But it just said CINGULAR, as usual.

"What did you mean now you're eating?" she said to Sarabeth. "When weren't you?"

Sarabeth colored. "In December for a while."

"Why? What happened?"

"Nothing."

"Sarabeth."

"Really, nothing."

"*Sarabeth.*"

"It was no one thing," Sarabeth said. "And anyway, I don't want to—" She hesitated, and Liz reached across the table and touched her fingertips.

"Whatever it was."

Sarabeth sighed and began telling a story about going to a play in Billy's neighborhood, and something about the neighbor children, and a missed appointment with Jim, and then some reckless-sounding intrigue with Mark Murphy. As she spoke she seemed to relax, her face losing its drawn look, her voice lowering a little. Liz tried hard to stay focused. Whatever was happening at home right now, however Lauren was: Liz was here.

"He looked so wiped out," Sarabeth said, referring to Mark. "*The* darkest circles under his eyes."

"Mmm," Liz said. With a new baby—she didn't doubt it.

Sarabeth leaned forward suddenly. "Do you think it's weird that I didn't have sex with him? *Why* didn't I?"

"Because you didn't want to make the same mistake twice?" Liz said, but she regretted it right away. "Sorry, I didn't mean that. It sounds to me as if you were trying to protect yourself."

"He brought a condom over," Sarabeth said. "The second time. It was kind of sad—he showed it to me like he wanted to admit what he'd been thinking."

"That's not the kind of protection I meant," Liz said, and then she sat there like a stone while Sarabeth's eyes widened in surprise. There was a tingling on the rims of Liz's ears, and her lips felt strange.

Sarabeth looked into her eyes, then quickly looked away again. She wore several slim silver chains around her neck, and she used her forefinger to separate them. Liz took a slow breath in, then released it even more slowly.

"Tell me about Brody," Sarabeth said. "And Joe. How are they?"

What could Liz say? That they were fine and also entirely ruined? Brody's shoulder was killing him, and she was sure it was stress, but when she asked how he was doing he brushed her off. "Getting through," she managed. "You know."

Sarabeth clasped her hands in front of her chest and leaned forward. "Are you mad at me?"

"Don't be silly."

Sarabeth's eyes filled again, and she closed them and pressed her fingertips against them for a moment.

"Maybe *you're* mad at *me,*" Liz said.

"What reason could I possibly have to be mad at you?"

"I have a reason?"

"I *failed* you," Sarabeth said, and Liz felt a wave of fury.

"What happened happened. What do you want me to say?"

"See, you are mad."

"Oh, Sarabeth."

Sarabeth put her face in her hands, and Liz was filled with remorse. What was her problem? She reached across the table and hooked a finger around Sarabeth's pinky, and now Sarabeth began to weep.

"What's going on?" Liz said.

Sarabeth shook her head.

"What? Sweetie."

"It's just"—Sarabeth raised her head and gave Liz a desperate look—"I had a really hard time."

"When? Tell me."

"Starting that day. That weekend."

Liz tried to remember what Sarabeth had said earlier, about the timing of going to the play in Billy's neighborhood. Hadn't there been something about the Sunday when Brody called her with the news about Lauren? A feeling of the story came to Liz, of how the time line of the story had in some sense been the story. But . . . was this actually happening? Was Sarabeth stationing her own misery in the field of what had happened to Liz's family? Was she saying she'd sat on the knowledge of Lauren's trouble, done nothing, because she was upset about having gone to Billy's neighborhood?

She was. She was even saying something about how she'd been alone with her pain because Liz had been busy. That *Liz* had failed *her.*

"I can't believe you," Liz whispered.

Sarabeth's eyes widened. "What?"

"You've been wanting to tell me this since then, haven't you? You've been waiting."

"I—"

"You probably wanted *me* to come see *you!*"

"I never asked you to!"

"You did," Liz exclaimed. "You wanted me to come see you. And you know what? You didn't have to ask. You knew I'd find out. Asking or not asking, you always want something!"

Sarabeth stared at her and Liz stared back. She felt that this was their truth, hers and Sarabeth's—that what she'd just said was the only true thing she could say about the two of them, and Sarabeth knew it. She looked at Sarabeth's crumpled face, and she said: "I'm not your mother."

28

Up in Tilden Park, the nighttime sky was hammocked with low fog. It was gray and gray and purple, and it clung to the treetops like spiderwebs or wasps' nests stuck to old wood. Sarabeth had not wanted to go home, and so she had driven up into the woods, to this place where a woman shouldn't be alone after dark.

The trails were squishy with mud, and the air under the trees was as damp as it would have been if it were raining. She walked until she was out of breath, and then she sat on a bench. All around her were the smells of the wet earth, the leaves. The bench was wet, and her skirt grew damp, followed soon after by her ass. She turned sideways and lay back, and she exhaled and watched the cloud of her breath float away. Away, away: she was in some sense gone herself, far from the agony of what Liz had said. How this could be she didn't know. How she had avoided crying, had left the restaurant and found her car, she didn't know. On the bridge she had imagined herself weeping on Nina's doorstep, collapsing into Jim's arms, but she had steered away from those possibilities. Here and now, they all seemed irrevocably distant, the people she knew: as far away as Earth was from the moon. The planets, the heavens . . . how sad it was that she had never thought of her mother as an angel watching over her, a guardian of her experience.

But how ridiculous: Lorelei could never have done that, never have been that. And Sarabeth didn't believe in stuff like that, anyway. Mystical phenomena, messages embedded in the everyday. "It was meant to happen." The truth was that nothing was meant to happen. Things just did.

She lay on the bench and stared up at the fog. The quiet itself seemed like a sound. She remembered being in Tilden Park one night during college—high on mushrooms, standing naked under a tree. She was with her boyfriend Timothy. Being undressed together felt different here: they were at once shier and emboldened, and they touched each other and separated to look and touched again. She learned that a hand on her breast was one thing in a bedroom, something else entirely when she and her lover were on their feet outside, moving slowly, stopping to watch. They were Adam and Eve. The expulsion from the Garden, the Fall— these took the form throughout the relationship of doubting feelings. She was uncertain, and that was the bed she made, the bed she lay in with him. Is this it? she kept thinking—after sex, during breakfast, in the car on the way to visit his brother at Davis. Then, one day, she was alone at the library, bored with a science textbook, and she realized this *was* it—all there was and all there was going to be. No great change was going to come over him; he was not going to become someone else. She broke up with him.

But the problem had been in her. She understood that now. It had been in the fact that she had wanted more, she had wanted him to make her life marvelous. She saw Liz's face across the table at the restaurant, heard Liz's voice saying *You always want something,* and she sat up quickly. Pinpoints of light swarmed before her eyes. Her shoulders began to shake, and in a moment she was sobbing. It was horrible, what she was, horrible: someone who always wanted something. Liz was right—she *had* wished Liz would come to her during that week in November. She had wished it without really even knowing she was wishing it. She knew it from how ashamed she felt now. She remembered lying on her couch one Sunday, looking at her bird picture and talking to Liz—it was *come to me* she had wanted, and why? So Liz could see her, so Liz could see how terrible she felt. It sickened her to think of it now. She had used Liz, hadn't she? She had used Liz for years, as a cauldron, a repository for everything that hurt, and it had been too much, she had been too much. *I'm not your mother.*

Was a mother a cauldron? What had she poured into Lorelei that had made her so ill?

But this thinking was dangerous, as she knew all too well: the bottomless bog of whose fault it was. Of causality. "The guilt, the guilt," she and her suicide sister used to say—like "the horror, the horror." "Did I drive her to it?" "I may not have driven him to it, but I didn't stop him—I wasn't enough to stop him." All of this was true and best forgotten.

She didn't know where she'd left her car, but she stood and began to walk. Her feet and legs were wet, her ass was wet, and she was cold, cold. She stumbled on rocks and brushed against bushes, but on she walked. Uphill, so that soon her breath came harder. She began to sweat lightly, a film at her hairline and between her breasts. There was the real and the metaphorical: the fact of her muscles and bones, their actualness, their ability to transport her; and this insistent new idea that she, her body, was a vessel for something that could pour out and fill other people, overwhelm them, poison them. That she was toxic.

She touched the trunk of a tree, felt its rough, creviced bark. She leaned against it and then slowly lowered herself to the ground. She had never felt worse.

29

*I*n some ways, it wasn't as bad as she'd expected. The first few days had been intensely weird, people staring at her, the guidance counselor popping up all over the place to see if she was OK, Amanda sort of hyperly nice—as if Lauren were a new girl and Amanda had been assigned the job of making her feel welcome—but now things were kind of normal. She was at school. That was that.

Except for Jeff Shannon. He knew where she'd been, and he knew why: she could tell. The first day, he blushed when he saw her, and then for the next couple days he was obviously pretending *not* to see her when he saw her, and now, every so often, she caught him staring at her from across the terrace at lunch or from his locker before or after class: looking and looking until he saw that she saw him and he quickly looked away.

Today was a Monday, which meant Dr. Lewis after school. She was wearing a top her mom had given her for Christmas and a pair of earrings she'd gotten from Steve and Kelly, very dangly and colorful, sort of like what you saw in magazines.

She ate a spoonful of yogurt. It was raining again, so she and Amanda were eating in the cafeteria, with its pizza smells and crowds of people. "So anyway," Amanda was saying, "he's just, like, different. It's like: *Oh, you're a girl? That's cool. We can be friends.*"

"But do you want to be friends?"

"It's very important to be friends."

"What?" Lauren said, but then she got it. "Oh—is that your mom?"

"Corinna in a mom moment." Amanda rolled her eyes and reached for a French fry. "She comes into my room all, 'I want to save you from making the mistakes I made. Newsflash: you should like the guy'? Like she's this big expert."

Lauren nodded, but she'd just seen Jeff Shannon come into the cafeteria, and she kind of lost a little bit of time whenever she saw him—a few seconds actually shrank out of her life. He was with Tyler Moorhouse and Daniel Black: the Three Stooges, Amanda sometimes called them. Jeff's blue North Face jacket was dripping, but though it had a hood he evidently hadn't been wearing it—his hair was drenched, and as he stood in the food line, he pulled one arm from his jacket and used his shirtsleeve to dry his face.

"So," Amanda said, "I go, 'Newsflash: I'm not taking dating advice from someone who used to think a hard-on was called a hard one.' "

Lauren made herself smile. Jeff grabbed a tray off the stack and reached for silverware. She forced herself to look at Amanda. "So why do you like him? Or how?"

" 'How'?"

This was something Dr. Lewis did, said "how" rather than "why"— she was embarrassed that she'd said it to Amanda. Dr. Lewis wanted her to tell him *how* she felt like a loser, and at first she was like, what's the difference? She kind of got it now: he wanted to hear *what her thoughts were* when she was feeling awful. The thing was, when she told him it made her cry.

"I just mean, you know, what do you like about him?"

Amanda shrugged. "He's nice. He doesn't, you know, goof off all the time. And—yeah."

He was in their chemistry class, but Lauren didn't know him, and the whole thing had started while she was away. He was a theater person, of course. Leaving class the other day, totally out of the blue, he'd said, "To pee or not to pee, that is the question," which might not count as goofing off but was definitely goof-y. Whatever, it was Amanda's problem.

Jeff came out of the food area, his tray loaded. He was following his friends, and with horror Lauren realized they were heading for the empty table next to hers and Amanda's.

"Oh, my God," she said.

Amanda glanced over her shoulder. "What? This is perfect, you can talk to him."

"No way."

In a moment Tyler and Daniel were setting down their trays. Jeff had stopped in the middle of the cafeteria, and as Lauren watched he began scanning the noisy room, looking like he was trying really hard to pretend he was alone, to pretend he hadn't been following his friends until the very moment he'd seen pathetic Lauren Mackay sitting right where they were headed.

"Dude," Tyler shouted.

The cafeteria was jammed with people and incredibly noisy, but Lauren could tell Jeff was faking that he hadn't heard.

Tyler and Daniel were both still on their feet, Tyler's sodden jacket close enough for Lauren to touch. "What's the matter?" Amanda whispered, but Lauren ignored her.

Daniel yanked out his chair but still didn't sit. He said, "What the fuck is wrong with him?" His younger brother had been on Joe's soccer team for years, but Lauren doubted he remembered her. She stared into her yogurt, scraping at the last bit as if she were starving, when in fact she was feeling kind of sick.

"Jeff!" Tyler shouted.

Amanda was staring straight at Lauren. She didn't know about the day, the last day, when Lauren had spoken to Jeff and he had smirked. Only Dr. Lewis knew. And Jeff himself, of course.

Tyler left his tray and headed for the middle of the room, and now Jeff took off, striding in the direction of the side exit, aiming for an empty table by the window. He managed to sit before Tyler reached him. Lauren's heart was racing. They spoke for a moment, and then Tyler headed back alone. She didn't want to hear what he would say to Daniel—yet she did. She reached for her backpack, unzipped it, pretended to look for something.

"What the fuck?" Daniel said as Tyler arrived at the table.

"He's an asshole." Tyler sat down and began to eat. Daniel was half-way through his burger, and they chewed in silence, picked up their sodas at the same moment, put them down, and ate again. Amanda had an obnoxious consoling look on her face, but Lauren ignored her. She watched Jeff's friends out of the corner of her eye. Tyler ate like a machine: bite, chew, chew; bite, chew, chew. He kept his eyes on his plate, even when he drank—he'd pick up his cup, sip hard, put it back down, bite into his burger again. Daniel was more restless—he'd look up and drum his fingers on the table every now and then, glance around the room, scratch his neck. Guys were weird—it was like the two of them weren't even at the same table. Why did they even want Jeff there?

"So," Amanda said. "Do you want to get going?"

"Hang on." Lauren picked up her water bottle and drained it. She looked across the room at Jeff's table, and there he was, head bent low, spoon going to his mouth over and over again, as if he had soup or something. The navy bean had looked disgusting—she hoped he didn't have that.

She stood and got into her jacket, then hefted her backpack onto her shoulder. At the next table, Daniel burped loudly.

"Dude," Tyler said, and then he went back to his lunch.

Dr. Lewis shared a tiny waiting room with three other therapists—just a couch and two chairs in what felt like a closet. Lauren was glad no one else was ever around. As she sat waiting for the door sounds that would tell her his current patient was leaving his office and then departing through what she'd learned was called the privacy exit, she thought that she'd never seen Jeff looking scared before, the way he had at lunch. She felt almost sorry for him, though he was the last person in the world anyone should feel sorry for. He was whatever the opposite of a loser was. Not a winner, that was too one-time. A king?

A jack of diamonds.

She heard Dr. Lewis's office door open. The person before her was a man; sometimes she heard him say goodbye, but not today. The door closed, and then the privacy exit opened and closed. Lauren picked up a magazine, then put it down again. Dr. Lewis had five minutes now, and she always wondered what he did. Listened to messages, returned phone calls? Or would he take off his shoes and lie down for a bit?

She pulled up her sleeve and looked at her scars. They were much lighter now, pink. She stroked them one by one and thought what she always thought: Jeff Shannon, school, how ugly she was, what a loser. The scars felt slightly softer than her regular skin, like short lengths of kitchen string laid on a piece of paper.

All at once she remembered her earrings, and her stomach tipped. Did she have time to get them off? They were kind of flashy; she didn't want Dr. Lewis thinking she'd dressed up for him. She pulled the backing off one, slid the post out of her ear, and then, fingers shaking, replaced the backing on the post and dropped the earring into her coat pocket. Was it safe there with her keys? She didn't have time to reconsider. She took off the other one, and it tapped onto the first just as the light next to Dr. Lewis's name went off. A moment later, he opened the door. He was wearing his purple-and-brown plaid shirt, the shirt she wished he'd throw away, and he smiled and said, "Hi, Lauren."

She had to pass close by him to get into his office. As always, she breathed in for his soap smell—which, as on most Mondays, was not as strong as it usually was on Thursdays, her theory being that he showered later in the day on Thursdays, maybe after going home at lunch to screw his wife.

In his office she took off her coat and sat in the leather chair. He came in after her, closed the door, and sat in the chair opposite.

"So," he said.

He smiled at her, and she looked out the window: at the bare trees and at the rain streaming down the glass. She hated this—hated it. She had no idea what to say. They had even discussed it once, how it was so hard, but that had been really embarrassing in and of itself. Last Thursday, in the morning before she left for school, she had written down some things to talk about with him, but once she was sitting here, feeling his eyes on her, it turned out that the idea of taking the little piece of paper out of her pocket and referring to it in front of him was far worse than miserably racking her brain as usual, and so the piece of paper stayed where it was. Later, at home, she flushed it down the toilet, too embarrassed even to read it again.

"How are you feeling?" he said, shifting a little in his chair and crossing his legs. When he asked questions he always had this concerned you-can-tell-me-anything look on his face, and he had it now.

"OK."

"Where would you like to start today?"

Behind him was a charcoal drawing of an old city street with some kids playing in front of an open fire hydrant. Sometimes, when she squinched her eyes, the arrangement of shapes looked a little like the face of a small, scared animal. Then she unsquinched and wondered how she'd seen anything but the street scene. She said, "Amanda has a new boyfriend. She was bragging about it all through lunch today."

He waited. After a while he said, "Can you tell me more?"

She felt a giggle rising inside her, and she fought to keep it down. In the hospital, Abby had told her about a therapist she'd seen for a while who had a Magic 8 Ball in her waiting room, but instead of stuff like "It is very likely" or "I don't think so," it had responses like "How did that make you feel?" and "Can you tell me more?"

"I don't know," she said. "His name is Noah."

Dr. Lewis made a steeple with his forefingers. "Two by two."

"What?"

"Noah made me think of Noah's ark."

Lauren considered this. "It's been raining a lot."

"It has."

She thought of Jeff coming into the cafeteria, dripping wet. Then, for some reason, of her dad at dinner last night, complaining about the rain like he was really angry, and how her mom acted like there was something wrong with him, minding the rain so much.

"He's avoiding me," she said.

"Jeff?"

She nodded. Dr. Lewis shifted again and recrossed his legs. He kept his eyes on her.

"His friends sat near me and Amanda at lunch today, and, you know, instead of sitting with them he went to this totally different part of the cafeteria."

"And you felt that was because he saw you."

"It *was* because he saw me! It was completely obvious!"

Dr. Lewis sat still for a while. At last he said, "It sounds like a hard moment for you," and she didn't like how she was starting to feel, kind of shaky. "It's very painful for you," he went on, "to think he might be avoiding you," and to her fury she felt an approach of tears. In a moment she was weeping into her hands. He stayed silent. He always did this: made her cry and then just let her cry.

"I would bet," he said once she'd calmed a little, "that Amanda talking about her new boyfriend made the feelings about Jeff harder to tolerate."

"Duh," she said. And then, confused, "Wait— Why?"

"Any ideas?"

She thought about it: Amanda talking about duder—Noah—and Jeff not coming anywhere near her. She pulled up her sleeve and looked at her scars. "They don't hurt at all anymore."

"How is that for you?"

"It's just a fact."

"It's a fact, true, but you might have feelings about it."

Actually, she did: she wished they still hurt. Sometimes she pressed on them to try to recover the way they'd felt as they were healing—so open, so raw. But she couldn't tell him that—he'd say something weird about it. When she told him once that she was afraid of people seeing the scars, he said maybe that was also what she *wanted,* for people to see them. *Maybe the cutting was a way of showing the world how much pain you're in. A way of making it visible.* Blech.

She reached for a Kleenex and folded it in half, then in half again.

"I have some ideas about why today might have been hard for you," he said.

"What?"

"If Amanda has a boyfriend, then she has something you want and don't have, so you might be having some pretty painful competitive feelings. In addition, you might worry that you won't see her as much anymore now that she's dating Noah."

"She isn't *dating* him."

"Oh. What would you call it? I don't know what you'd call it."

"She isn't *anything*ing him. She just likes him, and he likes her back. I—I lied earlier."

"You lied."

"I said she has a new boyfriend, but she doesn't really. Not yet, anyway. I lied."

"Imagining things can make them feel true."

"No, I lied."

"I see."

She looked down at the Kleenex, and all at once she began pulling it apart, shredding it until her lap began to fill with bits of fluff. There had been times when she'd forgotten what a geek he was, but here it was again. She didn't want to come here anymore. In the hospital she'd had this bizarre feeling that as long as she kept seeing him she'd be OK. Even this morning she had sort of wanted to see him. What was her problem? She was like some crazy person, always changing her mind. She had more than half an hour to go. Her mom would never let her quit coming, either. More than half an hour today, and hours and hours for however long it would take everyone to believe she wasn't "at risk" anymore. She hated that: "at risk." Like at any moment she'd do it again. She would never. Never. She hadn't even really meant it! Dr. Lewis had said so: she knew her mom was coming home; she knew she'd be found in time.

"Where'd you go?" he said.

He was watching her. The Kleenex was all over the place, and her face warmed as she plucked bits of it from her pants and tried to gather them in her hand. He was always so calm—she didn't think it was fair. She wondered if he'd ever had to do this. Maybe he was a therapist because he'd been "at risk" himself.

"I was wondering where you grew up."

"You're curious about me."

Her face burned, but she kept looking at him.

"I grew up in Sacramento."

"Oh." She was surprised. "Were you depressed?"

He did the steeple thing again with his fingers. He sat there without responding, as if he were thinking about it. *Don't you remember?* she wanted to say, but didn't.

"What do you imagine?"

"I don't know," she said. "That's why I'm asking."

"Sometimes," he said, "when teenagers feel alone with painful feelings, they want to know how other people have dealt with the same thing."

"So?"

"So maybe in asking if I was depressed, you were wondering if I'd gone through what you're going through—if I felt as bad as you feel."

She shook her head, but she was about to cry again, and then she was crying. Why had she done it—said *I'm Lauren*? Why, why, why? Everything was going along fine until then. Maybe that wasn't entirely true, but with Jeff it was. And if it hadn't been for her problems with Jeff, would she have been such a moper? Would she have been such a crier, such a loser? No. No, she wouldn't. Dr. Lewis had it backward. He thought her crappy life, her "low self-esteem," made it just *seem* like Jeff hated her. But she knew what she knew: Jeff hated her, and that made her life crappy.

30

*A*ll that lying in bed in December, all those tears—Sarabeth wondered where they'd gone. She'd had trouble getting herself out of bed then, but in an odd way she felt worse now—she couldn't get the bed out of her. Her legs, that had moved her through Tilden Park: they were full of sand, deadweights. Her head was full of sand, too, which made it hard to concentrate, hard to talk. She met Nina for coffee one evening and tried to explain what had happened, but she kept losing her train of thought or having trouble finding the right words.

"I'm worried about you," Nina said, and Sarabeth knew she meant well, but it made her feel worse. "Will you make an appointment with a shrink?"

Sarabeth shook her head. She didn't feel it was a bad idea, just that she couldn't do it. Besides, she was too poor. Real estate was dead, and though she had lampshade orders to fill, she couldn't make herself work.

Nina said, "Would you go if I made an appointment?"

"The lightbulb has to want to change," Sarabeth joked, but her face felt weird, as if something were crawling on her cheeks, and she gave up and shrugged. "Anyway, it's getting late—I should get going."

At home she sat on her couch. She felt tired in one way but wide awake in another. There would come a moment when she would feel it was time to go to bed, and she would go, but meanwhile she waited. Time moved slowly. She thought of a freeway just past the point of a huge jam, how each emerging car would seem to have the road to itself, minutes passing, one by one.

In a while she realized that she needed to pee, and then that she needed to pee very badly: the pressure in her bladder surprised her. She got up and went into the bathroom, and it was the strangest thing—at the moment when she felt the urine against her skin, her eyes welled. It was like that trick kids played, putting someone's hand in water to make him wet the bed.

Back in the living room it was very quiet—she could hear the tick of the clock in her workroom. She recalled a time when she almost always had music playing, but that was long ago. She hadn't opened her stereo cabinet in months. What would it be like to have the kind of terrible, wasting disease where your mind was entirely intact but you couldn't move or speak? She felt a little like that now, as if somewhere inside her there might be an urge to hear music, but that she lacked the means to bring that urge forward, to feel it.

She let Jim and Donald talk her into going to a cocktail party in Marin, at a stark hillside house in which just about everything was beige or white. The crowd was very upscale: she met a cardiologist, a landscape architect, a professor of sociology, a producer at KQED. She chirped her way through an explanation of her work, pretty sure they were all wondering how she supported herself. *Not very well,* she wanted to say.

At the hors d'oeuvres table she ate a handful of salty cashews, then a couple of mouth-puckering cornichons. She picked up a little plate and helped herself to a few sections of California roll, then added several leaves of pickled ginger and a knob of wasabi. She rolled a piece in the seasonings and put it in her mouth whole, and instantly the wasabi assaulted her sinuses, burning her nostrils and making her eyes water. She chewed quickly and immediately had another.

In the window over the table she saw her reflection, her pale face with its shadowed eyes, her mouth moving mechanically. Behind her, the party guests talked animatedly of art and Hawaii and feeling more grounded these days. She didn't know them, but she knew she wasn't them. *Is this it?* It was. She was where she'd been heading all along, though without knowing it. Liz hadn't put her there; she'd just turned on the light. There was a fluttering in Sarabeth, like wings, and she thought her task was to quiet that feeling, to soothe the bird inside her, reassure it that all was OK. She looked at the window again, but this time she tried to look through it. She believed she was looking into the backyard, but it was too dark and rainy to tell if there were dense trees out there, or lawn, or a neighbor's imposing house.

In the days after the party she began to think of her bedroom on Cowper Street, of how, because of an unfortunately placed streetlight, it had been very light at night, and of how when she couldn't sleep she sometimes pretended that the illuminated shapes she saw were other than what she knew them to be. Her fan-backed chair was a peacock, her coatrack was an antelope, and down the hall her mother's voice was just the cry of a monkey, a shriek that should be, or the soft, rhythmic cawing of an exotic bird.

The bird in Sarabeth grew more and more still. Without the beating of its wings it began to seem like something quieter than a bird, a small warm roundish thing in the middle of her chest, like an auxiliary heart. This thought pleased her for a very short time and then repelled her with its reach toward poetry. If not a heart, then a stone? But that was poetic, too.

So there was nothing inside her—she said goodbye to the bird and missed it only briefly. She was shedding what she could, though the pile of stuff on her floor remained.

31

*J*n the second half of January an acquisition deal of Brody's did an eleventh-hour stall, and though he could have dealt with it by videoconference he booked a flight to Boston instead, telling Liz it was the only way.

Bruce Sellers came along. They took a cab from Logan, arriving at their hotel a little before 11:00 p.m. Once Brody'd dropped his bag in his room and phoned Liz, he went down to the empty business center and spent an hour on e-mail, calling room service to bring him a burger while he worked.

He'd taken a midday flight because of a morning meeting he couldn't miss, so he'd been home at breakfast—unusual for a day when he had to travel. "Where are you going?" Joe said, and when Brody told him, Joe found the weather page of the newspaper and reported that snow was expected in the Northeast.

"Better take your galoshes," Liz teased.

"Oh, no—I don't *have* galoshes!"

"Maybe you could buy some at the airport." Joe looked serious, pleased to have this idea for Brody. "You know those stores that have everything, like suitcases and toothbrushes and stuff? I'll bet they'd have galoshes. Especially in January."

Lauren was watching Joe. "They were kidding," she said in a mean voice, and from across the table Liz met Brody's eyes and then quickly looked away.

Finished with his burger, he opened a new e-mail and addressed it to Joe. It was a little after nine in California; he might be online. Brody typed:

> It's the middle of the night here and twenty-three degrees out. It was a real shock when I walked out of the terminal. What's up there?

He went to the *Times* site and read an early edition of tomorrow's paper, giving Joe five minutes, ten, fifteen. At last, when he was close to giving up, a reply came.

> Not much—I have a ton of homework. Mom ordered Round Table for dinner.

Brody wrote back:

> She's slipping! I'll have to talk to her about that. (Just kidding.) I'm alone in a sterile "business center" in my hotel—a weird place to be in the middle of the night.

And Joe wrote:

> That would be a good opening scene for a movie. Businessman in the middle of the night in a strange hotel, no one else around.

Brody smiled.

Stop, you're scaring me!

Tracking shot up the hotel corridor, scary music. Sorry, I've gotta
get back to my math now.

No need to be sorry, Joejy. You don't ever need to be sorry you've
got other stuff to do, OK?

Brody thought for a moment, the cursor hovering over the SEND button. He moved it to the line he'd just written and backspaced until it was
gone.

"Go get 'em, kiddo" he typed instead, and he sent it, though he knew
Joe might not see it before tomorrow sometime. He did a few more work
e-mails and then logged out and wandered around the mezzanine level of
the hotel, passing an empty conference room and then the closed door to
the fitness center. A sign said it was available twenty-four hours a day, and
he opened the door: empty, though the lights were on, the machines lined
up against a black window. There'd been so much rain at home lately, he
and David hadn't played tennis in weeks, and he'd all but stopped his
nighttime trips to the high school. He imagined himself working out, and
the pain this would bring to his shoulder was almost a draw—as if hurting
it were a job he'd been neglecting.

Round Table. They delivered, was the main attraction. Their pizza
wasn't very good. Hound Table, the kids used to call it. Woof, woof.

An elevator took him to the main lobby, and he strolled past the
concierge. At the registration desk the lone clerk said, "Anything we can
help you with, Mr. Mackay?" and Brody did a double take, wondering if
this was the same guy who'd checked him in two hours ago. He didn't
think so. Another ominous touch for a movie: everyone knowing your
name.

In the bar there were several clusters of low, upholstered chairs, only
one of which was occupied, by a couple sitting as close together as the
furniture allowed. Brody took a stool and ordered a Scotch. The bartender was a young woman with long hair and a tastefully revealing
blouse, and he imagined saying, *I'll bet you get a lot of lonely businessmen
trying to talk to you*, but then he'd be one.

The first taste of his drink gave his throat a satisfying burn. He went to bars only when he traveled, drank Scotch only when he went to bars. It tasted good, better than he remembered. He sometimes thought that the main difference between life now and life in his parents' heyday was the decline of alcohol. He and Liz had talked about this: how, growing up, they'd lived with their parents' drinking the way farmers lived with the seasons. Spring, summer, fall, winter. Sober, tipsy, drunk, hungover. And none of the four of them—Robert and Marguerite, his mother and father—had ever had anything like a drinking problem. It was just how people lived then.

Liz, at breakfast this morning. That mischievous look when she made the galoshes comment. An idea had flashed through his mind in that instant: Don't go. Don't go to Boston. Then Lauren made her nasty remark to Joe.

He thought of an evening at Tahoe, over Christmas, when Joe switched his vote from the DVD his cousins preferred to the one Lauren wanted. "That's not fair," Austin said, but Joe wouldn't budge, and the only adult willing to intervene was Steve, who forced a coin toss and was thereby the agent of his boys' defeat. "I changed my mind," Brody overheard Joe saying later. "What's the big deal?" He didn't want to be caught protecting his sister's interests.

Brody took a long draw on his drink. In the mirror over the bar he saw the couple nuzzling, the man's hand so far up the woman's leg that he couldn't have had more than an inch to go. They were having an affair, of course. In Brody's experience this happened when someone wasn't moving fast enough, when someone couldn't get the hungry look out of his eye. An affair or a garage band, those seemed to be the options. Or a sports car. Russ had bought a Ferrari just months before his separation was announced.

"What's up?"

He turned and there was Bruce, looking a lot better than Brody felt: showered, maybe even shaved.

"There he is," Brody said. "I figured you weren't asleep. What can I get you?"

Bruce asked for a Scotch, and they sat and drank for a while, talking about tomorrow, their strategy for jump-starting negotiations again. It was one-forty when Brody got to his room. He brushed his teeth in the spotless bathroom, pulled down the sheets on the pristine bed, and climbed in.

He'd had a second drink, and he was a little woozy. Heat blew from the vents under the window, and he felt how dry the air was, could almost feel how dry he'd be by morning, his nasal passages, his throat. He got up and went back to the bathroom for a glass of water.

He blinked in the sudden light, then looked at his reflection. His face was changing: softening, falling. He was getting jowls, and his chest hair was almost white. He imagined Liz climbing into bed, three thousand miles away; Joe up in his bed; Lauren in hers. Thinking about Joe and Lauren when he was away: this always made him ache a little.

He turned off the light. Getting back into the hotel bed, he thought again of Lauren's nasty tone at breakfast: *They were kidding.* He understood that his not saying anything had made it worse than it was. It had been like telling her: *I'm afraid of you, I can't control you, I can't—I still can't help you.*

He had failed to help her. Her life had brought her to its own edge, and he had failed to step in and help her. He didn't want this to be true, but it was.

When Brody was away, Liz felt returned to a much earlier time, a time when he'd traveled less but worked much more. His years at start-ups—she'd often felt that he was much farther away than Mountain View or San Jose: hundreds of miles, thousands of aeons. Winter afternoons like this one, she made blanket forts with the kids: crawled inside with them and staged tea parties, Playmobil rodeos, Thumbkin sleepovers. Sometimes in those years he didn't get home till two or three in the morning, and he'd climb into bed next to her and seem for a moment like someone she didn't know. And then: *I'm finished,* he said, three or four years ago, and she knew right away what he meant. No more craziness. No more seventy-hour workweeks, no more Valley rules. They opened a bottle of champagne that night to celebrate.

But had he done it? Truly? She wasn't sure.

She let things go a little when he was away. Round Table last night, Chinese tonight—though tonight there was a good reason. She cleaned up quickly, dropped Joe at his science partner's, and drove with Lauren back to the high school.

"Women's History Project," the notice had said. "An evening of discussion and taking stock." Lauren's social studies teacher had organized this end-of-semester event as a kind of conference or colloquium, complete with focus groups, talks, and miniseminars. The participants were supposed to be the class's students and their parents and grandparents, but as Liz followed Lauren to the auditorium, she saw several other mother-daughter pairs and not a single boy or man.

Lauren's middle-school friend Jessica and Jessica's mother, Linda, were standing in the lobby. "Look," Liz said, "there are the Youngs. Shall we join them?" She'd always liked Linda, hadn't seen her in a long time.

Lauren stood still, not speaking, her arms crossed over her chest.

"Lauren?" Liz said.

"You can."

"Oh, that's OK. I just thought you might want to."

Liz tried to remember if this was a class Amanda was in. Would there be anyone here Lauren could comfortably approach? Getting in the car after school today, she'd seemed dull, listless. She'd been quiet through the afternoon, quiet through dinner.

"We can go in," Lauren said now, but she didn't move, and after a moment Liz herself led the way to the double doors.

The stage was set up with a microphone on a stand, and there were circles of folding chairs on the auditorium floor, six to eight per group. A woman Liz took to be the teacher stood on the steps up to the stage, talking to a couple of girls.

"Wow," Liz said, "very professional."

"Liz!"

She turned, and there was Pam Silk, another mother from the middle-school days—someone Liz hadn't always liked. She was one of those people who seemed to regard busyness as a contest you could win. "Three kids," she was always saying. "You can't imagine how big a difference that third one makes."

Now she approached, saying, "Long time no see! And Lauren—your hair looks *so cute.*"

"Thanks," Lauren said, and then, "I'm just going to go down there," and before Liz could follow, or ask her to wait, she took off for the front of the auditorium.

Pam moved closer and lowered her voice. "I've been thinking of you constantly. How are you? Are you OK?"

"I am," Liz said. "Thank you, yes."

"Alexis was really upset," Pam said, shaking her head. "Really upset."

This was not a conversation Liz could have. She craned her head back and forth as if she were trying to make out what was happening at the front of the auditorium. "It looks like things are getting started," she said. "I guess I'll—I think I'll head down there."

Pam colored slightly. "Oh, absolutely," she said. "Isn't this fun? I told Alexis, there's no way anything like this would've happened when we were in high school."

Liz made her way to the front, smiling when she saw an acquaintance but keeping a purposeful look on her face. She stopped at a folding chair and feigned interest in the contents of her purse.

Terri Mayfield arrived at her side.

"Terri, thank God."

"You OK?"

"Yeah, yeah. I wasn't sure Amanda was in this class." Liz glanced around, but Amanda was far from Lauren, standing with a group of girls Liz didn't recognize. She turned back to Terri. She'd been an angel during Lauren's hospitalization, dropping off dinners in disposable dishes, leaving messages of love and concern that insisted Liz not call her back unless she really wanted to. "I'm glad to see you," Liz said.

The teacher moved across the stage to the microphone. She welcomed the visitors and explained the format: first small groups, with the students asking questions and making notes; then a few short papers, to be delivered by individual students; and finally several concurrent discussions on a variety of subjects. "We're here," she concluded, "to explore the question 'Where are we now?'" She looked out at the group in the auditorium, perhaps forty girls and women ranging from adolescent to quite elderly. "Though another question might be: 'Where are they?'"

Everyone laughed, and Terri leaned toward Liz and muttered, "I know where mine is."

"Wouldn't you think some of the boys would have come, though?" Liz whispered back.

"If only for the extra credit."

Liz chuckled, but she felt a little disappointed; she hadn't known Lauren was getting extra credit for attending. *Mom,* she'd said. *Do you want to go to this thing with me?*

Lauren was standing outside a circle of chairs, and when the crowd broke Liz joined her and took a seat.

The girls had typed up questions. "Do you work outside the home?" "Who does the housework at your house?" "Respond to the following with a score of 1 to 10, with 1 being 'strongly agree' and 10 being 'strongly disagree': I am where I want to be in life. I felt free to make choices when I was 20. 30. 40. My daughter/granddaughter is likely to have a career. My daughter/ granddaughter is likely to have a family."

The mothers' answers were recorded on yellow paper, the grandmothers' on green. Lauren wrote with her head bent, then doodled on an extra piece of paper when another girl was up. Liz stole a look at the doodles: curlicues, parallel lines, nothing of real substance. She wondered if Lauren was drawing for real these days. She remembered a Saturday evening in October or early November when Sarabeth found a sketch of Lauren's on the kitchen counter. A sketch of a leaf. Later, Liz had taken it to a folder where she kept drawings of Lauren's that seemed in danger of disappearing, and when she opened the folder to put it inside, she noticed that the previous one she'd put there had been from months before.

I'm not your mother.

Liz felt the approach of a terrible feeling—of guilt, shame, and a miserable sense of righteousness. It was how she felt every time she thought of Sarabeth. The guilt was there, and the shame, but mostly she thought that after all the years she'd supported Sarabeth, she'd earned the right to expect Sarabeth to come through for her. Weren't there things you just *did*—because you cared? There'd been times over the holidays when she'd felt terrible about how long it had taken her to call Sarabeth back, but she knew now that she'd been on the right track.

"Liz?"

This was Lauren: addressing her, oddly enough, by name. Lauren had her pencil poised, her yellow sheet ready. The others in the group were waiting.

"I'm sorry," Liz said. "Could you repeat the question?"

" 'For you,' " Lauren read, " 'what is the most important issue facing women today?' "

The most important issue—Liz tried to think. There were so many. Abortion rights? Equal pay for equal work? Universal health coverage? Funding for education? She thought, oddly, of the billboards in the city, rising up from the tops of buildings and seizing your attention as you gained the freeway, exhorting you to think of Verizon, Rolex, Old Navy.

"Caring," she said. "In general." She looked around the circle, and a couple of the other women nodded. "That it's not at the forefront," she added.

The girl next to Lauren posed the same question to her grandmother, and attention shifted to them. Lauren finished writing and returned to her doodle page. She drew a little girl's daisy, shaded in the petals, then moved her pencil and spun a spiral from the inside out.

Last night she had been hard at work on chemistry when Liz went in to say goodnight. "Hi, Mom," she said, and then she returned to her work, and Liz ended up sitting on her bed for quite a while, just sitting and looking around, watching the way Lauren hunched over her desk, the way her heel jiggled under her chair. She looked at Lauren's tangled hair and after a while realized that she was longing to brush it, and she thought back to when Lauren was in second or third grade, how before school each morning she'd say, "Can we French-braid my hair?" and Liz would say, "Sure we can," and they'd stand together in front of the bathroom mirror while Liz ran the brush through Lauren's hair, then used her fingers to separate the strands.

What, Liz wondered, had happened to the word "we"? Where had it gone?

She watched as Lauren slid her pencil into the clamp at the top of her clipboard and then brought her purse from the floor to her lap. Hand hovering over the mouth of the purse, she waited a moment and then reached in slowly, with an obvious concern for the disruption she might cause. In a while, Liz saw that she'd taken hold of a roll of mints. One of the grandmothers was talking about the environment, and without removing the mints from her purse Lauren fingered one out and quickly slipped it into her mouth. Then she looked at Liz and raised her eyebrows. There was a little smile on her face, and it took Liz a moment to realize why: it was a family joke that there were a few questions in the world to which the answer was always yes, and *Would you like a mint?* was one of them.

She nodded, and Lauren freed another candy from the roll. In preparation to receive it, Liz moved her hand to the outside of her thigh, palm facing up. Lauren waited a moment, then moved her own hand to Liz's and released the mint.

"Thanks," Liz whispered.

It was a Mento—or would you say a Mentos? A hard candy shell over a chewy center. Liz's hand sweated a little as she held it. In a moment, another girl would ask a question, and Liz would raise her hand to her mouth. As she waited, though, a memory came to her, a picture of herself with chocolate melting in her palm.

She was eleven or twelve. Lorelei had planned a day in the city for her and Sarabeth, lunch at a special restaurant and then a matinee. That morning Liz crossed the street in a pair of brand-new cords and a sweater from Saks, and there, inside the Leoffler house, were Sarabeth and Lorelei dressed up in suits, Sarabeth's a miniature version of Lorelei's: tweed skirt, tweed jacket, small scarf knotted at the throat. "Well," Lorelei said, "don't you look comfortable, Liz," and Sarabeth blushed and looked away.

She was lost to Liz—all the drive up and all through lunch—deep inside being Lorelei's daughter. What did they talk about? Perhaps they didn't talk. Lorelei refused them dessert, then ordered coffee for herself, sending the waiter back twice to look for cubed sugar. Finally, when she left the table to go to the ladies' room, Sarabeth turned to Liz and said, "It'll be better at the movie, I promise."

But it wasn't. At the movie, *The Go-Between,* Liz sat in the dark next to her best friend, her best friend's mother two seats down, and something about the day kept her from taking in anything about the story on the screen beyond the fact that it was alternately boring and embarrassing. Lorelei had bought a box of Junior Mints to make up for the denied dessert, but Liz didn't like Junior Mints, and when they came her way she tipped out a candy or two to be polite, but then couldn't bring herself to eat them. Inevitably, in the heat of her palm, the chocolate coating began to melt. She got nervous and then more nervous about how her hand would look when the lights came up, until at last, her heart racing, she reached toward the floor and released the candies. Then, as subtly as she could, she kicked them forward, under the seat in front of her, out of sight. Finally, she leaned forward and glanced at Lorelei to make sure her eyes were on the screen, and then she licked her palm until it was certain to be spotless.

Lauren had returned her purse to the floor and was doodling again. Liz felt terrible. She *wasn't* Sarabeth's mother, and the habit of it, of pretending she was, had cost her family dearly: she'd grown certain of this. She'd have been a better mother to Lauren if she hadn't spent so much time trying to be a good one to Sarabeth. Period. And yet thinking about that long-ago day, about her own tiny episode of fear, Lorelei sitting near her in the dark like some kind of not-mother, some kind of antimother, she thought it was wrong, it was almost criminal, that Sarabeth had been forced to do without.

32

There was her mortgage; there was her property tax bill. There was the fact that she needed new tires on her car. The remains of Sarabeth's inheritance were supposed to be off-limits for everyday expenses, but as January progressed and her bank account dwindled, she considered making an exception. A thousand dollars—would that be so bad? She didn't know what else to do. She'd made no lampshades in weeks, and she was losing listeners at the Center; the stalwarts said it was because the book was so long, but she knew better. She was boring.

A new paper store appeared on Shattuck, and it occurred to her that the way back to work might be via design. She loved coming up with new ideas. At least she remembered loving it.

Carta, the new place was called. She went on a day that was strangely warm, parking out front and wondering as she approached the door if they could possibly have anything she hadn't seen at a dozen other stores. She said hello to the proprietor and sure enough: here were the eye-boggling geometrics she disliked, repeated rows of tiny bull's-eyes, of dice or perfect daisies. And there were the ubiquitous giant fruits, the tone-on-tone stripes. Hanging near the back, though, was an unfamiliar line, and she went for a closer look: very soft, almost silty sheets in pastel colors, with text printed on them in similarly pale shades. The type was fairly large, about a quarter of an inch high, and on one she saw *"Longtemps, je me suis couché de bonne heure"* and on another "It is a truth universally acknowledged, that a single man in possession of a good fortune must be in want of a wife" and on a third "Last night I dreamt I went to Manderley again." Each went on, through the familiar words, to the bottom of the sheet. She sort of liked them.

Paper stores made their money selling things other than paper: fine or silly address books, cellophane envelopes of confetti, expensive beaded picture frames. She fingered a flat plastic box of magnets bearing tiny photographs of pastries: éclairs and petits fours and meringues. The meringues were just the plain white kind, not nearly as good as the chocolate ones she used to make for Lauren and Joe. How they'd loved them! She remembered the two of them at her kitchen table, their legs dangling from her chairs. How were they? Lauren especially: did she know why Sarabeth hadn't been around? Sarabeth thought of buying the magnets, imagined sending them to Lauren and Joe in an envelope with no return address. Impossible. She left them where they were and returned to the draped sheets of paper.

"In my younger and more vulnerable years my father gave me some advice that I've been turning over in my mind ever since." "Her first name was India—she was never able to get used to it." "This is the saddest story I have ever heard." She got Gatsby and *The Good Soldier,* but who was India?

"Do you have a key?" she asked the proprietor.

"A key?"

Sarabeth indicated the sheets of paper. "The authors. The books. Do you know where each passage comes from?"

"Does it matter?" the woman said, and though this was obviously just a nasty woman in a nasty mood, Sarabeth was embarrassed and hurried from the store.

She got in her car and started the engine. Clearly, she had to force herself to do the work she already had. Maybe the problem wasn't that she had no energy; maybe it was that her old designs bored her. Surely she could deal with that. When audiences asked Joni Mitchell to sing old songs, she said, "People didn't ask van Gogh to paint 'Starry Night' again." As if she were van Gogh! Sarabeth took comfort in the fact that she knew she wasn't van Gogh. Or Joni Mitchell, for that matter.

"Her first name was India—she was never able to get used to it." The line stayed with her as she drove home, and she realized she was thinking of *The Raj Quartet,* which she had read over and over again in her twenties. It was *set* in India, during the Second World War; two of the main characters were a pair of sisters named Sarah and Susan, and where Sarah was thoughtful and full of reason, Susan was flighty, possibly hysterical. She ended up marrying a terrible guy, what was his name, the military guy who lost his arm. . . .

Sarabeth's boxed set of *The Raj Quartet* was on a bookshelf in her bedroom, and when she got home she took out the second volume and flipped through the pages. The military guy, the military guy . . . he had an inferiority complex because he hadn't gone to public school back in England. At last she found him, Ronald Merrick. Oh, he was horrible. But pitiful, too.

She went outside and sat on her filthy porch, then went in, found a broom, and swept it off. What it really needed was mopping, or better yet painting, but she sat down again and closed her eyes against the bright sun. Sarah and Susan. Elizabeth and Jane. Dolly and Kitty. Meg and Jo. She'd always been fascinated by sisters in books, especially paired sisters, with their insistent dichotomies: blond and brunette, innocent and experienced, sweet and sour, beautiful and plain.

Creative and smart.

She squeezed her eyes tight and then opened them. The two little girls of the Heidt household had appeared on their patio with Popsicles, and she stood up and brushed herself off and went inside. In the kitchen she filled a glass with water and sat at the table. *Anna* was in her shoulder bag, and she opened it, thinking that if she were better prepared people might be likelier to come back. She read the chapters she'd read aloud Thursday night, then she skimmed here and there until her eye fell on a passage about Seryozha, Anna's son. He'd been told, after Anna went away with Vronsky, that she was dead.

> Among his favorite occupations was looking for his mother during his walk. He did not believe in death generally and especially not in her death, though Lydia Ivanovna had told him and his father had confirmed it, and therefore, even after he was told that she was dead, he looked for her during his walks. Any full-bodied, graceful woman with dark hair was his mother.

Sarabeth thought of the picture she'd had in her mind, months ago, of a woman walking with a girl, the pair of them like something from a movie; and then she thought of Anna's suicide.

Anna was going to throw herself under a train. Sarabeth knew this at her core, and yet, here and now, she was surprised by it. This had happened with *Madame Bovary,* too; she remembered arriving at Emma's death and realizing that she'd somehow managed not to know it was coming. Suicide, these books were about. Not adultery.

She turned to the end of the book, looking for the scene; she had read *Anna* only once before, in college. She had to search and search, finally locating it not at the true end but fifty pages shy. Then she read, barely breathing, and at the end she knew two things: that Anna had given Seryozha scarcely a thought as she moved toward her death, and that, as she let herself tumble toward the train's giant wheels, she was horrified by what she'd done.

33

The day arrived for Liz and Brody to meet with Dr. Lewis. The appointment was for eleven-thirty, and after Liz dropped the kids at school she went home and wiped the kitchen table, then sat down with a notepad and pen so she could write out her questions. Outside, the wind was huge, blowing in a new storm that was predicted to last for days. She could hear the rattling of tree branches and, less frequently, the whimper of the wind itself.

She wrote: "1. Should I talk to M. and D. about how they are with her? 2. Should I encourage her to be more social?" She stopped and read what she'd written, then crossed out each "I" and wrote "we." Then she went back and crossed out the first "we" and changed it back to "I." She considered. She put a "3" below the "2," then set down her pen and rubbed her eyes. She knew there were other things she wanted to ask him, but what were they? "Prozac dose OK?" she wrote after the "3," then she crossed out the entire line, made a new "3," and wrote: "Is her Prozac dose where it should be?" Then she said, out loud, "This is ridiculous," and she crumpled up the paper and tossed it aside.

She had dreamed about Joe last night—she'd just realized. She had dreamed about him as a little boy playing with building blocks, which he had habitually done in the very corner of the family room at which she was now looking. Joe at three years old, or four. She could see him clearly, his munchkin smile and stubby little hands. She could see the blocks, too: red, yellow, blue, and green. Joe's blocks. And yet—was this true?—they'd been Lauren's. Yes, they'd been Lauren's to start with, a gift Lauren had received at the time of Joe's birth.

Sad but with toys. Who had said that? A woman Liz had known when the children were very young, Rachel something. Her husband was a lawyer, like Brody never home. She and Liz had been pregnant at the same time, she with her third and Liz with Joe, and when the babies were born and twenty-two-month-old Lauren started getting gifts from everyone who sent things for Joe, this Rachel told Liz that she'd asked people not to send things to her older two this time because the oldest, when the second had been born, had gotten dozens of presents, and they were really just an unsuccessful distraction, making this sad little girl *sad but with toys.*

God, it was the most ordinary things that caused the greatest misery.

Liz left the kitchen and went into her bedroom. Her desk was littered with papers that needed her attention, but she reached past it for her yoga mat. She unrolled it at the foot of the bed, kicked off her shoes, and lowered herself onto her back. She lay with her feet apart, arms at her sides. She had not lain like this in—how long had it been?—two months. She could feel her abdomen pulling at her lower back. She was so soft now—soft where she had once been firm. Did Diane wonder what had happened to her? She brought her legs into her chest, but the waistband of her jeans dug into her belly. Slowly, like the old woman she'd become, she rolled onto her side, got to her knees, and stood. She turned to the bed, hesitated a moment, then pulled back the covers and got in.

She lay on her side, facing her nightstand. She had not turned off the Krups, and from the kitchen came the smell of burned coffee. Her clock said 9:27, and if she left for Burlingame now she could shop first. But did she feel like shopping? It was January—"poor month," as she and Brody used to call it—and last week she'd taken Lauren to Burlingame Avenue after therapy and said yes to three pairs of pants and two tops.

4. Should I buy her new clothes? 5. Should I spend hundreds of dollars buying her new clothes that won't do anything but make her feel better for a day or two?

She reached for the book she'd been reading, a collection of essays about terrorism. Hand on the cover, she changed her mind and rolled to her other side. One of the pieces was about a Palestinian woman whose son had been a suicide bomber. It had broken her heart.

Brody's pillow was still in the place where he'd left it, askew, a dent down the middle. He was having trouble sleeping these days; she could feel it. She'd wake in the middle of the night and from the sound of his breathing know he'd been awake for a long time.

She sat up and plumped his pillow, then stood and made the bed carefully, smoothing out the wrinkles. Right after New Year's she'd ordered some luxurious new sheets from a catalog having a white sale: pale yellow Egyptian cotton, 420 thread count. She was sad but with bed linens.

In Burlingame Brody parked just behind Liz's van. He longed for a cup of coffee, but there wasn't time. In the building the stairs creaked as he climbed them, not a California sound.

He took a couple of turns down a hallway and found Liz in a tiny waiting room, a magazine open on her lap. She looked up when she heard him. "Made it," he said. He leaned down to kiss her, then took a seat in a canvas director's chair. He reached for a magazine but changed his mind. He could tell Liz was nervous; she kept clearing her throat, as if she were about to answer the phone.

"Here he comes," she said, and it was as if she'd conjured him: Dr. Lewis opened the door right then.

"Liz, Brody, hi, it's good to see you." He looked younger here than he had at the hospital, less experienced, a bit tentative. Then again, he wasn't wearing a tie. Or his white coat.

He shook hands with Brody, then shook hands with Liz and held out his arm. "Please come in."

In his office they all sat down. Lauren spent hours here, and Brody wondered: Which chair did she use? Did she stare at the clock, waiting for the minutes to go by? "Dad," she'd said at breakfast this morning, aware of this meeting. "I want to stop going."

"So," Dr. Lewis said. "I've talked on the phone with Liz, but it's been a while since we all met. How are you both doing?"

"Fine," Brody said, and at the same time Liz said, "Maybe a bit better," and Dr. Lewis clasped his hands together and leaned forward.

"How is that for you? That you're in different places?"

Brody felt a wave of irritation: he and Liz were not the patients. "How's she doing?" he said. "In your view."

Liz turned to him. "He asked a question." Then she looked back at Dr. Lewis and said, "It's hard. For me, anyway."

"Most couples struggle with this," the doctor said. "I don't know if that's helpful, but it's very common to feel angry when there are differences in how you're handling things."

"I said 'fine' as a pleasantry," Brody said.

There was a long silence, and then at last Dr. Lewis shifted, changing the cross of his legs and interlacing his fingers. "Well then, how are things at home?" he asked, and Liz began to talk: about Lauren's lack of energy, about her quietness, about how in many ways life felt just the same as before she—Liz hesitated—as before what happened. No, she said in response to a question, Lauren wasn't seeing friends out of school, though she talked on the phone with Amanda from time to time. Should she push Lauren to get out more?

Dr. Lewis hesitated before he spoke. "It would be nice to see her interacting with her peers, but that may not happen for a while."

Another silence.

"I wanted to ask you," Liz said. "My parents are kind of awkward with her, and I was wondering if I should talk to them about it."

"Awkward?"

The corners of Liz's mouth went inward. "My mother can't really look at her. I mean she does, but it's unnatural. She keeps her distance."

"It sounds like she's anxious."

"We went to the beach," Brody said, speaking before he'd really decided to. "She was pretty cheerful that day, don't you think?"

"That was six weeks ago," Liz said.

Dr. Lewis looked confused. "Wait—this is your mother-in-law?"

"No, no, Lauren," Brody said. "It was just the four of us."

"Before Christmas," Liz added.

Dr. Lewis took this in, and then he sat there silently, just sat there— Brody hoped he didn't do this to Lauren. At last he looked at Liz and said, "Regarding your parents, I suspect more contact would be the best medicine."

"Right."

"Local grandparents can create certain . . . issues in situations like this. But of course they can also offer a lot of support." He gave her an encouraging smile and then turned to Brody and said, "It must have felt nice to have a family outing."

"Should we do more of that?" Liz asked brightly.

"I think you'd enjoy it," Dr. Lewis said, and Brody longed to get up and leave.

Liz began talking again, something about the counselor at school and a comment she'd had, and Brody wanted to cut in and ask Dr. Lewis to talk to them. The minute hand crept on: toward and then past the halfway mark. Finally, after a silence, Liz clasped her hands together and said, "So do you think it's helping?"

"The treatment?" Dr. Lewis said. "It can be hard to assess this early, but I think she feels safe here. I'm hopeful."

"This early?" Brody said.

"This early in the treatment."

Brody glanced at Liz. "This is early? She was hoping she could stop soon. How much longer were you thinking it would take?"

"I think that depends on the goal."

"We'd kind of like her not to slash herself open again!" Brody snapped, and Liz gaped at him. "What?" he said. "You disagree?"

She shook her head quickly.

"That's the goal," he said to Dr. Lewis. "Any questions?"

Dr. Lewis waited—Brody had the infuriating sense that he was being given time to cool off. At last, lacing his fingers together again and speaking as if he'd weighed every word in advance, the doctor said, "Of course that's of primary concern—I know you have a great deal of anxiety about that, and whenever there's self-injury the treatment has to focus on the risk of repetition. But we also want to work on the underlying problem, which in Lauren's case is a pervasive feeling of worthlessness. She's quite depressed."

"Still?" Liz said, and she began to weep.

Brody looked at his hands. The weeks since that horrible day in November shrank away, and he recalled arriving at the hospital to find Liz marked with Lauren's blood and crying hysterically. He faced the doctor. "What can we do?"

"You're doing a lot," Dr. Lewis said. "Both of you." He glanced at the clock, and Brody saw they were down to their last few minutes. "The Prozac seems to have brought her to a place where she can function better. As she gains trust in me, I think she'll feel more and more that she can tell me about some of the painful thoughts and feelings she's having. We'll look at them together and talk about them."

"And then she'll feel worse," Brody said.

"No, she won't!" Liz exclaimed. She looked at him with something like hatred. "She won't."

"It can be very painful," Dr. Lewis said. "No question. But there's a good chance we can bring about some positive change. And the alternative can be very costly, as you've seen."

Brody lifted his hands from his lap, then let them fall again. He looked at Liz and then at Dr. Lewis and the clock. "This is hell," he said, and after a moment Dr. Lewis nodded.

"Yes, it is," he said. "It certainly is."

Outside, the wind whipped against her, and Liz zipped her jacket and crossed her arms tightly over her chest. She had the beginnings of a headache behind the bridge of her nose, and her mouth was dry and sour tasting. Down the block, she saw Brody's car parked just behind the van.

"Are you going home?" he said.

"Yeah."

They began to walk. She held her purse close, thinking ahead to the relief of being alone. She needed time to remember the whole fifty minutes with Dr. Lewis, to ponder the meeting and figure out what she thought. At the van she stepped into the street, and Brody followed, then stopped at her door. He said, "It's almost twelve-thirty."

She fished for her keys and pressed the unlock button on the remote. *Chink* went the locks. She opened her door and stepped up into the van, balancing her purse on the console. When she looked at him he was waiting to speak.

"What are you doing for lunch?"

"I'm not really hungry."

He frowned and said, "She's going to be unhappy."

"She is unhappy, that's the point."

Now the skin at his temples seemed to tighten, and his face took on the look of something inanimate, like meat or clay. She imagined pulling at his cheek and having it stay pulled.

"Liz."

"What?"

He shook his head. He started toward his car. He turned back just as she was closing the door.

"It's freezing," she objected.

With a frown he pushed the door to. He hesitated, then went around the front of the van and got in on the passenger side.

"What?" she said.

"What do you mean 'what'? I'm not standing for this."

"What choice do we have?"

"For *this,*" he exclaimed, waving his arm at her, at the space between them. Then he slammed his palm onto the dashboard and said, "He didn't say *how* she'll ever feel better! *How!*"

She turned away and put her hand up to hide her face. What was she supposed to say to him? Why was it her job to make sure the right thing was done?

"Liz."

She turned and looked at him. She saw how big he was, saw it so plainly: he had big, strong arms and big, muscular legs, and he was too large for the passenger seat of this minivan. She felt her pulse in her throat. She thought of the night when Lauren was still in the hospital, when he had pounded into her as if he had wanted to hurt her. Was that the last time they'd had sex? What would have happened if, instead of letting him leave, she had reached for his arm and said: *Wait, stay and talk?*

His face was a face again, a thin veil of skin over muscle and bone and cartilage. She began to cry. She wasn't up to the job of being *anyone's* mother—anyone's wife, anyone's anything.

He reached for her and then said, "Here, hang on." He got out of the van and then got back in, in the backseat. He held out his hand, and she sat still for a moment, then slid her seat back and crawled over the console to sit with him. Rain began to fall, lightly at first, and then suddenly it was pouring. A woman ran by on the sidewalk, holding her purse over her head.

"What can I do?" he said.

She struggled to swallow. She could perpetuate their difficulties with a single, cold word; she was capable of such cruelty. She shifted her weight so she could look at him. "What can I do?" she said. "What can I do for you?"

He squeezed his eyes shut. They were glazed when he opened them again. Speaking very slowly, as if each word were a separate effort, he said, "You . . . can . . . be with me."

34

*I*t was from *Mrs. Bridge:* "Her first name was India—she was never able to get used to it." She found out from Miranda, during an out-of-the-blue phone call that she suspected Nina had engineered. "I was just thinking about you," Miranda said by way of explaining the call, but how likely was that? They talked about *Mrs. Bridge* and about the movie version of *The Raj Quartet,* with its images of the spoiled British being waited on hand and foot by Indians, being called sahib and mem-sahib while the clock ticked toward their departure. "Speaking of literary adaptations," Sarabeth said, and she apologized again for having walked out of Miranda's play. Miranda said her only regret was that she'd wanted to introduce Sarabeth to her cousin, a single man.

And so they were having lunch. Not Sarabeth and Miranda's cousin: Sarabeth and Miranda.

Sarabeth arrived first. At her request they were meeting at a cheap place, a café that didn't even have table service, and as she stood out in front waiting she hoped she hadn't made a mistake; it was not the kind of place where one comfortably lingered. She wondered if they would talk easily, or if it would feel forced, with lots of silences. She'd never been alone with Miranda before.

Miranda came into view at the far end of the block, her tall frame and long light hair, and as she approached she looked in store windows, at the sidewalk, into the street: everywhere but at Sarabeth. "It's a first date," she said when she'd arrived and they'd said hello, and Sarabeth realized that she felt awkward, too.

Standing in line at the counter, they talked about the book group, about the weather—about nothing. Once they'd found a table, though, they moved easily to more personal things, including the fact that Miranda was divorced.

Sarabeth was astonished. "You are? You don't seem divorced."

"What does divorced seem like?"

"I'm not sure—I guess it's one of those things where you know it when you see it."

"Like pornography," they said in unison, and they both smiled.

"So what happened?" Sarabeth went on. "If you want to tell me."

"Oh, sure—it's nothing to not tell. We were incredibly young, for one thing. And we had very different ideas about what marriage was. Or what we wanted ours to be."

"So it was amicable? You realized you wanted different things and went your separate ways?"

"Oh God, no. We fought like crazy, and lied and cheated—well, I did. I had this ridiculous affair with our super."

"Your super? Was he some magnetic Stanley Kowalski type or something?"

Miranda laughed. "He was a Ph.D. candidate in art history at Tufts. He was the super so he could live rent free—he couldn't fix anything."

Sarabeth tried to imagine Miranda minus twenty years: a married Miranda, an adulterous Miranda. Today she wore a gray wool turtleneck and not a trace of makeup. Though what did that mean? Sarabeth wanted to make adultery something other women did—women in sexy clothes, women unlike herself. A week or so ago, she'd seen Billy's wife standing with another woman in a housewares store she'd been about to enter, and she was filled with shame. Guilt *wasn't* a useless emotion; it made the guilty suffer, as they should.

"Speaking of fixing things," Miranda said, leaning forward. "I can definitely fix you up with my cousin if you're interested, but I had dinner with him last night, and I think he's too staid for you."

"Staid might be good," Sarabeth said. "But somehow . . ."

"It's not the right time?"

She hesitated. "I guess not." She was tempted to explain, to tell Miranda about Liz, but she didn't want to; she didn't want it to be the thing she talked about—or didn't talk about—with everyone. She ate some tabbouleh, wishing for a moment that she'd gotten the pepper noodles, wishing it almost enough to get up and go order some. She was so weird; she'd wanted nothing but spicy food for weeks. "Back to your art historian," she said. "I'm curious. Did your husband find out?"

Miranda shook her head. "Not officially, but he was aware of it on some level. His mother had this very flamboyant affair when he was a child, so he had almost . . . antennae for it."

"My mother committed suicide when I was sixteen," Sarabeth said. And then, "Oh, my God. Why did I say that?"

"Maybe so I'd know." Miranda watched her for a moment and then reached for her water and took a sip. "I'm really sorry," she added. "That would be hard anytime, let alone at that age."

"Thanks," Sarabeth said, but she felt embarrassed, and also a little empty. What a blurter she was. And hard or not hard—that wasn't the right set of possibilities. The right axis. Her mother's suicide had been . . . a devastatingly welcome relief. Which itself had occasioned . . . an endlessly burning shame.

Endlessly.

"Do you miss her?" Miranda said.

"Not really. She was sort of out of it for most of my life."

"She was sick?"

"Depressed."

"But she lived with you?"

"You mean as opposed to at a hospital? She was never that bad off."

"She must have been," Miranda said, and after a moment Sarabeth saw her point. She was right, of course: when you looked at it from this end.

After lunch they walked down the street. It was the beginning of February, cold and raw. They came to Carta, and through the window Sarabeth saw that a different woman was behind the counter today. "This is the store I was telling you about," she said to Miranda. "With the paper. Want to go in?"

The *Pride and Prejudice* sheet had been bought, as had several of the others; she could tell from how depleted the display looked. There were perhaps a dozen left, including "Her first name was India—she was never able to get used to it."

Miranda said, "After our conversation I went to Cody's and bought myself a copy of *Mrs. Bridge*. Do you ever do that? I don't even necessarily want to read it again—I just want to have it."

"All the time," Sarabeth said, but she was looking at the sheet of paper, not quite attending. "Her first name was India—she was never able to get used to it." It didn't actually make sense, now that she thought about it, because if you grew up with the name India you wouldn't *have* to get used to it: you wouldn't know anything else. India would be you before it would ever be a country. It came to her that Lorelei had been like that for her—that Lorelei's depression had. She had been how she had been before Sarabeth could understand that there was a difference between her and what other people meant by "mother."

Miranda had wandered to the other side of the rack, and she began reading aloud: " 'Last night, I dreamt I went to Manderley again.' God, I loved that movie. I could go for a Maxim de Winter, couldn't you? Then again, maybe it's Laurence Olivier I really mean." She came back around. "So are you making lampshades out of these? They'd make great 'reading lights.' " She did air quotes on "reading lights," but it took Sarabeth a minute to get it. Then: lights you could read, not just read by. It was a cute idea.

But what if she got the paper home and then for whatever reason couldn't work? Her resolve to start cranking out some lampshades had not exactly borne fruit.

"You should do it," Miranda said. "Go, Sarabeth! Don't you hate cheerleaders? But I think they would be great."

Mark would probably really like the idea—it was just the kind of larky thing he'd go for. Straight sided, they'd have to be, and probably square, though circular could work, too. She lifted a sheet from the display and carried it to the window. Light filtered through, separating the text from the background: pale pink words on a yellow field. She put it back, told Miranda she had to make a quick call, and stepped outside. She found Mark's work number and then stopped, heart pounding. *Hi, Mark?* she imagined herself saying. *This is Sarabeth.* She hadn't seen him since the night when he'd been waiting for her on her porch. She took a deep breath and sent the call.

He sounded surprised to hear from her but covered it quickly, chatting casually for a minute or two and then listening closely once she started explaining what she had in mind.

"It's a cool idea," he said when she was finished, "but of course I'd need to see a prototype."

She felt herself begin to wilt. She imagined having one sheet of the paper in her workroom, having one lampshade to make. She said, "The thing is, they're selling. I was here last week, and they've sold maybe half the stock in that time. There are maybe a dozen left, that's all."

"I like the sound of it," he said. "But wait—people wouldn't be able to choose the passage they wanted? No two are alike?"

"No two here. I suppose I could find out who the manufacturer is, and—"

"Why don't you?" he said.

"What?"

"Find out who the manufacturer is. Look into what the options are."

"No."

There was a silence, and as she stood there with her back to the shop, people passing by on the sidewalk, cars whizzing by on the street, she felt an urge to giggle.

"What's happened to you?" he said, and now she did giggle.

"Yes or no, Mark," she said.

"Am I doing this?"

"I think you might be."

He laughed, and after a moment she laughed along with him. "Someday," he said, "I'm going to have to figure out what just happened."

"I wouldn't worry about it," she said. "You think far too much as it is."

They finished the call, and she went back inside, where she bought all of the remaining sheets of paper. Would she have called his bluff like that if it hadn't been for his nighttime visits? The force of the word "no"—it was almost titillating.

"It would have been cool," Miranda said as they headed toward their cars a little later, "if you could have chosen the passages yourself."

"I thought of that," Sarabeth said. " 'One may as well begin with Helen's letters to her sister.' "

"What's that?"

It was the beginning of *Howards End;* it had just popped into her head, whole like that—she hadn't even known she knew it. She thought of Liz, telling her Lauren hadn't liked the book. What an idiot she'd been, going on and on about how she should have suggested something different.

She wondered how Liz looked at what Lauren had done, at Lauren's suicide attempt, or gesture. Was it the same as with Lorelei? Did it change the way you saw what came before it?

"It's Forster," she told Miranda. *"Howards End."*

"Of course!" Miranda said. " 'Telegrams and anger.' 'Only connect.' I have to ask you, did it drive you crazy that they cast Emma Thompson and Helena Bonham Carter in that movie? As sisters?"

Brainy, sensible Margaret and softhearted, impetuous Helen: two more sisters for Sarabeth's list. "It did," Sarabeth said. "It definitely did."

The time had come to part. Miranda leaned down and kissed Sarabeth on the cheek. "Let's do this again," she said. "OK?"

"Definitely," Sarabeth said, but as she watched Miranda walk away she imagined the "again"—another restaurant, another table—and she wondered if there were any other setting possible for friendship.

Liz at the Thai restaurant.

Liz's face last time, the way it went from soft to hard to soft again.

What did you mean now you're eating? What happened? What? Sweetie.

How had Liz found the means to sound so concerned? To *be* so concerned? This question had never occurred to Sarabeth before, and she stepped back from the sidewalk and leaned against a wall. *What happened? What? Sweetie.* She'd sounded genuinely concerned, when clearly, and with good cause, she'd been furious. Sarabeth thought of the moment earlier that same evening when she asked how Liz was, and Liz said: *How are* you? And then, right away: *How* are *you?* Trying to fix it, trying to correct her tone so Sarabeth wouldn't know how pissed off she really was.

What an effort that must have required.

Sarabeth remembered what Liz had said about Joe, last time she was over there: they were talking about how cute Joe was, and Liz said she was afraid Joe felt he *had* to be cute—that he saw it as his job.

What was Liz's job? To be good, to be kind in every instance no matter how she felt?

Poor Liz, Sarabeth thought. To have to work so hard, always.

35

*W*eekends dragged. She either saw Amanda or she didn't, and neither felt right. Amanda treated her weirdly: sort of fakely polite, too careful about what she said. "I don't know what her problem is," Lauren had said to Dr. Lewis one day, and he'd said, "Maybe she's worried about you," and now she was sure he thought she was a brat.

One Saturday afternoon she lay on her bed doing nothing, a practice her parents had always frowned on, but these days they didn't seem to care. She'd told them it was normal for people on Prozac to need a little extra sleep, and she guessed they believed her.

In fact, being on Prozac was having no effect on her at all. "Are you sure?" Dr. Lewis had said. "Have you had the kinds of thoughts you used to have?" He meant the pill thoughts, the falling-out-the-window thoughts, and she hadn't really, but how could that be the Prozac? A pill couldn't make you think or not think something.

There was a knock, and her dad leaned in, said he was heading out to do errands, and did she want to go.

"Come on," he said. "Keep me company."

And so they drove around town, dropping off DVDs at Blockbuster, stopping at Longs, getting cash at the ATM. "One more?" he said, and next thing she knew they were heading down 101.

"Wait, where are we going?"

"Expo."

"You never said we were going down there."

He gave her a sheepish look. "I never said we weren't."

Expo was miles away, on the edge of East Palo Alto in a huge lot of horrible megastores. It was supposed to be a fancier Home Depot, but when they arrived, Lauren found it was just another airport inside, way too much undivided space. The ceiling was about sixty feet high, traced with pipes, and the whole place smelled of something not natural— chemical finishes, plastic, she didn't know what. She wished she'd stayed home.

Her dad wanted to redo the storage system in the garage, and he led her past tiles and flooring and a bizarre display of shower stalls. There were a lot of people, and it was noisy in the way she didn't like, sort of a loud hum behind all the other noises, behind the voices and laughter.

"Huh," he said when they got to the storage section. "I thought they'd have more."

How far out of the way had they driven for this? "Dad," she said.

"I wonder if Ikea—"

"Dad!"

He frowned and turned to leave, and she felt bad; he didn't have many chances to do stuff like this, especially lately—he seemed to be working all the time. It was sort of his own fault, though; he never should have asked her to come along. Why hadn't he asked Joe? Because Joe had a life.

"Oh," he said as they stepped outside. "I almost forgot. I told your mom we'd run by Grandma and Grandpa's."

Lauren stopped.

"What?"

"I thought we were done."

"It won't take more than twenty minutes. I've got a recipe of Mom's that Grandma wants."

"I don't *want* to." Embarrassed, she turned away.

"What's the big deal?"

"It's not a big deal, it's just—" To her dismay, tears filled her eyes. "Can't Mom e-mail the recipe?"

"Laurie, what is it?"

Out of the corner of her eye she caught sight of a guy pushing a bare toilet on a cart. She wanted to laugh, but instead she started to cry. What was she doing here, in this parking lot with her dad, grease and beef smells wafting across the asphalt from McDonald's?

"Laur?"

She shook her head and started walking again. He caught up with her and stopped her with a hand on her shoulder. "We can go home. Mom can e-mail the recipe, or I will."

"It's OK, we can go."

"Are you sure?"

She looked at the ground and saw the scuffed toes of his shoes. There was something about them: she began to cry again. He stepped close and put his arms around her, and she let herself lean against him. The feel and smell of his shirt were like something she'd known once and forgotten. She cried harder. "It's OK," he said, "it's OK." His arms came up around her, and he stroked the back of her head. "Let's get in the car," he murmured, and she let him walk her, his arm around her as a guide. In the hospital, a girl had told her about being escorted by some weird escorting professional to a school for troubled teens in rural Idaho. The escort had insisted that they hold hands whenever they were in a public place. *It's your choice,* the escort had said. *I can cuff you instead.*

Lauren's dad produced his keys as they approached the car. "Do you want to drive?"

She was shocked. "Now?"

"Why not? Your permit's still in the glove compartment."

She hadn't driven since it happened. She didn't know if she still could—couldn't *believe* he thought she could.

With his remote he unlocked the car. He opened the driver's door and held it for her like a chauffeur. "Madam."

She hesitated. The world was impossible, pressing on you from the outside and then suddenly reversing, so that *you* tumbled toward *it.* She got in the car, and her dad closed the door and went around to his side. He buckled up and handed her the keys.

The seat was set for him, way back and low. She pressed the memory button for her setting, and the seat moved forward and up, the mechanism making its familiar *errrr* sound.

"See?" he said. "It remembers you."

She adjusted the mirrors, put the car in reverse, and slowly backed from the spot. She made her way to the parking lot exit and then to the stoplight at University. Across the freeway, she crept along in the line of cars heading for downtown Palo Alto, relieved when she could finally turn and drive more freely. The senior complex was on a street with towering pine trees, and by the time they got there she was liking the feel of driving, liking the way the car gave itself to her, followed her lead. She almost wished they had farther to go.

"Very nice," her dad said. "How'd it feel?"

"Good." She sat still for a moment. "I mean . . . it actually felt really good."

He smiled and cupped the back of her head with his hand. "That's great."

The sidewalk was shady, and she shivered in her sweatshirt, then said yes when he offered her his jacket. Her grandparents had a ground-floor unit, and her dad knocked on their door, using his knuckles rather than the brass-monkey knocker they'd brought back from one of their trips. Her grandpa answered, and there was a look of deep confusion on his face for a moment before he recovered himself and said hello. "My favorite local granddaughter and my favorite son-in-law! Come in, come in."

Lauren hung back for a moment, then let her dad push her toward her grandpa for a hug. Up close, he had begun to have a kind of bad smell, and she held her breath until he let go.

Her grandma came out of the master bedroom, hair tousled as if she'd been lying down.

"You were expecting us, weren't you?" Lauren's dad said. "I hope you weren't napping."

"Of course not," her grandpa said. "Please come in."

Lauren felt her dad's eyes on her, and she looked at him long enough to exchange a smile. Of course they'd been napping—but they'd never admit it.

"Let's have hot chocolate," her grandma said, and she led the way to the tiny kitchen, where she opened a cabinet for a box of Swiss Miss.

"Don't give them that," Lauren's grandpa said.

"It's fine—no one can tell the difference."

"I can."

"That was just when I accidentally bought the diet."

She got out cups and filled her kettle at the sink. She had the kind of Swiss Miss that had miniature marshmallows in a separate paper envelope, and while the water heated she shook a handful of the tiny white pebbles into each cup.

"Is that the new style?" Lauren's grandpa asked her, tweaking the sleeve of her dad's jacket, dangling way past her fingertips. "What's it called, oversize?"

"It's Dad's."

"In a catalog," her grandma said, "I saw men's underwear for women—with a fly and everything!"

"Everything?" Lauren's dad said, and her grandma flapped a hand at him.

"Honestly, Brody," she said, but she was smiling.

A little later, they sat sipping hot chocolate in the living room. This was the darkest room in the condo, too dark for daytime. Lauren let herself go, let her mind wander to her grandparents' old house, on a street with the biggest trees she'd ever seen. When she used to spend the night there, she slept in her mom's old room, imagined she somehow *was* her mom—that someday she'd have her mom's life.

"Have you made plans for the summer, hon?" her grandma asked her.

Lauren pulled herself back to the present. "Not really."

"Because I was wondering if you might want to travel. Your mom spent a summer in France during high school, and she had a wonderful time. She lived with a French family in Brittany, and she wrote letters back and forth with the daughter for years afterward." She turned to Lauren's grandpa. "Remember Marie-Sandrine?"

"Of course," Lauren's grandpa said. "Of course I do." He leaned forward and set his cup on the coffee table. "Funny when you think about it—she almost didn't go."

"Who?" Lauren's dad said. "Liz almost didn't go? To France?"

"Because of Sarabeth," Lauren's grandpa said. "That was the spring Lorelei died."

Lauren stared into her lap. If her dad was giving her grandparents a look, she didn't want to see it. Not long ago, she had told Dr. Lewis about Sarabeth's mom, and he'd said suicides often ran in families, which had made her feel very weird.

"But she did go," Lauren's grandma said, "and she had a great time, and Sarabeth . . . let's see . . . I think that was the summer she worked at the ice-cream parlor, wasn't it, Rob? She'd bring us pints sometimes. The boys loved it."

"Butter pecan," Lauren's grandpa said. "I had a bowl or two myself."

There was a silence. "Listen," Lauren's dad said, scooting forward and setting his cup on the table, "we should get going. I didn't realize how late it was getting." He hesitated a moment and then got to his feet, and Lauren's grandparents stood, too. Lauren took a final sip of the lukewarm chocolate and rose as well. Sarabeth at an ice-cream parlor: she couldn't quite picture it. Was her mom still fighting with Sarabeth? She had no idea.

"Dad," she said, remembering suddenly. "The recipe?"

He smiled. "I almost forgot!" He patted his pants pockets, then took out a folded piece of paper and handed it to Lauren's grandma. "Spare ribs à la your daughter."

Lauren's grandma unfolded the paper and pulled her glasses up onto her nose. "Soy sauce and ginger," she said. "This is the one."

They all stood there. The recipe was at the center of their circle, a small piece of paper covered with Lauren's mom's handwriting, an excuse, Lauren understood, for her grandparents' welfare to be evaluated. *Just checking on you,* she remembered her dad saying long ago, when she woke in the middle of the night to find him outlined in her doorway, the hallway bright behind him. *Go back to sleep,* he said, and she always did.

Valentine's Day fell on a Tuesday, and because it was their custom, Liz and Brody went out for dinner, to a little French place downtown that had been around for years. It was the kind of restaurant where the menu never changed, but the food was so good you didn't care. Brody had escargots for an appetizer, and Liz thought of a day maybe ten years ago when he told the kids to find as many garden snails as they could, because that was what they were having for dinner. The shrieks that brought on. The laughter.

She said, "Remember coming here when Lauren was a baby?"

He had finished the snails and was mopping up the butter with a piece of bread. He said, "I remember coming here a long time ago—maybe when we first moved here?"

"It was the first place we went after Lauren was born. The first place without her."

"Really?"

"My parents babysat."

"Did we have fun?"

"We did."

"My archivist," he said. And then, "Try this."

He held out a piece of butter-soaked bread, and she took it from him and put it in her mouth. It was so garlicky and delicious she nearly groaned with pleasure.

"Good, huh?"

"I could live on it."

"No, you couldn't. Not if you couldn't also have your coffee."

The entrance door swung open, and a couple they knew came in, the parents of one of Joe's soccer teammates: a former college basketball player and his tiny Japanese-born wife. Liz had spent long hours on the sidelines of games with Kiko, sometimes wrapped together in a single blanket if one of them had remembered and the other hadn't.

She said, "Look, it's the Morrises." She waved, and Brody turned and waved, and the Morrises hesitated for a moment and then smiled and waved . . . and kept following the maître d' to their table.

"Isn't it funny?" she said. "If it hadn't been Valentine's Day, I'll bet they would have come over and said hello."

"You think?"

"It's an unwritten rule, no tableside hellos on Valentine's Day."

"Thanks, Jerry."

She grinned; there'd been an era when one of their great pleasures was watching *Seinfeld* together. He was never home in time for the broadcast, or he'd have gone back to the office after dinner, so she generally taped it, and they watched late on Friday nights, when the kids were in bed.

He lifted his glass. "Here's to you."

"To us." She touched her glass to his, and as she looked at him, a surprising, happy feeling spread through her. This was Brody: Brody. He liked red wine and lamb, smelled a certain way after tennis, whistled when he did yard work. When they were first dating he'd had the sweetest way of kissing her goodnight: he'd put his hand on her shoulder, but just one hand on one shoulder, as if he didn't want to stake too large a claim.

You knew you'd slept when you woke, would know you'd been dead only if you were reborn. Was it the same with marriage, its renewal telling you how bad things had gotten? Something had happened in the last couple of weeks, some shift in how they were. The day they saw Dr. Lewis and then sat together afterward in the van: it had started then. Making love that night, they'd taken more time than they had in ages, moved from position to position—it was making love in the sense of making it, from scratch, there and then. At one point she was sitting on top of him, slowly rising all the way off him and then lowering herself down again, and when she finally stopped he reached up with his thumbs and forefingers and twisted her nipples in a way that was both familiar and astonishing. At breakfast the next morning they kept laughing, over the tiniest things.

After dinner they walked down the street, past the bank and the post office. She held his arm. She'd let him down, she felt; she wanted to do better.

At city hall they turned into the rose garden. In spring it would be full of colorful blooms, floodlit at night and a popular destination for evening strollers; but tonight the bushes were bare, and the paths were empty except for the two of them. They walked the outer lanes, gravel crunching under their shoes.

"Hey, I ran into Tom Shepard the other day," he said, "at Ace Hardware."

"You're kidding." She hadn't thought of Tom Shepard in years. Brody had worked with him at Xyno, the company he'd been at before Oiron. Tom had been single; she remembered because she'd tried to fix him up with Sarabeth. "How is he?"

"Great. Married. His wife was with him, she's from Cleveland."

"Oh, how funny. We should have them over."

"That's what I was thinking."

They had circled the garden, and now they left and headed back, passing the library and the fire station.

"How's Sarabeth?" Brody said. "You haven't mentioned her in a while."

They were in front of the town diner now, and Liz looked through the window: dark, though on weekdays it was full of old-timers, on weekends families with toddlers or hordes of soccer-uniformed kids.

She said, "Were you thinking of that time we did dinner with her and Tom?"

"They didn't exactly hit it off."

She let go of his arm and turned up the collar of her coat. "The thing is, I don't actually know."

"What?"

"How Sarabeth is."

He slowed and gave her a puzzled look. "What do you mean?"

"I think we're finished."

Now he stopped altogether. "What are you talking about? What's going on?"

"We aren't talking."

"Liz," he said. "My God, what happened?"

She shrugged.

"I can't believe this. I knew she hadn't been around, but—why didn't you tell me?"

She brought her gloved hands together and listened to the whisper as she rubbed them back and forth. She remembered a mom from the elementary school days, admonishing another woman: *Don't try to talk to your husband—that's what your girlfriends are for.* She thought of her parents' marriage, the absolute division of realms. But look at them now! Playing bridge together, taking each other to the doctor.

Her mother had made it all look so easy.

She looked into Brody's face, saw he was waiting for her. She said, "I don't tell you everything."

He opened his mouth and closed it again, his eyes full of hurt.

"Come on, let's go home," she said, and she took his arm and held it with both her hands, leaning into him as they walked. "Don't worry," she said softly. "It's OK."

He stayed silent until they got to the car. He opened her door. "You can't be finished with Sarabeth, can you?"

"No," she said. "Which is why I may have to be."

"What?"

She got in and adjusted her coat underneath her. "I don't know," she said. "I don't know what I meant by that. But really, don't worry. It's OK."

Kathy had foil-wrapped chocolate hearts on her desk the next day and a sign saying HELP YOURSELF. At first she affected an attitude of mystery, making Brody wonder if she had an admirer. Then she confessed she'd stopped at Walgreens on her way to work, for the half-off sale.

"When these are gone I've got a package of red and pink M&M's waiting."

He said, "You bring out M&M's, I'll rewrite your evaluation. I've gained enough weight this year already." He grabbed another chocolate and waved as he headed into his office.

In fact, he was softer at the middle than he'd ever been before; in bed last night Liz had rubbed her hand back and forth across his abdomen, and his belly had moved with it. He thought of that hand, its southward wanderings, its fingertips at his thighs—its perfect squeezing pressure. And then, at just the right moment, her mouth.

His in-box was already jammed, the usual distribution list junk plus at least a dozen messages requiring real attention. And he had to call Boston, to iron out a few last points with the guys there. He imagined flying out again—just for one day, for the advantages of face-to-face contact. But there was no need.

He made the call, wrote six or eight e-mails, went to a meeting with Russ and Dale Quigley, the CFO. Now there was a go-getter: three major promotions in two years. *Brody,* Dale always said when they ran into each other, *good to see you,* and he'd smile and offer Brody his hand even if they'd just seen each other the day before. (*Watch the smilers,* Brody's dad used to say. *Figure out a guy's smiles, and you've figured out the guy.*)

When the meeting was over, Russ asked Brody to stay. They remained at the conference table, Brody watching Dale as he passed by the interior windows, glanced in at them, walked on.

"He's going places," Russ said.

Brody nodded, then said, "Wait, *going* places going places?" Like Dale or not, he was the best CFO the company'd had; Brody didn't want to see him leave.

"Maybe," Russ said.

"Really?"

Almost imperceptibly Russ shook his head. "So you talked to Boston? We're good?"

Brody brought Russ up to speed, explaining what the CEO had told him. Russ asked some questions about another deal, and then they were finished.

"So what about Dale?" Brody said as he pushed back his chair, but Russ just shrugged.

"He's a striver. He's the only guy I see here after midnight."

"Jesus, Russ, what are you doing here after midnight?"

"It's when I get some of my best work done."

"You amaze me," Brody said. Whatever was going on with Dale, Russ wasn't in a confiding mood. Brody got to his feet and pushed his chair in. "Onward, then."

"Onward." Russ stood, too, and his bare scalp caught the light from one of the spots in the ceiling. He looked tired, but down at the bone level; his skin was tanned from skiing, ruddy from the sun and wind. He tightened his fancy tie, clapped Brody on the shoulder.

"I was thinking," Brody said, but he'd been thinking of the early years, pre-IPO, when he'd worked insane hours himself. He and Russ and a couple other guys had found a Mexican restaurant in Mountain View that would keep its kitchen open late if they had some advance notice, fire up chicken quesadillas at midnight, 1:00 a.m., for the guys at Oiron. It had been fun, crazy, ridiculous. He kind of missed it.

"You were thinking?" Russ said.

"Never mind—better let it percolate a little more." He saluted Russ and headed back to his office, grabbing a couple more chocolates as he passed Kathy's desk. He had phone calls to return, but he went to Google instead, typed "Sarabeth Leoffler" and "Berkeley, CA." Only seven hits, and none with any contact info. He tried People-Finder, but her number was unlisted, as he'd figured it would be.

Not that he would have called. *What's up with you and Liz?* Not in a million years. She was Liz's project, in his view. Liz's *project*. "I have this friend," Liz had said, early on, "she's sort of like a sister"—which had failed to convey the first thing about the reality of the matter. Five feet of chaos, that's what Sarabeth was.

Maybe this was better, actually. A little distance.

But no, he didn't really think that. He'd made his peace with Sarabeth long ago.

At six he wrapped things up and headed to his car. Six o'clock, and the sun wasn't all the way down yet. He liked the California dusk in late winter: pale sky reflected in the pale bay; hills green for the brief spring, little yellow and white flowers sprouting everywhere. And evenings like this: calm, cool, clear.

He wanted last night back again. He wanted all of it: the sex, the rose garden walk, the dinner. He wished he'd made a better toast. *To my beautiful wife* or something. She was, in fact. Beautiful. They hadn't had a weekend away in a long time. Why'd he punted his career, or at the very least plateaued, if he wasn't going to take his wife away for the weekend? He was. Soon.

36

Sarabeth was perplexed by a great many things, but mostly by herself, by the weird tranquillity she was beginning to feel—about Liz, about everything. Maybe it was just the way things were when you got older. You let go more easily.

She had with her house. Nothing bothered her anymore—not the falling-apart bathroom, not the makeshift curtain blocking her view of the Heidts', not the splintery porch nor the dusty pile of objects on the living room floor. The stuff on the floor had even taken on a feeling of permanence. Why not keep it there? It was as good as anywhere else.

In this mood she dug out a box of college papers and found one of her old journals, a blank book with a blue cloth cover. It was full of writing, page after page—not just accounts of her life, but all kinds of other stuff, too: lists of things she'd liked, juxtaposing the exalted ("Chopin's études") with the mundane ("Reese's peanut butter cups"). She'd written about her relationships: "Last night, Jerome said he thought he loved me but that it wouldn't be fair to either of us for him to say so until he was sure. I really respect him for that." Then she'd gone back afterward and annotated: "Hello, Sarabeth? He was an asshole!" She'd experimented with alternate handwritings—all caps, like her architecture-major roommate; the tiniest scrawl possible, to show how tortured she was. She'd even played with her name: Sara, Sara B, Sara-bande, Sarabé.

And then there was this:

> "Lorelei Leoffler is survived by her daughter, Sarabeth."
> Think about this. There's "survived by" and "survived
> by": "outlived by" and "tolerated by." "Lorelei Leoffler
> was tolerated by her daughter, Sarabeth." <u>How true.</u>

She'd been twenty-one when she'd written that—an adult. She couldn't believe the melodrama, the self-pity. Yet she felt in an odd way protective of that former self; when she packed the journal away again, she rubberbanded onto it a note that said "Fragile."

She was less so. One bright Friday afternoon she went window-shopping: peered into an exotic bird store, paused outside a boutique where she'd once bought a clingy red dress she'd never worn. She stopped in front of a brand-new spice shop and on a whim went inside and wandered around, looking into open bowls, leaning down for a smell of clove, of nutmeg and cinnamon. She found a tin labeled STAR ANISE and opened it to a collection of odd, woody flowers, not at all what she'd expected. Star anise—what *had* she expected? The smell was like licorice, and the flowers were exquisite, circles of perfect hard petals that dug into the pads of her fingertips when she squeezed one.

She was finally getting her act together lampshadewise, and she let herself buy the tin, all $5.95 of it, as a souvenir of she didn't know what. She lingered in the shop for an extra moment, reluctant to leave the rows of glass jars, the sound of the grinder as it pulverized hard pods into powder.

Outside, she hesitated; what now? Coldwell Banker had an office nearby, and she wondered if it was the one where Peter Something—Peter Watkins—worked. On tour with Jim last week, she'd seen him for the first time since the day he helped her, and she'd been mildly disappointed when he only smiled and nodded.

"He doesn't remember," she said to Jim.

"Of course he does."

It was the Rockridge Coldwell Banker where he worked, she remembered now. She went and stood in front of this one anyway, looked at the listings and recognized a house she'd staged for Jim a few years back.

She cupped her hands at her eyes and peered inside. There were five or six people at desks, talking on phones or tapping at keyboards. As she looked, a woman at the back saw her and waved, then held up her forefinger as if to say *Wait*.

Did she mean Sarabeth?

The woman smiled and nodded, finger still aloft, and Sarabeth turned around, looking to both sides to make sure there wasn't someone else right there. The sidewalk was empty, and she hesitated and then stepped to the door. She actually recognized the woman, from touring with Jim; she thought Jim had even worked with her once or twice. She was somewhere in that netherworld of fifty to sixty-five, with chin-length gray-blond hair and an Eileen Fisher outfit.

Once inside, Sarabeth took a few steps forward and then stopped. The place was dim, and though the woman smiled as she approached she looked almost surprised. What did she want with Sarabeth? Something about staging?

"Hi, there," she said. "Can I help you?"

Confused, Sarabeth looked around again, and now she saw that in fact a car had pulled to the curb right in front of the office, and the driver had lowered the passenger-side window and was leaning forward, waiting.

A young guy at a nearby desk hung up his phone and looked from Sarabeth to his colleague and back again.

"Do you have a minute?" the woman asked him. "Can you help this lady while I step outside?"

When she was gone, he cracked a wide smile. "Sorry, that was just so classic."

"You saw the whole thing?"

"Start to finish. But I was on the phone, and anyway, some things have to play out in real time."

He was in his early thirties, surprisingly young for a guy in real estate. Men usually came to it later in life; Jim had had a whole career as a high school English teacher before he made the switch. This guy had a pristine look: close shave, expensive polo shirt, immaculate fingernails. He could have been a pilot on his day off, even a male model, though he wasn't particularly handsome; just perfect.

"*Can* we help you?" he said. "Are you house hunting?"

"I was honestly just looking in the window."

"So what *are* you hunting for?"

She hesitated for a moment. "Peace and love, same as everyone else."

His smile was slow at first, and then his lips parted and he was grinning. He said, "Would you settle for coffee?"

"You're asking me to have coffee?"

"Technically, I was asking if you were *hunting* for coffee. But that might be splitting hairs."

"I'm way older than you."

"What does that mean—you have insomnia? A weak bladder? Your days of drinking coffee are over?"

Sarabeth shook her head, but she couldn't stop smiling. "Who *are* you?"

"Who are you?"

"Just a passerby."

"Oh, I doubt that."

The door opened, and the blond woman came back in. "Are we taking care of you?" she asked as she headed back to her desk, but she didn't slow for an answer.

"The royal 'we,' " the guy said under his breath. "What a gal." He lowered his voice even further. "My mother," he added.

Sarabeth looked at the woman, then back at him; she'd have sooner believed they were lovers.

"How old are you?" she said.

"Twenty-eight."

"I was in *college* when you were born."

He shrugged, and she stood there for another moment and then gave him a little wave and headed off, pushing through the door into the sunlight.

37

I don't know what to do for my birthday." Lauren looked directly at Dr. Lewis, then over at his desk, where, to her great frustration, he had no pictures. It was beyond unfair that she had no idea what his wife looked like.

"What would you like to do?"

"That's the thing, I don't know."

"Is there pressure to do something?"

"Well, yeah—it's my birthday."

She thought of birthdays in the past—two years ago, when her parents took her and three friends to *Mamma Mia!;* last year, when her mom paid for her and Amanda to go to a day spa. When she was younger, she'd loved studying magazines for party ideas, but there was really nothing to do that she hadn't already done, and besides, she wasn't in the mood.

His white coat was on a hanger on the back of the door, and she couldn't remember whether it was usually there or not. She had gotten kind of confused about his job—doing therapy here, seeing kids at the hospital. It seemed he should do one or the other.

He laced his fingers together. "I guess another question would be, what do you like to do?"

"For my birthday?"

"For anything."

Here he went again. Every so often he'd sneak this question in, like maybe he'd trick her into having an answer. She didn't like to do anything. That was her problem; she had no interests.

She wished she'd brought a bottle of water. Once, she'd seen a yogurt carton in the garbage under the Kleenex table, and she'd been awestruck that someone would eat in front of him. It wasn't his carton, she was sure—there was another garbage can under his desk.

"You mentioned once," he said, "that you like to draw."

She shrugged. "Yeah."

"Do you like to look at art?"

"I'm not going to go to a museum for my birthday!"

He pooched out his lips, then sort of shrugged.

"That would be incredibly geeky," she went on.

"Your friends aren't interested?"

"I don't *have* friends."

He watched her for a long moment. "You're feeling very empty," he said at last. "It's very painful."

She sighed and looked out the window. Fuck you, she thought. The trees on his street were getting green, and she thought of how she used to try to draw leaves—like, really draw what they looked like. It was hard.

She turned back. "What do you mean 'empty'?"

"No interests, no friends. No boyfriend."

"You mean I'm a total loser."

"I think that's how you feel."

"Because I am one."

"I think there's a difference," he said, "between what you are and how you feel. And I don't think how you feel now will last forever."

"How do you know?"

"I don't, but I'm optimistic. You're attacking yourself, but without as much passion or despair as a couple months ago. You're not as focused on Jeff. And while you can't decide about your birthday, you'd like to do *something,* which encourages me."

The session was over, and she got to her feet and put on her jacket. He stood and opened the door. This moment, passing close by him to get out of his office, was always the same—crowded with things she suddenly wanted to say.

At home that evening she waited until everyone was occupied, then crept into the guest room. In a bookcase there her mom kept several books about art—a big art history book that she'd had since college, a book about the Italian Renaissance, several books on specific artists. There was one Lauren wanted to look at—Alex Katz. She pulled it from the shelf and kicked off her shoes, then sat on the guest room bed. This was a book her parents had bought on a trip to New York before she was born. From all the stuff they'd told her about that trip, you'd have thought they'd been there for months, but it was only a week.

Was it true that she wasn't as focused on Jeff? She'd had some weird moments looking at him lately when she wasn't even sure she liked him anymore. But she did—of course she did.

Somewhere in this book was a picture of a canoe on water, but she couldn't find it. Instead, it was pretty much all paintings of people, and mostly of one person, a woman named Ada. The paintings had dates, and Lauren saw that over the years Alex Katz's painting style had changed from sort of blurry or muddy to really sharp, almost like cutout paper. There was one of a woman—it was Ada again, though it didn't say so—carrying an umbrella in the rain, and Lauren looked at it for a long time, focusing, finally, on the three white dots he'd put on each of her eyes. Those dots and the falling rain—it was as if she were crying, but she didn't really look sad.

At last she found the canoe. She couldn't remember the first time she'd seen it, but it was long ago, when she was a kid. It kind of freaked her out, actually, the canoe nearly filling the picture, blue all around it so you didn't know where it was: near a house and people, or out in the middle of a cold lake. There had been a time when Lauren had taken this book from its shelf quite frequently, had sat on the guest room rug and stared at this picture. The page was even a little smudged. When had that been?

The blue was as dark as the ocean. The canoe was pale yellow, with markings that suggested it was made of bark. It sat on its own reflection, its pale water-self black at one end, as if that end would pull the entire reflected canoe down into the depths, leaving the other one to try to go on by itself. Lauren closed the book and lay back on the bed. The house was quiet: her parents were downstairs somewhere; Joe was in his room doing homework. She had homework, too, a page of math problems she could never finish by tomorrow, which made her feel it was pointless even to start them. She pulled the book close, rolled onto her side, and rested her forearm on its cool, smooth surface. Maybe she would sleep here tonight, for a change.

38

As weekends approached, Sarabeth thought of making plans, but she was never sure she'd feel like following through, and she hated, above all, to cancel on people. It seemed so wishy-washy. It was.

One Friday evening, after opening a container of leftover pasta puttanesca and discovering that it was sprigged with mold, she simply left the house and got in her car and drove. Other people did this—just headed out—why not her? Something interesting would occur to her, and if not there was always Intermezzo.

She hadn't seen a movie in a while, and she headed for the likely theaters, but nothing appealed, at least not at the first few. She headed back to Solano, thinking there might be something interesting at the Albany Twin, and amazingly enough there was an open parking space right in front. She thought it might not even matter what the movies were, given how well everything else was working.

But it did matter. She didn't want to see Catherine Zeta-Jones as a woman with a dying child, nor Jude Law as a football coach. From her car she watched as people spilled down the sidewalk in twos and threes, chatting, laughing, ready for the weekend. She was within a stone's throw of great Indian food, but she didn't move. She couldn't get out of the car, couldn't join the strolling crowd, not by herself. She felt weak and useless for a moment, but then she summoned a positive thought and reached for her phone. She called Nina: no answer. Jim and Donald: no answer. Miranda: no answer. She had cell phone numbers for all of them, and a year ago she might have used them, interrupted them midevening for salvation. Not now.

She started the engine again and looked over her shoulder. Someone was already waiting for the spot, and she reversed with the sense that she could never keep anything, not even a parking place, for quite long enough. All the drive home she thought this, but without the kind of feeling by which such thoughts used to be accompanied. It was neutral, divested of freight. Maybe it was the truth.

The Heidts' house was bright with lights, and she didn't even slow down; she kept going right past it and on to the corner. The clock on her dashboard said 7:42. She reached the freeway quickly, the traffic fairly light for a weekend evening. What to do? She looked at the bridge, saw the way the lights traced the way to the city. Should she? Her last trip across the bay had been the night she saw Liz.

She merged into the bridge traffic. The approach to the toll plaza was a sea of brake lights, and as she neared the stalled cars she felt a sense of misgiving.

Across the bridge, the San Francisco exits offered themselves, but she let each one go by. Passing Cesar Chavez, she realized she was not going to stop, not going to find a little taqueria where she could have a bite to eat and then go home. Coming up was the exit for the Cow Palace, where she had gone with her parents to see Barnum and Bailey; all she remembered was the enrapturing smell of cotton candy and the serious tones with which her parents discussed whether or not to buy her a cone. Did they in the end? She couldn't recall. She drove on, hungry now, the bay on her left and the dark hills of Brisbane up ahead on her right.

In a while, she passed the airport. The network of skyways was still new to her, unnerving. A bit later she passed the exit for Liz's, and she imagined showing up and ringing the doorbell. *Surprise!* She was not about to do that. She was going to Palo Alto then, and she was now hungry enough to wonder what restaurant she could find there. When had she last been to Palo Alto? It had been years, and the restaurants changed all the time. What did she want to eat? Wondering made her ravenous, and it seemed nothing could be large enough, no amount of food huge enough, to satisfy her. She wanted a greasy, dripping cheeseburger was what she wanted.

She took University and headed toward downtown. Driving past one enormous house after another, she remembered a burger place farther south. Could she find it from here? She drove by feel, taking turns that seemed right and then were. She could almost taste the cheeseburger with its charred edges and delicious, soft bun. It had been around forever, this place; it had been a Castleberry tradition, Saturday lunch: Robert would grab a kid or two for the drive, load up on food and milk shakes, and head back home to Cowper Street for the actual eating. When Sarabeth and Liz went with him, they sat in one of the red leather booths while he waited in line, gradually approaching the crank-operated grill, where a woman in a smock stood with a spatula, pulling slips of thin white paper from slices of cheese and then laying them on the blackening rounds of meat.

But the place was closed. Not just closed: gone. Sarabeth gaped from her car. She was over an hour from home, and starving, and she had lost something she'd had at the beginning of this adventure, something vital. She went into a supermarket and bought the last rotisserie chicken in the place, and she devoured it in her car, tearing at the breast meat, gnawing on the legs until the bones were clean. She felt like an animal.

There was a kind of muscle memory to driving these streets, a knowingness activated in a not entirely conscious way. Heading for the freeway, she might not have turned on Cowper at all had she been prepared to see it. But no, it was a complete surprise: COWPER STREET on a sign, in advance enough of the actual corner so that there was time to get into the left lane. As she turned, she slowed down and cracked the window, and cold air came in, along with a tree smell from her childhood.

She parked in front of what had been the Castleberrys' house. Across the street, the streetlight that used to keep her awake was gone.

Her parents' bedroom window was dark. She got out of the car and jaywalked, then stood still on the sidewalk. It was a stucco house with shutters and a turret with a conical roof that her mother had despised. "My Hansel and Gretel house," she used to say. Standing in the cold night air, Sarabeth wondered at the sheer energy it must have taken for her mother to be dissatisfied by so much. Her psyche was like a huge grid of mousetraps, set to spring at the lightest touch. There were traps for Sarabeth's father, traps for Sarabeth. The biggest trap, though, was the grid itself, the trap of being Lorelei.

Sarabeth thought of her own miserable time around the holidays, how at certain moments she had feared that she might decide she couldn't do it anymore, couldn't stand it anymore, feeling as she felt. Was that what Lorelei had lived with? Feeling horrible, and feeling that her stamina for feeling horrible might run out? They had been so awful, those feelings: the tiny bit of them that Sarabeth tasted. Did they go away for Lorelei, the morning she took the pills? Was there a period when she felt better, relieved? Sarabeth thought of Anna, tumbling toward the wheels of the train and hating what she'd done. She so hoped Lorelei had been calm as she went.

She looked at the house again, took herself back thirty-five, forty years. She imagined following the brick walkway to the front door, stepping into the entryway, and having in her possession the thing that would lift Lorelei's spirits forever. She imagined this Lorelei, her spirits forever lifted, greeting her and asking: *How was your day?* She let this image stretch out, expand: herself in school clothes, carrying a metal lunch box; Lorelei calm and combed and cheerful. *How was your day?* She imagined a Lorelei with room inside herself for the response.

She remembered the damp air in Tilden Park, the mud. The things inside her that she had wanted help in carrying—would they have been so poisonous if that help had been available when she was younger? Maybe a mother *was* a cauldron, or something simpler: a plain round bowl.

And if so, what was a friend? She looked at the Castleberrys' old house. Love, she thought. Kindness.

In fact, she'd had both from her mother, in bits and pieces. She could remember Lorelei sitting at her bedside when she was sick, bringing her toast and ice water, playing cards with her if she felt well enough. And Lorelei's excited applause when she learned to ride a bike, watching from the sidewalk as Sarabeth's father trotted along holding the handlebars and then, at just the right moment, let go.

Do you miss her?

Maybe so—despite the dark corners, despite the cold winds. Maybe she missed not only the Lorelei who was but also the Lorelei who wasn't: the one who might have been. Maybe that Lorelei even more.

39

I thought of something," Lauren said.

It was her birthday, and though she'd managed to come up with a dinner Liz could make—spaghetti and meatballs with garlic bread, followed by chocolate cake—she had insisted that there was nothing she wanted in the way of a present, not one single thing.

Liz waited, and she saw that Brody, at the sink washing dishes, was waiting, too.

"Art books," Lauren said. "Or an art book—I know they're expensive."

Liz was thrilled, beyond thrilled, ecstatic—she'd been agonizing over Lauren's apathy. "Great idea," she exclaimed. "Really great—that's something that'll give you a lot of pleasure for a long time."

"Do you want us to choose?" Brody said, turning off the water. "Or would it be more fun to choose yourself?"

"I don't know," Lauren said. "Choose myself, I guess. But I won't go crazy, I promise. I know they're expensive."

Brody winked at Liz. "Are you kidding? I don't know about Mom, but I was afraid you were going to say a car."

"Yeah," Liz said. "A Mercedes SUV."

Lauren cracked a smile—an amused, knowing smile that buoyed Liz's spirits even further. Liz had been referring to a story of a few years back about some private school parents who agonized over whether or not to buy their daughter a brand-new Mercedes SUV for her sixteenth birthday. They went back and forth, back and forth, and finally they bought the car . . . but they had it distressed before they gave it to her.

"I still think that was an urban myth," Brody said.

"It was a suburban myth," Lauren quipped, and Liz thought her heart might burst with joy.

Later that evening she lingered in Lauren's room, listened as Lauren told her she wanted to get a job this summer, either something incredibly boring that paid well or a nonpaying internship doing something really cool. "Just—I don't want to be greedy," she said. And then somehow, a little later, Liz began telling Lauren the story of her own sixteenth birthday, how all she'd wanted was a certain pair of platform sandals she'd found at Macy's, how she'd written down the style number for her mother and then gone back and taken a picture of them so there could be no mistake. But next to her plate at her birthday breakfast was a package far too small to contain any shoes, let alone platform sandals. "Happy birthday," her parents said together, and inside was a beautiful ring, gold set with her birthstone. "We couldn't get you sandals for your sweet sixteen," her mother said. And all day Liz wore the ring and tried to be happy with it, tried to love it, but in truth she was crushed. The sandals—they'd be gone for sure now. And they'd been so right, so perfect. After the birthday cake that night, John and Steve said they were going upstairs to do homework, but back down they came, carrying a wrapped package just the size of a shoe box. Which in fact it was.

"And the moral of the story?" Lauren said.

"What should it be?"

"Never give up hope?"

"That's a good moral."

Lauren tucked her hair behind her ears. Liz was making sure not to look right into her eyes, or to do so only briefly. I'm talking to my daughter, she thought. We're talking, right now.

"Did you think about getting me a birthstone ring?" Lauren asked.

Liz thought of the conversations she and Brody had had about this, how in some sense they had decided against a birthstone ring, in that they'd decided against anything that would push her, preempt her.

"We didn't know if you'd like one," she said, not untruthfully. "Would you?"

Lauren held out her hands. She'd gotten a couple new thick silver rings lately and now wore them in stacks. "I guess not."

"There's always eighteen," Liz said. "If you change your mind."

"Mom," Lauren said. "I might want to go to art school instead of college."

"Really?"

"Or at least to a college where you can do a lot of art."

Two years from now, Lauren would be about to graduate from high school. Today, for the first time, Liz could imagine it.

She was wired. Brody could tell even before she got into bed: by the way she moved around in the bathroom, the sounds she made as she closed the medicine cabinet, rinsed her mouth out, turned off the water. Pulling back the covers and climbing in next to him, she said, "I want to take her for the books tomorrow." And then, "Did you *hear* her *voice*?" And then, "I am *so* not tired. Maybe I'll get up. But what would I do?"

"Clean the kitchen?" he said.

"Paint the kitchen!" she said with a laugh. "Paint the whole house! Sorry, I'll calm down in a while. I'm just— I don't know what."

He squeezed her hand. "You're relieved."

"No, I'm . . . I'm . . ." She chuckled. "I'm relurved."

"What?"

"Remember that part in *Annie Hall*? When Diane Keaton asks him if he loves her, and he says 'I don't love you, I . . . I . . . I lurv you.' "

"I lurv you," he said.

"Do you think we should tell Dr. Lewis?"

"That we lurv each other?"

She laughed with delight, and he brought her hand to his mouth and kissed her knuckles.

She fell silent, and he thought of how things had been between them during the worst of it. *It's very common to feel angry when there are differences in how you're handling things.*

He said, "Can I ask you a question?"

"Sure."

"How guilty did you feel?"

" 'Did'?"

"Do."

"Incredibly," she said. "Completely, absolutely, totally. Solely."

" 'Solely'?"

"I was *here*. Why didn't I go back to work when Joe started school? So I could be home with my kids."

"Liz," he said. "It was nothing you did."

"I don't believe that, and I'll bet you don't either. About yourself."

Brody sighed. The thing was, what could you pinpoint? And it was more about what they hadn't done than what they had. Stopped her— that was what they hadn't done.

Joe had scarfed his slice of cake tonight and then headed to Trent's for an evening of poker. You had a girl who fell into misery, a boy who skipped from school to soccer to five-card stud. But that didn't really say anything.

"What do you think you did?" he said.

She'd been on her side, facing him, and now she rolled onto her back. She lay there for a long time, and he thought maybe the question had been too much. *I don't tell you everything.* At last, when he wondered if she would speak again all night, she began.

"I let myself get hurt when she yelled at me. I didn't encourage her enough when she was scared to try something new I didn't show I believed in her. I let her see me crying on her first day of kindergarten, for God's sake." She paused. "I had Joe."

Brody rolled to face her. "We both had Joe."

"No, not really. Not really."

He thought about this, remembered the long-ago days right after Joe's birth, the way Lauren would ask him: *Is he drinking milk? Is he still drinking milk?* He said, "Do you really think those things caused it?"

"Dr. Lewis?" she said. "On the phone once? He said it's easier if you feel it was your fault."

"That's absurd."

"I know, it sounds crazy, but the point is: if it was your fault, then you weren't powerless—you weren't at the mercy of stuff just happening."

"You're always going to be at the mercy of stuff just happening, no matter what."

She moved closer, draping her arm across his middle and tucking her hand into the space between his elbow and his side. "You're right," she murmured. She pressed her lips to his chest, and he leaned down and kissed the top of her head. He imagined wrapping both arms around her, holding her so close they could almost merge.

"Let's go away," he said, but she just nestled closer and perhaps hadn't heard. They were moving toward the moment when one of them would fall asleep. Early in their relationship they'd enjoyed arguing over who'd gone first: "It was you," "No, it was you, I heard you snoring." This would be in the morning, their legs intertwined, the outside world farther away than it ever was now.

The next day, Lauren spent over an hour browsing through art books, thinking, as she pulled volume after volume from the shelves, that two hundred dollars was both an insane amount of money to spend in a bookstore and barely enough to satisfy her longings. Other customers stepped around her, but she barely noticed them, she was so taken by the smooth, heavy pages, by the shapes and colors they revealed. "Couldn't find anything?" her dad asked when she rejoined her parents in the café next door. "More like the opposite," she said. "I'm going to need to come back."

"You're excited," Dr. Lewis said when she told him about it.

"So?"

"I guess I'm noticing that your mood seems lighter."

It was true, she supposed. One thing was, at school she actually had a new friend. Amanda was off with Noah all the time, and Lauren was now eating lunch with this bizarre, morose-looking girl who wore fishnet stockings and tons of black eyeliner. Her name was Myrna, and she'd been new at the beginning of the year: the victim, as she put it, of her dad's midlife crisis. "Most men are content to start fucking their secretaries. My dad has to surf the California coast." He'd taken early retirement from his lawyer's job and talked her mother into giving up a perfectly happy life in New York for the insane Bay Area.

"New York?" Lauren said.

"Oh, calm down—it was just Poughkeepsie."

It was a friendship that shouldn't have been, except Lauren had something Myrna needed: school-wide indifference. For months Myrna had been an outcast, an East Coast freak, but once she started hanging out with Lauren, the bitchy whispers ebbed, and she could, as she put it, just kick. She said, "We don't even have to like each other, you know? It's like, hanging out as camouflage." They were at lunch, and she dug in her backpack and pulled out a spotted banana. "I mean, I do like you," she said as she began to peel it. "But that's just sort of a bonus." She lifted the banana to her mouth and took a bite, and Lauren almost choked on her sandwich. No one ate a banana that way at school. Then she realized Myrna was right: as much as she helped Myrna blend in, Myrna helped her disappear. Who would notice the girl who slit her wrists when another girl was giving a public blow job to a piece of fruit?

It turned out Myrna didn't know what Lauren had done—which Lauren didn't know until one day when Myrna started talking about a girl she'd known back home who'd actually done it: killed herself. Lauren was all, "It's OK, don't worry," but Myrna didn't seem to get it, so Lauren finally said, "You know about me, right?" and Myrna's eyes widened. Then Lauren told her, and Myrna turned purple and almost started crying. "Oh, my God," she said. "I'm such a fucking asshole."

"Why?" Lauren said. "Because you didn't know? How were you supposed to know?" She felt almost like Dr. Lewis saying that, and it actually calmed Myrna down a bit.

"So we're the freak and Sylvia Plath," she said the next day.

"I'm not Sylvia Plath!" Lauren said, laughing a little. "She stuck her head in an oven, for one thing."

"Then someone else. Who slit their wrists? What did you use, any-way—a razor blade?"

"An X-Acto."

"That's cool, that's very artsy. Aimee Berman would use a nail file."

They were united in their hatred of Aimee Berman, which was fitting, since it was Aimee who had united them—chosen every other girl in PE to be on her volleyball team. Well, half the other girls; her friend Sierra—her bitch, as Myrna put it—had chosen the other half. "I don't care," Aimee had said when confronted at the end of the selection process by the sight of Lauren and Myrna still waiting to be chosen. Sierra said she didn't care either, and then the entire class stood there until at last the teacher woke from her daze and assigned Lauren to one of the teams and Myrna to the other. "Serve into her head," Myrna whispered as Lauren headed for Sierra. "I'll do the same with Little Miss Cunt."

"Wow," Dr. Lewis said about Myrna.

"What? She's just this girl."

"Six months ago," he said, "I'm not sure you'd have been able to start a new friendship."

"I didn't know her six months ago."

He smiled.

"What?"

"You may have a future as an attorney."

"What's that supposed to mean?" she said, but now she was fighting a smile, and she gave up and laughed.

"You've got a pretty persuasive argument that you're not *feeling* better—life is just suddenly better."

"It is," she said, but now they were both laughing, and she had to bite the inside of her lip to stop.

She bought a book: Richard Diebenkorn. He painted sort of geometric abstractions in soft colors, and they reminded her of maps and also of quilts—modern quilts like she'd seen once at a shop, without patterns. Looking at one of his paintings, she imagined lifting up the edge of a pale blue rectangle and lying down underneath it.

She kept the book in the guest room, and maybe because she was in there a lot she started using the guest bathroom—she even moved her stuff in. It was about like her and Joe's bathroom, but the tiles were light blue instead of peach, and it had this sort of clean-hotel feel to it. Plus, obviously. She wasn't sure why it had taken her so long to see that she really never had to go back into her and Joe's bathroom again.

One Sunday afternoon she sat on the counter and shaved her legs. She'd brought along a bar of Ivory, but she used the special guest soap instead, its rose smell opening up as the bathroom filled with steam. After she rinsed, she dried off and chose some honey-almond lotion from inside the medicine cabinet, where there was a whole range of fancy stuff that her mom kept there for guests—which basically meant for Sarabeth. Or had.

Lauren's grandparents came for dinner that night, and it reminded Lauren of long ago: her grandma brought these addictive spiced pecans she used to always make, and her grandpa got her dad talking about some new company he'd read about in *Wired* magazine. He'd worked in the computer industry himself, back when there barely was one.

At dinner, during a lull in the conversation, Lauren turned to her mom and said, "How's Sarabeth?" Being in the guest bathroom had pushed her. She'd gotten tired of wondering when she'd ever see Sarabeth again. There was something Lauren needed to say to her, though she wasn't sure what.

The lull turned into a void. Her grandma looked at her mom; her mom looked at her dad; her dad looked at her.

"I've been wondering that, too," her grandma said.

Color filled her mom's cheeks, and Lauren wondered if she'd made a mistake.

"Well," her mom said in a light voice. "I can give you her number if you want."

Lauren felt a rushing sensation, as if she were falling through the seat of her chair. It was as if her mom had said: *I don't know and I don't care.*

"Hey," Lauren's dad said, standing up, "who wants more salmon? Marguerite? You sure? How about you, Robert? I've got a nice crisp end for you."

"Got to watch my waistline, Brody," Lauren's grandpa said. "Thanks, anyway."

"Honey?"

Lauren's mom didn't respond. Her face was still pink, and Lauren wondered if she'd even heard him.

"Well, I will," her dad said. "How about you guys? Laur? Joe? I don't know how the rest of you can resist, it's so good." He picked up his plate and headed for the salmon, whistling as he walked. He forked a piece of fish onto his plate and brought it back to the table. Lauren watched him take a bite, chew, drink some wine. He was pretending it hadn't just happened, her mom saying what she'd said.

Across the table, her mom and her grandpa had started discussing a trip her grandparents were planning, to Scandinavia, and she watched her mom, saw how she nodded while she was listening, her head cocked a little to the side. She was pretending, too. What was Lauren supposed to do? She wished she could leave the table, but she didn't want to do that. *I'm not going to school today.* She didn't want to be that.

"June," her grandpa said, "is supposed to be the best month for the fjords." He turned to Joe. "What about you, Joe? Going back to camp this summer?"

"Definitely," Joe said.

Lauren looked at her dad again. He was watching her mom, and she thought suddenly of the portraits by Alex Katz, how there were three things that told you what kind of mood the person was in: the set of the mouth, the shadows on the face, and the reflection of light—the little white dots—on the eyes.

40

Temperatures were rising, and Sarabeth called Miranda, suggested a walk around Lake Merritt. They went on a Sunday, passed picnicking families and couples on Rollerblades, and a pack of teenagers who were perched on a pair of bike racks: talking loud, chiding one another, laughing. Sarabeth imagined a time in the future when Lauren would look her up, and the two of them would have dinner and talk first about the present, and then about the recent past, and only toward the end about this year. *I thought about you,* Lauren might say, *I wondered what happened to you,* and Sarabeth would say, *I thought about you, too.*

Because she did. She thought about Lauren much younger and also Lauren now, about the things inside her that had caused her to do what she'd done. Sarabeth wondered what those things had been, what they'd felt like, sounded like. How much they'd been like the things inside Lorelei.

The song was quieter. It was hardly there. *It was so familiar,* she would tell Lauren. *I was sure I knew it. I was always trying to hear the words.*

Don't worry about the words, she imagined Lauren saying. *You don't want to hear the words.*

Another day, she set about washing the outsides of her windows. The sky was a soft, hazy blue, and it was so warm she stripped down to the camisole she wore under her sweater. It was satisfying to stand on a ladder in the sun, satisfying to give her house a little elbow grease. Windex hooked to her belt loop, she moved from window to window, until at last she arrived at the big front one.

The red tablecloth looked pretty bad from out here, and as she sprayed she thought she should get a real curtain. She wiped the running Windex and then rubbed the glass in circles, imagining something sheer, something that would let in some light. The window was a little wider than her arm span, and she found that she couldn't quite reach to the far side. She considered repositioning the ladder but instead stepped to the window ledge, where she found her balance and sprayed again.

"You're kind of like Spider-Man," said a voice.

She turned, and there was Pilar, standing in the middle of her family's backyard, wearing too-small flowered bike shorts and a tank top.

"I guess I am," Sarabeth said.

"I'm not allowed to see that movie," Pilar said, taking a step closer. "My sister isn't, either."

"If you're not allowed to see it, then how do you know what he's like?"

"I snuck."

"You snuck into the movie?"

"I snuck watching the preview. Dummy."

"Oh," Sarabeth said. "Got it." She hesitated for a moment and then turned back to the window. She wiped it, sprayed again, wiped again. She hooked the Windex back in her belt loop, stepped onto the ladder, climbed down.

"Fighting is worse than kissing," Pilar said from very nearby. "In movies."

"Goodness, you're very quiet," Sarabeth said. Pilar had moved—as stealthily as the Indian whose headdress she'd worn on Thanksgiving— and was now just a few feet away.

Pilar shook her head. "No, I'm not. My teacher says I'm too loud."

"Oh. That's not very nice."

"Well, my mom says I have to cooperate or I'll get a consequence."

Sarabeth looked Pilar over. She wore orange plastic sandals and glittery purple nail polish, and a dirty Band-Aid flapped from her knee. This was the first time Sarabeth had seen her up close since Thanksgiving, and she thought Pilar was not as fetching as she had been. She was growing and leaving her cuteness behind.

They stood there looking at each other. Sarabeth considered taking the ladder back to her shed, but she wasn't sure how to walk away. "Would you like to come in?" she said.

"Do you have any cookies?"

"I may." She led the way up the porch steps and into the house. In the kitchen she opened a cabinet. "I have some digestive biscuits," she said. "Do you like those?"

Pilar stared up at the shelf. "What are they?"

Sarabeth handed Pilar the package. "They're pretty tasty, actually."

"Are they good for you?"

"I think so. I think they're high in fiber."

Pilar handed them back. "My dad eats cereal like that. To help him poop."

"Ah."

"Do you have any lemonade?"

"You know, I don't. I have tangerine-grapefruit juice, though."

"That's OK. Look, I lost a tooth." Pilar thrust her jaw forward and pulled down her lower lip, revealing a tiny space right in front.

"Very cool," Sarabeth said. "Did the tooth fairy come?"

"She gave me a dollar."

"Wow. She's gotten a lot nicer since I was a kid."

"Were you fast on teeth?"

Sarabeth didn't understand this. "Fast on teeth?"

"I'm slow on them. My sister is superfast. When she was my age she'd lost five teeth already."

"Oh," Sarabeth said. "I see."

"I'm fast on height. I grew three inches since my last birthday. My sister only grew one." Pilar looked at Sarabeth. "What are you fast on?"

"Me?" Sarabeth said. "Grown-ups can be pretty slow, actually."

"So can kids. My brother is very slow on table manners."

"He'll get there."

"That's what my mom says. My dad says, 'Isaac! Use your fork!'" For this last, she nearly shouted. "My dad thinks you're pretty," she added.

"You know," Sarabeth said, "you might not want to tell people what other people think about them."

"It's OK," Pilar said. "Beauty is in the eye of the beholder. There's really no such thing as pretty."

Sarabeth smiled. Pilar *was* still fetching—but in a different, more complicated way. When you didn't see people for a while, you could see the changes in them more clearly.

"I have to go now," Pilar said. "But I could come back over sometime, when you have other cookies."

"I'd like that," Sarabeth said, and she walked Pilar to the front door and then watched as she trotted home. When the Heidts' patio door was closed again, she went down the porch steps and circled her house, admiring her cleaned windows. She liked the way bits of branches and sky were reflected in the glass. It was quite cool in the shade now. She remembered springtime in her own childhood, when the nights were so much cooler than the days, and the house in the late afternoon was chilly and dark. She pictured Pilar inside her house, shivering in her bike shorts and tank top but refusing to change.

41

*L*iz returned to yoga. She felt so stiff and weak—far more so than
when she had first started, years ago. "Take it easy," Diane told
her, but she pushed hard. She pushed against her burning hamstrings,
against her tired arms and resistant hips. She pushed against having let
yoga go for so long and against how difficult it was to return.

Next, she went back to the bench. She wrote up a schedule for herself, a habit from long ago—from junior high, in fact, when she and Sarabeth would plan their assaults on the boys they liked, down to *Hi* on
Monday and *Do you have a pen I can borrow?* on Wednesday or Friday.
Making the schedules was far more fun than talking to or even kissing the
boys, though they hadn't known that then. They spent hours at it, laughing over the question of which was a bigger step, asking a boy for the time
or saying *Hey, cool bike.*

Over many days, she got the blue and yellow lines she'd painted in
the fall to intersect in green, a slow process of taping and painting and
waiting and taping and painting and waiting. At last, her plaid finished,
she was ready for the final touch.

So many things could suggest a flower: a circle of dots, a dot surrounded by zigzags, a series of soft arcs to imply a rose. She used them all.
She painted tiny red snapdragon-like flowers and tiny orange zinnia-like

flowers and tiny daisies of yellow and white. The work was slow and painstaking. At first, she tried not to repeat herself, but she had too much space to cover for that. And who ever heard of a garden in which every flower was unique?

She finished late one Sunday afternoon, her legs and arms stiff and aching as she straightened up and dropped her brushes into the garage sink. Brody and Lauren were in the family room, Brody grubby from an afternoon spent in the yard. "I'm done," she said, stepping up into the kitchen.

Brody looked up. "*Done* done?"

"I believe so."

"Your hands," Lauren exclaimed, coming over. "They're like a Seurat."

Liz turned her hands over, turned them back. They were dotted with color.

"Hang on a sec," Lauren said, and she ran up the stairs and returned with a piece of paper. "Here, do a print." She laid the paper on the counter and directed Liz to press her palms to it.

"Cool," she said when Liz lifted her hands away. "Check it out."

The paper bore two ghostly handprints, patterned with what looked like pastel camouflage.

"Now that," Brody said, "is a fine collaboration."

They followed her back to the garage, Lauren slipping past her and saying, "I can't *believe* how many flowers you painted. That is so OCD." She looked back at Liz. "But in a good way. It's really cool."

Liz leaned against the washing machine as they bent to look closer. She wondered if there would come a time when this bench would stop reminding her of the split in her life, when she would no longer think that the yellow and blue represented innocence while the rest was from After.

She'd planned nothing for dinner, and Brody suggested going out for pizza. She headed upstairs to tell Joe, passing by the bathroom that only he now used.

He was at his desk with a book. His room was immaculate, bedspread pulled tight, not so much as a single sock in sight.

"What are you doing?" she said, and he turned to look at her.

"Reading."

"You OK?"

He gave her a puzzled look, as if to say: *Of course I'm OK. Why wouldn't I be OK?*

No reason. Anxious expectation, that's what she had. Her new companion. Mother's little helper, but in reverse. Mother's little hindrance.

"You know," her own mother had said to her in the kitchen before Easter dinner, the two of them working together, arranging asparagus on a platter, tossing tiny boiled potatoes with butter, "you know, you kids really raised yourselves. I was just there in case things went wrong." Which had made Liz want to take her mother by the shoulders and shake some sense into her, shake some memory into her. *Hello?* she'd wanted to say. *Remember the day John was born? Remember the day Steve left for college? Don't you remember being kind of busy for the twenty-five years in between?*

"We're going out for pizza," she said to Joe. "Ten minutes."

"Can we get pepperoni?"

This was because Lauren didn't like pepperoni; Lauren preferred veggie or pesto chicken. His diffidence broke her heart. She went to him and kissed his head, smelled soap and a trace of unfresh scalp. She put her hand in his hair and ruffled it a bit. "Absolutely we can get pepperoni," she said. "We'll get whatever you want."

Suddenly the end of the school year was in sight. It was still seven or eight weeks off, but Lauren believed in it now, knew it was a matter of actual days beginning and ending rather than a miraculous lift from here to there. This was partly due to the weather, partly due to a plan she and Myrna had to get Myrna's dad to teach them to surf, and partly due to the fact—the *fact*—that she was feeling better.

Leaving math on Wednesday, she scanned the courtyard for Myrna, eager to tell her about the crazy thing that had just happened, Aimee Berman getting busted for using her cell phone during class. Mr. Pavlovich had humiliated her, demanding that she come up to his desk, and then flourishing a yellow principal's ticket at her as if the whole thing made him happy. Aimee's phone would be confiscated and kept in the office for a week. Far worse, she'd be barred from attending the next—and as it happened final—school dance.

People were moving here and there across the courtyard, but Myrna was nowhere to be seen. Lauren figured she was already at her locker, and she headed in that direction, looking the other way when she passed

Amanda and Noah on a bench outside the cafeteria. A year ago, she would never have believed that not having Amanda as her best friend might be OK, but somehow it was. They still sat together in the classes they had together, and they talked a bit, but the rest of the time it was as if they barely knew each other.

Lauren wondered what you did if you were Aimee Berman and in deep shit. Aimee Berman busted just didn't compute.

Mr. Greenway walked by, nodding at her as their paths crossed. She nodded back. She received a strange kind of recognition from certain teachers, almost a sanction. It was like they were saying: *Yes—yes, you.* It bugged her, but seeing as she couldn't stop it, she hoped it would help with her grades.

There was Myrna, coming out of the locker area, scanning the court-yard herself. Lauren raised her hand and waved, then quickly dropped it. She'd just seen Aimee. Aimee and Tyler and Jeff, standing near the science complex. Why hadn't Aimee gone to the office? She was crying, and Tyler's arms were around her, and Lauren thought, How pathetic, though she also felt kind of sorry for her. She made sure Myrna hadn't seen her and stepped back into the shadows.

Jeff was just standing there, a few feet from Tyler and Aimee. Do something, Lauren thought. Leave. But he didn't. His pack hung from his shoulder, and he moved the toe of his shoe back and forth over the asphalt.

Tyler put his hands on Aimee's shoulders and bent to look at her. He would graduate in six weeks, and Lauren had heard he was going to the University of Oregon in the fall. What would happen then?

He took Aimee's backpack from her and slung it over his free shoulder, and then, one of his arms around her, they began walking toward the office. Lauren tracked their progress, thinking, Dead Girl Walking, though it didn't seem all that funny. She watched for a while and then looked back at Jeff, and to her surprise he was looking right at her. Immediately her heart raced, but she didn't look away, and after a moment he kind of smiled and shrugged, then he turned and headed out of sight.

"Because he's an artiste," Myrna said a little later. "He has to suff-aire."

They were at the Jamba Juice across from school, sipping smoothies and talking about a cousin of hers who lived in New York City, in an apartment the size of "your average bathroom," as Myrna put it.

"I mean, you should see the cockroaches in that place—they're like the size of mice."

"OK, I take it back," Lauren said. "I'm not jealous."

"If it was Paris I'd let you be jealous."

"If it was Paris I'd be on the next plane. I'd be all, *Hi, Myrna's cousin, I'm just going to unroll my sleeping bag here, OK? Don't mind me, I won't be any trouble.*"

"Au revoir, Mom and Dad."

"No kidding." Lauren pried the lid off her cup and used the straw to stir her smoothie. "Dear Mom and Dad," she'd write on a postcard of the Eiffel Tower. But then what would she say?

"He even had a real mouse once," Myrna said.

"Who?"

"My cousin. And listen to this—instead of setting a trap he fed the fucker."

"Gross," Lauren said, but she'd begun thinking of Dr. Lewis, of something he'd told her last week. They were talking about Prozac again, about whether or not it did anything, and somehow they got onto the subject of how antidepressants were first tested, back when they were new. Drug testing always started with animals, he explained, and he described how the researchers would give one mouse the antidepressant drug and another nothing, and then they'd put them both into buckets of water and see which fought harder to stay afloat. They were measuring the drug's effect on mouse despair.

Mouse despair. Something about that really got Lauren.

Myrna's mom arrived a little later to pick them up. She drove a funky old Saab, and when she saw Lauren she said, "Hey, doll—how're things?"

"Fine, thanks," Lauren said as she got into the backseat. The car was messy and smelled of Myrna's dog, but she was happy to be in it. She had only been to Myrna's house once, but she was dying to go again. Everything about Myrna was interesting.

They left the shopping center and drove past the high school and then up the hill. Myrna's mom glanced over her shoulder and said, "So Lauren, what are you two beauties up to these days? My daughter won't tell me anything."

"Mom," Myrna said from the passenger seat. "Don't call us beauties."

Her mom shrugged. "Damn—busted on my first sentence."

"You said 'Hey, doll' to Lauren when we first got in."

"That's true, I did."

In the backseat, Lauren closed her eyes. She felt a smile pulling at her mouth, and she let it pull, let her lips come apart and her teeth feel the air.

At home she dropped her backpack at the foot of the stairs. "Picking up Joe," said a note on the kitchen counter. She went up to her room, found a sketch pad, and flipped through it to a clean page. She thought of Jeff after school today, that little smile he'd given her—or had she imagined it? The little smile, the shrugged shoulders. He was going to Chico. Party school, everyone said.

She started to draw a mouse in a bucket. The problem was, she kept making it cute: Its little face peeking over the edge. Its big eyes and long, silly whiskers. She didn't know how to get the despair in. It might work better if it were a view from above, but how to put despair in a mouse's ears and tail? Desolation in its legs and terror in its lumpish little body.

Jeff, staring at the ground. What was he looking at? What was he thinking? She wondered if she was going to laugh about him someday, like Sarabeth with the guy Doug.

Puppy love, she thought.

Mouse despair.

Mouse-*sized* despair, as if it were small, what she'd felt: a junior version of something adults experienced, of something she might experience someday. On the Internet she'd learned that depression often came back. Did it come back bigger?

What are you doing? Dr. Lewis might say.

I don't know—trying to scare myself? As a way of attacking myself?

I can see that. But I think there's another possibility. Maybe you're trying to prepare yourself for something that's very scary. So you won't be surprised if it happens. I could make an argument that you're not attacking yourself, you're trying to take care of yourself. Do you think?

Sure, Lauren said. She flipped the page and started to draw again. *If you say so.*

Brody had a busy week, including a quick trip to LA and a management meeting late Thursday afternoon. It was Russ and all the VPs, gearing up for the first-quarter board meeting. Last time around, Brody had been caught short—how he'd gotten anything done in December he didn't know—and so he was actually ahead of the game. He sat and listened to the other guys—plus Joanne Ramirez, from HR—talk about how they were ready with their updated PowerPoints, knowing full well they'd spend their weekends here.

At home that evening, Liz asked him to help her move the bench to the entry hall. He got the old one out of the way first, then carried the new one in and stood with her while she appraised it.

She held her right arm across her stomach, tucked her left fist under her chin. He could tell she was disappointed, and he said, "I think it looks good."

She shook her head. "No, it's all wrong here. I don't know what I was thinking."

The entry hall had a serious look: grayish-green walls, some botanical prints he'd given her for Christmas early in their marriage. The old bench had fit better—a woven straw seat on dark wood legs.

"It kind of livens things up," he said, but she grimaced, moved to drag the bench away from the wall, gave up and headed for the kitchen.

He followed after her. "Maybe it could go in here," he said, glancing around the family room and knowing even as he spoke that she'd say no.

"That wouldn't work, either. It doesn't matter. When you get a chance can you just take it back to the garage?"

Lauren was sitting at the coffee table doing homework. She looked up and said, "What are you guys talking about?"

"The bench," Liz said. "It doesn't really go."

"You're kidding." Lauren got to her feet and made for the living room. In a moment she was back.

"See what I mean?" Liz said.

"It totally doesn't go."

"I didn't think it was so bad," Brody said. "I thought it was kind of cheerful."

"Dad, you're high," Lauren said. She went to the refrigerator and got an apple; Brody watched as she cut it into slices and arranged them in a pinwheel pattern on a plate. Back at the coffee table, she took up her pencil again and said, "You know who it reminds me of?"

Liz looked over at her. "What?"

"The bench," Lauren said. "Sarabeth."

Liz looked as if she'd been punched. Brody didn't understand what Lauren's problem was. Why was she bringing up Sarabeth again? Surely she'd noticed the effect on Liz the last time.

He moved to the drainboard, where Liz was putting things away. He said, "Here, I've got that." He took a platter from her and reached it to the high shelf where it was kept. He put away a colander, a mixing bowl.

She hadn't spoken, and he said, "I think you should give it a day or two. Or you know what? It could go upstairs, on the landing. Wouldn't it be nice to have something there?"

She was looking at Lauren, and he wondered if she'd even heard him. "But it's plaid," she said to Lauren. "With preppy colors."

"I know," Lauren said. "But it made me think of her." She picked up an apple slice, then set it down again. "What's going on with you guys?"

"Honey," Brody said to her, "why don't you go upstairs?"

"Don't *do* that," Liz said to him. She turned to Lauren and said, "I don't mind your asking. It's just that the situation is complicated."

Lauren glanced at Brody and then looked down. "I'm sorry."

"There's nothing to be sorry about," Liz said. "Really. And you know what? You *know* what's going on. It's no big secret. We're out of touch."

There were footsteps on the stairs, and Joe came in. He looked surprised to Brody, but just for a moment; he crossed the kitchen, opened the cookie cabinet, and helped himself to a handful of gingersnaps.

Liz went over to him. She said, "How many of those do you have, mister? At least drink some milk with them."

Joe gave Brody a quick smile. "OK."

She poured a glass of milk and slid it close to him. "I'll take my tax now," she said, holding out her hand for a cookie.

Lauren went back to her homework. Joe ate his cookies. Liz returned to the drainboard. Brody sat at the table and paged through the business section of the *Times,* feeling uneasy. Should he ask Liz about Sarabeth? Press her to tell him what happened? He had work to do, and in a while he headed upstairs, thinking he'd figure it out later. There was an e-mail from Russ, sent just twenty minutes ago to the product development team working with the Boston company; things had gotten off to a rocky start, and Brody had suggested a quick intervention now, before the situation got more complicated. "Let's tread softly here, folks," Russ had written. "Cook it like an egg, not a steak." Amused, Brody composed a reply: "Well put, boss." But he dumped it without sending it.

He stayed at his laptop for about an hour, then went back downstairs and carried the bench through the now-empty kitchen to the garage. He set it against a wall and stepped back for a better look. It *was* very flowery—maybe that had been Lauren's point. Sarabeth's house was full of flowery stuff. He'd always felt uncomfortable there, afraid he might break something.

Liz was asleep by the time he got to bed and up by the time he woke. At breakfast she seemed cheerful, chatting about plans for the weekend.

He was taking both kids to school, and when they were ready he kissed her goodbye and followed them out to the car. He unlocked the doors, then hesitated. "Hang on a sec," he said, and he went back inside.

She was at the sink, a dishtowel tucked into the waist of her black yoga tights. "Forget something?" she said.

"No, I just—" He crossed the kitchen and touched her shoulder, then bent to kiss her again. "Just that. Are you OK? Last night?"

"I'm fine."

"I didn't mean to cut her off, I just—"

"You wanted to protect me."

"I guess so."

"You'd better get going," she said, but he didn't want to; he wanted her to talk to him. Didn't she *need* someone to talk to at this point? With Sarabeth out of the picture? The dishes were right there, a stack of plates with silverware piled on top like kindling, and he pushed them away with the back of his forearm.

"How are you?" he said, and she gave him a puzzled look.

"Fine."

"No, really. I want you to tell me everything—I *want* you to."

"Brody."

He looked across the kitchen table and into the family room. Over the years he'd missed hundreds of hours here: weekend hours taking the kids on outings; evening hours sitting up with Liz, listening for peeps and murmurs from upstairs. Nighttime hours, pillow to pillow.

"Hey, let's plan a weekend," he said. "Let's go to Napa, just the two of us."

She held her palm to his jaw. "That sounds very nice. But come on, you better go—look what time it is."

In the car the kids were quiet, Lauren beside him and Joe in the back-seat. When they arrived at the high school, Lauren got out and said good-bye, but Joe stayed in back, the ride to his school too short for it to be worth his while to move.

"Cook it like an egg, not a steak." That was a new one. Mike Patterson had a collection of corporate lingo, scrawled on Post-its stuck all over his office: "We're not trying to boil the ocean here, folks." "That's like trying to roll Jell-O uphill." Brody would forward Russ's e-mail to him, soon as he got in.

"Joe?" he said, glancing at the rearview mirror.

"Yeah?"

He adjusted the mirror so he could see Joe's face better.

"What?" Joe said.

Brody took in Joe's patient expression, his willingness to listen to whatever his father wanted to tell him. "Nothing," Brody said. "I just wanted to hear your voice."

Not much later, a few blocks short of Yoga Life, Liz pulled to the curb and stopped. She was on a quiet street, commercial but far enough from the main shopping district that some of the storefronts were vacant. Four minutes till class, and she suddenly wasn't sure she wanted to go.

But that was silly. Of course she'd go.

A row of flowering plum trees had been planted along the sidewalk; she'd always liked the deep burgundy of their leaves. She turned the radio on, then turned it off again. There was a car parked ahead of her, the only other stopped car on the block.

Napa with Brody. They'd gone a few times when the kids were younger, rented bikes one springtime, lazed around the pool at an insanely expensive hotel one summer. Gone wine tasting on both occasions. She didn't think she had an appetite for wine anymore. She pictured herself in the passenger seat of Brody's car, Brody standing on the sidewalk waiting for her to get out. Herself, not moving.

Two minutes. She hadn't driven all the way down here to turn around, had she?

Don't be late.

Don't be lazy.

Don't be weak.

I can't help it, she thought, and she lowered her forehead to the steering wheel. She lifted her foot off the brake, felt the car roll forward, slammed the brake down again. Heart racing, she looked up, but the car in front of her was still a good five feet away.

One minute—she'd walk in breathless just as Diane was telling everyone to lie on their backs and take a minute to go inside. Her heart would be pounding as she pulled her knees to her chest and rocked back and forth.

She made a U-turn in the middle of the block and drove away. It was nine o'clock on a Friday morning, and she had no responsibilities for the next six hours. What did she ever used to do with herself?

She thought of the front yard at home, the greening hydrangeas and the leafy shrubs, and the bare spots where she usually planted annuals. There was actually a wonderful nursery in Napa; if she and Brody went up for a weekend they could stop in on the way home. She pictured zinnias, daisies, some color to fill in the garden while she waited for the perennials to bloom. Maybe they could even buy a tree; there was a spot in the backyard that needed some height.

But could they really go? The kids were too old for a babysitter but way too young to spend a weekend alone. She could ask her parents, but she hated to ask them for something they'd feel compelled to say yes about. They had their own lives now—though according to her mother at Easter dinner, they'd had their own lives for just about ever.

When she got home it was only 9:23. She'd been gone such a short time she could still smell coffee and even a trace of toast.

There'd been an e-mail plea last night from the middle-school vice-principal, saying parents were needed to organize the eighth-grade graduation dance, and she thought now was as good a time as any to write back. She'd worked on the dance Lauren's year and had a file she could offer the committee—if she didn't volunteer herself, which she ought to.

But first, to find the file. It was stuffy upstairs, and she opened the kids' windows before going to the file cabinet in the TV room. There was a bulging Pendaflex labeled MIDDLE SCHOOL, and she pulled it out and took it over to the old plaid love seat, a relic from the house on Cowper Street. BOOK FAIR, PTA, HOT LUNCH: folder after soft-edged folder, papers jutting out of all of them.

And then there it was: GRAD DANCE.

Grad dance. She clasped the folder to her chest. There was something so innocent about that—"grad" instead of "graduation." Her mouth felt dry. She looked again and saw the hurried scrawl, pictured herself just two years ago, quickly labeling this thing she'd need again very soon—in no time at all, in the blink of an eye. Before anything could possibly change.

Having no idea.

She leaned back into the love seat, held the folder close again. How nice it would be to think that in the end it would merge, life before and life after: into life itself—just life. She longed to believe this, but she thought something permanent had come into being at the exact moment Lauren touched the blade to her skin.

Liz dreamed that night that she was trying to reach a red Frisbee that had lodged on someone's roof. She had a mop stick screwed onto the extension handle, and she was leaning out Joe's window, except that it wasn't Joe's window, it was the window of a huge loft place, and she was reaching and reaching for the Frisbee, and missing and missing it.

Brody dreamed of his father, sitting behind the wheel of the Cutlass he'd bought in '71, tan with a dark brown roof. He was smiling. He was in the middle of a vast, sunny field, no road in sight: just sitting behind the wheel, windows open, smiling. In the dream, as in life, Brody thought the Cutlass was the coolest car his dad could have bought and still been his dad.

Lauren dreamed she couldn't find her little pillow. She needed her exact pillows, a big one under her head, a small one over it. Myrna had confessed one day that she still slept with a stuffie, so Lauren's extra pillow was nothing. She woke and found it, and when she slept again she dreamed about Ada, sitting in the canoe.

Joe wasn't dreaming. He wasn't sleeping, and he wasn't at home. Fridays were turning out to be poker nights, and he was at Trent's, lying in a sleeping bag in the family room, wide awake though it was almost one-thirty. Nearby, Trent snored, and Anthony whacked the floor every now and then as he tossed in his bag. They'd played till midnight, till Trent's dad pulled the plug on them. Conor and Elliot had gone home, and Joe had thought at the last minute about getting a ride from Conor's dad, but he'd decided to stay. It would've been hard to explain to Trent why he was leaving, harder still to explain to his parents why he'd come home. They'd've been in bed, and he'd've had to use his key to get in, and he didn't like the look of that in his brain, tiptoeing into his own house, uncertain whether or not his parents were still awake. Not wanting to bother them.

Rosie, Trent's golden, twitched in her sleep, then whimpered a little. She was on the couch, in her usual spot; Rosie in that spot on Trent's couch was as old as anything.

He'd won. They only played for pennies, so it was just a few bucks, but still, he'd cleaned up. "Lucky," Trent kept muttering, but Joe wasn't lucky, he was good. He knew something the other guys didn't: the cards didn't really matter. What mattered was how you played. What mattered was your face.

The ice maker in the freezer clicked on, water filling the reservoir. Joe moved onto his other side. He didn't mind being awake here, at Trent's house. He could pretend he was anywhere.

An hour later he was still awake. Still not tired. The clock on the DVD player said 2:43. He pulled his legs from his sleeping bag and got to his feet. He knew Trent's house almost as well as his own, and he walked slowly and quietly to the family room door.

Out in the hall, he had to be even quieter. Trent's parents' room was directly above the back door. He twisted the knob slowly and pulled, but nothing happened. He let go of the knob, quietly unlocked the dead bolt, then twisted again. Outside, he pulled the door after him to within an inch of the jamb.

It was colder than he'd expected, and he crossed his arms over his chest. He could see a fair number of stars—nothing like what he'd see at camp this summer, but not bad for here.

He couldn't wait for camp.

Trent had two little brothers, and the backyard was full of sports equipment: bats and balls, a pitchback, two different-height basketball hoops on stands. There was some really old little-kid stuff, too, and he waited till he could see, then picked his way across the grass to an ancient plastic seesaw. He could barely get his butt between the handholds, but he wedged himself in anyway. He and his sister had had a seesaw exactly like this. And a little green sandbox in the shape of a turtle.

His sister had scars, two on her right wrist and four on her left. She touched the ones on her left wrist a lot. One, two, three, four: he imagined her counting. They were at home, the three of them—his father, mother, sister. He was here. One, two, three, four. When she was doing something else, he sometimes looked at them. The third was the longest, the fourth the darkest—the slowest to heal. A day would come when they would be close to invisible, and he wondered: Would she touch them still?

He looked at the sky again. In less than two months he'd be at camp, in the mountains, and the sky would swarm with stars—all that pinprick, enormous light. He thought of the impossible truth that they were finished despite their brightness. They looked motionless, but they were on their way away—they were going, they were already gone.

42

On a sunny Saturday at the beginning of May, Sarabeth stopped at Andronico's on her way home from a paint consultation. She was starving, and though she needed to do a big shopping, all she wanted right now was to address how hungry she was right now. At the deli she asked for a quart of asparagus and pasta salad, then she went to the baked goods and selected a full-size loaf of *pain levain*. "Pane levane," as Nina had pronounced it once, and it had become this joke of theirs: Pain le Vain, and le Conceited, and le Grandiose. Pain was all of those things.

The Heidts' driveway was empty, and she went inside for a fork and a bottle of water, then sat on her porch, took off her sweater, and pried the top off the salad. She ate a piece of asparagus, tangy in its lemon vinaigrette.

A minivan pulled into the driveway, and for a moment she wondered if the Heidts had finally gotten rid of the Volvo. But no: it was Liz, Brody and Liz, Brody driving all the way to the end of the driveway and Liz wearing such a stern expression that Sarabeth was certain they had come to tell her something terrible.

There was a swarming feeling inside her, and she set her food down and got to her feet. Brody cut the engine and held up his hand in greeting, and then no one moved.

She went down the steps, and as she approached, Brody opened his door and got out. He left the door open, and Liz leaned over from the passenger seat and called, "Hi."

It was dark in the van, and Sarabeth couldn't quite see Liz, couldn't see her expression anymore. "Hi," she said back. Brody just stood there, then he moved forward and gave her a light hug.

She stepped closer to the van. She could see Liz now, looking not so much stern as frightened. "Hi," Sarabeth said again.

Liz gave her a quick smile. She hesitated, then opened her door and got out. Sarabeth waited, and Liz walked around the front of the van and stopped a few yards away from her. She was wearing black-and-white-checked pants and a black polo shirt and gleaming red loafers. She said, "I don't know if it's OK that we came."

"It is," Sarabeth said. "It definitely is." She glanced over her shoulder at Brody. They had not come with news, she didn't think, but she couldn't understand why they had both come, why they had come together.

"We brought you something," Liz said. "I couldn't bring it by myself."

Brody ran his toe over a crack in the concrete. "Are you sure you want to do that now?"

Liz lifted her hands, then let them drop again. "I don't know." She pinched the bridge of her nose and looked at Sarabeth. "I missed you."

"I missed you, too."

Liz dug in her purse for a Kleenex and dabbed at her eyes.

"Do you want to come in?" Sarabeth said. She looked over at Brody. "Do you want something to drink?"

"Um," Liz said. "Brody's going to do an errand, but I want him to help me with something first." She set her purse on the driver's seat and moved to the back of the van. Brody followed. He opened the gate, and Sarabeth watched as he maneuvered something that was evidently quite heavy to the mouth of the van. It was a bench, a painted bench. He carried it over and set it at Sarabeth's feet.

"I don't know if you might have any use for this," Liz said, "but if you do, I'd like you to have it."

It was the bench from Liz's garage, from last fall. It had been painted a bright, insistent plaid, topped with a confetti of pastel flowers. The plaid was strident, its colors the colors of nursery school, and against them the pale flowers didn't stand a chance: grayish against the background more than pink, lavender, peach. Sarabeth could tell Liz had labored over it for a long time.

She said, "This is that bench, isn't it? That you showed me last fall?" Liz nodded.

"God, it's amazing, it's beautiful. But—you shouldn't give it away, should you?"

"If you don't want it," Liz said.

"No, of course I do. I love it."

Brody said, "It might look good on the porch."

Sarabeth looked at the porch. It would be the first thing anyone saw, coming to visit. A plaid bench.

"Do you sit out here, though?" Liz said. "I mean, you just were, but—"

"I do," Sarabeth said. "I definitely do."

Brody carried the bench up the steps and positioned it next to the door. He stepped back, looked at it, moved it a little to the left. "Good?" he said.

Sarabeth smiled at Liz. "Perfect."

Liz went to the van for her purse, and Brody came down the steps and stood by her.

"So I'll call you," she said to him.

"OK."

Sarabeth watched as he looked at Liz, as he stepped toward the van, as Liz reached for his arm and stopped him for a kiss that seemed almost . . . apologetic? Sarabeth wondered how things were between them these days.

"Thanks, honey," Liz said, and he cast a glance at Sarabeth and then stepped up into the van, raised his hand to them, and started the engine.

Sarabeth and Liz stood side by side and watched as he backed out of the driveway.

"So," Sarabeth said.

"So," Liz said.

They stood there awkwardly, and then Liz moved closer and put her arms around Sarabeth, and her shoulders began to shake. "I'm sorry," she said. "I'm so sorry."

"*I'm* sorry," Sarabeth said. "I'm sorry it was so true."

"It wasn't."

"No, it was. Is. Was."

Liz let go of her. She stepped back and looked at Sarabeth with her wet eyes wide.

"Love the red shoes," Sarabeth said, and Liz let out a single, loud laugh.

Up the steps Sarabeth went, and across the porch to the bench. It was, or you could choose to see it as, a rather delightful piece of furniture: a burst of fruity candy in the middle of a bland meal. She was beginning to love it already, how Liz it was. She sat down and rested her elbow on the little armrest. "Come," she said.

Liz stepped up onto the porch and then stopped and leaned against the corner post. Her eyes were still wet.

"Sit," Sarabeth said, and after a moment Liz came over and sat next to her, but tentatively, her butt only half on the seat, her body angled toward the yard. Sarabeth said, "This is so strange. Are you really here?"

"I'm not sure," Liz said. "I'm not sure how much I am." Her head was turned away, but she reached back and gave Sarabeth's fingertips an awkward squeeze. "Sorry."

"No, that actually makes it more real," Sarabeth said. "Don't be sorry."

Now Liz looked at her. "Really?"

"Yeah."

With a sigh, Liz moved herself back, settled onto the seat with her elbow just inches from Sarabeth's. She had the heavy, brooding presence of some kind of huge creature; but it also seemed she might skitter away at any moment. Sarabeth wanted to leash the skitterer, make room for the weighty other.

She touched the back of Liz's hand. "How's Lauren?"

"She's doing better," Liz said. "I don't know how. Sometimes it doesn't even seem real."

"Real like permanent? Or real like you're not sure you're right?"

"Both, I guess. Or no—just the first. Real like permanent."

"Is she still in therapy?"

"Oh, yeah. I think that's going to go on for a while."

Sarabeth's stomach growled, and she went and got her food, then returned to the bench and sat again. She tore off some bread and offered the loaf to Liz, but Liz waved it away. The sun shone brightly, hit the wall behind them and made this corner of the porch feel close to hot.

"That year I lived with you guys?" Sarabeth said. "I think that's when it started."

"What do you mean?" Liz said.

Sarabeth knew she knew. She took a sip of water and went on. "You know that doll you had? That you'd brought from Swarthmore? And she could pee?"

"Baby Betty?" Liz said.

"Baby Betty. Did you ever wonder what happened to her?"

" 'It.' What happened to 'it.' "

"Did you?"

"I can't say I did. Why? Do you know?"

"I stole her," Sarabeth said. "I put her out with the garbage one morning; I set my alarm. I wrapped her in a grocery bag."

"You've got to be kidding. Why?"

"It bugged me that you still had her—I thought you were too old. I mean, that's what I thought then. Now I think I was jealous."

"Oh, that's silly," Liz said. "You weren't jealous."

"No, I think I was." Sarabeth brought one foot up onto the bench and swiveled to face Liz. "I went back there, about a month ago—I parked right outside your house. I got out of the car, and it even *smelled* the same. Remember that spring, when my father sent me money for a car and I got that little white Pinto? I can remember the sound it made while it was cooling, this kind of ticking sound, but I can only remember it at night, and I wonder, Am I remembering it from one night or am I remembering it from a whole bunch of nights?"

Liz pulled her own feet onto the bench. She wrapped her arms around her shins and rested her cheek on her knees.

"What?" Sarabeth said.

Liz's eyes filled, and Sarabeth reached out and stroked her hair, hot in the sun and lit with red and blond.

A bee dove at them and flew away. Liz lifted her head; the side of her face was red. She said, "I don't know how I survived." Her hands were curled loosely on her bent knees, and Sarabeth ran a forefinger over her knuckles.

She said, "You must be very strong."

"No, it's a brute thing. It's almost animal."

"Well, in whatever way, you did." Without me, she thought, and she minded less than she once would have.

"Yeah," Liz said. "I guess I did. I did and I am."

Sarabeth fanned her face and looked out at the yard. Climbing the wall of the Heidts' bike shed was a tangle of nasturtiums, yellow and orange flowers amid a profusion of round green lily-pad leaves. She ate a piece of asparagus, waved away a fly. "Want to go in?" she said. "Let me get you a nice cool drink."

The corners of Liz's mouth lifted.

"What?"

"Thanks, Mom," Liz said, and they both smiled.

Inside, they leaned against the kitchen counter and drank tall glasses of tangerine-grapefruit juice. When Sarabeth was finished drinking, she ran cold water into the sink and wet a paper towel, then held it to her forehead.

"How've you been?" Liz said.

Sarabeth kept her eyes averted, moved the towel to the back of her neck as if she were absorbed in the work of cooling herself off. What she thought of, for some reason, were the weeks during the worst of it when on several occasions she'd come to herself, from a kind of daze, to find that she was smelling cloves or sucking a lemon—seeking an extreme for her dulled senses. All that spicy food she'd craved.

She looked over at Liz and smiled, and Liz's face changed, a look of understanding appearing as she realized what she'd asked, how impossible it would be for Sarabeth to answer.

"It wasn't the whole story," Liz said. "Ever."

"It's OK," Sarabeth said. "Thank you so much for coming."

"Actually, it's Lauren you should thank."

"What do you mean?"

"I'll tell you later."

In the living room they settled onto opposite ends of the couch. Sarabeth sat sideways with her legs folded underneath her, while Liz faced the fireplace, one leg crossed over the other. "What's with all that?" she said, waving her hand at the stuff on the floor.

"Oh," Sarabeth said. "My life in a nutshell."

"An abalone shell."

Sarabeth looked at Billy's shell. It was off to the side, and she couldn't remember whether that was where she'd first put it or whether at some point she had moved it away from everything else. She said, "Did you want to kill me through all of that?"

Liz opened her mouth, then shut it again.

"You can tell me," Sarabeth said.

"I was going to say no, but"—Liz shrugged—"I guess at times I did."

She thought for a moment. "But you know what? Not really. It was more that I wanted to shake you."

"To my senses."

They sat and talked, and then after a while they got up, and Sarabeth showed Liz the new batch of "reading lights" she'd begun, with some additional paper she'd managed to special order. When they returned to the living room, she stooped to pick up the abalone shell, and because she was standing there holding it, just steps from the bathroom door, she took it back and put it where it had been, long ago. Liz was holding the pink dish when she got back, and she took it from Liz and returned it to its old place. In five minutes the floor was clear, and they had not even discussed what they were doing.

Not much later, Liz looked at her watch and said she should call Brody, and together they went outside to wait. The Volvo was back in the driveway, and it struck Sarabeth that now he would have to return on foot. She pictured him walking up the driveway, maybe tossing his keys, maybe whistling, and for some reason she felt a little sad for him.

She sat down and stretched out her legs. "I love my new bench," she said. "I can't believe you gave it to me."

Liz was leaning against the post. "What are friends for?"

"You know, that's actually a really interesting question."

"Whoa," Liz said. "Philosophical."

"That's me—a philosopher."

Liz stood still for a moment, a pair of lines appearing between her eyebrows as a thought occurred to her, as her lips parted so she could say, Sarabeth felt certain: *And what am I?* But she closed her mouth again, and with a look of wild uncertainty on her face, she stared into the Heidts' backyard.

Once more, Sarabeth had the idea that Liz might flee. Sarabeth was going to have to be very careful with Liz; that was clear.

The Heidts' patio door opened, and Chloe came out, glancing at Sarabeth and Liz as she moved to the grass. She stood at one edge, raised her arms, hesitated, and then took a couple steps and turned a perfect cartwheel. As Sarabeth watched, the worried look left Liz's features, and she smiled a small, private smile. She came and sat next to Sarabeth and said, "Remember our gymnastics show?"

Now Sarabeth smiled, too. In the Castleberrys' backyard she and Liz had spent several afternoons one summer doing somersaults and clumsy cartwheels, until the only possible next step was a performance. Her parents must have come to watch, but she couldn't remember them. She couldn't remember Liz's parents either, for that matter. What she remembered was how perfectly bright the sky was, though dinner was long over, and how she and Liz hid around the side of the house while everyone settled in, holding hands for moral support, for courage.

Acknowledgments

Many thanks to Jordan Pavlin, my wonderful editor, and everyone else at Knopf and Vintage for their kindness and hard work.

I'm very grateful to Drs. Charlie Goldberg, Nancy Marks, Luke Moix, Lynn Ponton, Steve Sturges, and Patti Yanklowitz for providing medical information and guidance. For offering expertise on a variety of other technical matters, my appreciation goes to Ben Goldstone, David Ewing Duncan, Chris Hunt, Ken Kornberg, Jan Seerveld, and Andy Wolff.

Thank you for reading and commenting on early versions of this book: Jane Aaron, Hallie Aaron, Jamie Eder, Ruth Goldstone, Alice LaPlante, Cornelia Nixon, Katharine Noel, Sydnie Nugent-Pierce, Ron Nyren, George Packer, Rachel Pastan, Tony Pierce, and Vendela Vida. For multiple readings and conversations, an extra helping of gratitude goes to Sylvia Brownrigg, Ann Cummins, Ryan Harty, Nancy Johnson, Veronica Kornberg, Lisa Michaels, Julie Orringer, and Sarah Stone.

Finally, I would like to thank and honor my agent, Geri Thoma, for her embodiment of the word "grace."

A NOTE ABOUT THE AUTHOR

Ann Packer received a Great Lakes Book Award and the Kate Chopin Literary Award for *The Dive from Clausen's Pier,* a national best seller that has been translated into ten languages. Also the author of *Mendocino and Other Stories,* she lives in northern California with her family.